The Freak Foundation Operative's Report

THE FREAK FOUNDATION OPERATIVE'S REPORT

TOM JOYCE

Codorus Press | NYC

This book is a work of fiction and satire, and is not intended maliciously. Names, characters, places and incidents are either the products of the author's imagination or used fictitiously, except in cases where public figures are being satirized. Any other resemblance to actual events, groups or persons, living or dead, is entirely coincidental or used as a fictional depiction or personality parody, which is permitted by precedent of the case Hustler Magazine v. Falwell (1988). Thanks, Larry and Jerry.

Copyright © 2013
by Tom Joyce

All rights reserved, including the right to reproduce this book or portions of it in any form, save for quotations in criticism or in a review. For permissions, contact publicity@coduruspress.com.

FIRST EDITION
July 2013

10 9 8 7 6 5 4 3 2 1d

ISBN: 978-0-9839783-4-3
Library of Congress Control Number: 2011937811

Cover and design by
Wayne Lockwood

Cover faerie photo
by Dana Stout

Author photo by
Scott B. Pruden

www.tomjoyceauthor.com
www.coduruspress.com

Thanks to the whole crew at Codorus Press, including:

Scott Pruden, author of "Immaculate Deception" — How often does a writer get a chance to have one of his favorite authors read and critique his first book? Thanks for the feedback.

Wayne Lockwood, author of "Acid Indigestion Eyes" — What can I say? You're a genius. I STILL can't believe you conceived this whole thing and made it work.

Mike Argento, author of "Don't Be Cruel" — You're an inspiration as both a writer and a fashion icon.

Tracy Vogel, you made some excellent suggestions. Man, I am so glad you talked me out of going with that original ending! (Seriously. It sucked.)

Ted "Eagle Eye" Palik, you've got my vote for world's greatest copy editor. Some of those mistakes you caught would have had me tearing out my already dwindling supply of hair. So thanks.

Thanks to the friends and family members who encouraged me (too numerous to list here) and the women who threw themselves at me (too nonexistent to list here). And to everyone affiliated with the Spoutwood Farm May Day Fairie Festival. Thanks for being a bunch of cool people with a great sense of humor.

This is dedicated to you, Mom and Dad. Though I really think you'd be better off not reading it. Seriously. There's no sex in it, but there's lots of violence and like A TON of bad words. Anyway, love you both.

THE FREAK FOUNDATION OPERATIVE'S REPORT

Who are the SLAIN?

TOM JERKFACE

AUTHOR'S INTRODUCTION — BY TOM JERKFACE

PUBLISHER'S NOTE: *The author's last name is pronounced Jerk – FAH – chay. It's Italian. Or possibly Native American. I don't care anymore.*

I can't vouch for the truth of the following narrative. Only for the truth of my experience relating to it.

You will not be provided with my name, only with the pseudonym that my pompous ass of a publisher has been instructed to select for me. More on that presently.

For a number of years, I have worked as a reporter for the Batley Daily Needler, the newspaper serving the small, Central Pennsylvania city of Batley. The following account came into my possession when Sister Pilar Lopez dropped it off at my desk one day. She knew I was familiar with both its author and the events it described, and wanted to know if I could do anything with it. This is a question I have been contemplating for a long time as the account sat on a shelf in my home. To be perfectly honest, I wasn't sure what to make of it.

The account is, to be certain, outlandish. But, it could be said, no more so than many of the verified facts surrounding the events to which it pertains. The assault by The Slain upon the city of Batley is undisputed. It has already been the subject of three rather slipshod nonfiction books and one awful made-for-TV movie, which mentioned the Friedrich K. Schulze Foundation operative who wrote the bulk of the following report as a marginal figure, if at all. All have dealt with the events as a mere act of thuggery at best; a minor if bizarre act of domestic terrorism at worst.

I have tried to some extent to verify the events outlined in the account, but found it difficult in the extreme for reasons that should become clear to the reader. I will indicate in notes the episodes in which my personal experience has impinged on the events described.

The account was, frankly, a mess. It consisted of reams of sloppily typed pieces of paper contained in manila file folders wrapped together with a length of twine. Enclosed were a number of other documents included with the main narrative, most notably the account of William "Wild Billy" Cleary. Some of my articles for the Daily Needler were included as well. The files had apparently been prepared and collected in haste, with a cursory attempt to keep them in more-or-less chronological order. I've tried to preserve that order in the presentation, dividing the account by files.

As I stated, the account sat in my home for a lengthy period of time. Ultimately, I attempted to get it published for an admittedly unprofessional reason. I knew the author. He was my friend.

Batley is a small place, and I'm personally acquainted with most of the people who figure in the narrative.

Though I considered the report's author my friend, I wouldn't characterize us as close. It occurred to me as I worked on the volume you are now reading how little I really knew about him. And in my subsequent research, I learned that few people who interacted with him knew more about him than I did.

The following is what I knew.

He was an employee of the Friedrich K. Schulze Foundation, known colloquially as the "Freak Foundation." Because I cover city government, I knew he and his foundation were involved in providing services for Batley.

He and I had some similarities, which may have served as the basis of our friendship. We're both originally from New Jersey. We shared a fondness for Scotch, cigars, and cards.

He was middle-aged, and spoke with a heavy New Jersey accent. He was a stocky man — quite short, with a muscular build and a thick neck. He usually wore a jacket and a tie. Sometimes he skipped the tie. He was surprisingly strong for a man his size. I know this because I also attended Ty Bacon's martial arts gym, where he trained. The others in the gym considered him a good fighter, though not an exceptional one.

In all candor, I found him rather coarse. Even oafish at times. But I thought he was essentially a good man. And so I endeavored to find a publisher for this account.

I failed scores of times before I encountered one who was willing to publish it. That publisher is, I regret to say, a puffed-up popinjay of a man with whom I have developed a strong, mutual dislike. Our animosity culminated with a visit to his home during which he actually ordered me to clean his living room. I, naturally, refused and left abruptly.

PUBLISHER'S NOTE: For the record, I did not "order" Mr. Jerkface to do anything. He had visited my house, ostensibly for the purpose of discussing his book. In Mr. Jerkface's estimation, this meant drinking a bottle of my wine while complaining stridently about my "bourgeois sensibilities." At one point, while he was making his unsteady way to the bathroom, Mr. Jerkface stumbled into a shelf and knocked it over, smashing a very expensive stereo system into many small pieces on my hardwood floor. I merely asked for his assistance in cleaning it up, at which point he became indignant and left. And that about wrapped things up for the night, unless you count the irate phone call from my next-door neighbor inquiring about the man urinating on his lawn. I didn't even ask Mr. Jerkface to pay me back for the damage. Though after weeks of getting up in the night to use the bathroom and stepping in my bare feet on a sharp plastic shard of what was once my stereo system, I had ample opportunity to regret that decision.

My publisher and I quarreled incessantly about the presentation of the account. He was cravenly concerned about the legal ramifications, and proposed the absurd artifice of presenting it as a novel. Lacking any other options, I eventually relented on that score.

Over time, I became so disgusted with the whole thing that I informed my publisher I wanted him to use a pseudonym. He asked what it should be. I told him to just go ahead and pick one, as I was thoroughly bored with his corporate chicanery.

Here, then, is the account as it was presented to me. Make of it what you will.

FILE ONE

September 26

I'm not proud of my reaction when I first saw those assholes in the masks attacking the people downtown.

Concern for the people? Absolutely. Concern for myself? You're fuckin-A right. But my first reaction was a long, internal groan. Because I just knew this would turn out to have something to do with my job, and it would be a major pain in the ass.

It was early on a Saturday afternoon, my day off, and I'd been out drinking the night before. I'd spent most of that morning and a chunk of the afternoon nursing my hangover before I finally came to grips with the realization that a Bloody Mary was the only thing for the job.

I left my apartment in downtown Batley, and suddenly I needed the Bloody Mary even worse. Some kind of street festival was happening downtown. Brass bands and kids clog-dancing and craft booths selling windchimes and glass unicorns. That kind of thing.

TOM JERKFACE: The festival was the annual Warm Hearths Festival, which takes place in downtown Batley in late September. The title comes from local historian and politician Buck Rockbaugh's book about Batley history, "Echoes of Destiny." In one section of the book, he deals with the fact that members of the Second Continental Congress passed through Batley while fleeing the British army, which occupied Philadelphia during the Revolutionary War. They stayed for a number of days. According to Rockbaugh's account, they did so because "the warm hearts and warm hearths of the city were a great comfort to them in those trying times." Though most historians agree that a more likely explanation for their extended stay was that several of their number had contracted diarrhea.

Even though it was still cloudy, it looked like some earlier rain had cleared up, and now the festival was in full force. Nothing wrong with that, in itself. But cymbals and kids and civic pride are three things you don't feel like dealing with when you're hung over. I started walking faster, heading for the nearest downtown watering hole.

"Hey man? Can you spare some cash? Gotta feed my family."

I looked to my right and there was a skinny guy with long, gray hair sitting on the sidewalk near an alleyway entrance. Leonard. There'd been a lot more homeless people hanging around downtown lately, and Leonard was a regular on my block. The "feed my family" routine would have been more convincing if he was younger and didn't smell like a distillery. But what the hell. Who was I to begrudge anybody a drink on a day like this?

I handed him a couple bucks, he said thanks and I kept walking. Dozens of people surrounded me. But the big concentration, hundreds of people, was a few blocks up ahead at the city's Center Square.

At first I thought it was my imagination. Maybe hangover-induced hypersensitivity. But the crowd noise ahead seemed to change all of a sudden. Become louder and more high-pitched. I squinted to see what was going on up ahead. Definite screaming and some kind of commotion. A fight?

Then a large mass of the people from the Center Square was running in my direction. But they were getting in each others' way. The ones on the sides seemed to be pressing away from something, tangling up the people in the middle of the pack. No mistaking the change in the sound now. Lots of screaming.

I stood still, trying to make sense of it. Behind me, Leonard started yelling.

"Get away from me man! I don't want no trouble! Just get away!"

I turned. A tall man advanced on Leonard with a baseball bat. He wore workboots, jeans, and a black T-shirt. A scattering of dreadlocks hung down past his shoulders.

I ran toward him, hoping to get him before he saw me or hurt Leonard, but no chance. He was too close to Leonard, raising the bat and getting ready to swing. Leonard had his skinny arms up, cringing.

"Hey," I yelled and continued running at him. He looked up at me. I got there in exactly the amount of time it took for him to decide I was a bigger threat, face me and pull back for another swing in my direction.

I took in the facts that he was pretty big and wearing some kind of weird mask, neither of which seemed like particularly good news at that moment.

I was right up on him as he swung. I knew my best bet at that point, counter-intuitively enough, was to step into the swing. This I did, turning my left shoulder toward him. The lower third of the bat thunked into my shoulder, lacking the momentum to do any damage.

He paused for a second, maybe considering the vagaries of physics and their effect on sporting equipment. I took advantage of the pause to reach up and grab him by the neck, hand clamped hard at his jaw hinges. I twisted his neck while at the same time swinging my leg around behind his and stomping on the back of his knee.

He arched his back, screamed and dropped to one knee on the sidewalk. I then torqued my upper body around, slamming an elbow into the side of his head. He went sprawling to the ground and didn't move.

I reached down, grabbed him by the shoulder and turned him over. His mask was dun-colored leather, rough and ragged looking, stitched together with coarse, black thread. It covered his head like a hood. What I'd at first mistaken for dreadlocks were long, black hanks of hair sewn into the crown. Horse hair, by the looks of it.

The front of the mask bore an abstract but unmistakable representation of a skull marked out in black pigment, with a triangular hole for the nose and a long, grinning crescent of lipless teeth for the mouth. On his hands were leather gloves. Not coarse leather, like the mask. Refined leather. Like the kind you'd wear to get a job done without leaving fingerprints.

I recognized the get-up, of course. I hadn't personally witnessed the infamous Halloween Parade Massacre 15 years ago. But I'd been in town. Specifically, I'd been in a bar on the other side of town, where I'd ordered another drink – a stiff one – when the 10 o'clock news had come on and I'd found out what was going on in this city I'd moved to.

The Slain. This was getting worse by the second.

I took the mask off him. White guy. Maybe 25. Shaved head. Ugly. Slack-jawed and unconscious. Didn't know him.

But I had more than 300 clients in the Greater Batley area, and didn't have all their faces memorized. If he was one of my clients, I had an interest in knowing as soon as possible. I checked his jeans pockets. No wallet. No nothing.

"Watch out!"

That was Leonard. He'd retreated into the alley entrance, and pointed at two more guys in leather skull masks heading toward me. One held a length of pipe. The other held a bicycle chain. I picked up the baseball bat from the guy I'd taken out and ran into the alley, standing between them and Leonard.

"Run!" I yelled at Leonard over my shoulder.

The guys in the leather masks ran over to their buddy and hoisted him up between them, his arms draped over their shoulders. They scurried away, the unconscious guy's feet dragging on the ground as they went. But first they paused for just a second so one of them could glare through his mask's eyeholes and point at me.

I later found out that they and about 30 others dressed like them had run into the crowd, swinging various blunt weapons. Each of them took out a handful of people. They didn't seem to care whether the victims were men or women, but they'd left the kids alone, bless their fucking hearts.

Then they'd run down the side streets they'd originally emerged from. They'd piled into stolen cars and driven them a short distance away to several downtown parking lots. There, they'd boarded some other vehicles, leaving behind the first ones. Then they'd disappeared.

The whole attack had taken only a few minutes. But it left hundreds of people screaming and running in panic along the festival route. That part I saw, as I watched the goons head down a side street and then lost sight of them with all the panicky people running around.

"The fuck was that?"

That question came from Leonard, who hadn't heeded my advice and remained in the alley behind me. I didn't answer, because I had no idea. But the glare and the point? I knew exactly what that was. The universal sign for "This ain't over, asshole."

FILE TWO

WARM HEARTHS FESTIVAL ATTACKED
At Least 50 Injured, 12 Seriously, in Festival Melee
By Tom Jerkface, Daily Needler Staff

Rain failed to dampen the spirits of Warm Hearths Festival-goers on Saturday. But a vicious attack by unknown assailants did.

Rains earlier in the day kept attendance at the annual community festival sparse. By 2 p.m., however, attendance had swollen to about 400 attendees along Main Street. At that point, according to police and eyewitnesses, approximately 30 men brandishing various types of blunt weapons emerged from side streets and attacked members of the crowd.

Batley Police Chief David Sanderson, during a press conference on Saturday evening, said at least 50 people were injured, 12 of them seriously. Those 12, whose names have not yet been released, were transported to Batley Community Hospital, Sanderson said.

Sanderson described the attack as only a few minutes in duration, and said the assailants quickly retreated afterward in vehicles that had been strategically positioned for that purpose. He declined to speculate on what the underlying motivation for the attack might have been.

"The matter is still under investigation," Sanderson said.

Sanderson would neither confirm nor deny that the assailants were wearing grotesque leather masks such as those sported by The Slain, the name by which members of a mysterious criminal gang that terrorized the city 15 years ago identified themselves in a series of cryptic communications to local police and press.

Members of The Slain staged an attack on the annual Batley Halloween Parade 15 years ago, during which explosives were detonated along the parade route and unknown gunmen fired into the crowd. In the ensuing panic, 11 people were trampled to death and more than 200 were injured.

No arrests were ever made. There had been no subsequent Slain-related activity since then. Until Saturday.

Thelma Dubler, 60, of W. Pine Street in Batley, said she was present both at the event that's come to be commonly known as the "Halloween Parade Massacre," and at Saturday's festival. She said that 15 years ago, she saw members of The Slain.

"They were wearing the exact same masks," Dubler said of the assailants who attacked the crowd on Saturday. "I have no doubt in my mind. The Slain are back. God help us all."

TOM JERKFACE: The following is a copy of the agenda from a City Council meeting that took place the following Monday.

BATLEY CITY COUNCIL MEETING AGENDA
7 p.m., Sept. 28

1) Roll call
2) Flag Salute
3) Opening invocation, delivered by Pastor Anthony Rosatti of Our Lady of

Perpetual Melancholia Roman Catholic Church

4) Resolution honoring Batley Junior High School Scrabble Club for third-place finish at regional "Scrabble Smackdown" competition in Liberty Township, Pa.

5) Public comment period on non-agenda items.

6) First passage and discussion of Ordinance 633435MK1JM346 pertaining to placement of historical resources.

Description: Acting on Batley Historical Preservation Advisory Committee's report regarding the ongoing problem of patrons of tavern district using historic butter churn replica in lieu of lavatory facility. The ordinance resolves to move historic butter churn replica to an as-yet-to-be determined location outside the tavern district. In the interim, violators will be assessed a fine on a sliding scale with the amount dependent upon the orifice utilized in the commission of the offense.

7) Special presentation by Police Chief David Sanderson regarding recent attack on Warm Hearths Festival, with public comment period to follow.

8) Additional public comment on agenda items.

9) Adjournment

10) Executive session to discuss personnel matters

TOM JERKFACE: The following is one of my own articles about that meeting.

RESIDENTS DEMAND ACTION AT CITY COUNCIL MEETING
By Tom Jerkface, Daily Needler Staff

Rain failed to dampen the spirits of angry Batley residents who went to the city council meeting Monday night in search of answers.

On a drizzly evening, more than 100 people packed the meeting room in City Hall and spilled out into the hallway to hear a special presentation by Police Chief David Sanderson following a baffling attack on the public during the Warm Hearths Festival Saturday.

Sanderson reiterated earlier statements that the episode is still under investigation. He said he's working with surrounding municipalities to resolve the situation. But he cautioned the residents to keep things in proper perspective.

"At this point, for all we know, it may be an isolated incident," he said.

Mayor Buck Rockbaugh also assured residents that all municipal resources are being brought to bear on the investigation, including the Friedrich K. Schulze Foundation – a national nonprofit with a branch in Batley that specializes in dealing with anomalous phenomena such as Saturday's attack.

He also urged residents to refrain from panicking until authorities have properly assessed the situation.

"We fully intend to find the people responsible," Rockbaugh said. "We ask that you assist us in this endeavor by remaining calm."

But councilmember Ernest Bixler said he shared residents' concerns, and urged them not to let "career politicians" get away with ignoring the situation.

"We've got a responsibility to defend this city," Bixler told the crowd. "I call for aggressive, immediate action."

"We're doing all we can to address the situation," added councilmember Daniel Oliphant.

During the public comment period following his presentation, one resident after another reiterated their belief that the assault marked the re-emergence of The Slain, a mysterious criminal gang that terrorized the city 15 years ago and then abruptly disappeared – leaving behind no indication of their motive.

George Hoffman of Gardiner Avenue claimed to have witnessed a gathering of men whom he believed to be The Slain during an incursion into some nearby woods.

Michelle Kendall of Slate Street drew applause from other audience members when she urged council members not to forget the most vulnerable members of the community.

"Remember, it's not just us," she said. "We're also here for on behalf of our children."

After the meeting, Buck asked me to hang around for an "executive session." I figured he was ticked. I guess I couldn't blame him. He'd specifically asked me to be on-hand for the meeting, to reassure the public that the Friedrich K. Schulze Foundation, my employer, would help out as much as possible.

As it turned out, I was out of the room when he called for me. When I came back in, the public comment period had already started. Buck had to ask for permission to cut into the middle of the public comments, all so I could say a couple reassuring things.

I doubt it did much good anyway. During the public comment period, one after another, the people started repeating the rumors they'd heard over the years about The Slain. How they'd been in hiding, waiting for a chance to come back and attack us again. How a diner waitress said she heard they'd kidnapped children in New Hampshire. How someone's cousin's brother's golf partner said he heard they butchered and dismembered five people in Texas. After a while, the people seemed to take a weird enjoyment in it, like kids taking turns telling scary stories around a campfire.

The highlight, hands down, was lumpy, bearded old George Hoffman.

In my opinion, Hoffman was always the most entertaining part of the city council meetings. For years, he'd been fighting attempts by the city to collect back taxes he owed on his broken-down shithole off Gardiner Avenue.

His financial problems were mostly from his aversion to work and his tendency to spend what little money he did scrounge on booze or new additions to his gun collection. But George decided he was fighting a Holy Crusade, based on the sacred principle that an armed American owed nothing to any government, ever. Every month, he'd drive his beat-up old pickup covered with custom-made "Proudly Armed American" bumper stickers – probably the only thing holding it together – to council meetings so he could tell them that they'd get nothing from him.

During his talk about The Slain, though, Hoffman acted a lot different. I'll admit it. He spooked me, just like everyone else in that meeting room.

When Hoffman approached the microphone, Buck warned him that the current public comment period was for the matter at hand only. Ordinarily, Hoffman would have answered a challenge like that with a bunch of cusswords, and probably got himself kicked out. But this time, he just nodded with a serious look on his face, and said he wanted to tell about something he'd seen in the woods the night before.

He said he'd driven out to a clearing he knows, to "get away from this damn city. Just get out in nature."

Someone in the back of the room yelled "You use a spotlight and a shotgun for that, George?" Some people laughed a little too loud. Most stayed quiet, especially when Hoffman didn't even get mad.

He only said, in a quiet voice, "I seen them. The Slain. They was out there."

He went on to describe how he'd been driving along a narrow trail, wide enough only for his pickup. He slowly became aware of a haze of smoke and a strange light around him, both of which grew steadily more intense as he approached the clearing.

Thinking it might be a forest fire, and being a "concerned citizen," he decided he should investigate. When he poked the front of his pickup into the clearing, he saw it was full of men.

He couldn't rightly say how many, and they didn't seem to notice him at first. The reason in both cases was a huge bonfire in the center of the clearing throwing off a lot of smoke. Which seemed to be the point. Green wood wouldn't blaze like that and old wood wouldn't smoke like that. They must've done something to it.

The men danced around wildly, like a barroom full of drunks fired up over some particularly rocking song on the jukebox. A rhythmic pounding filled the air, punctuated by whoops and screams.

Then he saw it. A wavering figure loomed above the fire. He couldn't make out whether it was formed from darker smoke, or whether it seemed to be wavering because of the smoke around it. It was shaped like a man, but bigger than any man. It had a bull's head, with long curved horns. And it was moving.

That's all Hoffman took in before a man stumbled near his truck. He was shirtless, wearing jeans and clutching what appeared to be a whiskey bottle. He glanced up toward Hoffman. He wore a leather mask, stitched together with coarse thread, a skull painted on the front and long, black strands of hair framing it.

Hoffman threw his pickup in reverse, and for he didn't know how long made his way backward through trees he could barely see. He wanted to do nothing more in the world than stomp on the gas pedal. But some rational part of his brain that somehow survived the decades of booze-inflicted damage told him that would be a bad idea.

He slowly backed up, his familiarity with the trail likely the only thing that made it possible, until he reached a section that was wide enough for him to make a turnaround. Then, at last, he stomped on the gas and got the hell out of there.

"There it is," Hoffman finished. "You can laugh at me if you want. But I know what I seen."

They probably would laugh at him. The next day, everyone would likely dismiss it as crazy rambling. Right then, though, everyone was dead silent.

"It's Cabot's Master," a woman's voice whispered.

Buck was never a stickler for Robert's Rules of Order. But I guess he could feel the panic rising in the room and wanted to put a stop to it.

"Ms. Gaffigan, please. If you want to make a public comment you can ..."

That just made her stand up. Skinny little Becky Gaffigan, with her pancake-sized glasses rims, big dangly earrings and hair spiking off her head like a giant, gray sea anemone. She had a shop downtown where she offered reflexology, psychic aura readings, and Tarot-based chiropractic.

"It escaped when Cabot did," Gaffigan said. "It's been waiting. And now it's back. Cabot's Master. We all know it. Why won't we acknowledge it?"

Everyone started talking at once, and Buck had to do some hammering with his gavel that would have done the legendary John Henry proud. He finally managed to restore just enough order to officially bring the meeting to a close.

I stood near the back, with the late arrivals. I positioned myself into a corner as the room full of people filed out. During the meeting, I'd taken note of one man sitting in the front row. I felt sorry for the lady sitting behind him. Even sitting down, he was a giant. He wore a leather jacket with some kind of patch on the back that I couldn't quite make out. He had long, blond hair.

"Great," I thought. "As if The Slain weren't enough, now we've got a Viking invasion."

He stood up and turned, revealing chiseled features and a close-cropped, blond beard. In his 30s, maybe. Even across the room, his ice-blue eyes seemed to give off an electric glow. I'd never seen him before. But he made eye contact and gave me a "How you doin" nod as he made his way out the door with the rest of the people.

Chief Sanderson – tall, gray-haired and looking every bit the ex-military man he is – gave me a considerably less-friendly look on his way out. One that says "Whatever you're planning, don't even think about it."

Once the last of them left and the door closed, I walked to the dais where Buck and the two councilmembers flanking him sat.

On Buck's left was old Dan Oliphant, with his thick glasses that always caught the overhead light in such a way that it obscured his eyes. Because of this, I had long-since given up trying to decide whether he actually closed them when he invariably nodded off seconds into every meeting. Just as I'd given up trying to decide whether to chalk up that tendency to narcolepsy, an improbably wild nightlife, or some change in brain structure that results from hearing too many Shade Tree Committee reports over the years. Whatever it was, he'd developed an uncanny ability to rouse himself just in time to vote with , or to say something like: "We're doing all we can to address the situation."

Bixler – young, jug-eared, skinny and twitchy – sat to Buck's right and looked a lot more animated.

Bixler had hosted a call-in show on a local radio station, which mostly consisted of him railing against "career politicians" and insisting that the country return to a "Christ-centered focus." Then he'd decided to run for city council, as part of what he called the "Feet to the Fire Campaign," based on the idea that people had to hold local politicians' feet to the fire for their lavish public spending.

Buck seemed to be exactly the type of "career politician" that Bixler targeted. Maybe it was a matter of political survival that Buck endorsed Bixler over long-time councilmember and political ally Anne Swanson nearly two years ago. Whatever the reason, I suspect Buck had ample occasion to regret it, judging by the pained expression on his face just about every time Bixler opened his mouth.

"Well," Buck said in his habitual slow drawl, steepling his fingers and addressing me. "Let's cut to the chase. What do you think? Was Cabot behind this?"

"Of course he's behind it!" Bixler cut in. "You should have arrested him years ago! It was a gross dereliction of duty on your part that you failed! And now the people of the city are paying the price!"

"Ernie, I've told you," Buck said. "We had no legal basis for arresting him."

Bixler gave a small yelp of indignation.

"No legal basis? The man's a godless heathen! What about the Declaration of Independence? 'One nation under God!' It's right there in the First Amendment!"

"We're doing everything in our power to rectify this dilemma," added Oliphant, before lapsing back into silence.

After a few seconds, I spoke up.

"You know why I was out of the meeting for so long? I saw a soap smear on one of the bathroom mirrors that looks just like the face of Jesus. Fascinating."

Bixler gasped and rushed from the room.

Buck sighed in relief and leaned back in his chair.

"Thanks," he said. "But you still should have been in the room when I needed you, buddy."

"I had to hit the bathroom."

"From that whiskey smell, I'm guessing you hit more than the bathroom."

"Sorry," I said. "That Historical Preservation Advisory Committee's presentation was pretty brutal."

"Yeah it was," he said. "You mind?"

"Not at all."

I reached into my pocket, pulled out the metal flask that contained my emergency Scotch supply, and handed it to him. He took a couple gulps, smacking his lips in appreciation.

Whether he was enjoying a drink or facing a roomful of angry people, Buck always carried himself with the same sense of laid-back ease. Handsome and white-haired, he was the type of guy people in another age called a "country gentleman."

He'd been a local hero in his youth, carrying statewide titles in a variety of youth sports including skeet shooting, pole vaulting, and jab-n-grab wrestling.

TOM JERKFACE: Jab-n-grab wrestling is a sport once popular in the region with rules essentially identical to collegiate wrestling, but without the prohibition on eye poking.

He'd worked briefly as a local lawyer before winning a bid for mayor. Since then, he'd been content to "serve the good folks of my hometown," as he put it during every re-election campaign.

"So getting back to my original question, what do you think," he said. "Cabot?"

"If I was a betting man – and I am – that would be my guess. Maybe he wants revenge for Paul Bacon. Maybe he's just feeling ornery."

Rockbaugh nodded.

"That's what I was afraid of. Don't suppose I could trouble you to investigate? Maybe prepare a report ..." he nodded toward the door through which Bixler had scampered "to convince certain people that the city's contract with the Foundation is worth renewing?"

"Hell, I got nothing better to do."

He handed me back the flask.

"How'd you get that past the metal detector anyway?"

Bixler demanded drastic cutbacks in every other area of the city budget. But he'd insisted on installing a metal detector at the front door, in case "foreign insurgents" tried to infiltrate City Hall.

I explained my technique to Buck. A surly rent-a-cop with a flat-top crewcut who was probably in his 20s but looked about 16 usually manned the metal detector before meetings. Bixler insisted on a private security company, because he said he didn't trust "political appointees." When I'd approach, I'd take off my jacket, sling it over the back of the folding chair the rent-a-cop never seemed to sit in, and make a big show of going through my pants and shirt pockets.

I'd walk through the metal detector, it would beep, he'd find a small pocket knife on me, then he'd announce that he'd just hang onto this until I left. I'd whine that's it's just a tiny little thing that I carried as a good luck charm, and couldn't I hang onto it?

He'd say no. I'd get huffy, grab my jacket from the back of his chair and walk inside. He'd watch me with a smug grin on his face – so pleased with himself for finding the knife, he'd never pick up that my jacket hadn't gone through the detector.

"Nice to know the taxpayers are getting their money's worth out of that thing," Buck said, kneading his forehead. "You mind?"

"Not at all," I said, passing the flask back to him.

TOM JERKFACE: The following is the text of a crudely hand-printed note, written in black marker, left in the mail slot of the Batley Daily Needler several days after the Warm Hearth Festival assault. It was deposited sometime in the late-night or early morning hours.

WE ARE THE SLAIN. 15 YEARS AGO YOU DIDNT TAKE US SERIOUS AND YOU PAID. YOU WILL PAY AGAIN. THE ONE WHO TAKES DEMANDS BLOOD.

FILE THREE

It was about a year and a half ago that I stood across the street from Gary Cabot's house on Maple Street, wondering exactly how big a shitstorm I was about to unleash.

I wore a dark sweatshirt, a pair of camouflage pants I'd picked up at the local Army surplus store, and sneakers. Slung over my shoulder was a small backpack containing bolt cutters for the front door lock, which could also double as a weapon in a pinch, a heavy metal flashlight that could also work as a weapon, and a bag of plastic zip ties. My pants pockets held a tension wrench, a lockpick, and a small plastic flashlight. All for the purpose of breaking into an abandoned house.

I make a point of never carrying anything that could be immediately identified as a weapon, convenient as one might be on occasion. I get away with a lot in the course of doing my job. Truth be told, I'm sometimes amazed just how much. But I suspect that toting a gun would sweep me into the dark, uncharted waters of "Too Far" in a hurry.

Still, I figured things might get messy before the night was over.

At this point, it might be useful to explain the nature of my job. I'm a hardworking employee, "operative" is my official job title, of the Friedrich K. Schulze Foundation. Known to both employees and members of the general public as the Freak Foundation. It's a nonprofit that the wealthy family of Friedrich K. Schulze established after his death as a way of assisting people harmed by their infamous scion's misdeeds.

I'm very familiar with Schulze's life, of course. And whatever view of him you subscribe to – visionary genius, diabolical fiend, self-promoting huckster or plain ol' nutjob – you gotta give him credit. He was a pretty interesting guy.

He started out from around these parts. At least, his family did.

An ancestor of his, Otto Schulze, moved to Central Pennsylvania from his native Germany in the 18th Century and established a dairy farm. But Otto's claim to fame was a book he published titled "A Friend for the Knowing Ones." Basically, it was a collection of folk cures and magic spells collected from the old country. It dealt with everything from curing a toothache to stopping a slanderer's tongue.

The book proved a hit and is still in print. Schulze's brood turned out to be a generally level-headed lot and invested the money wisely. Mainly in real estate.

TOM JERKFACE: To provide an example, the following is a spell from "A Friend for the Knowing Ones," to serve the stated purpose of protecting the user from witches and evil spirits: "Cut off a chicken's foot and roast it. Make a cross on your forehead with the grease, then bury the foot under the eaves of your house. Spin around widdershins thrice and say the following: 'Fiends, I forbid thee my house; I forbid thee my horse and cow-stable; I forbid thee my bedstead that thou mayest not breathe upon me.' Then spit over your left shoulder."

By all accounts, later generations of Schulzes were more interested in pork bellies and rate fluctuations between the yen and the U.S. dollar than they were in magic. Until Friedrich came along.

His interest in magic started when he was attending college. He went into academia himself, getting a doctorate in anthropology and landing a teaching gig at a Massachusetts university where he taught courses in occult studies. His lectures on topics such as human sacrifice and ritualistic sex magic were very popular.

But he eventually left the university in disgrace. He reportedly had a thing for young, female students. At the university, rumors of sex-and-drug orgies dogged him from the beginning. Those rumors turned out to be well-founded when police busted his place. Among those arrested was the daughter of conservative senator who, according to the arrest report, was naked, covered in goat's blood, and whacked out on a tincture made from hallucinogenic toad secretions.

When the papers got hold of the story, Schulze denied nothing. By all appearances, he relished the label that the tabloids gave him: Most Evil Man in America.

After his banishment from the university, Schulze spent some years traveling the world on his family's considerable dime, studying various occult traditions. Then he returned to America, where he began writing. His first book was titled "Business Success for the Knowing Ones: A Guide to Folk Magic for the Busy Executive." It drew on the practices of his famous ancestor's work. And like the earlier book, it was a runaway bestseller.

TOM JERKFACE: The following is an excerpt from "Business Success for the Knowing Ones: A Guide to Folk Magic for the Busy Executive," by Friedrich K. Schulze. The author claims it's a spell by which you can banish a business rival: "Take a personal effect of your rival, such as a portrait of his family or a favorite golf club, and bury it in a graveyard at midnight. Cross yourself thrice, spin around counterclockwise thrice then say the following: 'I forbid thee my office; I forbid thee my bedstead; I forbid thee my portfolio that thou mayest not breathe upon me.' Then spit over your left shoulder. If that doesn't work, spread a rumor that he's gay."

That was his only time on the bestseller list, although his books picked up quite a following in the ensuing years. They still have healthy sales. Wander into the "Occult" or "New Age" section of any bookstore and you'll likely find two or three of them.

His earlier books were relatively tame. Self-help with a sprinkling of Jungian mythology. Later works were darker, more intense, and weirder. He wrote about casting off your false mantle as a civilized human being, and embracing your true identity as mythical creature. He claimed to have the ability to summon up spirits, demons and ancient gods, and to be able to pass those abilities on to those who followed his teachings.

No different from plenty of other authors favored by the type of people who have lots of unicorn art in their homes. But Schulze showed an entrepreneurial bent that went beyond selling books.

Schulze established a national organization – he'd bristle if anyone called it a "religion" in his presence – called the "International Society for Mythical Studies and Personal Development." He then left its operation to his staffers so he could travel and continue his "research," which included frequenting S&M clubs and satanic masses. He even traveled with a carnival freak show for a while, showcasing his purported magic powers alongside some characters named Rubberella, Mr. Masokismo, and Fat Clem. That was when he'd reportedly first met Cabot, who was working for another sideshow.

Sixteen years ago, Schulze announced he was opening a "Spiritual Healing and Exploration Clinic" in a sprawling, three-story house in Batley. His brochures claimed he'd picked the spot from "psychic mapping" that showed "the barriers between worlds were thin" around Batley.

A few religious types squawked. But by and large, the city was grateful for any tax revenue.

So he set up shop. He brought in staffers from his organization who bought or rented homes around Batley. Patients came to his center, to judge by the brochures, to be treated for everything from drug addiction to a general case of the blahs.

After establishing the center and leaving its operation, Schulze published his last book. And it was a doozy.

It's called "When the Ancient Ones Feed." I slogged through it because I figured it's part of my job. I damn near went cross-eyed in the process, and felt like I needed a shower afterward.

Basically, it's one long, crazed rant that appears to draw on some personal mythology he never bothered to explain to anyone else. I'm no prude, but I found it pretty goddamn revolting. Some of the more noteworthy passages call for "celebrating the blood harvest" with sex orgies – he specifically recommends that sex acts with animals be included – and cannibalism. The paperback edition I read is 600 pages, with no paragraph breaks and damn few periods.

Let's just say it didn't burn up the bestseller lists. To this day, some of his more indulgent apologists try to explain it as an attempt to disorient and shock the reader into a higher state of consciousness. Most write it off to brain rot, brought on by heavy drug use or possibly syphilis.

About the time of "When the Ancient Ones Feed's" publication, Schulze disappeared. In a final communication to his followers, he stated that he was going on a dangerous "vision quest." In case he didn't return, he was leaving young disciple Gary Cabot as his "spiritual successor."

I was already knocking around Batley by the time all this happened. Cabot was a recluse even back then, and I never saw him. I did see a guy who worked with Cabot. He was a dwarf. A black guy in his fifties. Sometimes I'd see the dwarf in bars, nursing a beer, reading a newspaper and muttering to himself. His arms and legs were short, but he looked like he had some muscles on him. I never talked to him. He seemed grouchy.

For a while, Schulze's whereabouts were a subject of great speculation. That ended a few years after all the shit around here went down, when somebody found his remains on the remote slope of a mountain in New Mexico. He'd apparently decided to make an ascent with few provisions and less experience. Dental records can be pretty handy sometimes.

One day 15 years ago, most of the staffers of Schulze's Spiritual Healing and Exploration Clinic left town without a trace. And in what absolutely nobody on this planet believes to be a coincidence, The Slain staged its first attack on the city almost immediately afterward.

The residents of Batley became aware that something hinky was going on over at the clinic when a ghost showed up walking the streets of the city.

That's what he claimed, anyway. When police picked him up, he said he was the spirit of a murder victim temporarily inhabiting the man's body to look for justice.

Like most police, they probably heard weirder stories on a daily basis. But this guy didn't fit the mold of your typical crazy person wandering the streets. Well-dressed and well-fed. Relatively coherent. No signs of intoxication or drug use. Social workers tried to find out who he was, and eventually tracked him back to Nevada. Turned out he'd signed on for Schulze's clinic a year ago, and hadn't been heard from since.

During the investigation to come, the headline "Chamber of Horrors" showed up on the front page of quite a few newspapers. Among the findings at the Spiritual Healing and Exploration Clinic:

- Examination rooms, with two-way mirrors in the walls.
- Electroshock tables, complete with restraining straps.
- Sensory deprivation chambers.
- A collection of mind-altering substances beyond the most debauched hippie's wildest dreams. Legal and decidedly illegal. Common and exotic.

And last but not least? People. Hundreds of them. Some were near catatonic, or sobbing and screaming incessantly. A lucky few were just fine, if a bit confused by all the fuss, and returned home promptly. Between those two poles was a broad range of fucked-up.

That particular brand of fucked-up was eventually termed "Schulze Syndrome" in the Diagnostic and Statistical Manual of Mental Disorders.

Some were ghosts. Others were lycanthropes. Werewolves, mostly. And a smattering of vampires, demons, and elves.

A couple of their identities required me to do some research once they became my charges and I figured I better educate myself on their backstories. There was a hamadryad, a Greek nymph that inhabits trees. One young guy claimed to be Anu, the Sumero-Babylonian god. An improbably Teutonic-looking woman presented herself as Xilonen, an Aztec maize goddess. Speaking of Teutons, there was a kobold from their tradition — an earth spirit that lives in mines. I thought that particular guy kind of looked the part.

No need to go into all the variations. Let's just say that damn near every major culture had at least one deity or mythical creature stumbling around that place and generally getting in the way of police trying to investigate.

They were both male and female. Different ages and ethnicities. Just regular people, aside from the fact that they were totally delusional.

So I waited, that night a year-and-a-half ago when I went out to Maple Street. Across the street from me sat two adjoining houses. The one to the left, surrounded by a wall, was Cabot's house. It was two stories. White. Well-kept-up and pretty innocuous looking. Aside from the wall, that is, which was brick and about eight feet high, with a gate that apparently could be unlocked by hand or electronically from inside.

The decrepit, boarded-up house to the right was supposedly vacant. Surrounding it was chain-link fence, which was also about eight feet high and might as well have been a solid wall because of all the vegetation that had grown up around it.

From observing the house through binoculars, I knew its front was spray-painted here and there with a crude "DTM." This was the tag for "Downtown Mafia," the street gang that supposedly controlled this block. Their only block, it seemed. And since this block consisted of nothing more than Cabot's house, some vacant properties and a few residents who'd never see 70 again, that would make them about the least ambitious street gang in the history of urban settlement if they really existed. And I had good reason to suspect they didn't.

I checked my watch. Right about 10. On schedule, a guy sauntered out of the gate in the chain-link fence surrounding the property next to Cabot's and into view under the streetlight. He was taking the last drags off a cigarette. I'd say he was in his mid-thirties. Black. Looked a bit doughy. Wearing a black nylon jacket and a knit hat. Not very convincing as a soldier in a street gang. But then, I'd been dubious about the Downtown Mafia before I even started investigating them in earnest.

Don't get me wrong. There's plenty of gang activity in Batley. The big drug dealers from Philadelphia, Baltimore and even Washington, D.C., long ago identified it as a potentially lucrative secondary market, and dispatched young men with guns and packets of illicit powders to stake out turf, make sales and occasionally shoot at each other.

When I was checking in with my contacts around town, I kept hearing that the Downtown Mafia controlled that particular block. I asked my buddy Tom, who works as a reporter at the local newspaper, to look in the files for any shootings reported on that block. The closest thing he found to a shooting was three years earlier, when a street punk died from an asthma attack on Cabot's property after he was causing a disturbance and a purported member of the Downtown Mafia pepper sprayed him.

I asked Tom to double check that. Because gang members shoot people. They stab them. They beat them with fists or feet or whatever's lying around. But they do not, in my experience, pepper spray them.

A look at court records confirmed my suspicion. The street soldier in question was acquitted because he was not a street soldier. He was an employee of a private security firm based in Maryland called "Security Concepts, Inc." And it seemed a safe bet that the doughy gentleman across the street flicking his cigarette butt in the gutter worked for the same employer. He gave one more look around, then started down the sidewalk. I took a deep breath and got ready to make my move.

Cabot's house, like the others on the block, was a remnant of more genteel days in the city of Batley. They had sizable front yards, unlike most city dwellings. Although the yard of the building on the right, my target, was now choked with weeds and untamed bushes.

Waiting. Waiting. Sure enough, a young white guy attired like his heavier black co-worker emerged from the chain link gate, made a right, and walked up to Cabot's gate. Another guy, also young and white, opened Cabot's gate and let him in.

I'd been observing them for a couple weeks, and taking notes on their patterns. At any given time, two guys were stationed in Cabot's front yard, and another two in the yard next door. I don't know whether it was the guys themselves or some error in planning, but the setup was pretty slipshod.

The doughy guy had finished his shift and about now would be climbing into his car around the corner and driving off. The fact that his habitually late replacement hadn't yet arrived didn't seem to be a problem, as far as he was concerned.

A minute or two after the black guy left, the young white guy also supposedly doing guard duty in front of the abandoned house next door would slip over to Cabot's place. Maybe he was shooting the shit with the other guys. The important thing, from my perspective, is that he appeared to leave the gate in the chain-link fence unfastened. I could probably have scaled the fence if I had to, but not without making a lot of noise. I like when people make my job easier.

I knew I had ten, maybe fifteen minutes before the guard wandered back over, which is about the time it would typically take for the doughy guy's replacement to show up. I scurried across the street, trying to stay out of the streetlight's direct circle of illumination. In the gate. Good.

I hunkered down behind an overgrown bush and listened. I could make out some muted conversation from the lawn next door. And I picked up a distinct whiff of ganja, which suddenly made the routine I'd witnessed more comprehensible. Staying low, trying to avoid making noise, I slunk toward the front porch. Slow, I had to remind myself. No point tripping over something in the overgrown yard and giving myself away. Eventually, I reached the wooden porch and climbed the steps, taking care not to make noise.

Sure enough, as I'd observed from a distance, boards covered the windows. The city would have done that. But the city hadn't installed the padlock on the front door. That meant I could remove it without legal ramifications. I set down my backpack and took out the bolt cutters.

See, the city contracts out to the Freak Foundation to perform certain vaguely defined tasks connected with cleaning up the big, steaming mess that Schulze left here 15 years ago. Does that make me a city employee? It's debatable. But I'd yet to find an element of ambiguity in that relationship I wasn't willing to exploit. I started in on the lock.

I'd checked the ownership on the house, and discovered a baffling succession of shell companies culminating with an anonymous P.O. box in Delaware.

City housing rolls officially listed the property next to Cabot's as abandoned. Which meant the Batley Housing Office would attempt to clear the title and eventually sell or demolish it. Given the city's current financial situation and the backlog at city hall, that might happen mid-to-late next geologic epoch.

Batley has plenty of abandoned homes. Some are even guarded, if the downtown gangs are using them for one reason or another. But I'd wager this was the only "abandoned home" in the city that somebody'd hired a private security company to guard.

I pulled out the bolt cutters and positioned them over the lock. And then, just for a second or two, I hesitated while two words went through my mind. "Cabot's Master."

It was the kind of story that kids scare each other with on campouts or sleepovers, with flashlights held under their chins to give themselves spooky face shadows while they tell it.

Except in Batley, adults would tell each other this story. During whispered conversations in the breakroom at work. Or during the half hour before closing time, when people at the bar were good and liquored-up and the conversation turned to subjects nobody was supposed to talk about.

Technically, it wasn't really a story. A story has a beginning, middle, and end. Something happens. Things are different afterward.

This was just – I don't know what you'd call it. An image. A concept. An under-the-bed boogey man. Cabot wasn't alone in that house. Something else was in there with him. Cabot's Master. The one he served.

Details? Descriptions? Nobody had them. Nobody needed them. Cabot's Master was in there, that was all. Waiting. In case some fool should happen to...

OK, I didn't have time for this bullshit.

The bolt cutters did the trick. I winced as the lock clunked onto the wooden porch, but the conversation next door seemed undisturbed. I hoped the guards wouldn't notice the missing lock.

I tried the door, but another lock held it. A deadbolt, by the looks of it. I took out the small flashlight, the tension wrench and the pick. Holding the flashlight in my mouth and shining it on the lock, I inserted the wrench — a tiny, hooked piece of metal. Just a little bit of pressure as I turned it. Then the pick, a small flat piece of metal with a triangular bump on the end. I inserted that as well and worked it up and down, raking the pins in the lock.

It was meticulous, frustrating work. I had to remind myself to stay calm and take deep breaths. Getting frustrated and sloppy wouldn't accomplish anything. As the lock turned and the bolt slid out, I was grateful for the hours I'd spent practicing in preparation for this.

I waited until I swung the door shut behind me to look around with the small flashlight. I was in a vestibule, with a couple coat hooks on the wall and another door in front of me. I tried it. Another deadbolt lock. I was a bit more relaxed as I went to work on this one. Eventually, it gave way too.

I took out the big, metal flashlight and looked around. I was in a carpeted hallway. In front of me, a flight of stairs led to the second floor. To my left was a big living room with a hardwood floor, a fireplace and no furniture.

I made my way around the first floor. Living room. What I assumed to be a dining room. Kitchen. Bathroom. No personal effects left around anywhere. I scanned the floors, looking for obvious signs of foot traffic, but it was hard to tell in the dim light.

I tried every door I could, discovering a few closets and a pantry and finding nothing in them other than some hangers and cardboard boxes. Underneath the stairs, a door opened onto a faceful of cold, dank air and some stairs leading down to the basement. That could wait.

First, I'd check out the second floor. I walked over to the stairs and started to climb.

Nobody ever connected The Slain to Cabot. Truth be told, nobody ever officially connected them to Schulze, either. In their semi-coherent communications to police and the media, The Slain used lots of rhetoric that seemed lifted straight from Schulze's books. "Opening the soul gate." "Madness that transforms." That kind of shit. Between that and their emergence around the time the clinic got busted, everyone pretty much assumed they were tied in.

The only staffers left at the clinic were a few low-ranking flunkies who claimed they didn't know the extent of what was going on.

That's what Cabot claimed too. Nobody believed him. But he lived away from the local clinic. No witnesses ever placed him there. He was on the Schulze organization's payroll, but didn't appear to be in charge of anything. In the long run, investigators came up with nothing to charge him with, let alone convict him. Once in a while, someone would spray-paint a few choice remarks on his front wall or wing a rock at his windows, but that seemed the extent of the consequences he'd faced.

In public statements, Cabot took the stance of condemning Schulze but not his teachings. He continued the International Society for Mythical Studies and Personal Development. Incredibly, despite everything, it still did a healthy business. Thousands of people worldwide still signed on to receive printed, audio and visual materials for courses with names like "Finding the Archetype Within" and "Harnessing Spirits for Social and Professional Success."

Cabot, already reclusive, became a virtual hermit. He emerged only twice a year for retreats out in the woods, for which people would pay steep prices. He'd demonstrate his otherworldly powers by getting buried alive. Then hours later, followers would return to the flag-marked location where he was interred and dig him up to find him dirty but otherwise just fine.

Personally, I didn't much give a shit what he was up to, as long as he was keeping out of trouble. Then a couple weeks earlier, my boss Sister Pilar Lopez got a photo in the mail that she passed on to me. It showed Cabot sitting on a bench next to a boy, about 12, against a backdrop of overgrown bushes.

It was taken from a high angle, apparently the second floor of a nearby home. The two appeared to be talking. Accompanying it was a typed, unsigned note that read: "I am sending this to you because I don't know what else to do. As you can see, that monster Gary Cabbot (sic) has a young boy staying with him. I don't usually take pictures of people like this and I don't want no problems with him or with anyone. I'm just scared about the boy and hope you folks can do something."

Cabot, supposedly, was living alone. He had no children. He also, according to my research, had no siblings. So that put the kibosh on any visiting nephew scenario.

I camped out in the building across the street for a while. Yes, there was a kid. And yes, that fact scared the shit out of me.

See, in "When the Ancient Ones Feed," Schulze goes on at length about how people once had the power to call certain beings to the "physical plain," and the powerful role that sacrifice – particularly human sacrifice, particularly children – played in that process.

Was I being paranoid? A few years back, I asked myself that same question. I decided to go with my gut anyway. And holy shit am I happy about that!

One of my clients was Cliff Norris. Before traveling to Schulze's clinic in search of help overcoming his awkwardness around women, Norris had been an office manager in Kansas. In recent years, however, Norris was convinced he'd become a vampire after pledging his soul to Satan.

The whole scenario was woefully unoriginal. But give him credit. He certainly was dedicated to it. That much became clear when he went after me with a steak knife in his kitchen. I doused him with a jar of lukewarm tap water that I'd told him was holy water, and he collapsed to the ground screaming in pain. Later in the emergency room, they refused to believe I'd only used lukewarm water because his skin blistered. I don't blame them. Emergency room technicians see a hell of a lot, but you could say my clients are a special breed.

In Norris' basement, I found two-year-old Jamaad Richardson, who Norris kidnapped in the belief that sacrificing him would make the boy his undead servant. Jamaad was sitting in the middle of a pentagram painted on the floor, and was alive and well. In fact, he looked happy as a clam and only started crying after I took away the shiny dagger he was playing with.

Norris' case set a precedent as the first time Schulze Syndrome was successfully used as a legal defense. Norris now lives in a hospital ward. He's doped to the gills and spends most of his time smiling vacantly at a TV, regardless of whether it's turned on or not. I'm glad Jamaad's safe. But a big part of my job is preventing shit like that from happening in the first place, so I still feel pretty lousy about the whole thing.

At this point, I should say I have nothing but the highest respect and esteem for our local police. But Chief Sanderson, for all his competence and dedication as a lawman, does not like shit-stirrers. Since occasionally stirring up shit is part of my job description, it's maybe inevitable that he and I weren't gonna be pals.

Sanderson didn't like that I'd taken things into my own hands in the Norris case. Since I'd apparently prevented a child murder, he couldn't exactly nail me to the wall for it. But he made it clear that he'd welcome any future opportunity to bust my balls. Hard.

Which is why I wasn't eager to go running to him with suspicions I'd gleaned from peeping into someone's yard with a pair of binoculars. Still, those suspicions got worse and worse.

Every afternoon, before the guards showed up, Cabot would emerge from the front door of the house next to his, in the company of the boy. The kid was skinny, average height for his age, with long brown hair. At first, I thought he was a girl.

I never saw Cabot enter the house next door to begin with, so I figured it must have a shared basement with his place.

Screened from view by the vegetation lining the fence and protected by the locked gate, the two of them would just hang out in the yard. Sometimes they appeared to be talking. Other times, the kid would wander around or do a few clumsy cartwheels while Cabot sat on a bench and read. A couple hours later, they would re-enter the house and not show up again.

From watching the property, I also learned that Cabot wasn't quite the recluse his reputation suggested. A bunch of times, sometimes when the guards were there, sometimes not, he had visitors. Without exception, they were rough-looking guys. We're talking tattoos, bandannas, leather jackets, shaved heads or long hair with shaggy beards. Sometimes they'd stay an hour or two, sometimes longer. Then they'd leave by themselves, more often than not to climb on a motorcycle and ride away.

I figured it was worth taking a look around the house.

A light shone from the second floor. It wasn't bright. But the closer I got to the top of the stairs, the more evident it was.

When I reached the top, a big, mostly empty room opened to my left. Bare wood floor. Bare wood paneling on the walls. In the middle was a regular floor lamp, plugged into a wall socket. Near the front of the room, positioned at one of the windows, was a painter's easel and canvas. And sitting in a chair with a paintbrush in his hand was Cabot himself.

He looked over at me, started, then set down the paintbrush and stood up. He was tall. Older than in the pictures I'd seen of him. Maybe late thirties or early forties. Long, dark hair framed a clean-shaven, high-cheekboned face. He wore jeans and some kind of military surplus jacket, which hung open to reveal a lean, muscular physique.

"Can I help you?" he asked. "I don't have any money, if that's what you're looking for."

For a man some people considered to be the living embodiment of evil, he seemed strangely soft-spoken. Deferential, even.

I swallowed.

"No," I said. "Sorry if I startled you. I'm with the city. I was looking for a runaway, and I got a tip that he might be in here. I was told that this building was abandoned."

"Technically, it is," Cabot said. "My house and this one have a shared basement."

He motioned toward the window. He'd removed the board from the outside and it afforded a pretty spectacular view of the city, inasmuch as any view of Batley can be called spectacular.

"A tree blocks the view from my house," he said.

I looked at his painting. The foreground needed some filling in, but he'd captured the Batley skyline pretty well.

"Hey, that's pretty good!"

He smiled.

"That's very charitable of you. It's just a hobby."

"I see you're even hooked up for electricity over here."

He smiled again, a bit sheepishly this time.

"Since it's hooked into my meter, I decided I wasn't technically stealing from anyone. I didn't know if it was legal or not, but it's always easier to ask for forgiveness than permission. I certainly understand if you need to ..."

I waved a hand.

"No dent in my package. I'm strictly runaway kids. Don't suppose you've seen a kid around here? Boy? White kid? Long brown hair? Maybe about 12?"

"Well, I've been here for about three hours," Cabot said. "I would have noticed if he came up here. So if you didn't see him downstairs ..."

"Any idea what's past that door?"

One door was in the back wall of the room, with a bolted-on hasp and a padlock.

"No idea," Cabot said. "It's been like that since I moved here. Storage, maybe. Hey, I was about to pour myself a drink. Care to join me? I don't get many visitors."

"Not supposed to drink on the job," I said. "But I guess what my boss doesn't find out won't kill her."

"You look like a Scotch man. Am I right?"

"Got me pegged," I said.

"I'll be right back," Cabot said. "Please, take a seat."

I noticed several folding chairs leaning against the back wall. I unfolded one, but didn't sit in it. I strode over and took a look at the locked door. Put my ear to it. Nothing. Gave a soft knock. Nothing.

I walked back to the chair and sat down. A couple minutes later, Cabot returned. Each hand held a glass brimming with Scotch. He handed me one and sat down.

"Well, cheers," he said, raising his glass and taking a drink.

I raised my glass too, but just sniffed at it.

"Smells good," I said. "Single malt?"

"I like to indulge myself."

"I pride myself on being kind of a Scotch connoisseur. You mind if I take a look at the label?"

"Sorry. I left the bottle back at my house."

I set down my glass on the floor.

"In that case, I have to compliment you on your dexterity," I said. "I figure you were gone maybe three minutes. Four minutes, tops. You went down, what, two flights of stairs, across the basement, then up more stairs to your house. You poured a couple glasses of Scotch, then made the trip back. You must've really been hauling ass. But looks like you didn't spill a drop."

He set down his glass and stared at me, no expression on his face. I went on.

"I don't know what's in this glass. I can guess. So you didn't buy my story about being from the city. Fair enough. I don't believe you were up here for three hours, because I would've seen the light from the street."

Still no reaction from him.

"I'm guessing I set off an alarm when I was taking care of the locks on the front door, and you booked up here. And speaking of locks, that one behind you looks pretty damn new to me for a lock that's been sitting in an abandoned house for a decade."

Finally, he responded. He stood and walked over to the window.

"All I need to do is signal my men outside, and you're dead," he said. "I'll give you one chance. Get out of here right now."

"Well," I said, "I guess you gotta do what you gotta do. So go ahead."

He hesitated. And that hesitation told me that all my assumptions had been right.

I'd researched Security Concepts, Inc. They were a few pay grades above shopping mall rent-a-cops. But not the amount you'd pay if you wanted people who'd keep their mouths shut after witnessing a crime. And well short of plug-someone-and-disappear-the-body territory. I figured that's the whole reason why his last line of defense was a glass of Scotch as opposed to a shotgun.

"Look," I said. "I'm not a cop. I'm not here to bust you."

"I just want to see the ..."

He cut his eyes back over my left shoulder.

"Now!" he yelled.

I looked behind me. Nobody there. I looked back but he was already on me.

Stupid stupid fucking stupid! Oldest trick in the book and I fell for it like the rookiest of rookies. He straight-armed me, knocking me back in my chair, no way to make it a good fall now as I went over backwards, stunned for a second when the back of my head banged the floor. Then he was on my chest, knees up in my armpits, keeping his weight low, giving me no leverage. Good jiu jitsu position. Must've have training.

He raised his arm and I saw a small, black paddle-shaped object in one hand. A leather-wrapped sap by the looks of it. And it turned out that's exactly what it was as I shielded my face and it hit my left forearm, which went numb after the first flash of pain.

He raised his arm again. If that thing hit my head, the fight was over.

I curled my lower body, driving a knee into spine. You do it right, it hurts like a bitch. I guess I did it right because he yelled and arched his back. I slammed the side of my fist into his sternum like I was swinging a hammer and threw him off me.

Doesn't matter whether you're on your feet or on the ground. You lose your balance, you lose your advantage.

I jumped forward, hit the ground in a roll and then to my feet. I needed to put some distance between me and him. Get my bearings. Regroup. He was already on his feet and moving toward me. Strong, about six inches on me, looked like he knew what the fuck he was doing and armed. Not good. Not good at all.

I was next to his folding chair. Thought about picking it up and swinging it. But I didn't trust my left arm, which felt like a hunk of frozen meat below the elbow, to grip it. I grabbed the back of it with my right hand and winged it at him. As he raised him arms to block it I was on him. I feinted toward his face then ducked low, crooking a leg around his shins and driving my upper body into his legs. My signature move. Using my lower center of gravity. Height advantage, my ass. He went over backwards. I was on my feet first. Him already charging me as he got up.

But I was there first again, slamming my forearm down on the back of his neck while I brought my knee up into the point of his chin. "The button," as boxers call it. As in "the off button." He crumpled to the floor.

I stood there for a second. Hands on my thighs. Catching my breath. Damn.

Then I hurried to my pack and got out the plastic zip ties. I joined two of them together in a loop big enough for a man's wrist, and repeated the process with a couple more. I put them around Cabot's wrists and cinched them. I got his arms behind his back and used another tie to join the two loops together. Good as reinforced steel handcuffs, for my purposes.

Then I took the bolt cutters out of my pack and went to the door on the back wall. No deadbolt here. Good. I took care of the lock with my pick and tension wrench, then opened the door. It was a hallway lit by an overhead light, with several rooms branching off it.

The doors were open. They were all empty except for one bathroom. A bar of soap, a toothbrush and a tube of toothpaste sat on the sink. And at the end of the hall, one closed door.

As I approached it, I heard a voice. Small and frightened.

"Is somebody out there?"

"Hey kid," I said. "I'm harmless. OK if I open the door?"

A long pause.

"It's OK."

For once, I had no lock to deal with. Inside, a bedroom. Clothes scattered all over the place. A few paperbacks and comic books. The kid I'd seen through the binoculars sat on the floor in front of a TV, a video game controller in his hand. He looked up at me with big, frightened eyes.

Might as well cut to the chase.

"Are you OK?" I asked. "Do you want to get out of there?"

No hesitation on his part.

"Yes," he said. "I don't like it here."

I led him out through the room where Cabot lay, still unconscious. The kid looked at him, then at me. He still looked scared but he kept following me.

We went down the stairs. Then a thought occurred to me.

"Do you think he's keeping anyone else here?" I asked him.

The kid thought.

"He told me nobody else was here. But one time when he took me outside, I heard noises coming from the basement."

"I better check," I said.

I went to the basement door and got ready to open it. He looked scared before, but now his face showed outright terror. I guess he figured I was about to leave him alone in that dark house.

I gave him my big, metal flashlight, which seemed to reassure him somewhat. Then I took out my little plastic light, opened the door and went down the stairs.

I reached the bottom and swept the light back and forth, even though it didn't give off a lot of illumination. There was stuff around me. I gave it a quick once-over. Lots of cardboard boxes and crates. Some looked big enough to hold a grand piano.

On the floor sat a huge roll of striped canvas that I assumed was a tent. A long, dusty wooden sign painted in bright colors leaned against it. The sign read "WILD BILLY'S WORLD OF MARVELS! Curiosities and monstrosities to thrill and delight young and old alike!" The light didn't reach the end of the basement, which was farther away than I expected. I could just make out a set of stairs.

"Hey!" I called. "Anybody here?"

A door at the far end opened. I heard a kind of high-pitched, keening wail. Like "AAAAaaaaAAAaaaaaa!" And something started making its way down into the basement. It was enormous, whatever it was. Slow and lumbering. I could tell by the steps on the wooden stairs. Then I could see the shape. Just an amorphous shadow, really, but bigger than any man.

A blind, nightmare panic took hold of me and I ran back up the stairs behind me. I emerged and the kid was staring at me with eyes the size of billiard balls. I took the flashlight from him and grabbed him by the hand.

"Come on! We gotta go!"

We ran to the front door. I opened it and we tore down the porch steps and onto the lawn.

"Hey!"

The security guard I'd seen earlier was in front of us. He reached for me. I slammed my arm into his chest while sweeping his legs out from under him, and he made a "Whoof!" noise as he hit the ground.

We headed for the gate. I'd observed that most of the time, they wouldn't bother locking it after the first guard finished his shift. I hoped that would be the case tonight. I saw another guard, a tall black guy, running at us. I whipped my flashlight at him. It went end-over-end, then a metallic clang and a shout of pain as it hit.

They were just guys doing their jobs and I didn't want to hurt them. But we really needed to get the fuck out of there.

The gate was unlocked. Hallelujah and praise the Lord! I threw it open, then led the kid at a full run down the sidewalk for a couple blocks and around the corner to my car.

Soon after, we were in my apartment. The kid was looking around, still wide-eyed, maybe incredulous that a room could be even messier than his own.

I was on the phone with Buck.

"Buck? We got a situation here."

And that pretty much ended my involvement in the matter. Professionally, anyway. Buck ran interference for me with the police. Sanderson wasn't pleased with the situation, particularly since Cabot was packed up and gone by the time police got to the house. What can I say? My goals were to save the kid and cover my own ass. Probably in that order, but don't make me swear on a Bible.

The kid said his name was Paul Bacon. He'd lived his life up until that point in a commune in Colorado, but he knew he had family in Batley.

The Bacons are clients of mine, and I know them quite well. It seemed to make sense, inasmuch as anything in my job ever does.

A couple of my police sources, whose names I will not divulge as Sanderson would slowly flay them if he ever found out, said Cabot did a thorough job of cleaning out anything that might give a clue as to his whereabouts.

No electroshock tables or sensory isolation chambers this time around. The only narcotics came in the form of chloral hydrate added to a thermos of Scotch. More than enough to send anyone who drank it into a good, long nap. Police discovered the thermos, along with a regular bottle of Scotch, in a cardboard box in one of the abandoned house's closets.

The most ominous discovery, as far as I was concerned, was a room on the ground floor of Cabot's place that contained several mattresses lined up on the floor, some children's furniture — a dresser and a clown lamp — and a television set. Police also found a bunch of crayons scattered around.

But the basement contained the real find.

What I'd glimpsed were the packed-up remnants of Cabot's old carnival show. While that would likely be a fascinating haul for any aficionado of quirky Americana, police investigators tend to be a more hard-headed lot.

They were more interested in the amateurishly poured concrete that all the boxes and crates were arranged specifically to cover. They took a jackhammer to it, and their suspicions proved valid.

Buried under Cabot's floor were two skeletons. One was a woman. At first, police thought the other was a child. But forensic tests proved that it was a full-grown man. A dwarf.

TOM JERKFACE: The following is an excerpt from Friedrich K. Schulze's book "Evoking the Dark," reprinted with the permission of his publisher, Singing Earth Goddess Press.

For who can doubt these things exist? Indeed, we know they do. We know it with an understanding that transcends "rational thought." And what is "rational thought" but a rote negation of any deeper comprehension, which social institutions foist upon us at an early age for the specific purpose of stunting our souls and blinkering our perceptions?

Yes, some modern academicians will acknowledge the universality of mythical archetypes such as the ghost and the demon, the faerie and the demigod. They will tell us that they are some amalgamation of chemicals and electrical impulses within our brain tissue, projected on the world we perceive.

Or perhaps they're a childish coping method. The learned will tell us that we are merely seeking order by imposing anthropomorphic shapes on an inherently shapeless universe, much as a child will ascribe sentience to a stuffed animal and cling to it for comfort in a darkened bedroom.

They will never acknowledge the possibility that our perception of these beings, these phenomena, may have a real and objective basis. Perhaps they don't stand before us physically. Still we perceive their presence from somewhere, much as the moon does not produce light itself, yet still reflects that radiance which its source conveys across the frigid gulfs of space.

Consider, if you will, the staggering arrogance of modern-day humanity. In merely the last century or so, our "rational" thought has supplanted millennia of human experience and belief. How proud we are! How complacent in our certainty! How utterly foolish!

The deities of ancient people were not mere phantasms of the subconscious. Hecate an internalized fear of a scolding mother. Moloch a stern and imposing father who never gave hugs.

Even among the most genuinely devout in our modern times, the gods they worship are laughable abstractions. They'll come one day to redeem the world. They just haven't gotten around to it for century upon century, preferring instead to offer tiny mood uplifts to the needy and pathetic or manifest themselves in 'miracles' such as burnt toast that vaguely resembles a long-haired, bearded face.

Among the ancients, such insipid forms of worship did not exist. For the ancient people of the world possessed the power to open the gateway to the realm of the gods. They would not merely pray to their gods, but summon them to behold them in all their glory and terror.

Terror, because these were not the comforting, teddy bear gods which modern worshippers create for their own comfort and use as repositories for their own anxieties.

The gods that the ancients evoked cared not for human comfort. They demanded much, in terms of obeisance, ordeal in the form of ritual, and — quite frequently — blood. In return, they would offer their followers powers and insights that far transcend the vulgar parlor tricks modern science puts before us. The gods would offer a kind of madness, but a madness that transforms the banal lives of believers into a transcendent and splendid existence.

I know that the very real evocation of these gods is possible. Through ritual and belief. Through ingestion of mind-altering substances and self-flagellation. Through myriad techniques that are largely lost to us, but which the determined and adventurous might rediscover, ancient gods can indeed walk among us. I myself have witnessed it. I myself have performed it. I have seen ancient gods walk the face of this earth.

TOM JERKFACE: The following is an excerpt from Friedrich K. Schulze's book "When the Ancient Ones Feed," reprinted with the permission of his publisher, Singing Earth Goddess Press.

And as the sky breaks forward with the viscera of the gods, the cuntblood of the lost goddess with the thousand limbs chokes the seas and the dancing minions of the grasping hands cavort and laugh for the time has come oh the time the time the glorious time for the feasting upon the silky flesh of the young what rapture is the great hunger sated. And stretching to the sky stands Kerthlashan, Ancient Leper God whose deathstench fills the void as he strokes his rotting cock and from his cum riseth the ancient nightmares of those who fuck the dead the dead rise and the cycle is completed for the blood is the completion the blood is the glorious death that is not death but everlasting death upon your knees those who are stricken and give glory unto the blood.

TOM JERKFACE: *Six months after Schulze's clinic in Batley was shut down, the district attorney announced that Gary Cabot would face no criminal charges. Cabot issued the following news release.*

    First of all, I extend my deepest condolences to those harmed by the Spiritual Healing and Exploration Clinics and their families. I would like to state most emphatically that neither I nor any members of my personal staff knew of the illegal and unethical activities taking place there. Had I known, I would have immediately brought it to the attention of law enforcement.
    Compounding this tragedy is that Mr. Schulze had so much to offer. He had been a mentor to me. He was a man of great learning and insight, whose writings and discoveries represent a significant contribution to human knowledge and spiritual evolution.
    The fact that he used his status as a respected teacher to exploit those who came to him for help and guidance is inexcusable. Yet Mr. Schulze's deplorable actions do not negate the importance and value of his earlier writings and discoveries.
    Indeed, much of Mr. Schulze's work could be a powerful force for good, especially during an era in which so many people find themselves spiritually adrift and desperate for some higher meaning. Recent events would prove even more tragic if we were to lose all of that work because of them.
    I have thus decided to continue the International Society for Mythical Studies and Personal Development, in the hopes that some good might eventually come of all this.
    I thank all of the Society members and followers who have been supportive during this trying time. And I will close by expressing my sincere wish that the people harmed find some healing in their lives.

    In Transcendence,
    Gary Cabot
    Executive director, International Society for Mythical Studies and Personal Development

FILE FOUR

TOM JERKFACE: *The following is from a written account scattered in sections throughout the report. It appears to have been composed on an old-fashioned typewriter. Sections of it were evidently missing. Those included were labeled "FROM BILLY'S PAPERS" in felt-tip marker. I have included them exactly the way they appeared in the original document, labeled accordingly.*

AN ACCOUNT OF RECENT EVENTS CONCERNING
THE CITY OF BATLEY, PENNSYLVANIA
By William "Wild Billy" Cleary, showman and entrepreneur

If I had to identify the genesis of the whole sorry affair, I'd say it began with our arrival in a little, shitkicker burg in the hinterlands of Pennsylvania, which the local residents have the temerity to call a city.

Batley, Pennsylvania.

The afternoon of our second day in Batley that particular year, I stood at a table with three walnut shells in front of me and calculated our odds for the near future. I put them at dismal, with a 40 percent chance of dire. I did not yet realize just how optimistic that prognosis was.

The caravan of trailers, trucks, and cars transporting the component parts of Gypsy Sam's All-American Carnival had arrived at the dusty field on the edge of Batley early the previous morning. We'd spent the first day setting up in time for today's Grand Opening, an event which would prompt any man possessing an iota of discernment to re-evaluate his definition of the word "grand."

Pretty Joe, our new boss, made it clear that he expected efficiency and was prepared to enforce it with his own hairy knuckles if necessary. He was a thug who'd made his ill-gotten fortune with a series of girly shows on the circuit, supplemented with whatever opportunities for grift or extortion came his way. He was quick to snap up the carnival after Gypsy Sam made good on his often-repeated pledge to keep working until the day he died.

I've never put much store in grieving. You simply deal with life's myriad hardships, and if you're lucky things will go your way once in a while. Or you rail against them, which is an annoying and exhausting process that invariably accomplishes dick. Yet it pained me to see Pretty Joe taking over the carnival that Gypsy Sam built with his hands and oiled with his sweat.

Gypsy Sam was a good man. He took me on when I was young, helping me escape from the steaming dogturd of a town where I'd grown up and which would probably have driven me insane even if not for the bullshit I endured as a dwarf.

Were the folks back home unkind to me because of my condition? Absolutely not. They were just nice as can be. Leaning down with hands on their knees to speak to me in the high, singsong tones with which one might address an infant or a cretin. When Gypsy Sam agreed to hire me, I was off faster than a prom dress.

At the time, he wasn't running the whole carnival. He conducted a magic show that employed the standard repertoire of interlocking rings and rabbits out of hats during the day. At night, he'd switch to his spiritualist act. Since I could stuff myself into hiding places where most wouldn't fit, I became what one might call the unbilled star of the séances, rapping out messages from someone's dear departed Aunt Bertha Mae. Gypsy Sam taught me a great deal and I was about to put it to use.

Behind me was my tent with the sign that read "WILD BILLY'S WORLD OF MARVELS!" I scanned the carnival grounds. Within my immediate proximity were a few small-town moms with children, who tended not to be keen on the freak shows at this time of day.

"Come on honey, how about we look at something nicer?" they would say when they drifted near and the little ones began pointing at our tent and pulling at their skirts.

"Delay it all you like, ladies," I would think. "The children are going to learn of life's inherent ugliness sooner or later."

At night, by contrast, the women would drag boyfriends or husbands over by the arm. The garish paintings of monstrously deformed animal/human hybrids out front seemed to give them a strange little thrill inside. And their male companions would go along to demonstrate their virile stoicism in the face of those assorted horrors and grotesqueries.

Later, once the evening rush started, plenty of people would lay down money for both the shell game and the World of Marvels, though maybe not enough to keep us going. Times had been hard lately, necessitating a strategic approach.

So for now, I was laying out traps for men and adolescent boys. The carnival grounds weren't crowded at this time of day, but enough of them milled about. They were the boys skipping school or the men who had the day off. They were the second-shift workers or the habitual avoiders of work. They escorted women on their arms or leaned against walls and smoked cigarettes. Each, being a man, carried within him the conviction that he alone of every swinging dick who ever walked the face of this earth had all the angles figured. And each carried within his pockets the money that was rightfully mine.

That latter condition was about to change. Heralding that change was the waddling arrival of an obese and towering imbecile with a harelip.

Fat Clem wouldn't last for long so we had to move fast. His enormous girth precluded extended periods of walking or even standing. Secreted behind my tent was his modified wheelchair, resembling a weird piece of industrial transport equipment.

He looked at me. I looked at him and nodded. And then he commenced wailing and blubbering. As his howls grew louder and louder, people began to look and gradually drift over. Afternoons were slow on the midway and this was a spectacle, even if they didn't yet know what it was.

A bearded man in a baseball cap, probably at the urging of his bleach-blonde girlfriend, finally approached me. Giving Clem a wary look, he asked "Is he alright?"

"Couldn't tell you," I said, already starting to move the walnut shells in their circular patterns. "Never seen him before. He just wandered over and started blubbering."

"Hey there, partner," said the man with the baseball cap, approaching Clem. "You need any help?"

Clem doubled his volume, bawling openly and bouncing up and down as he waved his arms, fat jiggling all over his enormous frame. A crowd draws a crowd. If that's not one of Newton's laws, it should be. Before long, a small ring of people surrounded Clem, a few giggling at his antics as several good Samaritans tried to extract something coherent from him.

"You found my brother! Thank God!"

They turned to see a tall, long-haired young man in a T-shirt. The kid. With him was a teenaged girl going heavy on the makeup and hairspray, light on the clothes. Her look was clearly calculated to draw the notice of every slobbering lech for three counties. This needed to be addressed. Not now, but very, very soon.

The kid walked into the circle of people, thanking them as he went. Clem dropped the crying for an even more effusive display of elation. He squealed and bounced up and down, drawing more snickers from the onlookers.

"Come on, pal," the kid said to Clem. "You know better than to wander off like that! I was worried sick!"

I began moving the walnut shells in earnest, switching them around in ever-more elaborate patterns. Now was the crucial moment. We didn't want the rubes deciding the show was over and departing. Clem pointed at my table and let out a delighted squeal, seemingly transfixed by my prestidigitation.

"What's that, Clem?" the kid said. "You want to watch this man over here?"

I looked at the kid.

"Want a chance to double your money, sonny? Just keep your eye on the pea!"

I lifted one of the shells to show the pea beneath it.

"Double your money," I said. "One'll getcha two! Five'll getcha 10! Best deal in town but you can't win if you don't play!"

"What do you think, Clem? Want to play?"

Clem laughed and bounced up and down like a happy, 500-pound Jack Russell terrier puppy. I sneered.

"You think this fat retard's going to spot the pea?" I said. "Don't make me laugh!"

A gasp went up from the group watching and several cried out in indignation. Perfect. The kid balled his fists and leaned forward.

"That's my brother you're talking about, mister!" he said. Then he reached into his jeans, pulled out a 5-spot and set it on the table.

"Go ahead, pal," he said. "You show this jerk! Just tell him what shell the pea is under. It's alright. You can do this."

I switched the shells back and forth, making the patterns flashy but not too flashy. The rubes had to think they could tell where the pea was.

When I stopped, the kid directed Clem to pick one of the shells. I lifted the shell toward which Clem had pointed his fat finger. Applause and laughter broke out from the assembled group when the pea rolled out. People love to see the house lose under any conditions. And by now, the kid had them rooting for him. More people wandered over. A crowd draws a crowd.

I acted surprised and disgruntled, then handed the kid the money. The kid turned to Clem.

"Want to try it again pal? Teach this guy a lesson?"

Shouts of encouragement arose from the growing crowd. The kid laid down some more money. I shuffled the shells around. Clem pointed to one and the pea rolled out when I lifted it.

This happened a few more times, the cheers and laughter getting progressively louder as I really played it up, wincing, grumbling, and cursing as Clem picked the right shell over and over and I handed the kid bigger piles of money.

Finally the kid held his fistful of money aloft to the cheers of everyone around him.

"Maybe you'll think about this the next time you get the idea to insult my brother, mister!"

Then he turned and walked away with Clem and — goddamn it — that slutty looking teenage girl. Yes, this absolutely needed to be addressed.

There was no time at the present, though. The rubes swarmed around, practically elbowing each other out of the way to put down their money. After all, how hard could the game be if a half-wit like Clem could win it?

After the first few lost their money, one genius in the crowd announced that there was a system to it. He stepped up and I let him win a few times. He explained his system to the others. Some of them tried it and lost. The genius came back to demonstrate how it was done and lost big.

"That fat guy musta been one a them idiot savannas," the genius muttered as he walked away, replacing his now-lightened wallet in his back pocket.

Once the last of them had shuffled off, I wandered inside the tent. Sally was there, setting up signs, brushing the road dirt off the displays and keeping an eye on the front entrance in case anyone wanted to buy a ticket.

"Big haul?" she asked.

I showed her the handful of cash and gave an appreciative whistle. Yes, it did look like a lot. But I wondered if it would cover the money that the World of Marvels wasn't taking in any more.

I felt no desire to share those concerns with Sally. It wasn't her problem. Besides, she looked really happy as she wandered around the displays and I didn't want to ruin her good mood. If she wasn't so tickled just with the idea of working there, she might not work so cheap. For her, the carnival was a nostalgic reminder of youthful adventure, not a back-breaking routine of trying to wheedle enough money out of the rubes to keep going another week.

I knew her from a ways back. She was a Batley girl who'd joined up with the show for a spell years ago, just for kicks. She'd learned how to swallow swords and do a fire eater routine. Since she looked good in a little dress, she brought in the rubes and their money. She was OK, I guess.

These days, she was working a respectable job here in town. She mentioned to me that she had two kids, now both teenagers, and she'd just married some ex-ballplayer from the local minor league team.

She started singing to herself as she dusted off the display. It sounded like one of those godawful songs she was always writing about fairies and unicorns.

"Why don't you get something to eat?" I asked her. "We've got some downtime before the evening rush starts. I'll have you out front. Can you still do your outside talker routine?"

She spread her arms and threw her head back.

"LADies and GENTlemen! Are you prepared for the wonders and horrors that await you in the ONE! The ONLY! Wild Billy's World of Marvels! Featuring Billy! Sexiest man in show business! Lock up your daughters, ladies and gentlemen, because Wild Billy is …"

"Alright, alright," I said and handed her a pair of bills. "Stay away from the corndog stand. The kid who runs it is a nosepicker."

Outside, I heard her and the kid exchange greetings. Then the kid walked in.

"How did we make out?" he asked.

"What the fuck are you doing back here?" I said. "What if one of the rubes saw you?"

"Nobody saw me," he said. "Give me some credit, would you?"

His voice contained that aggrieved tone he'd always get when he felt I wasn't extending him his due respect. I'd been hearing that tone a lot lately.

I regarded him and had to admit he wasn't the same kid I'd taken in three years ago. He was a lot skinnier back then, for starters. The carnival was traveling through one more little cracker town when he showed up one day. He had a black eye and bruises on his face. He said his name was Gary Cabot, and he practically begged me to give him a job. When I asked him why I should, I expected him to tell me what a hard worker he was. But he surprised me.

"I just need to get out of here," he said.

I was about to tell him I was running a show, not a travel agency. But I detected the desperation in his voice and I thought of those people back in my hometown, bending down with their hands on their knees and talking to me in their high-pitched singsongy voices. Sometimes I think I'm too much of a goddamn sap for this business. He did good work, I'll give him that.

He'd picked up some exercise routines from an acrobat troop we'd traveled with one season. Between that and moving our displays, he'd become pretty strong.

He was good with people, too. When we had some downtime, like now, he'd wander the grounds, striking up friendships and talking up the show. He'd learned a lot, but not as much as he thought. Lately, he didn't like to hear that. And just now, there were some things he needed to hear.

"What were you doing with that girl?" I asked him.

"I met her when we came through here last year," he said. "She's a friend of mine. She wanted to be part of the routine and I thought having her along would give me some credibility. Don't worry, I trust her."

"For your information," I said, "that girl's name is Alice Kettner."

"I know that."

"Did you know her father's a local city councilman? A real mean sonofabitch. And that girl's trouble. There's a certain kind of local girl who sees us carnies as something exciting and exotic. She's one of them. She's been coming around here every year and shaking her titties before she even had titties to shake."

"I wasn't going to do anything with her. You know that."

"Of course I know that! But what if she or somebody else claims you did? What then?"

"I'll tell them I'm not into …"

"Not into women? Is that what you were about to say? So if you get into trouble, your strategy for defending yourself is walking into a courtroom in this backward-ass cracker town and telling them you're a cocksucker?"

He went quiet.

"I'm going to go work the crowd," he said at length.

"Fine. Do your job. And you think about what I said. We're in a bad situation already, and more trouble is the last thing we need."

He walked off, clearly steamed. Fuck him. Everything I said was true and I was just trying to protect his sorry ass.

I wandered around the tent, making sure all of the displays were set up properly. Near the entrance, a glass case displayed glossy photos of famous freaks from the past, such as Fish-Faced Flossie and Helmut Kissel the Monkey Boy.

Preserved animals in glass cases comprised most of our displays. We had a six-legged goat, and two-headed rabbits, otters and turtles. Some were getting pretty ratty-looking. Tighter environmental regulations in recent years had severely curtailed the supply of two-headed and multi-limbed animals. Goddam bureaucrats.

We had a few new entries that had set me back some serious cash. They included a chupacabra, which consisted of a coyote's head sewn onto a baboon's body, with a pair of horns attached to the forehead for good measure. I'd added a stuffed manatee to the piranhas and sandsharks in our "Horrors of the Deep" section.

We'd had live, human acts in the past, including myself. But Dietrich the Alligator Man retired to Florida a few years back and Fantasia the Tattooed Lady had moved out to Arizona to be closer to her grandchildren. Neither had been much of a draw toward the end, anyway. When half of the people in the audience have green hair and metal studs through their tongues, the dynamics of a "human oddities" show tend to shift radically.

Even that wasn't the biggest problem, which resided within the blue-and-white striped tent across the midway featuring the sign out front that read "MADMAN SKUNK'S NIGHTMARE FREAKATORIUM."

Clem was part of that show, putting himself on display along with a handful of other performers whose shtick primarily consisted of doing repulsive things with their own bodies. Skunk's show had already been the top draw at the midway. Then he brought in Friedrich Schulze, and suddenly it was the hottest ticket in whatever town we were traveling through.

Schulze was an individual who'd recently attained fame and accolades for being a crackpot and a pervert. God bless America.

I never spoke to Schulze, but I'd see him around the midway between shows. He's an odd-looking individual. His gaunt frame, scrawny neck and big nose give him a bird-like quality compounded by the brightly colored robes he typically sports over a pair of jean shorts. He wears his grey-flecked brown hair down past his shoulders, with a matching straggly beard.

Word around the carnival had it that Schulze was a serious horndog, always on the lookout for willing females, and a prima donna pain-in-the-ass who insisted as part of his contract that a steady supply of cognac be kept on-hand at all times.

How he wound up with Skunk's show, I had no idea. But he sure did bring in the rubes and their money, with our show suffering as a result.

Ordinarily, I wouldn't begrudge Skunk or anyone else the opportunity to make a buck. But I didn't like Skunk, who was a junkie and a thug. Big earner or not, Gypsy Sam would never have allowed someone like that in his carnival. Times had changed, alright.

I'd heard through the grapevine that Skunk, even though he was pulling in more money, still had it in for me, having decided that another freak show on the midway was necessarily taking money out of his pocket. If and when he decided to move against me, I knew I couldn't count on any support from Pretty Joe, who'd never shown the least compunction about expressing his dislike and distrust of black people.

While I considered this sorry state of affairs, a voice spoke up behind me.

"Hey buddy? Excuse me, I'm looking for Sally."

I turned around to see a big man walking into the tent. He possessed movie star good looks and was evidently cognizant of that fact, strutting as though he expected the stuffed animals in the cases to applaud his arrival.

"She's somewhere getting lunch," I said.

"I'm her husband. Name's Ken. You must be Billy."

"Your powers of discernment are impeccable. You can probably find her on the midway."

"Tell you the truth, I wouldn't mind getting a look at this World of Marvels I've heard so much about."

He grinned, hitched his thumbs in his belt and looked around, apparently considering his interest to be a form of benediction on the place. I didn't much like the idea of somebody getting a free look at the show, but didn't push it. Sally did work cheap.

"Suit yourself," I said. "I've got work to do."

I picked up a sponge and a spray bottle and began cleaning off some of the display cases. Ken wandered over to the stuffed wildebeest, located under a sign that read "Wildebeest: Man Eater of Darkest Africa."

"Are wildebeests really man eaters?" he asked.

"The rubes don't pay to see herbivores."

Then he sauntered over to the Horrors of the Deep section and examined the manatee.

"Looks pretty fierce," he said. "What does it eat? Wildebeests?"

"You know," I said, "I'll bet there are plenty of people out there who think you're fucking hilarious. Why don't you go find some of those people? I'm busy."

He laughed and continued to wander around the tent. Sally soon reappeared and smiled big when she saw Ken. They kissed.

Sally asked if she could take some time to show her husband around the carnival. I gave my assent. Anything to get rid of that guy. When they exited the tent, a man accompanied by a boy of about 10 approached Ken.

"Excuse me, are you Ken Bacon?" he asked.

Ken confirmed that he was. The man became excited, said he used to watch Ken and Bubbles McBride play back in the day, and asked if he could get Ken's autograph for his son. With a magnanimous smile, Ken signed a corndog stand napkin that the man presented to him.

The man then asked his son if he wanted to go on some rides.

"If I can make a suggestion," Ken said, "this is the show you want to see. Wild Billy's World of Marvels."

He leaned in close and spoke in a low voice to the boy.

"They've got a wildebeest in there," he said. "One of them can swallow a full-grown man just like that!"

He snapped his fingers. The boy's eyes went wide. While his father purchased two tickets, Ken turned and winked at me. There's never a big fucking brick around when you need one.

Skunk made his move that night. Business had been adequate. Sally and the kid split up the duties of outside talker and ticket-taker, bringing in a regular stream of goggle-eyed locals to view the displays. I worked the shell game outside the tent a few times. I had to do it without the assistance of Clem, who was doing performances at Skunk's tent. I also received no assistance from the kid, who was plainly visible as part of our show during the evening hours and thus unable to shill for me. Still, I did well enough.

After the carnival closed for the night, Sally went home and I let the kid knock off early. He'd gone back to our trailer and was probably asleep by now. He was still pissed off at me, and his sulking was beginning to get on my nerves. I swept up the gum wrappers and cigarette butts on the ground.

Then I picked up the spray bottle and the sponge to eradicate some smeary handprints left on a case, directly beneath a sign that said "Please Do Not Touch Display Cases."

"You owe me, son."

I turned. Walking through the entrance of the tent was Skunk. He was tall and lean, his head shaved and a long tuft of beard hanging down from the point of his chin to his waist.

From the looks of it, every inch below his neck was tattooed. At a distance, you might think he was wearing a tight, multi-colored, long-sleeved T-shirt beneath his black tank top. The preponderance of ink was probably useful for concealing track marks.

"I'm not your son and I don't owe you shit," I told him. "What exactly are you talking about?"

He stepped closer, exuding that air of perpetual sickliness so common among junkies. He didn't look strong, but he didn't look weak either. He towered over me, which was hardly a distinction on his part.

"That shell game scam. You got Fat Clem involved. Clem works for me. I want a cut."

"I did not ask Clem to get involved," I said, careful to let no anger show. Let the other man get angry. You stay in control. That's how it's done. "Clem has taken it upon himself to follow my employee, Gary, around like a puppy. Clem asked Gary if he could help and Gary assented. Take it up with Clem if you're displeased with the arrangement. I owe you nothing."

"Why's he hanging around Clem, anyway?" Skunk asked. "Everybody knows your boy is a faggot. He better not be doing any of that faggot-ass shit on Clem."

I set down my sponge and squirt bottle with slow deliberation.

"I do not inquire about my employees' sex lives," I told him. "If Gary does the work I pay him to do, that's all that concerns me. But from what I gather, he and Clem are friends. Even if Gary is homosexual, as you imply, I would surmise that a 500-pound imbecile with a harelip is not an object of lustful desire. And as you're no doubt aware of that too, I suggest you stop wasting my time and get to the fucking point."

Skunk looked confused for a moment, attempting to puzzle out the semantic content of my words before continuing.

"I already told you," he said. "It's real simple. You're making money off one of my people, that means you owe me money too."

"Clem's actions on our behalf cost you nothing," I said. "You weren't holding any shows at the time. Clem volunteered, probably to give himself something to do while you're tying off back in your trailer."

Skunk reached into his pocket and came out with a small length of chain, which he began slowly and methodically wrapping around his fist. He stepped closer still, obliging me to look up at him.

"You watch yourself, little man," he said. "My mamma didn't raise me to take shit off no half-pint nigger."

I punched him in the balls. He doubled over, trying to shout in pain but without the air in his lungs to facilitate it. I grabbed his long strand of beard, looped it around my hand and yanked him down to the hard, dirt floor. He went sprawling, face-first.

Before he could regain his bearings, I had a knee in the back of his neck and my straight razor out, laid alongside his face directly next to his eye. I was not cutting him, but giving it enough pressure so that he knew it was there.

He tried to say something. I warned him to shut the fuck up and pressed the razor just a little harder. He complied.

I let him lie down on the floor like that for a few heartbeats. Hurting, scared and acutely aware that he was not in control of the situation. Then I spoke.

"This is what will happen," I told him. "When I let go, you are not going to say anything. You are not going to pause in the doorway to favor me with one parting eyefuck. You are simply going to leave. Immediately. And if you ever set foot in here again, I will gut you like a fish."

I released him. He ran out, all the tough-guy bluster gone.

I folded my razor and replaced it in my pocket. This would not be the end of it, and much was at stake.

Skunk would not be satisfied with a single payment. A junkie will rapidly deplete every source of income he encounters, and so it would go with me if he was able to shake me down with impunity.

What's more, for all its geographical dispersion, the professional set in which Skunk and I operated is relatively small and tight. Word would travel fast, and other would-be extortionists would materialize. Simply getting away from Skunk was inadequate. No, I must demonstrate conclusively that fucking with Wild Billy is an exceedingly ill-advised course of action.

Even as he was running out the door, I had no doubt that Skunk was already planning his revenge. I too was already formulating plans, because I happen to be a firm proponent of the philosophy that the best defense is a good offense.

FILE FIVE

Ty Bacon had me in a chokehold, and was explaining in his typical laid-back monotone exactly what he was doing.

"Don't bother with the windpipe," Ty said. "Your opponent can go minutes without breathing, and that's plenty of time to do you serious damage. What you want is to squeeze shut the carotid arteries on the side of his neck and cut off the flow of blood to his brain. Do it right, and he loses consciousness in seconds."

He tightened the arm scissoring the sides of my neck, and my peripheral vision went gray, then black. Now seemed like a good time to tap out. I slapped my hand against my thigh, and he released the pressure.

He guided me down to the black wrestling mat on the floor, where I lay on my stomach and tried to do a good imitation of an unconscious person.

"If you keep up the pressure, he's going to fall forward when he loses consciousness," Ty said, addressing the semicircle of guys in T-shirts, sweatpants and army surplus gear who were watching us. He got down to his hands and knees alongside me.

"Depending on the circumstances, it might be a good idea to give him a couple extra shots to make sure he stays down. An elbow on the back of the head is good. Or get him with your knee."

He pantomimed drawing his knee back and slamming it into the side of my head. I knew Ty wouldn't hurt me, but it's hard not to feel nervous when he does stuff like that.

"So you hit a guy when he's down. Isn't that kinda pussy?"

That was Ezekiel.

Ty and I both stood and faced the smirking kid with the hair dyed green and the blue splotches on his arms where attempts at self-applied tattoos hadn't worked out so good.

"If you want to learn tournament fighting, you're training at the wrong place," Ty said, no anger in his voice. "I'm trying to teach you guys about real-life self-defense, and I don't expect you to use any of this unless your safety or somebody else's is seriously at stake. You choke someone out, that may not be the end of it. I've seen guys wake up swinging because they didn't even know they'd been choked unconscious."

Ezekiel's smirk never wavered.

After that, Ty divided us up for some free sparring. He took me to the side, and asked if I'd mind sparring with Ezekiel to see how he did. I did mind, but wasn't going to be a pain in the ass about it.

Turned out Ezekiel had some promise as a fighter. At 19, he was pretty skinny but strong. Quick, too. If I was to give him one piece of advice as a fighter, it would be stop watching stupid action movies. He'd apparently adopted "rock and roll, baby" as his tough-guy catchphrase, saying it before he was about to unleash a combo and helpfully telegraphing his intent.

He also liked to throw flashy high kicks. Some people can make those work in a real fight. I'm not one of them. Neither was Ezekiel. When he threw one, I shot in, hooked my leg around the leg he was standing on, then took him down to the floor. Got him in an ankle lock and made him tap.

"OK," I said when we were both standing. "That's pretty good. But you might want to stay away from those high kicks until you can really get 'em down. Think about it. You use a lot of momentum getting that leg up to head height, so it takes away your power and ..."

I pulled my head back just in time. I felt a whoosh of air as his foot missed my face by a hair. He was smirking again.

"No power?" he said. "Think you could take that one?"

"Ezekiel!" That was Ty, who'd seen everything. "That was totally out of line! You know what? Get out. You're done for today."

"Hey, we were just..."

"Now!"

Ezekiel sulkily hoisted his gym bag and walked through the big garage doors, which Ty had left open. The others in the class stopped to watch. Ty told them to go on with the sparring, then asked to talk to me outside. We stepped out through the garage doors into the warm evening, and sat down on a bench flanked by a couple six-foot-tall dragons that Ty had carved with a chainsaw. Several of his chainsaw sculptures dotted the backyard of the Bacon family's single-story house, which was tucked in among some vacant buildings downtown.

Ty favored dragons and sword-wielding barbarian warriors as his subjects. Kind of cool, actually. He installed floors for a living. He also occasionally played drums for a local heavy metal band called Grymm Reeper. I've seen them play a couple times. They're ... distinctive.

But teaching martial arts in his detached garage appeared to be his true calling. He taught mainly Russian martial arts, called Systema, with some muay thai and jiu jitsu thrown in. His students called it "Ty Kwan Do." What can I say? We're an easily amused bunch.

He charged a nominal fee for the instruction. That helped his family make ends meet, but never amounted to enough that he could quit his day job.

Ty, with his rangy build and long hair cut short in the front, didn't look like a bruiser. Still, he was the best natural fighter I'd ever seen. Whether he was grappling or throwing strikes, he moved with an effortless, sinuous grace that was a treat to watch as long as you weren't on the receiving end.

"Sorry about that shit Ezekiel pulled," Ty said. "I thought he was ready. I figure he's uncomfortable being around all these new people, so he tried to act like a big shot. Guess he needs more time."

I shrugged.

"What the hell. Kid's been through a lot."

Ezekiel's father had been a prominent, some would say notorious, local fire-and-brimstone preacher. A few years ago, the old man had gone to jail for fondling underage members of his congregation. Since then, Ezekiel had been in and out of various county programs for violent juvenile offenders. He'd managed to stay out of trouble since hitting legal adulthood, largely because of Ty.

He was part of what Ty called his "farm team." They were a bunch of youths, teens through mid-20s, with behavioral problems that Ty held special classes for at a farm called Moondog Organic Produce in the southern part of the county.

I was always urging Ty to make it an official nonprofit, and get some funding for it, but he never seemed interested. He was a hard guy to figure out sometimes. You'd look in his eyes and get the feeling someone else was driving.

But it didn't take a doctorate in psychology to figure out why Ty wanted to help those troubled kids. When he and his sister first came out of Schulze's compound, he'd been wild. Feral almost. It took a lot of effort on the part of his sister and his stepfather to get that part of him under control.

He said the martial arts training helped him, and he wanted to teach other kids who could benefit from it. He looked glum at the moment. He tended to blame himself when the farm team kids weren't progressing to the extent he hoped.

To cheer him up, I said "Looks like Paul's really getting good."

He smiled. "Yeah, he is. He made Tom tap out three times tonight."

TOM JERKFACE: *I was taking it easy on him, because of his youth and relative lack of experience.*

"Just to let you know," I said. "I've got to talk to Luanne tonight. That incident at the Batley Businessmen's Association."

Ty winced.

"She should be home soon. Picking up Dad from physical therapy. But I wouldn't try it tonight. Union meeting."

Luanne Bacon, Ty's older sister, was president of the union at her employer, a local firm that manufactures piston engines and one of the few local manufacturers that hadn't moved overseas in recent decades. She drove a forklift.

Ty was right. Her union meetings tended to be stressful, and she generally returned from them in a sour mood. But since my presence often put her in a sour mood anyway, I figured it didn't make much difference in the long run.

"Hey, I need to ask you something," Ty said.

He was quiet a moment, considering his words. That surprised me, because Ty wasn't a contemplative guy by nature.

"That attack downtown," he said. "You think it was really The Slain?"

"Seems likely," I said. "There's always a chance it's some kind of copycat group. But it sure looked like them."

Ty was silent a moment longer. Then he spoke.

"All that shit that happened 15 years ago ... You think there's a chance it might come back?"

He didn't sound frightened when he asked that. Just deeply sad. Like someone who'd survived a bout of cancer, and got news that his latest test results weren't looking good.

I was trying to think of how I might answer when Luanne's car pulled into the driveway. I wasn't sure whether to be relieved or not.

She walked out of the driver's side, then went around and opened the passenger door to help her stepfather, Ken, get out of the car. He slowly and painfully stood, and she handed him his cane. He began hobbling toward the house. She walked toward us.

Luanne is lean and sharp-featured, with long brown hair. A good-looking woman. Not that I ever noticed, mind you.

She had an annoyed look on her face, which deepened when she spotted me. Ignoring me, she confronted Ty.

"Did you pick up that ground turkey like I asked?"

Ty groaned.

"Oh shit, Luanne! I'm sorry! See, when I finished up work I was so focused on getting back to the class ..."

"Great," she said, hard creases forming around her mouth. "You know, I didn't have anything to do today either. Just working my ass off at the job, having everybody jump down my throat at the union meeting and getting Daddy to physical therapy before coming home and cooking dinner."

He held up a hand, silently asking for a brief reprieve, and turned back toward the class.

"Hey guys? I think we're done for the day. But if you all want to hang out and spar for a while, you can."

He then walked back to Luanne, who was waiting with folded arms. She started right in on him.

"Well, I guess it's pizza again. We can't afford to keep ordering pizza! And it's sure as hell not teaching that boy good eating habits! Is it too much to ask for just a little help around here?"

Not waiting for an answer, she walked past us and stuck her head in the garage, where about a dozen guys were wrestling, or circling each other and throwing kicks and punches.

"Paul!"

The teenager, not as skinny as when I'd seen him, looked up from where he had Tom in yet another chokehold.

"Homework," she said. "You've got some time while we're ordering dinner. Guess it's pizza again."

She gave Ty a poisonous look. Paul walked up to her.

"Is it OK if I play some games first? I can do homework after dinner."

"You know the rules," she said. "Homework first, then videogames. Go on."

She kissed him on the forehead, and he started toward the house.

"Looking pretty tough in there," Ty said to him.

Paul's face lit up like a floodlight. Since moving into the Bacon household, he'd taken to following Ty around like a puppy. And the slightest praise from his older brother was enough to make him ecstatic.

"Ah, it was only Tom," Paul said, looking down at the ground and blushing.

"Hey, don't put yourself down," Ty said. "You're really getting good at this."

Paul practically sprinted to the house, sheer joy in his every movement. At that moment, it would have been easy to assume he was doing OK. I knew for a fact that wasn't the case.

Earlier that day, I'd had a talk with Dr. Pigeon, Paul's therapist. He operated out of a little renovated house on the west side of town, indistinguishable from the homes around it except for the sign out front that read "Pigeon Clinic," featuring an abstract rendering of a bird.

Dr. Pigeon contracted with the city to provide counseling for kids who met — or rather, didn't meet — certain income parameters. Luanne didn't like that I consulted with him about Paul, but the Freak Foundation provided the Bacons with a small monthly stipend that they'd come to depend on, and that was one of the conditions.

I liked Dr. Pigeon. He was a small, bespectacled man who conducted himself with good-humored professionalism. He had an air of vague sadness I've often seen among people who work in the human services field. Doing his best, and knowing full well it might not be enough.

"Paul is a very troubled boy," Dr. Pigeon had told me that afternoon, after presenting me with a cup of coffee in his office and sitting down behind his desk. "I suppose that's not surprising, after what he's been through. It's probably a testament to his emotional resilience that he's doing as well as he is."

The woman's skeleton in Cabot's basement? That was Paul's mother.

She'd been Sally Bacon, a follower of Schulze who'd disappeared in the days immediately after his clinic's closure. Her remains showed no obvious signs of foul play, and police weren't exactly sure what the cause of death was.

The dwarf under the floor with her was William "Wild Billy" Cleary, proprietor of the carnival show Paul had been with. Police had an easier time determining his cause of death. Even after 15 years, a shotgun at close range is about as obvious as it gets.

A decade and a half ago, Cabot showed up at a commune in Colorado and asked to see Patrice Logan, a friend of Sally's from her days touring as a folk musician. He'd presented her with the infant Paul and a manila folder full of documents pertaining to him, much of which turned out to be forged. In it was a letter signed by Sally. She explained that she had advanced bone cancer — untrue, incidentally — and didn't have much time left. She identified Cabot as a cousin — also untrue — and stated that she'd given him custody of her son. She asked if Logan would raise him.

The whole thing was fishy on many levels. But Logan, by all accounts, was a free-spirited type very much dedicated to the concept of living "off the grid" and not particularly concerned with the legal complexities of modern society.

She was also a very kind woman. She and her husband raised Paul along with their four natural children on the commune. The two dozen or so families there were into the idea of living off the land, raising their own crops and animals and supplementing their income by making and selling furniture. They even had their own school.

Paul lived a happy and uneventful life until the day Cabot showed up nearly two years ago. Logan had tearfully informed Paul that he'd be traveling back to the East Coast with this supposed relative he'd never met until that moment.

Cabot brought Paul to his house in Batley. He seemed remote, but hadn't mistreated Paul in any overt way, other than locking him in his room with his videogames and books for much of the time. For a couple hours every day, Cabot would take him outside. When Paul would ask him what was going on, Cabot would talk cryptically about "safety concerns" and "making new living arrangements." On one occasion, Cabot told him that "should anything happen," he should know that he had family in town.

Then one night, something did happen. I showed up.

Paul was disoriented with his new life, but pleased with new discoveries such as pizza. He adjusted well to public school, and made friends easily. Every week, he wrote to Logan and her husband. He was planning a visit around Christmastime.

But he was having problems that went beyond simple culture shock. He had bad nightmares where he'd wake up screaming, and afterward be unable to tell what they were about. He was also sleepwalking. Once he made it outside into the street before Ty brought him back. It wasn't just at night, either. A couple weeks ago, he'd stood up during class and walked out of his school. Later, he said he didn't remember it.

Dr. Pigeon said it might all just be a complex reaction to the stress of having his life uprooted, although he wasn't ruling out an underlying mental disorder. He'd started Paul on antidepressants, and was waiting to see how he'd react.

"Sometimes, there's only so much you can do," Dr. Pigeon said that afternoon, in that mournful way of his.

As Paul ran through the back screen door of the house, he almost bumped into Ken, who was exiting.

"Sorry, Ken," he said. He'd grown up calling Patrice Logan's husband "Dad," and wasn't yet comfortable attaching that name to Ken, who smiled indulgently as he passed. Then Ken hobbled down the walkway to the garage, with the help of his aluminum cane.

He looked scruffy as usual, with his tattered green windbreaker, baseball cap and thick, gray beard that didn't completely hide the scar tissue covering much of his face. Years ago, he'd been an explosive ordnance disposal technician for the National Guard, and a mishap with an explosive left his face a jagged wreckage.

For years, Ken was on mental disability. Unlike Ty, Luanne and Paul, he wasn't technically one of the Foundation's clients and I'd never got the particulars. From what I understood, it had to do with traumatic stress disorder from the accident that disfigured him.

Still, he'd been relatively fit and strong until last winter, when he'd slipped on some ice and fractured an already arthritic hip. A series of painful operations seemed to age him decades in the span of months.

"How'd therapy go?" Ty asked him.

"Eh, it went," Ken replied. "You know, your sister's pretty upset."

Ty looked at his feet.

"Yeah. Sorry about that. I just forgot."

"You know, she carries a lot of weight around here. Maybe you should make more of an effort to help her out."

Ty met his eyes and smiled.

"Come on, Dad. You're just as relieved as I am that we're having pizza instead of her turkey loaf."

Ken tried to suppress the grin, but failed. When it broke out on his face, he suddenly resembled the young man whose picture dominated a framed sports page from the Batley Daily Needler hanging in the Bacon household. The star pitcher for the Batley Snippers.

TOM JERKFACE: At the time Ken Bacon was a pitcher for the local unaffiliated minor league baseball team, it was still called the Batley Consolidated Livestock Processors.

At that moment, inconveniently, Luanne stepped out the door and caught them both laughing. She fixed them with a glare that would blister paint and they stopped immediately.

"Well, I've ordered the pizzas," she said. "Guess I'll get in a workout while we wait for them."

By that time, the last of Ty's students had wandered off. She walked into the garage, put on a pair of gloves and started whaling on a heavy bag hanging in the corner.

Ken looked at me.

"You joining us for dinner?" he asked. "No turkey loaf. It's safe."

"We'll see how safe it is once I talk to Luanne," I said.

I took a deep breath, then walked into the garage.

"Luanne? I need to talk to you about what happened at the Businessmen's Association."

This time, her glare would have scorched the wood underneath the blistered paint.

"Just what I need tonight."

"Look, we have to do this sooner or later," I said. "Might as well get it over with."

So she told me.

Luanne, I should explain, is obsessed with folklore and mythology dealing with fairies. Every fall, she helped organize the Moondog Faerie Festival, where a bunch of like-minded individuals show up for three days to wander around the grounds of Moondog Organic Produce dressed up like fairies to mark a pagan holiday called Samhain. Hey, everyone needs a hobby.

During the rest of the year, she got her fix by dressing up as a fairie queen named Titania and lecturing historical societies, folklore study groups and book clubs about fairy lore.

She used to do kids' birthday parties, but that got awkward. Parents would expect some cutey-pie fairy in a frilly dress. But Luanne's get-up incorporated a tight black corset and skirt, elaborate shawl, primitive jewelry, a headdress of intertwined branches, face-paint and a pair of wings that looked like they came from a giant raven. She looked beautiful and dangerous in that costume, like some kind of Celtic warrior queen. I suspect the problems with the kids' parties were due, in part, to Mom not being pleased when Dad's eyes would pop out of their sockets at her arrival.

She advertises this service in the phone book under "entertainers," which she assumed was how the Businessmen's Association got her name.

She knew it was bad news the moment she entered the fire hall they'd rented for their monthly meeting. It was filled with disheveled-looking men in jackets and ties, most of whom appeared to be very drunk.

"You would have fit right in," she told me.

She introduced herself to the Association's president, local realtor Jack Lange. He seemed quite pleased to see her, and shushed the gathering.

"Gentlemen!" he yelled, waving a hand at her. "Here's our entertainment! Titania!"

The air filled with cheers and whoops as they all gathered around.

"Well," she said, as they quieted down to hear her, "the story really starts with prehistory. Every culture has some version of fairy lore, in the form of magical beings that supposedly coexisted and occasionally interacted with humanity ..."

I've heard her lecture before. She goes into how the cute, benevolent and child-like image of fairies is relatively recent, dating to the Victorian era. Before then, folklore was more likely to present them as frightening than benevolent, in stories where their appearance frequently coincided with sex, insanity, or death.

It's pretty interesting, really. But the businessmen looked bored with it, showing no interest other than breaking into guffaws at her mention of the name "Puck."

At length, Lange motioned her over to the side.

"Look, this is all very fascinating," he said. "But can you just go ahead and show them?"

"Show what?"

"Your ... titania."

Luanne was confused.

"I don't think you understand," she said. "Titania is the the character I appear as for lectures on fairy lore. It's the name of the fairy queen from Shakespeare's 'A Midsummer Night's Dream.' "

Lange's face drooped in an expression of dismay and alarm.

"What did you think it was?" Luanne asked.

"I thought it was a fancy word for tits," he said. "You know. Like 'genitalia.' "

Luanne said she was leaving. Lange hinted that she could make a lot of money if she stuck around. She hinted that he'd be wearing his nuts for a bowtie if he didn't drop the subject immediately, then demanded what he'd agreed to pay her.

He got pissed, and said he didn't have to pony up since she hadn't provided the service he'd hired her for. She pointed out that she'd used up time and gas to be there, and it wasn't her fault he's an idiot.

When he tried to argue further, she settled the matter by grasping the knot in his tie and twisting it until he dropped to his knees with his face turning purple and his eyes bulging out. He reached into his pocket and handed her a wad of bills, then collapsed into grateful gasping for air as she let go.

She barged toward the exit, drunken businessmen scurrying out of her path like they were in the streets of Pamplona. Except for one big, fat guy who suddenly materialized from the crowd and blocked the exit. He pointed to where Lange was gasping on his knees, then whispered in her ear.

"I'll pay you two hundred bucks to do that to me. Except could you dress up like a nurse?"

Her brother taught her a thing or two. That fat guy would be walking funny for a while.

"Well what the hell," I told her. "I hear the Batley Community Choir needs a new soprano anyway."

She went back to her workout in a way that made me pity the bag. I turned to exit, stopping at the sound of a staccato mechanical rumbling. Then he slowly glided into view.

On a low-slung, electric blue bike, tricked out like a Gothic cathedral rendered in steel, sat the enormous, blond man I'd seen at the the city council meeting.

"This Ty Bacon's place?" he asked.

"Can I help you?" Ty asked, walking up behind him. The big man disembarked from his bike and shook his hand.

"Name's Michael," he said. "I'm new in town, and looking for a place to train. I hear you're the best around here."

Ty shrugged and smiled.

"Don't know about that. We're very non-traditional here."

"That's OK. Never had much use for the traditional stuff. Ma'am."

He said the last word with a courteous nod of his head toward Luanne. If you ever feel you're overdue for a withering look, call Luanne "Ma'am."

"Well, we're here every night around 7," Ty said. "Usually go 90 minutes or so, but I let people hang out and spar if they feel like it. Drop by if you want. We're very informal."

Michael looked one of the chainsaw-carved dragons up and down.

"Your work? Nice."

Ty just smiled and shrugged again. Michael mounted his bike, then looked toward Luanne.

"Hope you don't mind if I make a suggestion, ma'am? You've got a lot of wasted motion in your swing. Keep throwing 'em like that and you might be setting yourself up for a rotator cuff injury down the road."

She didn't even stop punching.

"Remember when I asked for your opinion?" she said. "Neither do I."

Michael smiled, inclined his head deferentially and tooled toward the alley entrance from which he'd emerged. Then he rode up to me.

"I was looking for you," he said. "I know something about The Slain."

"I'm listening."

"Not here," he said, glancing back toward Luanne, Ty and Ken. "Where do the movers and shakers drink?"

"Excuse me?"

"The bar where the local politicians and judges go to get drunk and chase tail. Every town's got one."

"That would be Liam O'Shaunessey's. The 300 block of Main, a little west of Spruce. You see a guy in a black robe puking out front, you've got the right place."

"See you there tomorrow at 6." He roared out and disappeared down the alley.

FILE SIX

Michael and I sat at a table in Liam O'Shaunessey's. The bar owed its name to the fact that owner Drew Schicklgruber, through no fault of his own, was stuck with Hitler's mother's maiden name as his surname. He worried about the kind of clientele he'd attract with that on a sign out front. We were each nursing a glass of Drosselmyer's, a regionally brewed beer that is reason in itself to move to the region, and had each just drained a shot of whiskey.

At 7 p.m., both City Hall and the courthouse had closed two hours ago. Buck Rockbaugh had put in his customary appearance. He'd drained his customary glass of cranberry juice and excused his teetotaling with the customary "Gotta keep in shape or the missus'd leave me for some younger fella." Assorted City Hall types had made with their customary obliging guffaws in response.

Now that Buck was gone, it was time to start the party in earnest. The jukebox was thumping and the director of the zoning commission was doing a raucous bump-and-grind with the chairwoman of the Batley Parking Authority, to the hoots and cheers of the entire bar.

"Hey Katey?" I said to the waitress. "I think we're going to need another round of shots here. This is getting painful."

She gave a mock shudder of sympathy and walked toward the bar against the wall.

Liam O'Shaunessey's started a long time ago as a nameless speakeasy long since upgraded easily to a legal, licensed drinking establishment. No later owners ever bothered to build an addition. It was still a long, narrow corridor of a bar, with a street entrance on one end, a kitchen door at the other and a bar against the wall.

Its success as a bar was due to the exact same factor that made it a success as a speakeasy. Namely, its proximity to City Hall and the county courthouse.

Michael told me he'd moved to Batley, taking a house in Heritage Estates. That surprised me. I don't know if the adjective "ritzy" could comfortably attach itself to anyplace in the greater Batley area, but Heritage Estates probably came closest.

That's where the moneyed people who found themselves obliged for one reason or another to remain in the area tended to settle, amid a bunch of closely placed mini-mansions. They had a communal pool, a clubhouse, and an adjacent private golf course.

The main appeal seemed to be a sturdy wall surrounding the homes, with an equally sturdy guard or two providing access via an electronic gate.

And that, according to Michael, was the main selling point for him. But in his case, that impregnability served an important strategic purpose other than the more commonplace concerns of keeping out riffraff who might key one's car or marry one's daughters.

"I needed a place with good security and a home alarm system," he said. "The nature of my job makes it necessary. Not too many places like that on the market around here. Also, some of my higher-ups prefer to put me up me up in a fancy place. Say it helps our image in the community. Buncha horseshit if you ask me, but that's bureaucracies for you."

"OK," I said. "Why this bar?"

"I'm on duty," he said.
"You always drink on duty?"
"Only whenever I get the chance."
"Why this bar?"
"This is the kind of place they hit. They like to make a statement when they're arriving in a city. That means a place like this, where they'll get plenty of visibility. Our intelligence tells us they're not planning a one-and-done attack like 15 years ago. This time, they're in it for the long haul."
"Who's 'us?' "
"I'm with an organization that's been tracking them a long time."
"How long?"
"Long."
"And who exactly are The Slain?"

An ancient shamanic cult turned criminal gang, as Michael described it. They were one of the few criminal gangs to have academic papers written about them, linked as they reportedly were to what many scholars considered to be the first monotheistic religion in world history. They even declined to provide a name for their deity, claiming that worship of him predates human speech. They called him "The One Who Takes."

"Takes what?" I asked Michael.

"Everything eventually," he said.

Men who wanted to join The Slain — and they were exclusively men — had to go through a rigorous series of trials, ending with the commission of a murder. Those who passed the trials made a vow to surrender their lives to The One Who Takes. The name "The Slain" reflected the symbolic end of their previous lives.

With those previous lives over, they considered themselves dead servants of The One Who Takes. That was also the symbolism behind the leather, the dead flesh, covering their faces. As well as the skulls painted on those leather masks.

Those who didn't pass the trials? They faced death, too. Just not the symbolic kind.

Michael had taken off his jacket, and draped it over a chair. I wondered if that was to give him a chance to flex biceps like bowling balls at the Important People who occasionally threw a wary look in his direction.

They were very eloquent, those biceps. What they said was: "Don't like my element in your classy hangout? Then try throwing me out, pencil dick."

On the way back from taking a piss, I'd checked out his jacket. The patch on the back said "Order of Gabriel." Below the words were a set of wings, rendered in a spare, linear style I liked to call "Kind-of-Celtic-or-Maori-or-Something."

"So why are you here?" I asked.

"To stop them."

"They tied in with Cabot?"

"Yes. We're certain on that score. Most people think Schulze inspired them. According to our intelligence, the opposite is closer to the truth. Schulze was doing research that put him in contact with The Slain. You could say they took a liking to each other. It seems they considered Schulze a powerful magician. Same with Cabot."

"Any idea where Cabot is now?

"My guess is far away, but I don't know. Our sources tell us Cabot worked closely with The Slain behind the scenes. But publicly, he always tried to distance himself from them. Maybe he doesn't care about keeping up that pretense anymore since you took him out of commission."

"You know about that?"

Michael hoisted his beer glass in salute.

"Your little visit with Cabot? Don't sell yourself short, buddy. That's legendary in some circles."

At that moment, a chant went up from two young men and a slightly older woman clustered around the end of the bar nearest us.

"FLA-MING FIST FUCK! FLA-MING FIST FUCK!"

The bartender, a young Latino guy who looked vaguely embarrassed, set down a couple of mouthwash-colored concoctions in highball glasses, then topped off each one with a jot of rum. He produced a lighter and set each one to flaming.

The trio picked up their glasses and drank, the object being to drink it down fast enough to extinguish the flame without burning yourself. The high and well-documented number of failures did nothing to diminish the popularity of the place's signature drink.

I'd never tried one myself, as intentionally burning up perfectly good alcohol for purely theatrical effect struck me as borderline perverse.

"That Ernie Bixler over there?" Michael asked.

I looked at a table near the end of the bar farthest from us. Bixler was talking and gesticulating about something that evidently had him quite fired up. My guess would be one of his political rants. Across from him was a young, female intern who looked like she very much wanted to be elsewhere.

"The man, the myth, the legend."

"I should go over and introduce myself," Michael said.

"Voluntarily start a conversation with Bixler? Hope you don't mind if I sit this one out."

He shrugged. Then picked up his jacket from the chair and put it on — I guessed he wanted to be wearing his colors for the introduction — and walked down the bar. Another "FLA-MING FIST FUCK!" chorus started up. I contemplated my glass of Drosselmyer's and tried to ignore it.

For years, I'd harbored two related hopes. The first was that The Slain had nothing to do with Schulze. Schulze and The Slain ending up in Batley at around the same time would turn out to be sheer coincidence. Seemed unlikely, but a man can dream, can't he?

The second was that they were just an isolated bunch of nutcases who'd quit soon after the Halloween Parade Massacre so they could devote more time to screaming on street corners or rubbing tapioca pudding into their hair or whatever it is crazy people do with their retirement years.

Either way, it would have meant they weren't my problem, and I would have been able to go my whole career without tangling with them. If what Michael told me was true, both those hopes had just disappeared like a Flaming Fist Fuck down some public servant's gullet.

What about Michael himself? Could he be an ally? I sure hoped so. Because if I was going up against The Slain, I'd need all the help I could get.

The bar went dead quiet. No chants, no whoops. No conversation. I looked up. They stood blocking the front entrance. Both wore leather masks with big skull grins painted on the front. Both held baseball bats.

I scanned the bar. Where the fuck was Michael? He'd disappeared.

Maybe a dozen people remained, counting staff. About evenly divided between men and women. I knew most of them. I wouldn't put any of them on a short list of backup I'd want in a bar fight. Or a long list, for that matter.

The Latino kid working the bar stood frozen behind three glasses that were still flaming away, which the merry trio had forgotten. He looked as stricken as everyone else. I guessed there was no weapon under the bar.

At that moment, the other patrons and I realized our immediate future held pain and bloodshed. Maybe death. And we were utterly silent.

I moved, heading toward the front of the bar where the two masked men stood. A lot of people between me and them, but nobody else seemed to be moving.

The guys in the doorway saw me and hoisted their bats. They didn't move from their positions — a tactic that made no sense unless ....

Oh fuck.

I looked behind me. The door leading from the kitchen was already swinging outward. Behind it, I made out a group of guys in leather masks, all holding blunt weapons of their own.

I picked up one of the flaming glasses from the bar and hurled it at the kitchen door. It hit the first guy in the chest with a fiery burst.

He gave a yell and staggered back into the guys behind him. In the moment that gave me, I lifted a barstool, hefting it like a battering ram and charging at the kitchen door. It swung open again and I plowed into the first guy, knocking him backward along with his buddies crowded immediately behind him.

They kept their feet, though. For a few seconds, I held them at bay. Then one of them near the front got smart and dove in under the stool, driving the weight of his body into my legs and knocking me over backward onto the floor.

I tried to get up, but they were all over me, swinging and kicking. I curled into a ball. Nothing to do but turtle up and hope for a minimum of broken bones.

They stopped. A man's throaty voice hollered.

"Order of Gabriel! Clear out!"

Footsteps running away from me. I uncurled and opened my eyes. Tables and chairs fell over left and right as eight or so men in leather masks ran toward the front door and the bar patrons frantically scrambled to get out of their way. Michael was chasing them.

The last of them made it out the door before Michael reached them. He paused, his immense frame silhouetted in the doorway, and bellowed after them.

"You better fucking run!"

Then he looked back where I was getting to my feet.

"You coming?"

I took stock. Bruised, no question, but no broken bones as far as I could tell. Overall, I was in better shape than I had any business being in. I ran after him and we made it out to the sidewalk just as the doors on a black van parked halfway down the block were closing.

"My bike is parked down the block!" Michael said. "Where's your car?"

Right across the street, as it happened. I got behind the wheel and Michael took shotgun. The van pulled out from the curb and made a left into an alley entrance. We followed.

I knew the terrain. The alley ended in a T intersection at a chain-link fence surrounding a big scrap metal processing plant that had closed down a couple years ago. The van would have to turn left or right.

Except it didn't. It went through a van-sized gap that somebody had cut in the fence directly across from the alley.

I wondered briefly if we were heading into an ambush, then decided against it. Not mere yards from the bar where someone was almost certainly calling 911. Besides, in my passenger seat was a man who eight armed psychopaths had just run away from. I was still trying to make sense of that one.

I followed the van through a long parking lot, darkened industrial buildings on our right, then out through another van-sized gap in the fence at the other side of the property. The van cut left on a side street, then a quick right on Gardiner Avenue. Even through my closed windows, its tires squealed audibly when it made a quick right onto Route 26 east.

All in all, the driver had done a very efficient job of getting the van out of downtown and onto a major road in a hurry. "They planned the shit out of this!" I thought as I hit Route 26 myself and stomped on the gas, winding in and out of the sparse traffic while I pursued the van.

"So what happens when we catch them?" I said. "You got a gun?"

"Don't carry one. Let's just say I've got other tricks up my sleeve. And we're not going to catch them. Maybe we can see where they go and alert the police."

"Might not have to alert the police. I'm going 90. Good thing I wasn't just in a bar drinking whiskey."

I didn't know it at the time, but my chances of running into police right then was pretty slim.

At about 6 that night, across town from Liam O'Shaunnesey's, a man in a skull-painted leather mask ambushed 26-year-old Angela Bell as she returned home from her shift as day manager at the Lobster Palace. By all indications, her only qualification as a target was her status as a young woman living alone.

He held a gun to her head and warned her not to scream. He took her inside her home and duct taped her to a chair. He called police, informed them that he was holding her hostage and warned them that he'd shoot any fucking pig who came near the house. He held the phone to Bell's mouth, allowing her to confirm everything. Then he put duct tape over her mouth, fired several shots through the ceiling, ran out the back door and disappeared.

Soon after that, pretty much every police officer in town was part of either a close perimeter surrounding Bell's home, or a wider one in the several blocks around it. Bell eventually came out of it frightened but unharmed, after the police spent several hours pinned down there before discovering that the gunman was no longer in the house.

At about the moment Michael and I were in my car eastbound on Route 26, a bundle of TNT attached to a crude timer device went off in a municipal garage behind City Hall.

The garage was deserted at the time and nobody was injured. But Batley's two sanitation trucks were damaged beyond repair. The garage was also a total loss.

"Where'd you go back there?" I asked Michael. "Lost sight of you."

"A door behind the bar," he said. "It led to a hallway with a fire exit. I went up an alley along the side and into the back kitchen door. They like to attack in a pincer formation. Create maximum panic. I figured my best bet was to get around behind them and drive them all out. Looks like they're turning off."

They were. A quick right on an unmarked, barely visible road entrance. I slowed down and followed.

We were well out of the city now, on a road that was paved but just barely, lined with thick woods and unlighted. I kept up with the van, despite the occasional bone-jarring pothole that even under the circumstances made me think of mechanic bills.

The van made a sudden left. Just before I followed, my headlights fell on a beaten-up sign. "Whispering Woods Family Campground."

The van continued on a paved road even more neglected than the last one, then made a right-hand-turn into a clearing. I followed. It stopped. I stopped too, maybe a couple hundred feet behind it.

The van's lights went off. It occurred to me we were sitting ducks if anybody in the van had a gun, so I turned my lights off and killed the engine. I kept my hand on the key, ready to start up and haul ass at the first gunshot.

"Any suggestions?" I asked.

"Just wait. See what they do."

We seemed to be in a fairly large clearing. Dark woods ringed us. The sky, glowing from its proximity to the city lights, only threw the darkness around us into deeper contrast.

Suddenly, a mechanical buzzing sounded off to our right. Chainsaws? One by one, a series of lights blinked into existence and then rapidly disappeared, bouncing as they went, among the trees. Not chainsaws. Dirtbikes.

"Come on!" Michael said, opening the car door and running in the direction they'd gone. I wasn't sure if that was such a great idea. But I turned the headlights back on, grabbed the heavy metal flashlight from under my seat and followed him.

I joined Michael near a trail opening in the woods. Not big enough to accommodate the car. Looked like the end of the road for us. The ground was torn up from multiple bike tires.

"Any idea where it leads?" Michael asked.

"There's a big network of trails out this way," I said. "Hikers and mountain bikers use them. Even if the police could track them through all that, my guess is they'd be long gone by then."

"Yeah, that'd be the way they usually work."

I played my flashlight around. On the perimeter of our clearing were little cabins, big enough to sleep maybe four. Some looked in pretty serious need of repair.

"Looks abandoned," Michael said.

"Yeah, I'm guessing the whole 'Wilderness Adventure' selling point was a bust for the original owners. This close to the city, hell, they probably got the occasional stray bullet from — What the fuck?"

I said that last part as my flashlight beam hit a towering, ghostly figure in the middle of the clearing. An enormous wood carving.

We approached it as I played my flashlight beam around its base. Wood shavings. Looked like somebody sculpted it on the spot, likely from a fallen tree trunk scavenged from the surrounding woods.

Littered among the wood shavings were the remains of a serious party. Bottles that once held various types of liquor. Gin, whiskey, vodka. Various drug paraphernalia, too. If you could smoke it, snort it or shoot it, looked like this party had it.

"Guess this confirms it," Michael said. "They were using this place as a base. That's their style. When they hit a town, they like to crash in the woods or abandoned buildings. They never stay in one place too long."

"Are those boys we chased out here the whole crew?"

"Doubt it," said Michael, kicking at a drained tequila bottle with his boot. "We should be so lucky. Judging by the volume of this shit, I think we're looking at a larger group. 30 maybe. This is Sunday church for them. They make themselves a replica of The One Who Takes. Then they get fucked up until they can hear it talking to them."

I played my flashlight up and down the wood carving. It was about 7 feet high.

Whoever carved it hadn't much bothered with the base, which was sunk upright in the ground like a post. The first detail started at crotch level, with a wooden dick that would put the most freakish porn actor to shame.

Above that was the crude but unmistakable outline of a man's torso, muscular arms straight at his side. The head wasn't human, though. It looked more like a steer's, complete with long, curving horns that had apparently started out as branches. The facial features would need a lot more precision carving to even qualify as "abstract."

Still, I got the impression that the thing was snarling. Roaring maybe.

I reached into my inside jacket pocket. The cigar I had in there was broken, but the lower half looked salvageable. I broke it off. Then I found some matches in my pants pocket and lit it. I stood there for a minute, smoking and looking up at their god. The One Who Takes.

"If they got a little plastic one of these on that van's dashboard," I said, "I'm going to be disturbed."

FILE SEVEN

Sister Pilar Lopez walked into her office with two mugs of coffee, and handed me one. I took a sip. Black, unsweetened, and industrial strength. Just the way I like it.

"Major renovations in the works?" I asked.

Her work clothes weren't remarkable in themselves. I genuinely have no idea whether her order requires a habit or not. Just about every time I see her, she's in the middle of some improvement project around the place. To all intents and purposes, her habit consists of a pair of jeans and a T-shirt or flannel shirt, usually splotched with plaster or paint.

Today she looked particularly grimy.

"Trying to tackle the hot water heater," she said. "Warm weather's on its way out, and I'm already sick of cold showers."

"You're a nun. Figured you'd be used to cold showers."

"You know, celibacy's pretty easy with men like you around."

We sat for a little bit, drinking our coffee. She was behind her desk and I was in front of it.

I wasn't sure where the desk came from. Likely second-hand, like everything else in the building. A gunmetal gray number big enough to serve as a table should anyone find it necessary to dissect a rhinoceros in her office.

It used to crack me up, this tiny woman behind the big desk, but not for long. She was little, but she had presence.

I went to Catholic school back in Jersey. She was a type of nun I'd learned early on to identify, out of sheer survival instinct. The type who was tough enough to be nice under most circumstances. Because if smartasses like me gave them any shit, they were fully capable of putting our snotty little heads through a wall.

She was in her 30s. Delicate-featured. Strong and wiry with short, black hair. She was originally from Puerto Rico, then ended up in North Jersey. There, she'd done a lot of advocacy work for the poor. She'd been a bit too vocal and too successful in those endeavors for the tastes of some pretty powerful people, including the testosterone-saturated ranks of her own church's hierarchy. Hence, the relocation to Bumfuck, Pa.

She's my boss. And as far as I can determine, we both inhabit the same foggy netherworld of working and yet not working for a bunch of different people and agencies. Her title is regional director of the Friedrich K. Schulze Foundation.

The Foundation isn't officially affiliated with Catholicism or any other religion. The Catholic Church acted as a kind of contractor in the Schulze Foundation's operations in Batley. I never knew the particulars of the deal, but I imagine they involved lots of hefty checks going to different Catholic holdings with the names of various Schulze family members inked at the bottom.

Like me, Pilar doesn't give a shit about the particulars. Her job is to look out for the people harmed by Schulze's operations, including the delusional ones found in his clinic. "My babies," as she often calls them.

Her office is spare. The only decoration is a poster of a dubiously Nordic-looking crucified Jesus. It reads: "I asked Jesus how much he loved me. He spread out his arms and said 'This much.' Then he died on the cross."

I once suggested that the poster might be more appealing if the Jesus on the cross was replaced with a kitten, and it read: "Hang in there, baby! Friday's coming!"

Pilar didn't think that was funny.

Also on her desk is a little sign that reads "No Foul Language. Please Be Respectful of Others." She enforces that, too, which frequently makes my conversations with her logistically difficult.

"So what happened to the carpet?" I asked.

The now-visible wood floor was pitted and dirty, but still an improvement as far as I was concerned. The carpet had made it look like someone puked on the floor after eating too much pumpkin pie.

"Lycanthrope support group," she said. "I was letting the Cub Scouts use the main meeting room, so we took it in here. Jerome and Steve got into an argument and Steve decided he had to mark his territory. He's banned for three weeks, and he's paying for a new carpet."

"You rub his nose in it and smack him with a newspaper?"

"Wanted to smack him with more than a newspaper."

Believe it or not, Steve was one of our higher-functioning clients. That marking-his-territory instinct made him pretty effective in his job as a security guard. By now, his boss knew to restrict him to outdoor jobs.

Pilar's philosophy wasn't to "cure" our clients, in terms of getting them over their delusions. Past experience showed that could be traumatic for them. If they could live happy, productive lives believing themselves to be mythical creatures, she saw no reason to tamper with that.

The operation she oversaw, called the Hope House, was more of a support and administration center than a hospital. She did have the capacity to house people there if need be. A couple of really low-functioning residents — I used the term "basket cases" once and Pilar was pissed at me for a week — lived there virtually full time. Sometimes clients would live there for shorter spells if need be, like if they were between jobs. But for the most part, Pilar's goal was to get them living independently.

In addition to being my boss, she was the public face of our operation. She served on a dozen or so community boards and operations, and also made meeting rooms in the Hope House available for groups like the Cub Scouts.

I was more the guy in the trenches, as I liked to think of it.

"So," she said after a few minutes of quiet coffee-sipping. "Who's Jeff Reppert?"

Shit. Pilar had about as many contacts in the community as I did. I guess it was inevitable she'd find out.

"He was the one vandalizing Nyx's place," I said.

"Tell me about it."

Nyx was another one of our higher-functioning clients. She had a live-in boyfriend and a good job as a receptionist at an orthodontist's office. She just happened to believe that she was the Greek goddess of night.

She didn't bother anyone, but somebody took exception to her presence. Several times in a span of about a month, somebody left spray-painted messages on her house. Stuff like "SATAN 666" and "CRAZY BITCH."

I did some snooping around, checking in with my sources, and tracked it back to Jeff Reppert. He was 18. A recent high school graduate and a bit of a neighborhood bully.

"What happened?" Pilar asked.

"I told him I wanted to talk about it. He asked if I was police. I told him I wasn't. He told me to go fu ... to go away."

"And?"

"I persisted. I explained to him how hurtful that kind of thing was, and told him it would be a nice gesture on his part if he would apologize and help her paint over the graffiti. He attempted to hasten my departure by grabbing my jacket. I removed his hand from my jacket."

"Removed it?"

"He was getting it wrinkled. The removal process necessitated some wrist twisting."

"And?"

"Well, I think it's a laudable goal to remind today's youth of the day-to-day challenges that people with disabilities face."

"And?"

"I don't remember every exact word that was spoken. But before I relinquished my hold on his hand, I may have suggested that he consider what it would be like to spend the rest of his life wiping his ass – his backside, sorry — with a hook."

I stopped. She was mad. I could tell because I was getting the cockeyed look.

Pilar has a glass eye. When she's angry, she tends to tilt her head — tucking in her chin and staring from underneath furrowed eyebrows. At those times, her glass eye lags a bit behind the real one.

"We've discussed this kind of thing before," she said, not raising her voice. She rarely raises her voice, because she can be plenty intimidating anyway.

"Hey, it worked. He went by her house, apologized, offered to help her. ..."

"That's not the point. This is the kind of thing that can get us in trouble. If Chief Sanderson gets wind of this ..."

"Ah, he hates me already."

"I can't for the life of me figure out why."

We polished off our respective mugs of coffee. I sat back, waiting.

"So," she said. "The Slain. What's your assessment? Are they linked to Cabot?"

"Does the pope shit in the woods?"

I got the cockeyed look. She hates it when I say that.

"In my opinion," I went on, "they are linked to Cabot. Which would link them to Schulze. Which would officially make them our problem."

"What do they want?" she asked. "Do you think this relates to Paul Bacon?"

"Could be. But I don't think they want him anymore. If they wanted to grab a 14-year-old boy, blowing up a couple garbage trucks across town isn't the most efficient way to go about it. Could be a kind of citywide retaliation for my run-in with Cabot. I don't know if he's their leader or not, but I get the impression he's got some sway in their organization."

"It sounds to me like finding him would at least be an important step in answering some of these questions. What are the chances?"

I shrugged.

"How long is a piece of string? Hard to say exactly. Depends on a lot of things. But that's a big priority. I got a feeling Cabot will be key to all this."

"Speaking of Cabot. ..."

She reached into her desk and brought out a file folder. On the cover, her neat, block writing read "BATLEY CITY COUNCIL REPORT, SEPT. 28"

She started flipping through it. I shifted in my seat.

"I've been going through the notes you took at the last council meeting," she said. "Seems like there's a substantial gap in the middle."

"Yes," I said. "I had to excuse myself to visit the facilities."

"How long were you absent?"

"Seconds."

"And you did not invent any of the dialogue recorded?"

"Wouldn't dream of it."

"So during the discussion on the historic butter churn replica, Mr. Oliphant really did use the term 'P-I-S-S like a racehorse.'"

"In so many words."

"And Mr. Bixler really did say that he likes to sniff bicycle seats?"

"I was a little far from the podium, so I may have misheard that."

"I'm more concerned with the statements made by Ms. Gaffigan."

I felt a twinge of annoyance. Pilar's good people. But in my opinion, she can be a little too dedicated to the idea that everyone has a valid opinion.

"Come on," I said. "If Batley had a local Nutball Olympics, Gaffigan would get a silver medal to Hoffman's gold."

"Regardless, it appears that the subject of 'Cabot's Master,' as they call it, is on people's minds. What's your take on it?"

"Just a story. A stupid one."

Even as I said that, I found myself thinking of a night a few months back when I ran into Tim Rourke, owner of Rourke's Grocery Mart, at a bar.

We talked about local politics and the Batley Snippers. We had a few beers. Then a few more.

As closing time approached and most of the other patrons left, he glanced around to make sure nobody was looking. Then his voice dropped a few decibels as he asked me if I'd really been in Cabot's house. I told him I had.

"Was there anybody else in there with him?"

"Yeah, that kid Paul Bacon."

"I don't mean that," he said. "Have you ever heard the talk about Cabot's Master?"

I told him I'd heard the stories, but I hadn't seen anyone else in the house. Which was technically true. I didn't tell anyone but Pilar about the huge shape moving toward me in the basement. I still didn't know what I'd seen and heard, if anything. Hey, it was dark and I was confused. Could have been my mind playing tricks on me. Besides, I figured there were already more than enough bullshit stories making their way around town about Cabot, and I didn't feel like adding to them.

Tim started telling me about a business arrangement he had with Cabot. Every month, Cabot would mail him a check. And every week, Tim would deliver him a load of groceries.

Tim got in the habit of delivering the groceries himself most of the time. His employees were scared about going by Cabot's place, and Tim didn't like putting them through that.

Sometimes Cabot would give him a hand unloading the groceries. Tim had to admit that he was pretty polite, if not exactly friendly. And he was a good tipper.

The routine was for Tim to leave the boxes on Cabot's porch. It seemed kind of weird to Tim, since it would be just as easy for him to carry the stuff inside. But that's how Cabot wanted it.

One day, Cabot wanted to talk about a change in the order. It was a cold day and Tim left his jacket in the truck. Cabot noticed him shivering and invited him inside to talk.

While they were talking, Tim heard something elsewhere in the house. Something moving around. Something big, judging by the creaking floorboards. Then whatever it was made a sound. Tim imitated it, making a kind of a ululating wail.

"AAAaaaaaAAAaaaa"

Cabot abruptly told Tim that he'd call him about the change in the order, and asked him to leave. Tim didn't argue. He forced himself not to run back to his truck, then drove way too fast for a residential neighborhood on his way out of there.

I'd felt a chill go down my spine when Tim made that noise, and ordered a double bourbon for last call.

"In your report on the night you went to Cabot's house to rescue Paul," Pilar said, "you wrote about encountering something in the basement. You were unclear on what it was."

"That's because I have no idea what it was," I said. "It was just something in the dark, making a noise."

"Did you investigate?"

"I was in a hurry to leave."

"You felt threatened?"

"I think 'freaked out' would be a more accurate term."

"Were you under the influence of any mind altering substances?""

"I may have had a drink or two earlier on."

"Does alcohol cause you to hallucinate?

"There was this one waitress who looked pretty good at 2 a.m. Not so much eight hours later. But I guess that's not what you're talking about."

"So it's safe to assume you weren't hallucinating whatever it was you encountered in the basement. All I'm saying is that it may play a role in your investigation. Sounds like we've got our work cut out for us. You work your sources, I'll work mine. Check in regularly and let me know how it's going."

She looked at her watch.

How about that?" she said. "Just in time for a meeting. I'd like you to sit in."

"Who is it?"

"A group of our clients."

"Who is it?"

"The C.C. Support Group."

"Ah fu..."

I trailed off as she glanced meaningfully at the "No Foul Language" sign.

"Look, Pilar," I said. "You know I've got no problem whatsoever dealing with most of our clients. But that crew. They just ... creep me out."

"I know," she said. "That's why I want you to attend this meeting. You need to get over that. You can't be going around with an aversion to a large proportion of our clients and expect to do your job effectively. I think sitting in on the meeting will help you in that regard."

"Look, it's not just them, per se. It's that one bugfuck crazy lady who always ..."

"Hey! Language!"

I shut up.

"I know of your issues with Mr. Russo," she said. "Again, that's one more reason why it would be good for you to attend."

Looked like there was no getting around it. I resigned myself to being creeped out for the next hour or so.

"C.C." stands for "corporeally challenged." I guess calling them the "ghost support group" would feel too weird, even for this place.

My average workday brought me in contact with lots of strange and eerie creatures. Demons, werewolves, Ernie Bixler. It was usually no problem for me. This group was different.

Each of them had once gone by a different name and a different identity before showing up at Schulze's clinic. Now each claimed to be the ghost of a murder victim whose killer had never been punished, inhabiting their respective bodies. They said the souls that previously inhabited those bodies had become dormant and they — the murder victims — were trapped in them until they could "move on," as they called it.

That would happen periodically. One day, the person who had been walking around claiming to be a murder victim would suddenly revert to his or her old personality, with no memory of the intervening time. Like a coma victim waking up. The ghosts seemed to regard that situation as desirable.

They were delusional, of course, just like everybody else who came out of Schulze's clinic. More than the others, though, this group could be eerily convincing.

Take Carlos Paz. He was a hulking Mexican-American from California. When the police showed up at Schulze's compound and he couldn't speak any English, they sent around a Spanish translator.

That didn't do any good either. He wasn't speaking Spanish. He was speaking Cantonese. He claimed he was a 17-year-old Chinese girl who'd been left to drown by the "snakeheads" smuggling her into the United States.

Even that, I'd be able to cope with. My real problem was with Dom Russo. Except he wasn't Dom Russo. He was a sixty-ish black lady named Thelma Pointer.

When I'd first come to town, Dom was my jiu jitsu instructor. We got to be friends. He was a good guy. I tried to befriend his brother, Vince, too. But Vince was kind of a weird guy. Socially awkward. Hard to get to know.

One day, Vince killed Dom. The two of them were training alone in Dom's dojo. Dom was on his knees and Vince was practicing a military choke on him. Vince lost his balance and fell with all his weight on Dom's neck, breaking it. A freak accident, and a tragic one. Still, an accident. The police agreed.

Vince was still living in town. He'd gained a lot of weight. Every time I'd seen him recently, even in the morning, he'd been drunk. You could say the accident did a number on him, too.

So I didn't appreciate it when this Thelma Pointer woman showed up claiming to be Dom, and claiming that Vince broke his neck intentionally. I know she didn't ask to be the way she was, but I still didn't feel like hearing about it. I made that clear to her on numerous occasions when she tried to approach me.

Pilar and I walked down the stairs to where the main meeting room was.

"So who do you think's going to be the first to make the 'first day of the rest of your afterlife' joke?" she asked.

"I'll say Theo."

"Really? My money's on Jane."

"Your money? This a wager then?"

"10 bucks."

We shook on it, then opened the door. About a dozen of them sat around in a ring of metal folding chairs.

Theo, supposedly the ghost of a heroin addict who'd been slipped a hot shot, was at the coffee maker in the corner, pouring himself a cardboard cup. Reincarnation cured him of his heroin addiction, so I figured he was ahead of the game.

He made his way back to his chair — a tall, lanky white man in his 50s with a slight hitch in his gait. Many in the C.C. group seemed a little palsied in their movements, as though they were still figuring how to work the controls on their new bodies.

Pilar and I both took seats, roughly opposite from each other in the ring. She introduced me, said most of them knew me and she assumed they'd be OK with my joining the meeting. They said they were, killing my last hope for getting the fuck out out of there.

"Who would like to start today?" Pilar asked.

"I'll go!" said Jane, enthusiasm in her voice. Unlike some of the others, her body and personality seemed a perfect match. She was in her late 40s, bleached blond, dressed in sequined denim. Her meth-dealing boyfriend reportedly strangled her before heading off for Mexico, never to return.

"I was thinking about it today," Jane said. "And I really think I'm just about ready to move on."

"No you ain't," said Theo.

"How do you know whether I'm ready or not?"

"Cause you're talking about it. You go around saying you're ready to move on, it means you ain't ready. That's how it works. Everyone knows that."

"Who the fuck are you? Mr. Kung Fu Zen Master?"

"Hey!" Pilar barked. "None of that language. Jane, you know the rules. And Theo, there's a reason God gave us two ears and one mouth. You might consider hearing what people have to say before going all negative on them. Dom, we haven't heard from you in a while. What's on your mind these days?"

I had a feeling that was for my benefit. Great.

Thelma took a second to roll her shoulders and crack her knuckles. Same as Dom used to do.

"What have I got? Hmmmmm. Well, I got pissed ... I mean mad, sorry there Sister, the other day when I saw him on the street. My little brother. Geez."

She shook her head in an expression of exasperation. It really was eerie, the way her vocal and physical mannerisms mimicked Dom's.

"I mean, I hate the guy for what he did to me. You know why he did it, near as I can figure out? Because he hit on my girlfriend and she blew him off! How bout that?

"And you know what? I was nice about it. I confronted him, sure. What was

I gonna do? Pretend it didn't happen? He knew it would get back to me. I had to address it.

"I just said: Look Vince. Lisa told me what you did. It was uncool and I don't appreciate it. But you're my brother and I love you and we're gonna forget this ever happened and never mention it again. And what does he do? He turns around and breaks my neck. And he doesn't even have the balls — sorry there, sister — the guts to own up to it."

She was silent for a moment, staring at the floor. I noticed she was wearing a black T-shirt, jeans, and a gold chain. Dom's regular uniform.

"What happened when you saw him?" Pilar asked.

"I was walking down the street," Thelma said. "You know, I've seen him from a distance before. I thought how good it would feel to go into a sporting goods store, pick up a shotgun and blow him away."

Pilar bolted upright and started to say something, but Thelma held up a hand and quieted her.

"Relax, Sister. I wouldn't do it. Far as I'm concerned, my goal is to move on and let this lady ..." she gestured at her own body "get on with her life. I get her killed, I'm a murderer. No better than my brother."

She stared at the floor again. I noticed she was clenching and unclenching her fist. Dom used to do that when he was upset.

"He don't know who I am. Thought I was just some lady walking down the street. It's 3 p.m., you know? Middle of the day. And he's drunk. I could smell it when I passed him on the sidewalk. He always had trouble keeping his weight down, but he really let himself go. I mean, he's a fucking whale. Sorry, Sister.

"He's walking down the sidewalk and looking like he didn't even know where he was. Like he was the dead one, not me."

She paused again. Her jaw was clenched tight. She took a deep breath and went on.

"You know what I wanted to do, just for a second? I wanted to put an arm over his shoulders. I wanted to tell him to stop doing this to himself. After what he did to me! How nuts is that?"

"It's not nuts," Pilar said. "It's how you felt."

"No!" Jane yelled. "It is nuts! Think about what he did to you! Same thing as my old man did to me! You ever think what you might have done with your life if he hadn't come along and taken it from you? Where you might have ended up?"

A small man in the corner spoke up.

"He would have ended up dead. It might have taken him longer to get there, but he would have ended up just where we are now, same as every other human being ever born. Then whatever he accomplished wouldn't have mattered anywhere near as much as what kind of person he was."

That was Ed. He claimed he'd been a small-time dope dealer who happened to be standing on the wrong stretch of sidewalk during a drive-by shooting. Even in his current incarnation, he'd been a hellraiser for a while. During meetings, he'd shout down the others and kick over furniture. He was the only human being I'd ever seen — male or female, dead or alive — with the courage to tell Pilar to her face to fuck off.

A couple years ago, he'd just changed. Stopped yelling. Gone quiet and contemplative. He rarely spoke up during meetings. When he did, he tended to infuriate Jane. Like now.

"Don't start in with that forgiveness bullshi- crap again, Ed," she said. "I didn't ask for what happened to me!"

"None of us asks for what happens to us," Ed said. "We've got no control over that. All we can control is how we respond to it. Is this how you pictured your afterlife? Seething and lashing out because of some man you'll never see again?"

"No!" she shot back. "As a matter of fact, this is not how I pictured the afterlife! I never pictured it at all! What did you think it would be? Clouds and angels playing harps?"

Ed sat back in his chair. His mouth stretched in a small smile.

"When I was a kid," he said, "every August the neighborhood association would put on a street carnival. They'd close off a few blocks. Put up rides and food tents. Have games and jugglers and stilt walkers. Everybody I knew would be there. Walking around and laughing and saying hi to each other. I guess I thought ... hoped ... the afterlife would be kind of like that."

Theo rolled his eyes.

"A street carnival. That's great, Ed. Maybe there would be rainbows and puppy dogs and little unicorns handing out ice cream cones, too."

Theo took a swig of coffee, then continued in a mocking, motivational speaker voice.

"Hey! Buck up, everyone! Today is the first day ..."

"Of the rest of your afterlife," Jane continued. "Jesus. That one never gets old."

Pilar broke in.

"Allright," she said. "Remember what I was saying about the negativity? You keep sniping at each other like this, you're not going to get anywhere."

Theo and Jane both stared at her, then looked away. There was no defying Pilar. End of story.

"Dom," she said in a gentler tone. "Did you want to say anything more?"

Thelma, the woman who claimed to be Dom, still stared at the floor. She'd stopped clenching and unclenching her fists, and just shook her head slowly.

They went around the room. A few more spoke about their feelings. About pain and betrayal and hope.

Then, at Pilar's direction, they stood, joined hands and said the serenity prayer.

"God, grant me the serenity
To accept the things I cannot change;
Courage to change the things I can;
And the wisdom to know the difference."

Then they hitch-stepped their way out the door.

"Was that so bad?" Pilar asked me.

"Yes."

"Well suck it up. It's our job. Remember to keep me informed of how the investigation is going."

I held out my hand.

"Ten bucks," I said. "Theo made the joke."

"Nuh uh. Theo started to make the joke. Jane actually made it."

"I thought nuns were honest."

"That's what you thought? You want to find Cabot, you should get yourself some better sources."

I went out the front door into the night.

"Hey!"

I turned. Goddamn it. Thelma Pointer was walking toward me from where she'd been waiting on the sidewalk.

"I have a message for you," she said.

I held up a hand to cut her off.

"Look lady," I said. "I'm sorry about what happened to you. And I wish you the best. I really do. But I just can't deal with you. Sorry."

I turned around and started to walk away.

"You could never quite sink it, could you?" she asked.

I stopped.

"Excuse me?"

"That reverse military choke. You'd always try for it, but you could never sink it. Then you'd go for an arm bar when you could tell the choke wasn't gonna happen. See, that's why I'd tell you to vary your attacks. You were predictable. I'd wait for you to go for the arm bar, and I'd roll right out of it."

I stared at her, unable to speak.

"When you're ready to talk, you know where to find me," she said.

She walked away from me down the sidewalk, a slight hitch in her step.

I leaned against the building. Fall was setting in. Evenings were coming faster and getting cooler.

I reached into my jacket pocket, brought out a cigar and lit it. The whole experience had knocked me off-kilter.

I needed some perspective. And I suspected I'd find it wherever I found One-Eyed Slim.

FILE EIGHT

I checked a couple likely places before locating One-Eyed Slim. Eventually, I found him in a dimly lit bar. Or more accurately, an even more dimly lit bar behind it.

The bar up front looked like any downtown Batley hole-in-the-wall. It had a long room that smelled of stale beer and cigarette smoke. The handful of old guys at the bar ignored the TV in the corner tuned to a local news broadcast, seeming more interested in the drinks in front of them. The only conversation was a one-sided rant by a bearded codger who was quite incensed about some political matter, directed at another patron who ignored him.

A door in the back wall might have led to a closet or supply room. Except it didn't. I stood in its general vicinity and made eye contact with the skinny old-timer tending bar. He gave me a nod. I opened the door and walked inside.

The room I stepped into was almost as big as the one out front. The only illumination came from two light fixtures shining down in straight lines like mini-spotlights. One was behind the small bar against the wall, where a beefy young man with a crew cut polished glasses with a rag.

The other shone down on a card table, where four people sat. They looked up when I entered, then turned their attention back to the cards in their hands as I sidled over to the bar. Without asking, the young bartender brought me a Scotch.

No mistaking One-Eyed Slim. He was tall and lean, lounging back in his chair with a Stetson pulled low over his eyes and a long black ponytail protruding from the back of it. He wore jeans and cowboy boots. His sleeveless T-shirt revealed a tattoo on his upper right arm of a royal flush with flaming skulls on the cards. At his elbow was a glass of whiskey.

On his left sat a tall, young Asian guy looking elegant in a suit and tie. On his right sat a gorgeous woman, late 20s, with flowing red hair and a creamy Southern accent.

Directly across from him sat a chubby, bespectacled man who was middle aged, but whose thinning blond curls and soft, round features gave him a babyish appearance. The chubby man wore a polo shirt tucked into the waistband of khaki slacks. At his elbow was a tall, day-glo-colored drink ringed with fruit garnishes.

As I watched, the chubby man tried to engage the red-headed woman in conversation about the importance of his job in purchasing. He became flustered when the woman ignored him to exchange glances and smiles with One-Eyed Slim. I stifled a grin and took a drink. I didn't know exactly what was going to happen, but it promised to be entertaining.

So it wouldn't be too obvious that I was watching, I picked a magazine up off the bar. "Saltwater Fisherman Monthly?" Whatever. I pretended to leaf through it.

The tall Asian kid dealt. One-Eyed Slim appeared confident in his hand, raising with a big handful of chips. The Asian kid and the redhead dropped out early. The blond guy, a pouty look on his baby face, stayed in. One-Eyed Slim glanced at the redhead and gave her a slow, easy smile, as if to say "Watch this, honey." She smiled back, ran a hand through her hair and then slowly trailed her fingers down the side of her neck.

A phone rang behind the bar. The beefy young bartender picked it up.

"Is there a Herbert Diekendorf here?" he asked.

The pudgy man flushed a bright pink and made frantic shushing gestures.

"I'm not here!" he said in a squeaky voice.

The bartender got back on the phone.

"He says he's not ... oh." He looked up at the pudgy man and gave him a "my bad" shrug, then went back to the phone.

"OK, ma'am," he said, and set down the receiver. "That was your wife. She said she wants you home and you better not be playing cards."

The other three players did a poor job of stifling their laughter. The pudgy man flushed an even brighter shade of pink.

One-Eyed Slim raised again, dropping a handful of chips in the center of the table. The pudgy man stared at them for a moment, lower lip trembling, before slowly folding his cards.

One-Eyed Slim let loose with the slow, easy smile again as he slid the chips over to his side.

"Wow!" said the Asian kid, regarding One-Eyed Slim with blatant admiration.

"That was pretty ballsy," the redhead said, eyeing him up and down and drawing out the first syllable more than seemed strictly necessary.

"You see darlin'," One-Eyed Slim said, leaning back still farther in his chair and pushing the Stetson back from his face, "poker's more than just a game. It's a philosophy of life. Now Herbie over here ..."

"Herbert!" the pudgy man squeaked.

"... He'll get riled once in a while and get his back up. But by and large, he likes to play it safe. Me? I'll take a risk just to see what cards are gonna fall into my life next."

The redhead purred — actually purred — and seemed to melt a little in her seat.

The chubby man got the cards, clumsy in his growing agitation as he shuffled and dealt.

Once again, One-Eyed Slim raised. The pudgy man cringed when the phone rang again and the young bartender picked it up.

"Yes ma'am. I'll tell him." He set down the phone.

"Mr. Diekendorf?" he said, an apology in his voice. "That was your wife again. She said if you don't come home this instant, you're in big trouble."

This time, the others at the table made no effort to hide it. The Asian kid and the redhead laughed and One-Eyed Slim grinned openly.

"I ... will ... come ... home ... when ... I'm ... ready!" the pudgy man declared to nobody in particular, his face breaking out in a pink blush again. To punctuate the last word, he slid his entire pile of chips into the middle of the table.

"You sure about this, son?" One-Eyed Slim asked, still grinning. "Sounds like the missus'll be pissed off."

"Are you seeing my raise or not?" His squeaky voice had gone up several octaves.

One-Eyed Slim exchanged another glance and smile with the redhead, then pushed all of his chips to the center of the table. A duel to the death.

"Call," the pudgy man said.

One-Eyed Slim dropped his cards to the table with a flourish of his wrist.

"Full house, aces high." Then he immediately turned to the redhead. "Like I was sayin', it's a philosophy of life. You see, some men ..."

"Four of a kind," the pudgy man said, turning over his cards. With no visible emotion, he began scooping up the towering pile of chips.

One-Eyed Slim shut up and stared slackjawed at the other man's hand. He swiveled his head to the Asian kid and then to the redhead, as if seeking confirmation they'd all just witnessed something that violated the basic mechanics of the universe, like a dropped object falling up instead of down.

The two of them just counted their own chips, neither much interested in him anymore.

One-Eyed Slim stood and walked out of the room. He didn't look upset so much as dazed, like he was thinking this was all a nightmare and he might wake up at any second. The door closed behind him.

The redhead looked at the pudgy man.

"Nice job, Pinky," she said.

"Yeah man," added the Asian kid. "That was classic."

"Thank you," the pudgy man responded, the squeak gone from his voice. "As usual, you two were a liability and an embarrassment. How many times do we have to go through this? When I am handling the cards, you do not look at my hands. I don't care if it's just a glance. I don't care if it's just a fraction of a second. The space that my hands occupy is the one spot on this big blue marble we call the planet Earth where you do not want to direct the mark's attention and I would appreciate it if you two would get that through your thick fucking skulls!"

I no longer felt obliged to conceal my grin. Fuckin Pinky.

Among his friends, colleagues, and the constantly shifting crew of young trainees he always referred to as "these stupid fucking kids," an ongoing debate centered on his nickname. Some held that it came from his ability to blush on cue. Others that it referred to his aptitude at manipulating cards with his little fingers. I figured it didn't make much difference, since he could use both skills to devastating effect.

I was once in a position to do Pinky a favor. He showed me a few tricks in return, despite insisting that I was too clumsy and stupid by nature to do anything useful with them.

The redhead and the Asian kid were unfazed.

"Sorry Pinky," said the Asian kid, who went by the name Mako. "We're just trying to figure out how you reverse the cut. I mean, you never really show us so of course we can't help but be curious."

Mako buried his face in his hands and pretended to cry.

"We've failed you, Pinky! We were weak. So ... very ... weak."

The redhead, whose name was Veronica, chimed in.

"Maybe if you showed us, I'd find it a little easier to keep my eyes off you. But I'm not making any promises. That ass on you? MMMmmm!"

The purr was back in her voice, but all it got out of Pinky was an eye roll suggesting depths of martyrdom to make the very saints weep.

"You two are a riot," he said. "You think this is a big joke? Well guess what? You get cocky and try a move you're not ready for when you're in the wrong place, you're not gonna walk out on your own feet."

He took a lime slice from the rim of his glass, bit down on it, then threw the stripped rind in an ashtray.

"Fuck it," Pinky said. "I'm gonna regret this. Just sit tight a minute. I've just got some business to take care of first."

The other two shared a smug glance in the time-honored manner of kids who've just wheedled themselves into a cool gift. Pinky picked up his fruity drink, wandered over to the bar and sat down next to me.

"The many deaths of One-Eyed Slim," I said.

One-Eyed Slim was a generic term that Pinky used for a type of mark in which he specialized, based on the Old West-style monikers they liked to give themselves.

"You know, I was going to take it easy on him," Pinky said. "Then when he started calling me 'son' and talking that poker-as-philosophy bullshit ..."

Whatever else Pinky was, he was no coddler of preening jerkoffs.

"The Slain," I said. "What have you heard?"

"Well, they hadn't been in town since the Halloween Parade Massacre. I'd know."

"How would you know?"

"I'd know. Have you seen them close up?"

"Twice. I took one of them out during the Warm Hearths festival attack. Got a look at his face. White guy. Maybe 25. Never seen him before."

"And?"

I told him the story about the attack on Liam O'Shaunnesey's. I included what Michael told me, and what we saw in the clearing afterward. I also told him about my speculation on the link between them and Cabot.

Pinky listened in silence.

"What's their source of income?" he asked at length. "How do they support themselves?"

"Never really thought about it."

"Where do their women and kids live?"

"There has to be women and kids?"

"Here's this criminal operation. It's been around at least 15 years. Much longer, from what this Michael guy is telling you. And no member's ever had a girlfriend or a kid. That sound plausible to you?"

I didn't bother answering. Pinky took a long pull off his drink.

"Any criminal operation is a business, first and foremost," Pinky said. "Doesn't matter whether their ultimate goal is to rid the world of infidel capitalist pigdogs or to sell dimebags of skunk to college kids. They need to make a profit or they're not going to last a week, much less 15 years."

"Well this is also some kind of religion," I said. "Religions aren't businesses."

Pinky looked at me and cocked an eyebrow.

"OK," I acknowledged. "That's about the dumbest thing I've ever said."

"I haven't heard everything you've ever said, but I'm willing to take your word on that."

The beefy bartender approached and asked if I wanted another Scotch. I did.

"So Bob," Pinky said to him. "What did you say when you brought me my drink?"

"Excuse me?"

"My drink. When you set it down on the table, you said something. What was it?"

The young man looked puzzled.

"I don't know ... 'Here's your drink?'"

"You said 'There ya go, Mr. Diekendorf.' Then 15 minutes later, you're taking a phone call and asking if that's my name. Luckily, our friend over there couldn't tear his attention away from Veronica's rack long enough to notice. But I for one think the chance of our landing another mark who's even stupider than you is pretty remote."

"Sorry, Pinky," Bob said as he refilled my glass.

"These kids are getting dumber every day," Pinky said after he left. "Our species is devolving. Don't let anyone tell you different. So this guy you took out is about 25. He's not carrying ID. We can infer a couple of things from that. First, he wasn't with The Slain when the Halloween Parade Massacre happened. That means they're viable enough to get recruits. That means a source of income.

"Second, he wasn't going to cooperate with the police if he was arrested. If he's willing to do time for this outfit, that means they've got enough money to make it worth his while. Or he's fanatic for whatever it is they're about."

"Or he's shit scared of them," I said.

"Or some combination of the three," Pinky said. "Whatever it is, there's something bigger going on under the surface. Looks like it's your job to figure out what."

He finished his drink, then signaled to Bob that he wanted a refill.

"Can't say I envy you," Pinky said.

FILE NINE

I thought about the flask of Scotch in my inside jacket pocket. Its heft comforted me. If the municipal meeting I was currently attending got much more tedious, I could always duck out to the men's room and take a few slugs.

But this time, I was afraid the Scotch might not do the trick. Morphine might not do the trick. I did have a ballpoint pen in my pants pocket. Maybe I could ram it through my eye socket and directly into my brain. I figured I'd experience only a few seconds of pain before drifting away to some blessed realm where I'd never again have to hear the word "proactive."

It was an emergency meeting of the Batley Public Safety Committee. That wasn't the problem. I considered the meeting, in principle, to be necessary.

That much was obvious when I'd walked the several blocks from my apartment to City Hall. At first, I'd wondered why The Slain would blow up the city's garbage trucks. City council said they were looking at a couple different waste-hauling firms in the region. They told local residents to give it another week or so, and in the meantime asked them to drive their trash to the local dump.

All in all, it seemed more like a malicious schoolboy's prank than something a bunch of psychos like The Slain would pull off. But on my walk to City Hall, I realized the logic behind it.

Trash bags and assorted debris piled up along the sidewalks. The piles weren't huge. Yeah, some of it stank if you wandered too close, but it wasn't overpowering.

Still, every pile of trash lining the sidewalk might as well be a sign spelling out a single message in flashing neon letters: "We are here."

So what was the problem with the meeting? Ernie Bixler was chairman.

Also on the committee were Buck Rockbaugh, who was vice-chairman; Chief Sanderson; Lou Evans, chief of the Batley Fire Department; Susan Rothman, director of Batley Emergency Medical Services; and Burt Chandler, head of public works. Also present was Linda Goldberg, Buck's secretary who typically attended to take the minutes.

The meeting took place in City Council chambers. My presence at the meetings was pretty common. Sometimes they'd have questions about our clients, and I considered it part of my job to know what was going on in the city.

Luanne Bacon was there too. Again, that was common.

Luanne did a lot of work with homeless people in downtown Batley. She was particularly good working with the mentally ill. I'd seen this before. She'd drop the prickliness, and her voice would take on a soothing quality that could calm the most manic street people.

For years, she'd volunteered at the Batley Homeless Shelter, which provided a soup kitchen, a place for homeless people to sleep and referral services for other social agencies. At least, that's what it used to do until it closed down under Bixler's Feet to the Fire Campaign.

Michael was also at the meeting. And that wasn't so common.

I'd showed up early so I could go through my routine with the kid working the metal detector. Just as I was picking up my jacket with the flask, Luanne got there and we walked up to the second floor meeting room together.

Michael leaned against a wall outside the meeting room and read a copy of the Batley Daily Needler, decked out as always in his jeans, boots, and leather jacket.

He looked up and said "Here to give them some safe driving tips?"

"Sanderson insisted on it," I told him.

Private joke. After we chased The Slain out to the campground, we'd agreed on our story before heading back and giving our report to the police. We'd discovered that all hell was breaking loose in the police station because of the hostage situation and the blown-up trucks.

That was probably lucky for us, because nobody had time to dissect our story. Or give me a breathalyzer test, for that matter. Even so, Sanderson spared a few seconds to let us know our claim of simply being concerned citizens who followed all traffic laws past and present smelled like grade-A bullshit, and he didn't appreciate us trying to take the law into our own hands. He seemed to have taken a dislike to Michael, too. And Michael seemed every bit as heartbroken about it as I was.

"You remember Luanne?" I asked.

"Of course." He smiled and nodded. "Good to see you."

"Hello," she said. Not hostile but not exactly friendly either. She walked past us and into the meeting room.

"So what are you doing here?" I asked. "Nothing good on TV tonight?"

"Mayor Rockbaugh invited me. He heard about what happened at Liam O'Shaunnesey's. He invited me to his office, we talked about my job and I guess he thought I'd have something to contribute."

We walked inside.

Most meetings consisted of members talking about their departments' needs and what funding was available. After his election, Bixler volunteered — demanded, really — to head the committee.

That hadn't been much of a problem up until that evening. All it meant was that Sanderson, Evans and Rothman would have to waste the first 30 minutes or so briefing Bixler on the city's capability for dealing with "foreign insurgents" before getting down to business.

Not tonight. When Bixler was excited about something, he guzzled coffee by the potful and got himself worked up until he was practically frothing at the mouth.

He started out demanding to know why the agenda items were marked off with Roman numerals. Linda explained that was common practice, which led to Bixler ranting about how this is an English-speaking country and we don't need foreign languages on our very government documents.

Linda assured him that from then on, committee agenda items would have Arabic numerals. Bixler went batshit crazy at that, until Linda started calling them "American numerals" and calmed him down a little.

Buck asked Sanderson to give a report. Sanderson stood and was about to speak when Bixler interrupted him.

"Before you start," Bixler said, "I'd just like to say something on a personal note. You know, I always figured we'd end up like this sooner or later. A pair of ol' guard dogs protecting this city. Sandy, I just want to say it's good to know you've got my back. And I've certainly got yours."

"I would prefer that you not call me 'Sandy,' " Sanderson said, pronouncing his words like he was afraid he might bite his tongue in half. "If you're going to address me, please do so as 'Chief Sanderson' or 'Mr. Sanderson.' "

"Gotcha," Bixler said, and winked. "We've got to keep up appearances."

"Chief Sanderson," Buck interrupted, "what steps are your department taking to address this threat?"

"Sir, we've stepped up patrols as much as possible. We're somewhat compromised in our attempts to deal with this."

Bixler looked accusingly at Buck, then back at Sanderson.

"Are career politicians getting in your way?" Bixler asked.

Sanderson's jaw muscles clenched, then loosened.

"With all due respect, sir, my department's budget was cut substantially under the Feet to the Fire Campaign," Sanderson said. "We've been forced to delay making urgently needed hires and replacing two patrol vehicles that are no longer operational. We've also been obliged to continue using the breakroom sink as a urinal until such time as we can make needed renovations to the stationhouse men's room."

Bixler looked at Sanderson with doe-eyed sympathy.

"Sandy ... Chief Sanderson. I know you're being asked to do more with less. But look at it this way. In the past, you had to jump through a bunch of hoops — rules and regulations — to keep the career politicians happy. You can consider those days over. If you and your people need to twist a few arms to get the job done, if you know what I mean, let's just say nobody's looking over your shoulder."

Bixler gave Sanderson a conspiratorial smile that was not returned.

"Sir," Sanderson said, "I have instructed my officers to abide by all applicable procedures during the crisis, and have informed them that failure to do so will result in disciplinary action."

Bixler looked confused for a second. Then a smile broke out on his face again.

"Uh huuuuh. I get it," he said, then continued in a louder tone. "Of course, Chief Sanderson! You're going to follow procedures to the letter!"

He winked at Sanderson again. Sanderson sat, his jaw muscles clenched so tight that I expected to hear teeth breaking.

Next on the agenda was Luanne, to talk about the city's homeless population. She told committee members that several homeless people had been targeted during the Warm Hearths Festival attack. Many were still frightened, she said, and she asked if the city would be able to find temporary shelter for them until the crisis passed.

Bixler made a show of shuffling through papers as she talked. When she finished, he spoke.

"Ms. Bacon, I think I speak for my fellow committee members when I say we share your concerns. But during these times when we all have to make sacrifices, we simply cannot guarantee protection for these people."

Luanne swallowed hard. Keeping her temper in check was not what you'd call a natural aptitude for her.

With a slight quaver in her voice, she explained that the number of people living on the streets had more than tripled over the past year, mainly because of the city's funding cuts both for the homeless shelter and for a mental health assistance program under the Feet to the Fire Campaign.

A network of volunteers tried to find accommodations for them in church basements or anywhere that could spare the space, but with limited success.

"Mr. Bixler," she said, "most of these people have nowhere else to go. We put them out on the streets. And now that they're in danger we're just going to tell them they're on their own?"

Bixler continued to skim through some papers for a few seconds before looking up.

"The city just doesn't have the resources to make this a priority. That's all."

Luanne pointed a finger at him and looked like she was about to say something not very pleasant when Michael spoke up.

"Excuse me, may I say something?"

Michael stood. Bixler, not exactly the king of icy control under the best of circumstances, suddenly looked even more frazzled. Michael seemed to frighten him.

Buck nodded his head, and Michael spoke.

"The organization I represent makes a priority of looking out for those who can't defend themselves," he said. "I have no doubt that the citizen action groups I've discussed with you previously, Mr. Rockbaugh, can find some kind of accommodations for the homeless people that have Ms. Bacon worried."

"Pardon me," said Bixler. "But can I ask exactly who you represent?"

Bixler made a point of looking Michael up and down, apparently trying to convey through body language that men with long hair, beards, earrings, and leather jackets were not welcome in the hallowed halls of government.

"Certainly," Michael said. "I'm here at Mayor Rockbaugh's invitation to explain exactly that. I represent an international network of people dedicated to combatting The Slain. Our job is to monitor them and put a stop to them when we can. In situations like this where they threaten a specific community, we train and organize the people to fight back and ..."

Sanderson was on his feet.

"I will not tolerate vigilantes in this city!" he shouted.

Michael stayed calm.

"I'm not talking about vigilantes," he said. "We rely on citizen watch groups. Their main job is keeping an eye out for suspicious activity in their neighborhoods. And they cooperate fully with the local police, of course."

"Chief Sanderson," Buck said, "I can tell you that I've heard accounts by people who were in O'Shaunessey's about the effect that this man has on The Slain. He's also explained to me that he has experience dealing with these criminals. It seems to me that we should avail ourselves of anything that might help us."

Sanderson sat down. I wouldn't have thought it possible, but he looked even more displeased than he had a few minutes ago. Bixler glared at Michael.

"Sir, if you want to make suggestions, you're certainly welcome to do so," Bixler said. "But keep in mind that we have a certain way of doing things in this community. And somebody coming in from outside and trying to tell us how to conduct our business may find himself unwelcome."

"So tell me, Ernie," Michael said. "That 'certain way of doing things in this community' — think that would have got you out of O'Shaunessey's in one piece if I hadn't been there to save your ass?"

Bixler said nothing. He had a stricken look on his face, eyes going back and forth as if looking for someone to bail him out. Nobody did.

"I've said what I needed to say," Michael said. "If you'll excuse me, I have a lot on my plate right now. Buck, be seeing you tomorrow for our talk. You said 3, right?"

He looked around at the other people in the room.

"I'll probably be checking in with the rest of you in the near future. Take care."

Michael sauntered out the door. Conversation turned to whether the city could afford a training course for firefighters. Since they seemed unlikely to solicit my opinion on the topic, I also headed for the door. Luanne followed.

Michael stood in the hall outside, waiting for us.

Luanne asked Michael if he could really find some way to help the city's homeless. She sounded a lot more friendly toward him.

"I'm sure we can," Michael said. "The way I see it, my job wouldn't be worth doing if we didn't look out for the most vulnerable people. It would probably be a hell of a lot easier, though."

Luanne walked off. He watched her go. Then he looked at me.

"I've got a feeling I'm going to need both you and Luanne in the days ahead," he said.

The door to the meeting room opened. Sanderson exited and closed it behind him.

"You may have Rockbaugh's ear," Sanderson said, addressing both of us. "But know this. Either of you steps over the line and I will be on you like stink on shit."

He fixed us with a cold, appraising gaze that had probably made countless suspects soil their undies over the years. Unfortunately for him, Bixler exited the meeting room at that exact moment.

"I have instructed my officers to abide by all applicable procedures," Bixler said, in a goofy, deep-throated voice. Then he laughed and slapped Sanderson on the ass. "You're a sly dog, Sandy."

Sanderson watched Bixler walk down the hall. For just a moment, his hand hovered near his gun holster before he slowly and shakily pulled it away.

FILE 10

I blinked at the young woman working the concession stand, trying to make sense of what she was telling me.

"You're not serving Drosselmyer's?" I asked.

I was in Grossman and Grossman Podiatry Associates Stadium, home of the Batley Snippers.

The perky blonde behind the register explained that some brewer of mass-produced goat piss had bought itself a monopoly on the beer concessions at the stadium. So I couldn't drink the local brew while watching the local team play for its first division title in recent memory.

She did offer me a selection of Goat Piss, Goat Piss Light or Goat Piss Special Edition Harvest Ale. And we kid ourselves we're living in a sane society.

I went with the Harvest Ale on the assumption that there was probably some law saying a hoity toity name had to make it taste better, and decided not to obsess about it. I was determined to enjoy myself that evening.

I'd had a hectic few days. A partial list of my tasks included talking to witnesses of both the street festival attack and the brawl at O'Shaunessey's, checking with my sources in the police department and on the street, tracking down the previous owner of Whispering Woods Family campground — now a resident of California — and calling around at a bunch of dealerships that sell or rent dirtbikes.

I'd visited at least a dozen abandoned properties that seemed like good spots for The Slain to camp out, rendezvous, or stash equipment. In the process, I'd run into many homeless people, assorted narcotics users in assorted states of consciousness, and one none-too-pleased local businessman engaged in an act outlawed in some Southern states with a big-haired woman in pink spandex. All that got me nothing but tired.

So I was due for some beer and baseball. Most seasons, rooting for the Batley Snippers was a kind of masochistic ritual I put myself through. But this season, they were on fire. And this particular evening, they were taking on the Mullersport Smelters for their division championship.

I couldn't forget about The Slain entirely. That much was clear when I got to the front gates and saw a long line of people waiting to get in. The delay was due to security guards checking bags and doing pat-downs. This never happened before at Snippers games, and I assumed it was in response to the recent disturbances.

I thought I'd be watching the game on my own. But someone called my name when I was in line for a beer. There was Ken Bacon, leaning on his aluminum cane and smiling. I asked if I could get him a beer. He refused at first, but I reminded him of all the times the Bacons had me over for dinner and insisted. I carried it to his seat, because he had trouble managing the cane without spilling any.

It turned out he was in an area reserved for disabled people, which was right behind home plate.

"Why don't you join me?" he asked. "Gimps and their guests get the best seats in the house."

I took him up on it, and it was pretty sweet. Great view. Easy access to the beer stand. Beautiful evening. Warm with just a hint of autumn crispness. The nice weather and the division championship brought a lot of people out, too.

As the announcer informed us at the beginning, the place was filled to its 4,200 capacity.

The game itself started out as kind of a yawner. The Smelters managed to load the bases during the third inning, but the Snippers pulled off a pretty impressive double play and took care of that. Other than that, it was uneventful.

But I was plenty entertained, since I was sitting next to Ken. We started out talking about the Snippers and the local fans. I told Ken I wasn't a big fan of major league baseball, because these days it was all about steroids and big money. Minor league baseball just seemed like it had more integrity.

"I guess it was more honest back in your day," I told Ken.

He laughed out loud.

"You kidding?" he said. "We used to cheat like hell."

Then he told me a bunch of stories about his days as a pitcher for the Snippers. He said they didn't consider it cheating, since everyone did it. It was more a matter of survival than anything else.

It turned out Ken was indirectly responsible for Bubbles McBride's nickname, when he'd coached McBride on a technique that always worked for him. He'd put a smear of soap on the inside of his sleeve. During the game, he'd get some on his fingers and then on the ball.

McBride got it down pretty well. The only problem was that Ken forgot to tell him wearing a T-shirt on a hot day was necessary. So the umpire threw McBride out of a game when he saw soap bubbles coming out of his sleeve.

At one point, Ken got up to take a leak. I looked around me. The press box was right behind us. In front of it, I saw a photographer I knew from the Batley Daily Needler named Sheila, unscrewing her camera from a tripod. She nodded at me.

"Hey, Sheila," I said. "How are things at the paper? You keeping my buddy Tom out of trouble?"

She rolled her eyes.

"Don't talk to me about Tom," she said. "He left a poem on my desk. Something about comparing him and me to Pygmalion and Guinevere. It was supposed to be anonymous, but he's the only one creepy enough to do something like that."

TOM JERKFACE: I did no such thing. And it's Pygmalion and Galatea.

Ken came back and we had a great time throwing back beers, shooting the shit, and watching the game. Things got more exciting in the seventh inning, when the Snippers scored a run. Now they just had to keep the Smelters at bay for a while, and they'd be division champs.

The inning ended, and they had this thing that a local car dealership sponsors where kids dressed as different items from the concession stands race each other around the bases. I guess it's cute if you're into that kind of thing, but for me it was always a cue to go for another round of beers. Ken said he'd like one, and I headed back for the concession stand.

I was walking past the opening to the stairway that led to the main entrance when I saw something that made me very happy. A case of Drosselmyers. It was just sitting there. I figured someone from one of the concession stands must be about to return for it. Apparently there was one left from before the people at Goat Piss Inc. took over.

I waited for a minute, hoping the employee who left it there would come back and tell me the location of the stand where I could buy a couple bottles. Even warm, it would still be way better than the other stuff.

The crowd cheered as the teams took the field for the eighth inning. Fuck it. I'd just grab a couple bottles, take them up to the stand and pay for them. I walked over to the box and opened it. It wasn't sealed.

Inside was a leather mask and a handgun.

I recoiled from it, like it was full of scorpions. I stood up, my pulse racing. I looked around. There had to be someone I could alert. A cop. A security guard. A stadium employee. Anyone.

The press box! There'd probably be someone from stadium management in there. I started making my way through the stragglers who were back in the concession area, toward where Ken and I were sitting.

Then it occurred to me. I'd left a gun back there, probably loaded, where someone presumably planned to pick it up and use it. I should go back and take out the clip before I did anything else.

I turned around and saw him. He was a tall, white guy with long, dirty-blonde hair and a beard. He wore jeans, a black T-shirt and workboots. On his hands were what appeared to be nylon gloves. Flesh-colored. Easy to miss if you weren't looking for them.

He picked up the box and carried it with him as he started down the stairs.

I looked around again, frantic. Sheila had wandered off somewhere and left her tripod. I picked it up, and collapsed the telescoping legs so it was a long, metal rod in my hands. It would have to do.

I ran for the stairs, startled and irritated people ducking out of my way. I didn't know what was going to happen, but this most definitely did not look good.

As I went through the entrance to the stairs, I saw he'd tossed the cardboard box aside. I pounded down the concrete steps. He was approaching a small landing at a bend in the stairs. He'd already put on the mask.

He heard me coming and started to turn.

I jumped and kicked, taking advantage of my higher position on the steps. My foot caught him high in the back. He'd already been off-balance as he turned, and my kick drove him into the concrete wall in front of him. My ass hit the concrete steps, hard. No time to think about the pain now.

He was starting to get up when I swung the tripod and hit him in the side of the head. It knocked him into the concrete wall again and he slumped to the ground. I hit him again, just to make sure he stayed down. And again.

Someone was running up the stairs from the ground level. Michael. He looked at me, then at the guy on the ground. He didn't seem surprised at what he was seeing.

Before I could say anything, I heard it. Explosions and screaming from the stadium above.

Michael ran up to the landing, scooped up the guy in the leather mask and threw him over his shoulder in a fireman's carry. He did it as easily as if the guy was a papier mache dummy.

"Come on!" Michael shouted, and he started running down the stairs.

"Wait!" I yelled. "I need to ..."

I was thinking I needed to head back and make sure Ken was safe. Then the screaming got louder, accompanied by the clomping of feet on the steps above me. A human stampede heading straight in my direction, from the sound of it.

I turned and ran down the stairs. I cleared the entrance and saw Michael off to one side, setting the guy in the leather mask down on the ground. A stadium employee — an older guy in a polo shirt with a laminated badge — was poised near the entrance, staring wide-eyed into it. I guessed he was trying to decide whether duty obliged him to go running in there, and hoping that it didn't.

I had just seconds to look around. Maybe a couple hundred feet to our right and left, parked cars idled in front of the other exits. Too far to see who was behind the wheels.

Somewhere, a gun was firing. Before I had time to take stock of that, a torrent of people erupted out of the opening that I just exited. Old people. Young people. Men and women. Parents hoisting or dragging screaming kids. Within seconds, a jabbering crowd surrounded us.

"What's going on?" I yelled at Michael.

"Don't know yet," he said. "The Slain are up to something. Just stand tight."

"There's one of them!" a voice screamed.

A small, silver-haired woman pointed at the guy in the leather mask still unconscious at Michael's feet. For a moment, the crowd converged on where we stood. I thought they might rush the unconscious guy.

Michael stood over him and raised him arms at shoulder length, palms out.

"Everyone, please! The police will be here soon! We need to remain calm!"

And the people immediately around us, miraculously, settled down. Something about Michael's size, his aura, his mere presence as a man issuing orders in the absence of any other authority, had that effect.

Instead of rushing the guy in the leather mask, they stood in a rough circle and gawped at him. Like he was some kind of dangerous beast brought down with a tranquilizer dart.

Sheila from the Daily Needler snapped a picture that would make the next day's front page — Michael towering and authoritative, holding out his arms to keep the crowd at bay while standing over the prone body of the enemy.

The next day's paper would include more details of the attack as well. At more or less the same time I was clubbing the guy in the mask unconscious, a bunch of pyrotechnic devices went off around the stadium, both in the seating and concessions area.

The newspaper account referred to them as bombs. But according to some of my sources, they were closer to theatrical flashpots, crafted for the primary purpose of creating a lot of noise and smoke.

The explosions around the stadium directly caused only two minor injuries. The real damage came when the people hit the exits.

In addition to the main stairway where Michael and I were standing, there were two other major exits. Each had a set of concrete steps.

When the people at the front of the panicked crowd tried to run down those steps, they'd encountered men in leather masks standing on the landings. Those men pulled out handguns and fired shots into the oncoming crowd.

As the injured went down and the others at the front tried desperately to run in the opposite direction, they'd blocked the surge of people trying to get out from behind. The result was a crush of people pressing in opposite directions.

Screaming. Clawing and trampling each other. Hell in the cement stairways.

Meanwhile, the police were responding to a disturbance across town, where 60 or so members of Christ Our Redeemer A.M.E. Church on Bower Street were holding a picnic. At about 40 minutes before I chased the guy into the stairwell, the picnickers were milling around, eating chicken and potato salad off paper plates, when someone started firing into the group from a nearby building with what police believed was a hunting rifle.

When police tried to get to the scene, they found torched cars blocking Bower Street about a block away from the church in either direction.

The ultimate count when it was all over amounted to 105 hospitalized and seven dead. In the next few days, eight more would die from their injuries and one would go into a coma.

So many were hurt that Batley had to send a school busload of the injured to a hospitals in an adjoining county, because the local hospital couldn't handle them all.

I found out later that Ken was OK.

A couple hours later in the police station, Michael and I were sitting on a wooden bench, waiting to be called into an office for questioning. In the lobby outside was sheer pandemonium, with crowds of people screaming at a poor, frazzled receptionist behind bulletproof glass, demanding to know what had happened, and whether family members were safe.

The cinderblock hallway in which Michael and I and other selected witnesses waited was a slightly more subdued version of pandemonium, with people urgently pressing the occasional and increasingly pissed off uniformed officers as to when they could leave.

People kept walking up to Michael and asking him what happened. I guess some of them had seen him outside the stadium, and figured he had some kind of authority. The others saw people asking him questions and apparently came to the same conclusion. Michael told them they'd have to talk to the police.

"So what were you doing there?" I asked Michael.

"I was patrolling on my bike," he said. "I had a feeling they might pull something. You get to sense it after a while. Like an oncoming storm. But this magnitude? I had no idea. If I had known ..."

His face and fists both clenched in a gesture that seemed equal parts sorrow and anger.

"I heard the sirens," he said. "I saw some police cars and ambulances headed for the east side of town. I turned around, headed west and tried to think of somewhere in that direction where there'd be a lot of people.

"I know these sons of bitches. That's their favorite tactic. There's a disaster in one direction, you immediately head the other way because that's where they've got an even bigger disaster working. You'll need to know that."

"Why?" I asked.

"You've been chosen," he said. "You're going to be very important."

"Chosen? What the fuck ..."

But right then a uniformed officer called him into a room off the hallway for questioning.

And I sat there by myself amid all the commotion and fear.

So much for my day off.

VOLUNTEER GROUP FORMING TO PROTECT LOCAL POPULACE
By Tom Jerkface, Daily Needler Staff

Rain failed to dampen the spirits of Batley residents who turned out at a meeting convened for those interested in joining a citizen watchdog group in response to recent attacks in the city by a criminal group assumed to be The Slain.

More than 50 people braved a torrential cloudburst on Wednesday night to attend an organizing session for the proposed group at City Hall.

Mayor Buck Rockbaugh, who presided over the meeting, said he's been working in conjunction with The Order of Gabriel, a national nonprofit organization devoted to assisting communities that are experiencing problems with The Slain.

A representative of the organization who would identify himself only as Michael referred all questions to members of city council, stating that his organization's policy is to defer to civic leaders. A call placed to the organization's headquarters in Philadelphia was not returned as of Wednesday night.

Rockbaugh told the assembled group that their responsibilities would consist of patrolling the city, and reporting to police if they observed any suspicious activity. He stressed that they were not to confront anyone they observed breaking the law, but leave that to police.

"Remember folks, you're just going to be our eyes and ears," Rockbaugh told the crowd. "The police are still the police."

Batley Police Chief David Sanderson, who was not at the meeting, could not be reached for comment as of deadline.

Tim Rourke, owner of Rourke's Grocery Mart on Main Street, was among the volunteers present. He said business has fallen off since the disturbances attributed to The Slain have begun.

"As a local businessman, I'm very concerned about all this," Rourke said. "And as a member of this community, I want to do my part to protect it."

During the two-hour meeting, volunteers discussed plans for the new organization, including establishing both car and foot patrols, and coordinating schedules to make sure someone is keeping an eye on the city around the clock.

The formation of the citizen watchdog group is not the only grassroots response to the recent attacks by The Slain.

The Batley Interfaith Council of Churches is planning an event called the "March for Batley."

Sister Pilar Lopez, assistant director of the council, said in a phone interview that the march's purpose is to "demonstrate our resolve as a community." Plans include a march through downtown Batley that will include members of the Interfaith Council and a number of local civic groups, followed by a rally featuring guest speakers and music.

Lopez said the point of the rally is to show the people of Batley that they shouldn't be intimidated by recent events in the city.

"The people behind these disturbances are clearly attempting to create fear and despair in Batley," Lopez said. "They're bullies, to put it simply. And any bully is just a coward at heart."

FILE 11

FROM BILLY'S PAPERS

A shirtless young man sporting an orange Mohawk, who went by the asinine moniker of Mister Masokismo, announced to the audience that he was about to lift a pair of concrete blocks with the rings piercing his nipples.

Paltry applause greeted this announcement. I wish I could attribute that lukewarm response to some modicum of taste among the 150 or so people seated in the bleachers surrounding the dirt ring where this ugly spectacle was about to transpire. But I found it more likely that everyone's attention was still riveted on the black flag bearing a skull and crossbones, which was protruding from the ground near Mister Masokismo.

I sat among that audience for the afternoon matinee showing of Madman Skunk's Nightmare Freakatorium. Under ordinary circumstances, I would have gone to great lengths to avoid being in that situation.

I'd wondered beforehand whether the others in Skunk's crew, Clem excluded, knew about Skunk's attempts to shake me down and decided the answer was probably no. This was an attempt on Skunk's part to line his own pockets. He wouldn't want to cut the others in, and thus would have no incentive to inform them of his efforts.

At any rate, Skunk wasn't present when I purchased my ticket and nobody gave me any trouble. The dirt circle in the center of the tent was approximately 30 feet in diameter. Opposite the entrance, an aisle stretched between the bleachers to a flap in the rear of the tent, opening onto a dark space from which the performers emerged.

Several torches set in the ground at intervals around the ring provided scant illumination. Making the sinister atmosphere still more pronounced was a hole in the ring's center, with a pile of dirt and a shovel beside it. Long and rectangular, it resembled a shallow grave. Which was precisely what it turned out to be.

The first to emerge from the flap was Skunk himself, wearing jeans and cowboy boots. He was shirtless, but sporting a long-tailed tuxedo jacket with the sleeves torn off to reveal tattooed arms. A top hat adorned his head.

"Welcome to Madman Skunk's Nightmare Freakatorium!" Skunk bellowed. "You paid money for this? Y'all are some sick motherfuckers!"

That brought cheers, laughter, and howls from the crowd, which consisted primarily of young people whose taste in hairstyles and clothing tended toward the flamboyant and bizarre. I noticed Alice Kettner among them, wearing a costume that made her get-up the day before look positively puritanical by comparison.

"Well, I know what you came for!" Skunk went on. "Are you ready to meet the Most Evil Man in America? We're talkin the Devil! The Antichrist! Mister Six Six Fuckin Six! Give it up for Friedrich K. Schulze!"

The crowd was on its feet as Schulze emerged from the flap in back. As usual, he wore jean shorts, sandals and a robe opened in front, revealing his ectomorphic torso. Schulze rotated slowly to acknowledge the applause from all directions, clearly relishing the attention.

When the applause died down, he grasped a microphone that Skunk handed him and spoke. His tone was low-key and conversational. Yet his voice possessed an underlying intensity, which prompted the audience to lean forward in their attempts to absorb every word.

"Welcome," he said. "I must compliment you on your bravery in coming out here today. Or perhaps it's mere foolhardiness that draws you. Regardless, we are about to venture into some extremely dark places. You will see things that will make you question the very nature of the universe you inhabit."

The place had gone utterly silent, with a stillness from the crowd more befitting a church service than a carnival show.

"I have no doubt that you know who I am," Schulze said. A few people clapped and then stopped almost instantly. "You may have heard the rumors about me. That I possess unearthly powers. That I came by these powers through tampering with forces that any sane man would leave well alone. That I commune with dark entities, the knowledge of whose very existence might drive one mad with terror. Let me say this about those rumors …"

He paused, then his voice dropped to a stage whisper.

"They're all true."

He swept an arm toward the back of the tent. It may have been a hidden string or someone concealed on the other side, but the flap seemed to fly open of its own accord. A fiery light flared up for just an instant, illuminating something back there in the darkness. A statue? It had a human shape but some kind of animal's head. A harsh, bestial roar accompanied the flaring light. Throughout the tent, people jumped in their seats and even screamed aloud.

Then it was over. The flap closed again. Some audience members laughed nervously, then went silent as Schulze began to speak again.

"Today, I'm going to demonstrate to you that the forces to which I refer give me the power to transcend death itself. Yes, just as many fabled mythological figures have done before me, I will now descend into the kingdom of the dead. And just as a few of them did, I intend to return from that shadowy realm to the land of the living."

He walked over to the hole in the ground, taking off his robe and laying it down next to the hole. He then picked up a pole topped with a skull-and-crossbones flag.

"I'll just use this to mark my position," Schulze said. "It wouldn't do to have Mr. Skunk here forget where he put me."

There was more nervous laughter from the crowd, which turned to gasps as Schulze lay down in the open grave and Skunk picked up the shovel.

I supposed this was as good a time as any. I stood upon my seat and yelled at the top of my voice.

"That's bullshit!"

In the silence, my voice carried. Every head in the place swiveled in my direction.

"Can't you people see what a scam this is?" I said, waving my arms as I strode down the aisle to the ring, making myself as conspicuous as possible. "The whole setup is fake!"

A buzz arose from the crowd, consisting of puzzled murmurs combined with laughter. They seemed unsure whether I was part of the show or not. Regardless, I had their attention.

The ticket-takers from out front came running in, looking for the source of the disturbance. Skunk gave me a look that was pure homicidal intent made manifest.

Schulze sat up in the grave. Rather than looking upset, he favored me with a beatific smile. He gestured for the microphone, which Skunk handed him.

"It appears we have a skeptic in the crowd," Schulze said. "How delightful! What fun would any of this be without the occasional skeptic like our outspoken friend here? Please!"

He gestured for me to approach, then asked: "Now what do you believe is the precise nature of this 'bullshit' to which you so passionately referred?"

He handed me the microphone.

"I'm guessing that's not really a hole," I said. "It's a tunnel. Once he starts shoveling in the dirt, you've got a cover you're going to close and then you're going to crawl out of there. Either that, or you have some kind of oxygen tank hidden down there."

"Interesting theories, both" Schulze said. "I give you credit for creativity. Well, either one should be easy enough for you to prove."

Schulze stepped out of the grave and gestured, inviting me to inspect it. I jumped into the hole. I'd estimate that it was four feet deep, which means the sides came up slightly higher than my head when I stood. I felt a moment of uneasiness, then shook it off, having no time for such foolishness.

I examined the sides and the bottom of the hole, poking my fingers into the dirt and finding no indication that it was anything other than what it appeared to be: a human-sized, four-foot-deep grave.

Schulze extended a hand to help me climb out, which drew laughs because dwarfism is inherently comical. Just ask the bent-over people with the sing-songy voices in my hometown.

"So," Schulze said. "Were your suspicions borne out? Was that a tunnel? Or did you find any concealed oxygen tank?"

He held the microphone to my face.

"No," I grumbled. "I still say it's bullshit. But that's just a hole in the ground."

"A hole in the ground," Schulze said. "And since presumably you can now tell your ass from it, we will proceed."

Skunk smirked. Some laughter and catcalls from the audience followed me while I returned to my seat.

Schulze repositioned himself in the grave, holding the flag straight up as Skunk shoveled in the dirt. At length, he had it all filled in, leaving a slight mound with a skull-and-crossbones flag surmounting it. I soon realized the purpose of that flag, which served as a constant, silent reminder of Schulze's presence under the ground.

Skunk brought out the other acts. First was Clem, who played a hamfisted number on a ukulele, but whose real act consisted of being imbecilic, cleft-palated and improbably obese.

Next came Rubberella, a female contortionist who bended her body in a variety of odd shapes. It might have been erotic if your tastes run toward underfed, pale girls whose fashion sense is reminiscent of something Edgar Allan Poe might have hallucinated in the midst of a laudanum bender. As mine do not, I found it rather tedious.

Then Mister Masokismo "entertained" us by lifting buckets of gravel and concrete blocks with his facial, nipple, and genital piercings.

Throughout it all, everybody remained intensely aware of that flag. While

Clem played his ukulele, audience members contemplated it and unconsciously held their breath, wondering if it was truly possible for Schulze to hold his that long.

While Rubberella placed her ankles behind her neck, they regarded the flag and thought of the lethal suffocation that must surely be taking place a mere four feet underground and unwillingly found themselves envisioning what it must be like to undergo such a fate. The desperate pushing against the earth holding you utterly immobile. The searing pain in your chest as you tried again and again to inhale the oxygen that wasn't there.

While Mr. Masokismo placed a hook in the ring piercing his flaccid penis and stood to hoist a bucket of gravel, they still could not refrain from cutting looks toward the flag. Might they have been unfortunate enough to wander into some bizarre public suicide? When Skunk dug up Schulze's contorted and lifeless body, would they be required to give a deposition to the police?

After Mr. Masokismo pulled up his pants — to my intense relief — and exited the ring, Skunk stepped out once again and picked up the shovel.

"Well folks, he's been down there for a while," Skunk said. "Guess we might as well dig him up and see how he's doing."

He started in on the dirt around the flag. Mister Masokismo appeared once more to hammer a nail into his nostril as Skunk shoveled away. But all eyes were riveted on Skunk, who shoveled more gingerly the deeper he got in an apparent attempt to avoid decapitating his star attraction.

Eventually, Skunk stepped out of the hole and stood alongside it, looking down. Everyone gasped as a dirty hand reached out and skittered along the edge of the grave like a disfigured brown tarantula. Schulze pulled himself to a sitting position, no longer resembling the man who had addressed the crowd earlier. Dirt caked his long hair, face, and body. That, combined with his natural thinness, lent him the aspect of an animated mummy.

He smiled with stark white teeth, drawing scattered applause from the audience. But most onlookers appeared to be in a trance, equally awed and frightened.

Schulze raised a hand toward Skunk, who handed him the microphone.

"Rubberella, may I have some cognac please?" he asked.

Rubberella emerged from the back flap, holding a glass, which she handed to Schulze as he languished in his unearthed grave. Schulze swirled the contents, in no apparent hurry, and drank. Then he raised the microphone to his lips.

"I have journeyed to the kingdom of the dead," he said. "Its denizens send their regards. They had little to say, other than a reminder that they will see each and every one of you sooner or later."

When I filed out with the rest of the crowd, Skunk shot me a pleased, "see-ya-later" look. Indeed he would see me later, although he would look considerably less pleased on that occasion.

I went straight to our World of Marvels tent, where the kid was working the front.

"Did you do it?" I asked.

He nodded.

"Did anybody see you?"

"No," he said. "There were a couple guys out front, but they ran back to look when you made a scene."

"Good," I said. "Later tonight, be ready to pack up. When you see Sally, ask her if she can give us a hand. We'll have to move fast."

I went to our trailer to change my clothes, donning a T-shirt, pair of jeans and sneakers. A baseball cap went on my head. The final item was a hooded sweatshirt with a garish cartoon character adorning the front. I raised the hood and pulled the drawstring, partially concealing my face.

I regarded myself in a mirror and concluded that anyone could easily mistake me for a child wandering the midway.

I purchased some cotton candy to complete the effect and watched Schulze's trailer behind the Freakatorium tent. Several people from the audience waited outside it, pens and paper at the ready. Among them was scantily clad Alice Kettner, in all her meager post-pubescence.

Schulze emerged at length, showered and dressed in a clean set of clothes. He dispensed autographs to the group of fans. Alice Kettner approached him. I edged in closer that I might hear their conversation.

"I liked your show," she said. "But it was scary."

She shuddered, giving her hips a sinuous little twist as she did so.

"Yes, there are frightening truths out there," Schulze said. "They can be exciting as well. Many people find them so disturbing that they choose to look away. But you strike me as a young woman of unusual discernment."

I followed them from a distance as they purchased corndogs and wandered, conversing while strolling the area adjacent to the midway where the trucks and trailers parked. That area was sparsely populated at this time of day, which I concluded was the reason that Schulze had taken her there. Fewer witnesses.

They were too focused on each other to take any notice of me. It continued thus for approximately two hours. When she followed him back to his trailer and the door closed behind them, I took off at a run.

The carnival was busy that night. Skunk's Freakatorium was not, as he'd been obliged to close it after the police showed up and arrested Schulze at his trailer for his attempt to initiate sex with a minor. The police, from what I'd heard, were unsympathetic to Schulze's protestations that he had not yet done the deed, as it were. With our main competitor shut down, we received a good deal of business.

About half an hour before closing, I told the kid and Sally to make themselves scarce. I ran the place myself while the last of the rubes made their way through and then left. After closing, I picked up the sponge and the spray bottle and began cleaning the cases. I surmised that it wouldn't be long, and once again I was proven correct.

A pair of burly shitkickers stormed into my tent and informed me that Pretty Joe required my presence at the Freakatorium immediately.

When I arrived, flanked by the hulking crackers, electric lights had replaced the torches as the source of illumination in Skunk's tent. Skunk stood in the middle of the dirt circle, conspicuously failing to make eye contact with Pretty Joe. Although even under normal circumstances, an aversion to looking at Pretty Joe's countenance is eminently understandable.

Pretty Joe was about six-foot-four and very fat. His face resembled that of a toad with an appalling skin condition. He wore a white suit with a bolo tie, and clasped a paper cup into which he spat tobacco juice as he spoke.

Pretty Joe motioned me over to stand beside Skunk. Then his two lackeys took positions on either side of him.

"I understand we had us a little trouble out here earlier today," Pretty Joe said.

"Joe, I ..." Skunk started.

"Shut up," Joe said. "Now I know the fellas working here are going to want to get themselves some pussy from the local girls. Hell, that's probably why half of them are working here in the first place. But I don't like it when somebody from one of my shows goes after underage pussy. You know why? Cause that makes problems. And I can't watch everyone all the time, so I expect you all to keep an eye on your people."

He looked hard at Skunk now. Skunk met his gaze then looked away quickly, his body quaking slightly.

When Pretty Joe shifted his stinkeye toward me, Skunk visibly relaxed. Pretty Joe may have been unhappy with Skunk, but I was clearly the primary target of his wrath.

"But you know what gets me madder'n a hornet?" Pretty Joe asked, his query directed at me now. "It's when people don't understand the rules. And the rules are when we have a problem, we take care of it our own selves. In-house, you might say. Because when somebody brings the police down on us, that means trouble for me. And trouble for me means bigger trouble for somebody else. You understand, Billy?"

"No," I said. "I do not understand. What does any of this have to do with me?"

Pretty Joe spat into his cup.

"I got contacts in this town," he said. "It's part of doing business. And from what I hear, the man who called the police from a pay phone on the grounds sounded like one of your kind."

"You're saying I was the only black man at the carnival today?"

"Nope. But you're the only one I know of's got a beef with Skunk here. I understand you were making a fuss at his show today."

The crucial moment had arrived. I needed to inject a note of fear into my voice so Joe would feel he was getting his due respect, mixed with aggrieved righteousness.

"Of course I have a problem with Skunk," I said. "You should too, the way he disrespects you."

"What the..." Skunk started to say.

"I said shut the fuck up," Joe growled. "What are you talking about, midget?"

"You're lecturing me about the rules?" I sputtered. "I've been in this business since you were just an itch in your daddy's balls! I know the rules! And the rules say you pay your honest percentage to the carnival boss. Whatever you think of me and 'my kind,' I've always been straight with you. Not like this dirtbag. You might want to take a look at the cigar box under the cash register stand."

Joe told one of his goons to check it out. Despite whatever else might be transpiring, this was an allegation that Pretty Joe must investigate immediately. More than run-ins with local police, more than black people, the one thing Pretty Joe hated above all else was skimming.

The goon approached the stand and sure enough found a cigar box beneath it. Precisely where Clem told the kid it would be.

"Come on, man," Skunk said as Pretty Joe began to untie the length of twine holding the box closed. "It's just a little bit. Everybody does it."

Skunk sounded worried, but not frightened. For all of his bullying tactics, Pretty Joe remained a practical man. Skunk was rightfully confident that Pretty Joe wouldn't take out a top earner over whatever piddling amount he was putting aside for his heroin fund.

So Skunk's eyes practically bugged out of his head when Joe reached into the box and extracted two sizable wads of bills bound together with rubber bands. One of the goons let out a low whistle.

"Doesn't look like no 'little bit' to me," Joe said.

"Aw fuck, Joe!" Skunk protested. "That's not mine! I have no idea how that got there!"

Pretty Joe looked at me.

"Go," he said.

When I returned to the World of Marvels tent, Sally and the kid were already at work on packing up the display cases. All Sally knew was that we had to get out in a hurry. I saw no need to get her caught up in the whole ugly clusterfuck.

The kid had hired a pair of local boys who agreed to give us a hand. Sally's husband came by too and worked hard. I guess he wasn't so bad. At 4 in the morning, we had the last of our belongings packed in our trailer and our truck.

I gave Sally an extra 50. After some thought I handed her another 20.

"And that's for your husband," I said. "Tell him to buy himself a case or something."

"Will I ever see you again?" she asked.

"I don't know, honey. I really don't."

She kissed me on the cheek.

"You take care of yourself," she said.

I walked to the truck. The kid stood beside it.

"What about Clem?" he asked.

"What about him?"

"You said we'd bring him with us."

"I said I'd think about it. The answer is no."

The kid tried to argue. He worried that Skunk might deduce what had happened and hurt Clem. I told him Skunk couldn't figure out how to pour piss out of a boot if the instructions were written on the heel, and by the time Joe and his boys were done with him he wouldn't be in shape to hurt anyone.

Besides, I told him, we'd used half our funds to pull off the stunt with the cigar box. Feeding Clem alone would likely bankrupt us before we made it 10 miles.

"You save who you can, kid," I told him. "Now let's get going. We're short on time."

We drove out of town in the pre-dawn glow.

FILE 12

"So we'll start at the Congregation Beth El parking lot," Sister Pilar said, tracing a finger along the Batley map spread out on the kitchen table. "I'm thinking ... two miles. We want this to be long enough to make a statement. But if any of the older participants kick off from heart attacks, I think that would be counterproductive."

"Good point," said Rich Zuckerman, rabbi from Congregation Beth El and executive director of the Batley Interfaith Council. He was a professorial-looking guy in his 30s, partial to tweed jackets.

Also seated at the table in the Bacon household kitchen were the other members of the March for Batley Organizing Committee: Buck Rockbaugh, Luanne and Michael. Since the Interfaith Council's makeshift homeless shelters were running low on provisions, they decided to also make the March for Batley a food drive. Luanne, to show her appreciation, volunteered to help with the organizing.

Michael had volunteered, too. A couple days ago, he'd gone around to the Hope House and introduced himself to Sister Pilar. He told her he thought the March for Batley was a good idea, filled her in on his background dealing with The Slain and offered to help out. Since community activists like Pilar don't generally spend a lot of time fighting off volunteers with a stick, she was pleased to take him up on the offer.

I was there because Pilar said I should be. Lucky me.

"We'll go along Main Street," Pilar said. "That's where most of the people would see us. Then we can turn east along Schimmel Street ..."

"Wait," I said. "Schimmel Street? Popularly known as Shemale Street?"

"I know they've got a problem with the sex trade," Pilar said. "But would it really be an issue at that time of day?"

"I'm afraid so," Buck interjected. "It got so bad that the district attorney from Haddon County conducted an undercover investigation there."

"Why would the Haddon County D.A. investigate something in Batley?" I asked.

"I don't know," Buck replied. "That's just what he told the police when they picked him up in a cocktail dress. How are we fixed for entertainment at the rally?"

"The Unitarians have volunteered one of their musical ministry acts," Zuckerman said. "They're called 'Ascension.' They incorporate bongos and interpretive dance."

Pilar winced.

"How about speakers?" she asked.

"Well," Zuckerman said, "the only positive response we've received so far is a gentleman from the D.C. area named Brad Muncy. He's written a book called 'Eat Thy Bread With Joy: The Biblical Way to Colorectal Health.' Buck, I don't suppose we could prevail on you to give a talk about local history? Maybe something emphasizing the courage of local people?"

"I'd be delighted," Buck said.

I heard laughter from the living room and turned to look. Ken, Ty, and Paul sat on the couch. Ken, it seemed, found it highly amusing that Paul was repeatedly kicking Ty's ass at some fighting video game. It looked like they were having a hell of a lot more fun than we were having in the kitchen.

After some more discussion, we agreed on the route. We would direct the 150 or so marchers we figured would show up to a trail that ran along Kendle Creek, which flowed through the center of the city. Once they'd skirted – no pun intended – the Schimmel Street regulars, they would get onto Drake Avenue and circle back to the Congregation Beth El parking lot.

That established, Pilar asked if there were any other topics to discuss.

"Look," I said. "I've talked to Sister Pilar about this before. And I'm really not trying to be a pain in the ..." Pilar shot me a look. "... neck. But do you really think this is a good idea? Especially since Sanderson says he can't spare any cops to accompany us?"

Pilar started to talk, but Michael held up his hand.

"Sister, if I may," Michael said. Pilar nodded.

"I understand your concerns," Michael continued. "But for what it's worth, I think the benefits here outweigh the risks. The Slain prefer to strike at night. When they attack during the day, it's usually because they're going after big strategic targets like the Warm Hearths Festival. My guess is they're not going to consider 150 church people out for a walk to be worth staging a daytime attack.

"I also agree with Sister Pilar here. They're trying to panic the city. The best way to defy them is to refuse to give in to that. This walk may be a small gesture, but every little show of defiance is important."

"So what exactly do they want?" I asked. "I'm still not clear on this. What kind of profit do they get out of coming in and fu ... – sorry, Sister – messing with us?"

Michael was quiet for a few seconds, staring at his hands folded on the table. Then he looked around at each of us, as if trying to figure if we were capable of understanding what he was about to say.

"This may not make a lot of sense to you," he said. "I'm not going to pretend it makes sense at all. But it's all about the god they worship. The One Who Takes. In ancient times, they considered conquering and subjugating other people for his sake to be the ultimate form of worship. That's still a big part of their mindset."

"And if they feel someone has disrespected their god or one of his followers ..." his eyes flicked toward me for a second, then out toward the living room where Paul sat "... they believe it has to be answered in blood. Not just the one person, but the whole community. Fear? Chaos? Destruction? Those are like prayers to their god, The One Who Takes."

We all sat quiet for a moment, as more laughter came in from the living room.

Then the doorbell rang. A big smile broke out on Michael's face.

"I think I know who that is," he said. Then he called out to the living room. "Hey Ty, you ready?"

Ty set down his controller.

"Thank God!" he said. "This kid's murdering me!"

He tapped Paul's arm, then the two of them got up and walked through the door leading to the basement.

Michael had been showing up for Ty's martial arts classes. He'd turned out to be a really good fighter, and Ty often asked him to demonstrate some move or other. A bunch of times, the Bacons invited him to stay for dinner after class.

Michael walked over to the front door, and I heard him having a conversation. Then he walked into the living room, followed by a couple teenage boys wearing baseball caps that said "Takeout Delivery."

Luanne stood up. "What ... What are you ..."

Michael looked at Ken and smiled.

"See, I've been hearing this rumor," Michael said, "that it's somebody's birthday. Somebody who likes barbecued ribs."

A smile spread over Ken's face. Paul and Ty came out of the basement, each holding the handle of a picnic cooler. They set it down in the kitchen. Ty opened the lid to show that it was packed with ice, bottles of beer, and cans of soda.

"Happy birthday, Dad!" he said.

Paul eyed the contents of the cooler and picked up a beer.

"Could I try one?"

Ty and his father exchanged shrugs.

"Hell, you're 14. That's practically grown up," Ty said.

"I suppose one beer won't do any harm," Ken said.

"No!"

That came from Luanne as she took the beer out of Paul's hand and replaced it with a soda. He looked disappointed for a second, then headed over to the table where the delivery boys had set the bags. Michael rifled through a stack of bills and handed the delivery boys something that left happy expressions on their faces as they headed back out.

"Dig in!" Michael said. "Plenty for everyone! We've got ribs, fries, coleslaw. Ty told me Ken's favorite place is Hank's Hog Heaven, and I ... ah ... Hey Rich, I didn't realize you'd ..."

Zuckerman held up his hands and smiled.

"That's quite alright," he said. "I'm very fond of french fries and coleslaw."

Everyone else headed for the food. I headed for the beer. Luanne waved Michael over to one side, not appearing to notice that I was in earshot.

"What is this?" she asked. "Think you could have checked with me before you decided to throw a party in my house?"

"I didn't want to create a problem for you," Michael said. "Ty told me you were planning to do a little something for Ken. My bosses gave me a huge expense account. I thought since I was here anyway, I could pay back some of the courtesy your family has showed me."

"We were just going to have a quiet, family dinner," she said.

"That's right," Michael replied. "After a long day at work, and hosting the meeting, and making sure Paul does his homework, and telling Ken and Ty to get their feet off the coffee table, you were going to cook dinner."

Luanne was silent.

"I've got news for you." Michael touched her chin and raised her face slightly. "You're allowed to take a night off, enjoy yourself and let someone else take care of things for a change."

He turned around and walked over to the kitchen table. Luanne continued standing there for a few seconds, her face flushed. Then she looked up, realized I'd seen her and her face turned an even deeper shade of red. I made a beeline for the table myself.

A couple of hours later, Ty, Ken and Michael whooped with laughter as Paul gave me a solid beatdown. The ninja he worked was mercilessly smacking the crap out of my character, who appeared to be a geisha with a samurai sword.

"Oh. Sorry," Paul said as his ninja delivered a kick that sent my geisha flying.

I gritted my teeth. Paul kept apologizing in all apparent sincerity every time he clobbered me, which was very annoying. Worse still, Ty, Ken and Michael had picked up on my growing annoyance, which apparently made the whole fucking thing twice as funny.

My geisha got to her feet and did a saucy little dance before resuming the fight.

"You're a lousy fighter, but hey. At least you've got a perky set of tits," Ken said.

"Old goddamn perv," I muttered as the three of them laughed again, followed by Paul unleashing a flurry of kicks that finally finished me off.

"Sorry," he said.

I tried and failed to conceal my shiver of irritation, which got another round of guffaws out of the other three guys.

"Ah, I'll get over it," I said, handing my controller to Ty. "Nice job. Now give Ty an ass-whuppin. He's overdue for one."

I started toward the kitchen, planning to get another beer. Everyone was still hanging around with the exception of Buck, who'd eaten some ribs, then said he had to get home. His wife, Bess, hadn't been feeling well lately.

The Bacon house was small. Ty had given up his bedroom to Paul, and fixed himself up in the little basement. You could tell Ken's bedroom was originally built as a kitchen pantry .

The place was never dirty but always cluttered, with lots of books and magazines lying around. Since Ken, Luanne and Ty all played a part in the decorating, framed posters and knickknacks featured an eclectic mix of baseball memorabilia, fairies and sword-wielding barbarian warriors.

On the coffee table was a gift for Ken from his kids. They'd found an old bobble-head doll of him from when he was with the Snippers. Those things creep me out, personally. But I had to admit, that was one handsome bobble-head doll.

Ken had a thing for old doo-wop records, and was currently playing a stack of them on an antique phonograph.

Before I got to the kitchen, Pilar walked over and intercepted me. She looked around to make sure the others weren't paying attention and said "I think we should speak to Luanne about Paul."

I hesitated. Luanne had been in a good mood since her conversation with Michael. She even got a little giddy after a couple beers. Laughing, joking, and dispensing hugs and kisses on the cheek whenever Ty, Ken or Paul were in range.

I hated to broach a topic likely to bring her down. Then again, catching her in a good mood was so rare that we might as well seize on the opportunity.

Pilar and I walked out the back door. Luanne and Zuckerman sat on a couple of lawn chairs, sipping beers and talking. Pilar apologized to Zuckerman, and asked if we could talk to Luanne for a few minutes.

Pilar sat down and I pulled up a chair as Zuckerman went inside. I felt bad. I could see the cheerfulness go out of Luanne. Her posture tightened up, signaling tension, exhaustion, and just a little bit of hostility.

"It's about Paul, isn't it?" she said.

"Yes, it's about his treatment," Pilar said, in a soothing voice. "Is this a bad time? We can talk later if you'd prefer."

"No, we might as well do this," Luanne said. She wasn't happy, but seemed a lot less crabby than when I talked to her alone. Pilar's a lot better at that kind of stuff than I am. No question about it.

"We've been discussing Paul with Dr. Pigeon," Pilar said. "I guess you know, the doctor's been talking about more intensive treatment. The good news is that I've spoken to our board of directors, and they've approved funding it."

Luanne seemed to relax a little bit. The Bacon household wasn't exactly swimming in spare cash.

"For now," Pilar went on, "Dr. Pigeon wants to start with medication and see how Paul responds. But depending on the outcome, he's not ruling out eventual residential treatment."

"Dammit!" Luanne punched her fist against her own thigh. "Somebody's talking about taking him away? Don't we get any say in this?"

Pilar was silent for a moment, waiting for Luanne to calm down. Then she spoke.

"Luanne, I know you're worried about that kind of thing, based on your family's experiences. But this is a question of what's best for Paul. And of course your family gets input into his treatment. Nobody is going to just take him away from you."

Luanne remained silent. She set down her beer, hunched over and stared at the ground. Pilar looked at me. My cue.

"At first," I told her, "Pigeon figured Paul was responding to the disorientation of it all. Leaving the home where he grew up. Being kept at Cabot's place. Finding himself with a family he never knew he had. Now he's afraid it might be something bigger."

Luanne looked up at me. She didn't look angry this time. Just stressed-out and kind of sad.

"Like what?" she asked.

"Well, Schulze Syndrome is a hard diagnosis to pin down," I told her. "From what Dr. Pigeon is telling me, not every doctor out there is convinced it even exists. But Paul's showing some signs. 'A disconnect with reality', is what Dr. Pigeon calls it. Paul wasn't at Cabot's for long. He still says nothing much happened while he was there. But Dr. Pigeon figures maybe there's more to it."

"He thinks Paul's lying?" Luanne asked.

"Maybe there's some stuff he's blocking out. Jeez, half our clients can't tell reality from their own ..."

Luanne's breath hitched. Pilar turned to look at me, her glass eye slightly off-kilter.

"Luanne." Pilar reached out and put a hand on her arm. "Please remember. We all just want to help Paul. Has he been acting strangely in any way?"

Luanne picked up her beer, thought better of it, then set it back down.

"Sometimes ..." Luanne said. "Sometimes it's like he's a different person."

"How so?" Pilar asked.

"I've found him walking around at night," Luanne said, her voice just a little bit shaky. "I'll be talking right in his face — Paul! Paul! But he won't respond. Sometimes I'll find him staring at the television. I'll turn it off. He won't react at all. After half an hour or so, he'll drift out of it like he was sleepwalking. The next day, he won't remember any of it."

She picked up the beer again and just held it, still not drinking.

"So the other night," Luanne said, "this is going on. And I tried to take his arm and lead him back to his bedroom because I'm afraid he's going to fall over something. And he looked at me, and he said some of the most foul things I'd ever heard anybody say. He didn't remember any of it the next day."

Pilar said "What kind of foul things?"

"Curse words," Luanne said. "I don't know where he'd even pick them up! I tell Dad and Ty to watch their mouths around him. He must have picked them up at school, because he's not around any adults who use that kind of ..."

Very slowly, she turned her head and began to glare at me. Sister Pilar, grasping her meaning, slowly swiveled her head as well. The pupils of her eyes were in different zip codes.

"Anyone need a beer?" I asked. "I'm getting one. Be right back."

I managed to walk, not run, to the kitchen door. Running would be unprofessional and I'm all about the professionalism. I grabbed a beer from the fridge and headed into the living room.

Zuckerman had joined the other guys. They'd put the video game aside and were sitting around talking.

"Amateurs," Ken said. "I saw the explosions in the stadium myself. Poor placement. Poor timing. And from what I heard about the garbage truck explosions, a six-year-old could have made that timing device. These aren't professionals. Just a bunch of punks. Eh, I need another beer."

I got to my feet to fetch him one.

"No!" he said. "Bum hip doesn't mean I can't get my own beer. And no helping me stand, either."

We pretended not to watch as he painfully got to his feet, then headed for the kitchen with the assistance of his cane.

"So what does Ken mean by a timing device?" Paul asked after a little bit. "I mean, how can you time a bunch of dynamite? Is it about how long the fuse is?"

Ty laughed.

"Nah, it's not like dynamite in cartoons," he said. "Here's the deal. You're not triggering the TNT directly. You're triggering a blasting cap to set it off. A battery-powered, electric blasting cap. You need to complete an electrical circuit. If you rig it up so the hand of a watch — just an ordinary watch — completes the circuit, you can time it down to anywhere within an hour. See?"

"You seem to know a lot about it," Michael said.

"Learned it all from me," Ken said, making his way back to the couch. "Back when Ty was younger, he wanted to know all about my work with explosive ordnance disposal. I finally stopped telling him about it when he damn near blew his balls off in the garage playing around with some degreaser and a box of matches."

He laughed, then remembered Paul's presence.

"I mean," Ken went on, "that was very dangerous of course and there was really nothing funny about it."

I'd seen better attempted saves in my time. But I didn't think Ken needed to worry. The wild streak that possessed Ty when he was younger seemed to have bypassed Paul. Maybe.

After a little while, Ty challenged Paul to a match.

"Don't pick the geisha," I advised Ty. "She sucks."

In my peripheral vision, I saw Michael waving. He'd got up from the couch and was now in the kitchen gesturing me over. He held up a beer for me. Sold.

"What's up," I asked him.

"Has Dudek been talking?"

That would be Joseph Dudek, 32, from Detroit. Got kicked out of the Navy for dealing weed, and since then had done time for liquor store robberies and a couple cases of aggravated assault. Most recently seen at the receiving end of a photographer's tripod in a stairwell at Grossman and Grossman Podiatry Associates Stadium.

(By the way, Pilar let me tap our expense account for $80 to buy Sheila from the Batley Daily Needler a new tripod. Pilar had lectured me about how tight on funds we were. She probably would have been even more annoyed if she knew the tripod really cost $70. But Theo made the joke first and a bet is a bet.)

I'd contacted a few of Dudek's family members and past associates to see if I could get some leads. Every one of them had asked if I was a cop, then effectively told me to perform an act that to the best of my knowledge is physically impossible.

"Tell you what," I said. "You're so curious about what I'm finding out? You know so much about these assholes? You just tell me exactly how to find Cabot."

No reaction.

"You done?" he asked.

"Fuck you."

"You done?"

"Yeah, I'm done. And fuck you."

"I can't intervene directly," Michael said. "Wish I could. I mean – I can jump in if people are in danger. I can patrol around and stop them if I see them doing anything. I can even organize citizen patrols. But you know what would happen if my organization made a practice of conducting our own investigations? We'd be in nonstop pissing matches with everyone from the feds down to your local meter maid. All I can do is point you in the right direction."

"If you're going after criminals, why would law enforcement have a problem with you?"

"Think you'll get a Christmas card from Sanderson this year? Neither do I."

"No, Dudek is not talking. What did you mean when you said I'd been chosen?"

"In time."

"What does that mean?"

"It means 'in time.' "

"Have I mentioned fuck you?"

"I seem to recall it coming up once or twice. Shot?"

"If you insist."

He picked up a bottle of whiskey from the counter and poured it out into a couple shot glasses. We downed them, then I filled him in.

According to my sources, Dudek was sitting in state prison. The feds had a go at him, but so far he hadn't said anything, which was baffling everybody involved with the case. Small-timers like Dudek didn't usually have the luxury of clamming up. In fact, I was surprised that a little fish like Dudek would be running around with an outfit like The Slain to begin with.

But Michael said he wasn't. In fact, he said it fit the profile of The Slain perfectly. They tended to attract losers who wanted some kind of structure in their life. They also wanted some nominal authority figure to give them permission to do all the twisted shit they always wanted to do, but never had the courage on their own.

"So how about the investigation?" he said. "Any ideas where this is going?"

"The problem," I said, "is that Sanderson clamps down pretty tight on my police sources. There's information that would be very useful to me. Like where they're getting their cars."

I explained that every one of The Slain's stunts so far involved stolen cars for getaway or to leave behind and torch. And stolen cars aren't something you get off a corner dealer.

Michael said The Slain were known to work with organized crime.

That sounded unlikely to me, I told him. The Baltimore and Philly dealers running operations in Batley never bothered much with anything other than selling drugs. And the last thing they wanted was a bunch of freaks like The Slain taking random potshots on the street and driving customers out of downtown.

"I'm thinking more old school," Michael said. "The people running things behind the scenes."

It took a few seconds before the name occurred to me.

"Amos Keller," I said.

A couple of decades back, I told Michael, the Philadelphia mob had a dispute with some of the boys operating out of New York City. The resultant dust-up produced an inconvenient number of discharged firearms that certain people didn't want showing up as courtroom exhibits.

Through a convoluted chain of events, they got Keller on the payroll. He was an Amish blacksmith.

"Beats me what an Amish guy would even spend the money on," I said. "Hats, I guess."

Whatever Keller used the money for, he made a lot of it melting down Mafia guns. Then his name came up as part of a big FBI investigation and he did some time. The Amish kicked him out of their community.

He'd remained in the area, though, operating a ring that stole cars and farm equipment, and dealt some weed and meth. Different client base than the downtown Batley gangs. They stayed out of each others' way for the most part.

By all accounts, Keller still did favors for the Italian mob out of Philadelphia on occasion. In return, they'd occasionally lend him muscle if someone tried to move in on his turf. He was small-time by any objective standard, but as big as they get in our humble little corner of the world.

"That sounds about right," Michael said. "This Keller is exactly the type that The Slain typically deal with."

"Not much I can do about it," I said. "It's not like I can throw Keller into a back room and sweat him. But it might give me a lead."

"Let me know if there's anything I can do."

"Now that you mention it, you can pour me another shot."

We eventually called it a night. Luanne offered to wrap up some of the leftover ribs for anyone who wanted to take them, but we all insisted the Bacons keep them.

Out in the street, I sat behind the wheel of my car and lit a cigar. I watched Michael say goodnight to Ken and Luanne at the door.

Michael walked to his bike, mounted it and rode off. I followed.

I kept him at a distance as he rode. There were still enough cars out that I could keep several between us. Since his was the only bike on the road, it was easy to keep an eye on him.

He made his way out of downtown, headed for the more suburban stretches on the edge of the city. Then I saw Heritage Estates. Or rather, its surrounding 15-foot-high encircling brick wall tucked in among a bunch of single-family homes like a fortress. A very quaint fortress.

I pulled off onto a side street, finishing my cigar and chucking the butt out the window. Then I pulled back out onto the main road.

I passed a dark sedan parked off another side street closer to Heritage Estates, not directly in front of any house, the front of the car pointed toward the road. A driver and a passenger, two men, sat side-by-side. I couldn't make out their faces. The headlights were off and the engine wasn't running.

I drove slowly past the front entrance to Heritage Estates. An enormous black man wearing a white shirt and visored cap sat in a booth, next to a metal gate that was currently shut. He smiled.

"How are you this evening?" he asked.

"Hey, John," I said. "Keeping out of trouble?"

"Doing my best."

I glanced at my watch and drove off. It was time to meet my buddy Tom for a beer.

PONDERINGS AND RUMINATIONS
By Tom Jerkface, Daily Needler staff writer

Hail and well met, fellow travelers upon life's winding byways! The time has come once again for us to take rest and refreshment within the tavern of the mind that is my weekly newspaper column.

Therein, we may shake the dust from our garments, sit down over a glass of ale (or non-alcoholic equivalent for my underage readers) and share tales of our journeys.

My tale this week is one of courage, as embodied in community activist Sister Pilar Lopez, regional director of the Friedrich K. Schulze Foundation and assistant director of the Batley Interfaith Council.

For those of you who have never encountered this remarkable woman personally, Sister Pilar is small in stature. But she exudes dauntless determination with her every word and gesture. This quality was very much in evidence when I visited her office at the Hope House in downtown Batley to interview her about an upcoming community march that the Interfaith Council is sponsoring.

The catalyst for the event, of course, is the recent series of craven attacks on innocent people by the cabal of masked buffoons who call themselves "The Slain." Sister Pilar likened them to a gaggle of schoolyard bullies who attempt to intimidate through senseless acts of violence but are, in fact, cowards beneath the swagger.

I cannot think of a more apt analogy.

As a journalist, I assure you that I know what courage is. I spend my worklife intrepidly seeking out truth and exposing injustices, which frequently obliges me to delve into the dark places from which most people would flee.

In composing this weekly column, I also fearlessly expose myself to the ridicule and scorn of the many wags among our readership who find great sport in deriding me in letters to the editor. (As a personal aside to Mr. "Heywood Jablome" of West Batley: I don't care if you disagree with my opinions. Speculating about my sexual proclivities is both rude and juvenile. And I've figured out that your name is made up, even if our editorial page editor has not.)

The Slain are not courageous men. They are bullies and punks. Kudos to community activists such as Sister Pilar Lopez for pointing it out.

FILE 13

"See, Jesus preached that the capital gains tax is against God's will, if you interpret his word properly," Jack Lange was saying. "Now, in the Sermon on the Mount ..."

Sister Pilar had somehow got stuck next to him during the March for Batley and was now staring straight ahead as she walked with an expression of mute suffering on her face.

Lange was there as a representative of the Businessmen's Association, and as a lay preacher for his church. They brought up the rear of the ragged line of about 200 people walking along Market Street.

I could tell Pilar was biting her tongue, because the Businessman's Association helped finance the march and rally, providing bottled water for the marchers and red buttons everyone sported that read "We Believe in Batley."

I considered going over to rescue her, but decided against it. She didn't like it when I drank from my flask in public. A music ministry act from a local Baptist Church called Jammin' for Jesus was scheduled to play a few songs at the rally afterward, and I figured I'd need a good buzz going by then if I was going to get through it.

I took a slug and offered one to Ty, who was walking beside me, but he turned it down.

Ahead of us, Luanne walked alongside Paul. She said Ken wanted to come along, but the walking would have been too much for him.

Up ahead, Rabbi Zuckerman led the march. Walking along with him was Pastor Cooke of Christ Our Redeemer A.M.E. Church. Before we got started, a lot of people shook Cooke's hand and expressed their condolences for what happened at his church the day of the stadium attack. Now Zuckerman and Cooke hoisted the two ends of a banner that read "We Believe in Batley."

Buck Rockbaugh and Dan Oliphant were also near the front of the pack. So was Bixler, which was why I was hanging near the back.

Michael was there, too. We'd talked before the march started at 2 p.m. He was betting that the The Slain wouldn't try anything. Still, trying not to be too obvious about it, he made his way back and forth along the line of people, keeping an eye out for any signs of trouble. Tom and Sheila from the Daily Needler circulated in the crowd too, interviewing people and taking pictures respectively.

Garbage sat in big piles along most of our planned route. Though the city found a contractor to remove it, the new hauler still had a pretty big backlog and hadn't gotten to most of the city yet. The smell wasn't exactly overpowering, but it was definitely present.

Still, as the organizers agreed beforehand, we couldn't have asked for a nicer day. It was sunny and warm, but not too warm. Even though the underlying cause was serious, it was kind of nice to be out walking that afternoon.

The word "Batley" doesn't exactly lend itself to catchy chants, so we were mostly quiet aside from individual conversations in the group.

Fire police from the Batley Fire Department, wearing orange reflective vests, manned stations along the route, making sure the marchers stayed on course. As we headed toward Kendle Creek, I saw one positioned at the intersection with Schimmel Street — a small, old guy waving the people along.

The group ahead of me was turning right, onto a paved path running along the creek. At the front of the crowd, Zuckerman and Cooke had turned the banner sideways so they could both stay on the trail.

Once you got out of the downtown area, the path eventually led to some pretty nice, wooded areas. But the stretch we were walking along was nothing too spectacular.

The creek was about 100 feet wide at this point, its steep banks lined with rock to prevent erosion. The water coursed slowly along the creek bed about 20 feet below us to our left on the other side of an iron hand rail. To our right was a railroad track. A train that once connected Baltimore to Batley and then to points north used to run along it. The train hadn't run for years, although some Chamber of Commerce types had been talking about possibly getting rail service started again.

Trees lined the other side of the creek. Our side had mainly industrial buildings, either shut down for the weekend or shut down permanently.

Ty and I had been talking about fighting for a while. The relative merits of staying on your feet vs. taking it to the ground. Then he said he was going to hit Luanne up for one of the granola bars in her backpack, and asked if I wanted one. I said no. He walked up to where Luanne was and I took another swig from my flask. Granola bars weren't going to get me through Jammin' for Jesus.

"Not a bad turnout, considering."

That was Michael, who'd made his way up to my side.

"Anything new?" he asked.

I told him I'd been investigating Keller. I'd checked out his spread, located in the boonies on the edge of the county. From a distance with binoculars, of course. I wasn't about to knock on his door and ask if he was providing stolen cars for The Slain. I hadn't seen any fleet of vehicles on his property, but there was a big barn that could have hidden plenty of cars.

I'd also been checking in with stadium employees, trying to get some idea of how somebody might have smuggled the boxes with the guns and masks in. I'd narrowed the possible scenarios down to about 50,000. It's not like anybody'd considered a minor league ballpark to be a matter of national security.

Not until recently, anyway. When I started sniffing around the stadium, I'd encountered some guys in suits who wanted to know what exactly I was doing and didn't seem too pleased once I'd explained. They turned out to be feds, who were distinctly uninterested in my assistance. Not surprising, since in my experience law enforcement types tend to be more territorial than hornets with obsessive compulsive disorder.

Since I wasn't getting anywhere anyway, I left them to it at the stadium. If they could find something, shut down The Slain and spare me the trouble, that would make my week.

In the meantime, I figured I still had to make some effort. I'd gotten myself a property map of Batley from the local tax office and was still checking out abandoned buildings.

"That's a good way to go," Michael said. "But keep in mind, they tend to move around a lot for that very reason."

"You mean I might have to go back and check the places I already checked? Halle-fuckin-lujah, that's just what I wanted to hear. So how goes the citizens defense?"

Pretty good, as Michael described it. The Businessmen's Association, recognizing the P.R. potential, kicked in a bunch of money. Michael said it could pay for stuff like radios for citizen patrol cars. Also windbreakers and badges, which could be important psychologically if you were trying to get volunteers motivated. And he had plenty of volunteers. Nearly 100 already signed on for citizen patrols, with scores more expressing an interest. Buck, Oliphant, and Bixler all offered to let people call their offices if they wanted to sign up.

"I guess people feel better doing something, anything, rather than just sitting around and waiting for the next attack," Michael said.

"Excuse me, are you affiliated with any of the churches organizing the event?"

Ah fuck. It was Bixler. He'd somehow managed to sneak up without my noticing, and directed that question in a none-too-friendly tone at Michael.

"No sir, I am not," Michael said. "My understanding is that this march was open to anybody who wanted to show support for the city. If there a problem?"

"Well, there's..." Bixler appeared to be trying to marshal his thoughts. "I've been thinking about all of it. You show up in this city right at the time these attacks begin. I suppose you're going to say that's a coincidence?"

"No," said Michael, "It's not a coincidence at all. I came specifically because The Slain are here, to protect the people. I believe I've mentioned that more than once."

I suspect that when Bixler rehearsed this exchange in his mind, he'd pictured things going very differently. He seemed nervous, although Michael didn't do anything threatening. Just something about confronting a guy who could obviously break you in half and clearly wasn't intimidated by your authority, I guess. As Bixler's Adam's apple jumped up and down in his skinny neck, I imagined he was reliving some high school experiences that involved being suspended upside down over a waiting toilet. After a couple of awkward minutes, Bixler just drifted off without saying anything more.

Michael smiled, shook his head, then said he wanted to talk to Lange about organizing. I told him Pilar would likely appreciate that. I walked on for a little bit, not talking to anyone around me.

The creek bed below us had widened, and now included a grassy shelf leading up to the rock-lined sides. The crowd started slowing down, then bunching up. Something was going on up ahead.

As I got closer, people from the line were walking down a small, unpaved trail that branched off the paved one. They proceeded down to a grassy area right alongside the creek.

Closer still, and I saw a fire policeman, wearing a baseball cap and an orange vest over his denim jacket. This one was a guy in his late 20s, by the looks of it, his hair tied back in a ponytail. Behind him was a length of yellow police tape stretched across the paved walk, tied to trees on either side. He waved people down the trail leading to the creek.

I stepped off to the side, allowing the people behind me to walk on, and approached the fire policeman.

"What's up?" I asked.

"Emergency up ahead," he said. "Police wanted a detour."

"What kind of emergency?"

He leaned in close and spoke softly, after checking to make sure none of the other marchers listened in.

"They don't want to panic anybody," he said. "Somebody found a body on the trail. Likely no big deal. Probably an overdose."

That would be typical for this part of town. I nodded, and started down the trail myself. It was steep, with rocks protruding, and required some slow going. I assisted an older woman wearing shoes that weren't meant for that particular job, then joined the others.

Overhead, an unused railroad bridge stretched the width of the creek. Nothing fancy. Basically a big girder with tracks running across it. A couple of big birds wheeled against the blue sky. Crows, maybe.

The procession kept walking. There was no trail down here and the ground was rocky, but it was pretty easy going overall.

Now that they didn't feel obliged to walk along the trail, the crowd spread out more. I hung nearly at the very rear of the crowd now, because of my stop to talk to the fire policeman. Pilar hovered near me.

Michael and Lange now walked at about the middle of the pack. Ty, Luanne and Paul were near the front. And at the very front, Zuckerman and Cooke hoisted the banner again.

"Who do they think is going to see that banner down here?" I asked.

"We paid for it," Pilar said. "Might as well use it."

We continued on for about half a mile, following a more-or-less straight course. I'd never been down there before, and it was pretty nice. We could still hear occasional barking dogs or cars above us. By and large, though, it was like a remote wilderness right in the middle of Batley. Boulders sat along the rock-lined sides of the creek, some as big as cars. I assumed some civil engineers must have moved them down here for erosion control, though it beats me how they did it.

Trees still lined the opposite bank. The bank on our side rose at such a steep angle that you couldn't see beyond it. We were in our own little world.

Here and there on the ground were scattered plastic food wrappers and small lengths of what appeared to be fishing line. I guessed anglers must come down there. I could see where it would be a nice spot to get away from it all, but I personally wouldn't want to eat anything out of that creek.

Even now, sunlight slanting down behind us revealed rainbow patterns from some kind of oily film swirling on the water's surface.

Up ahead, Cooke and Zuckerman approached a bend in the creek that I couldn't see beyond because of some piled-up boulders. I wondered if another fire policeman would be waiting beyond it to wave us up another trail past the dead junkie. Though I was in no particular hurry to leave this spot. It was nice.

Then I had a thought.

"Hey, Sister," I said to Pilar. "That fire policeman seem kind of young to you?"

Cooke and Zuckerman went around the bend. The crowd followed. They bunched up a little, because the space between the rocks and the water narrowed to a couple yards or so. Luanne and Ty and Paul went around the bed. So did Michael.

"What do you mean?" she asked.

"See, the fire police. They're the ones who stand out in the road and direct traffic around the spots where they've got fires and accidents ..."

"I know what the fire police are."

"Well, most of them tend to be the older guys in the fire companies. The ones who have trouble lugging a hose or swinging an ax anymore. That guy who directed us down here? Looked like he was in his 20s."

Nearly all of the group had gone around the bend. It was just me and Pilar and a few straggling old-timers waiting to go.

"So what are you ..." Pilar began.

Then the screaming started.

It came from the other side of the bend. A bunch of people, from the sound of it.

Pilar and I hurried around the bend ourselves.

The relatively narrow gap between the rock wall to our right and the water continued on for a few yards, then widened into a broad, grassy swath bounded by thick brush along the creek bank. The end of the line, it seemed. We'd been led into a dead end.

The people from the march were crowded around some kind of statue, propped up on a bunch of boulders along the bank. Some screamed. Some averted their faces. A few were crying.

I couldn't get to the clearing where most of the people stood because the path in front of me was blocked.

I ran into the water and splashed toward the clearing, trying to get a better view of the thing they all stared at. Even as I did, I realized the oily muck on the water's surface clung to my pants legs. Dry-cleaning bills in my future. Great.

As I got nearer, I saw that some people close to the statue on the rocks were trying to get away from it. Others pressed forward, trying to get a look. The result was a lot of confused pushing and pulling.

I ran onto the bank. Now, I'd be the first to admit there aren't a lot of circumstances where you're justified throwing elbows to get through a crowd composed largely of older church folk, but this was definitely one of them.

Then I took a look at the thing on the rocks. I guess you could call it a statue. Or a sculpture, maybe. One made out of meat and bone.

It was about 12 feet high, in a sitting position on several boulders that had a natural, chair-like contour. It stank. A few late-season flies buzzed around it.

At that moment, I had no idea of the logistics that went into making it. I found out later the construction material was steer carcasses. Or rather, sections of steer carcasses that somebody had fashioned into component parts with a chainsaw and fastened together with lengths of stout wire and bolts. Ribcages for the trunk, leg bones for the limbs and a horned skull sitting on top, forming a humanoid shape. All of it covered in ragged strips of putrefying meat.

Lying on the ground at its feet was the face-up, naked body of a fat, bearded man. George Hoffman, the Proudly Armed American. His face was bruised, but recognizable. The top of his skull, though, was stove in like an overripe pumpkin. His eyes were torn out. His cock and balls were cut off.

I had just a few seconds to take it in. Then the creek caught fire.

Not a big flare-up, but a trail of low flame making its way from around the bend and following the sluggish flow downstream. The flames were hard to discern in the sunlight, but they were definitely there. I could feel the heat. The whole creek wasn't aflame. Just a strip near the bank where we were. Engineered for our benefit and lit by someone farther upstream at the precise moment we hit this spot, it would seem.

The screaming and shouting increased in volume, as people backing away from the water and away from Hoffman's body began to jostle each other.

In one corner, I spotted Ty with an arm over both Paul's and Luanne's shoulders, as though the three of them were huddling together for protection.

Michael stood between the marchers and the flaming water.

"Keep back," he yelled, though that hardly seemed necessary, given the way everybody pressed away from the flaming creek.

Buck was trying to position himself between Hoffman's body and the crowd as if he could somehow prevent them from seeing it, and as if that would make any difference at this point. Oliphant and Bixler stood off to the side, gaping.

Buck held out his hands in what he might have intended as a calming gesture.

A lot of the people seemed to get the same idea at once and made a break toward the narrow strip between the boulders and the creek from which we'd entered this clearing. Then they abruptly stopped as a sharp, clear voice cut through the air like a bonesaw.

"Stop! Get back in there! Now!"

It was Pilar. She was blocking the path, all five-foot-nothing of her. The people trying to exit backed away from her as she advanced on them.

"Fuck that!" yelled Jack Lange, who was near the front. He broke from the group and ran at Pilar, as if intending to barrel over her.

She brought up an index finger and stuck it in his face, simultaneously yelling "MISter Lange! I told you to get back there!"

Lange started to protest, then she thrust her finger forward again and let out with another "MISter Lange!"

In spite of everything, I felt an urge to laugh. I remembered from grade school that if a nun ever addressed you as "Mister" in that tone of voice, your ass was oatmeal. Even a shithead like Lange understood that on a primal level.

The crowd had gone quiet, as they watched Pilar back the group of would-be escapees into the clearing with everyone else. Whether she knew what she was doing or not, she gave every appearance that she did, which seemed to put her one-up on anyone else in the clearing.

Buck spoke up.

"Sister Pilar is right," he said. "If we start panicking, somebody's going to get hurt. Please. Just stay calm and we'll figure out the best way to handle this."

Some protests, muttered and shouted, came from the crowd. But nobody else made a break for the exit.

Pilar motioned to me. I wandered over.

"What do you think?" she asked in a low voice.

"They wanted to attack us here, they'd have done it without giving us a warning first," I said, talking in a low voice myself. "I think this is another one of their panic-the-herd, showpiece numbers. It's like they're trying to stampede us in that direction." I pointed where Pilar had stopped the people from running.

"You think they've got an ambush set up?" Pilar asked.

"My guess," I said, "would be the railroad bridge. Maybe somebody with a rifle to pick people off when they head that way. Couldn't get everybody, but just enough to send a message. They seem to like that kind of thing."

"Why not just get us when we passed under it the first time?" Pilar asked.

"They wanted you to see this," said Michael. He had walked up to us, and was gesturing toward Hoffman's body and the meat sculpture sitting over it.

"You're right," Michael said, nodding at me. "They are sending you a message. I blame myself. Again, I underestimated just how much they have it in for this city."

"So what do we do?" Pilar asked.

"I'll handle it," Michael said. He looked at me. "You get near the bend over there. Take a look around every few minutes. You should be out of range from here. I'll signal you from the bridge when it's clear."

Michael started walking toward the steep, rocky incline leading out of the creek bed.

"You're going alone?" Pilar asked.

"It's better this way," Michael said. "Trust me, I've got lots of experience handling them."

"No, he's not going alone," I said. "I'm coming too. Pilar, you can handle lookout."

I walked toward Michael.

"Look, I appreciate the gesture," he said. "But really, you'd only get in the way. And maybe you noticed, we got a real situation here."

"Too bad, I'm going," I said.

For just a second, Michael looked like he was about to take a swing at me.

"Goddammit!" he said. "You can be a real pain in the ass sometimes!"

I looked at Pilar, half expecting her to reprimand him for his language. Instead, she muttered something that sounded very much like "Tell me about it."

Without another word, Michael turned around and started scaling the bank. I went after him. I was a slower climber, but I caught up with him as he crept along a brushy stretch near the edge of the creek bed.

"Wait up," I said, just loud enough for him to hear me.

"Shhh!" He gave me an irritated look and made a shushing gesture.

He was quiet for a minute, looking around and listening closely.

"Stay behind me and keep your mouth shut," he said in a whisper. "I don't think they've got anyone planted here before the bridge. We're probably safe taking the path until we get close. I'm going to try to end this without a fight. I don't want anyone getting hurt. Including you and me, understand?"

I nodded. We found the paved path, and crept along it. When we got close to the bridge, we crouched down behind some bushes.

"Stay right here." He whispered it, but gave each whispered syllable an emphasis that meant he wasn't going to accept any argument.

I heard him skulking through the brush some more, getting closer to the bridge. Then he spoke. Not yelling, exactly. But in the silence around us, he might have been talking through a megaphone.

"You! On the bridge! Listen to me! This is Michael from the Order of Gabriel and I have the Godknife! You know who I am and you know what I'm capable of! I will give you 30 seconds to vacate your position, or I will come after you! Do you understand? I have the Godknife! 30 seconds!"

Nothing happened for a few seconds. Then through the bushes, I saw two men stand up on the bridge. They held hunting rifles and wore leather masks. One wore camouflage. The other wore a denim jacket and had a ponytail protruding from his mask.

They ran toward the opposite bank from where we were, picking their way carefully along the railroad ties but going as fast as the circumstances would allow.

"Wait," Michael said, addressing me. And I did. For about five minutes, I remained motionless.

Then Michael stood. In his hand was a black knife. It was maybe 10 inches long. The blade had an elongated wedge shape. But it was jagged and uneven, as if carved out of rock with rough tools. I started to stand too, but Michael motioned for me to get back down.

"I need to make sure it's safe," he said.

He walked out of the bushes and down to the bridge. Then he strode out to the center of it. He looked around, contenting himself that all was well, and lifted his jacket to place the knife in a sheath that was cinched against his lower back.

He waved his arms over his head a few times, then stopped. Pilar must have seen him.

I stood and made my way to the side of the bridge. To my right, down the creek bed, marchers emerged from around the bend. Michael waved his arm, gesturing for them to head in our direction.

The waning sunlight hit him from the side, making him look like some animated gold statue. I could only imagine what he looked like to the people on the ground as he beckoned them toward safety away from that nightmare in the clearing.

"You gotta be kidding me," I said.

"What do you mean?"

"So I've already seen you chase eight guys armed with baseball bats out of a bar. Now I've seen two guys with guns run away just because you said you were coming after them. Why would they do that?"

"Because they knew the guns wouldn't do them any good."

"What does that mean?"

"In time."

"You know, it's really starting to piss me off when you say that."

"I know. Kinda makes it more fun to say."

FILE 14

A few hours later, I looked at George Hoffman's home and thought to myself "Yeah. Definitely the right place."

Trash cluttered its overgrown lawn, much of it empty bottles and cigarette packs. The backyard was crowded with rusting and partially disassembled lawn mowers, four-wheelers and other machines that George must have lost interest in around beer number 12 or so.

Officer X took a look around, made sure none of his colleagues were paying attention, then gestured me over.

Officer X is one of my sources. I suspect Sanderson is aware of this arrangement, because Officer X gets at least as much information from me as I get from him. But just in case Sanderson should ever see this account, I won't name him. (Or her. Never know, do you, Sandy? Mind if I call you Sandy?)

A few hours ago, everybody had made it back safely, if traumatized, from the March for Batley. The police had plenty of people to interview, as did the reporters and news crews swarming around outside the police station. By that time, a bunch of national news outlets had taken an interest in the city's story. Around town in recent days, you'd occasionally spot people toting cameras or notebooks, interviewing locals. None of them had shown up for the march, aside from Tom and Sheila, but they were all sure as hell interested in its aftermath.

I'd swung by Hoffman's place to see what was going on, hoping Officer X would be on the scene.

He made it clear that he was busy, so we didn't take any time to shoot the shit. I gave him an account of what happened on the march, and he told me what he knew.

It wasn't much so far. An autopsy was scheduled on Hoffman the next day, though it seemed pretty clear the cause of death was "blunt force trauma" — a fancy way of saying somebody pounded the living fuck out of him with clubs of some kind. The mutilation of the corpse, the missing eyeballs and wedding tackle, in other words, likely happened post mortem.

Judging by the blood on the carpet inside Hoffman's house, they'd done it there and then transported his body out to the creek for the big show. No shots fired, from the look of it. No signs of forced entry. No sign that the place was robbed or ransacked. But given Hoffman's housekeeping skills, the last one was purely a guess.

"No shots fired?" I asked. "Seems kind of weird. A guy like Hoffman spends his life looking forward to the day he gets to shoot an intruder like a 14-year-old boy looks forward to his first lay."

"We're still investigating the scene, but that's the way it looks," Officer X said.

"Between that and the lack of forced entry, can we assume that he let whoever did this into his home?"

"Officially, the investigation is ongoing. Unofficially, that's where my money would be."

Officer X also filled me in on the latest concerning Dudek, my pal from the baseball stadium. He was dead. Somebody'd shanked him in the prison shower. Investigators didn't have anything promising yet.

On my way out, I took a look at the shiny new pickup in the driveway. Its bumper bore a single sticker: "Proudly Armed American."

I looked at my watch. About 8. I had to be someplace in 90 minutes. Meanwhile, I figured I should check in on Pilar and make sure she was OK.

I drove downtown, parked, and walked half a block to the Hope House. It's a free-standing, two-story building at the end of a block that consists mostly of row houses. I believe it started as a family home for one of Batley's better-paid citizens in the 19th century. Despite Pilar's constant efforts to keep everything in it sturdy and functioning, it isn't much to look at.

I stared at it for a minute. I knew a few people had been staying there, in addition to Pilar. It wasn't late by any stretch, but the place was dark and quiet.

As I approached the front door, I got an uneasy feeling. It was locked, which was unusual. I had a key, which I rarely had to use. I used it now.

I walked through the front door and into an entrance hallway with another door at the end. It was dark, so I hit a switch. A bare lightbulb in the ceiling gave off a dim light as I went to the second door.

That was locked, too. I unlocked it and swung it open, peering into the darkness inside. Was that movement?

Someone came barreling out the door and head-butted me in the solar plexus. I went over backward, my assailant tackling me and then straddling my chest.

No time for a counterattack. I raised my arms, protecting my face from the punches that were about to start raining down.

The punches didn't come. I lowered my arms. Sister Pilar was on top of me. She had a fist cocked. On it was a set of brass knuckles.

"You know we do have a doorbell," she said.

Not long after, I sat across from her in her office. We were drinking coffee. Her hands shook slightly. I offered her my flask. She declined at first, then shrugged and poured a small dollop into her coffee.

As she sipped, I looked at the papers on her desk. My eyes settled on an envelope. It was from the Pigeon Clinic. Something occurred to me and I held it up.

"What's this?" I asked.

"Just an update from Dr. Pigeon about Paul. Why?"

"I want to check something out. Mind if I hold onto the envelope?"

"Whatever."

"So," I said "You seem jumpy. I've got an amazing knack for picking up on these things."

She handed me a folded piece of paper and I read it.

STUPID CUNT YOU THINK YOU CAN MOCK THE ONE WHO TAKES AND NOT PAY? THOSE IN THIS HOUSE WILL PAY IN PAIN AND BLOOD!

"Somebody put it through the mail slot during the march," Pilar said. "We have three people staying here. A couple of lower-functioning clients, two homeless men and Theo. He lost his job and was having trouble keeping up with the rent. Rich Zuckerman is finding places for them to go. He thinks he can have them out by tonight. In the meantime, I told them to wait in the basement."

"You informed the police?"

"I called them. For some reason, they're a little busy at the moment."

"OK," I said. "You've got a place for Theo and the other four. Now we've got to get you out of here. Understand?"

"No," she said. "I won't give them that."

"Come on," I said. "Don't be stupid. And I have no idea where you got those brass knuckles, but how about you give them to me? Do you have any idea what those can do to someone?"

She stared at where they sat on her desk. I started to reach for them when she gave me a look that stopped me cold.

"Yes," she said. "I have these because somebody once used them on me."

She told me the story. There wasn't much to it.

When she'd first gone to North Jersey to work at a homeless shelter, they'd temporarily put her in a crappy, one-room apartment until she could find something more permanent.

One day not long after she'd arrived, a teenage girl wearing fishnet stockings and a short skirt showed up at her door. Pilar never did learn how the girl found her, or what her story was. But it wasn't that hard to guess.

The girl managed to convey in heavily accented, barely understandable English that she needed help. She panicked and started crying when Pilar suggested trying the police.

Pilar wasn't sure what to do and let the girl stay at her apartment when she went to work at the shelter. When Pilar returned that night, the girl was gone but two large, expensively dressed men waited for her.

One of them stood lookout outside the apartment while the other worked her over with the brass knuckles. Pilar was dazed from the beating but still conscious for what he did next.

Something must have spooked the guy acting as lookout. Pilar's assailant was in such a hurry to get his pants back on and leave that he left the brass knuckles behind. She never saw the girl again.

"I keep them in my desk drawer, so I can see them every day," Pilar said. "That way, no matter how much I talk about God's love and mercy, I'll never forget what people are capable of doing to each other."

She got a hitch in her voice and didn't say anything for a minute while she composed herself. When she started talking again, her voice sounded strong and angry.

"Yes. I know very well what these can do to someone. So don't you dare — don't you dare! — talk to me like I'm some poor, helpless woman who doesn't know what she's getting into!"

She was really upset now. I could tell because her glass eye ...

Her glass eye.

The brass knuckles.

Oh Jesus.

"I am not going to run away when so many people are depending on me!"

She was yelling now.

"Sister, I just mean ..."

"And what are you doing to find Cabot?"

"I'm looking into a bunch of things. See, I'm starting to get an idea that this is more complicated than it looks and ..."

"I don't care how complicated it is! You get out there and you find Cabot before these people hurt my babies!"

She punctuated that last declaration by slamming her fist down on the desk. Since there didn't seem to be any more for me to say at that moment, I got up and left.

Goddam. It had been so long since a nun put my head through a wall, I'd almost forgot what it felt like.

I looked at my watch. The visit with Pilar took longer than I expected, but I still had plenty of time. I sat down in my car and examined the envelope from the Pigeon Clinic by my overhead light.

Specifically, I looked at the stylized bird on the logo. Its wings. Hard to tell without holding it up right next to the patch on the back of Michael's jacket. But I was pretty sure it was the same design. That Kind-of-Celtic-or-Maori-or-Something motif.

Not long after, I drove past the entrance to Heritage Estates. The dark sedan was still parked in the side street, lights off, engine off, two men in the front seat.

I slowed down near the gatehouse. John, the big security guard, met my eye.

I made the next left. Then another. I pulled over to the curb, then walked up a paved path to the back wall of Heritage Estates. The path ended at a metal security door.

A minute or two later, it swung outward. John the security guard was on the other side. He poked his head out the doorway, then glanced around.

"Anyone see you?" he asked.

"I'm assuming the boys in the sedan out front saw me drive by. Nobody else, so far as I know."

"I need this job, man."

"Look John, I wouldn't be asking you to do this if I thought your job was at serious risk. It's important. There's a kid involved."

John looked resigned, if not real happy.

"Come on in," he said.

I stepped onto a very clean sidewalk among the generic, pint-sized, closely packed mini-mansions of Heritage Estates and John shut the door.

"How you going to get out?"

"Shouldn't be a problem," I said. "Anything goes wrong, slap the cuffs on me and make it look convincing, but I don't think it's going to be necessary. Just get the info. I'm not planning to check back with you tonight, but it shouldn't be long."

He still looked unhappy.

"So how's Jamaad?" I asked.

He smiled.

"That boy's a handful," he said. "You know he started kindergarten this year?"

And to think the last time I saw him, he was playing with a dagger in Cliff Norris' basement. Time does fly.

He pointed me in the right direction, then made himself scarce. Michael wasn't trying to hide his presence in the neighborhood, judging by the motorcycle parked prominently out front.

Like the rest of the Heritage Estates dwellings, his was brick with columns out front and some other decorative architectural doo-dads here and there. Two-story. Probably accommodate a family of four comfortably enough.

I went around back and climbed up on a small wooden deck. No furniture on it. Michael must have inherited it with the house and likely hadn't hosted any backyard barbecues since his arrival.

The window on the back door and another window in the rear wall were both shuttered. I gave an experimental tug on the doorknob. Nothing. I lightly tapped on the window.

Then I walked around to the side of the house. No neighbors were about, so far as I could see. I stepped up to a side window, shuttered as well, and lightly tapped on it. Then I leaned forward to peer in. Some light was visible, but nothing more.

A pickup truck hit me. Or that's what it felt like. I'm not sure which impact was harder — him slamming into me, or me hitting the ground. That's where I ended up, anyway, the air knocked out of me and a hand clamped tight on my throat.

Then Michael let go and got off me, letting me gasp and cough as I tried to fill my lungs again. He didn't look surprised or angry. If anything, he looked a little amused.

"So it's you," he said.

He looked around, then reached down, threw one of my arms over his shoulders and hurried me through his back door, which was still open. He helped me through a small hallway and into a living room, dumping me onto an upholstered chair. A buzzing noise, not real loud but hard to tune out, filled the house and all the overhead light fixtures were intermittently dimming then brightening again.

"Sit tight a second," he said, and stepped out his front door.

He was gone for about a minute and I looked around. The chair I was on matched several others and a sofa with its floral design. Matching cream-colored carpet and wallpaper, with light-blue curtains. A TV set. No pictures on the wall.

None of it Michael's choosing, I guessed. A few newspapers and empty beer bottles seemed to be his only contribution to the decor.

Michael stepped back in the front door, then through a door off the hallway leading to the kitchen. The buzzing and blinking stopped.

I heard him banging around in the kitchen. Then he re-entered the living room with a whiskey bottle and a couple of glasses. He put the glasses down on the coffee table and poured us both a hefty portion.

By that time, I was breathing relatively normal again. I picked up my glass and took a drink.

"Well," said Michael, sitting himself down in an upholstered chair across from me, "at least I know the alarm system works."

"The police going to show up?" I asked.

"Nah. It might surprise you, how many times The Slain have managed to get eyes and ears in local police departments when they hit a town. Our policy is to rely on our own resources as much as possible."

"Who's 'we'? You and Dr. Pigeon?"

"So you've connected us? Congratulations. You did that sooner than I expected."

He sat back and took a long swig of whiskey.

"I'm not even going to bother asking how you got past the gates, since you'd probably bullshit me anyway. Doesn't matter. I figured you'd show up here sooner or later."

"Bixler may be a dumbass, but he does have a point," I said. "Seemed kind of convenient, you getting here right about the same time as The Slain."

"Fair enough. The truth is, my organization's been here for longer than I have. We try to keep an eye on towns The Slain have hit, because they have a way of coming back. They tend to target places they think have some kind of mystic significance. 'The veil between worlds is thin,' as that esteemed philosopher Friedrich K. Schulze might put it."

"So what, you sent some pediatric psychiatrist as your advance guard?"

"We didn't know The Slain were planning a full-on assault, or our operations would have been different. Maybe. That's for folks higher up the command chain than me. Somebody got word about what happened with you and Paul Bacon. Dealing with what The Slain do to kids — that's Pigeon's specialty."

"And what exactly do they do to kids?"

"Sometimes it just a matter of recruitment. They'll snatch kids around Paul's age and subject them to a bunch of brain-washing techniques. Drugs. Sleep deprivation. Hypnosis. That kind of thing. But they seemed to have something special planned for Paul."

"Like what?"

"We're not sure. They're known to use human sacrifice. The younger the victim, the more bonus points they get with The One Who Takes. But Pigeon thinks they had something different in mind for Paul. Cabot really got into his head somehow."

"If they want him so bad, why haven't they just tried to grab him?"

"Could be that whatever they wanted to do, they've already done," Michael said.

We both took a drink and set our glasses down.

"So," Michael said. "You want a tour of the place? Not much to see. The previous occupants didn't leave a lot behind. And aside from food and booze in the kitchen, all I got here is a rucksack and a sleeping bag in the upstairs."

"And the Godknife. Let's not forget that. The fuck is that, anyway?"

"In time."

"Goddamn it!" I yelled, banging on the coffee table with my fist. "I am sick of you jerking me around! People are getting hurt, and you're playing games!"

Michael shook his head.

"I'm not playing games," he said. "There's nothing I take more seriously. I know this may sound like bullshit. But there are certain truths you're just not ready to know, for the sake of your own mental well-being. People have literally been driven insane by getting too much of this knowledge at once."

"You're right," I said. "It does sound like bullshit. You want to know the truth?"

"In whiskey veritas."

"Your whole act. I'm Michael. I'm with the Order of Gabriel. I'm fighting a long-running battle against the forces of darkness with the Godknife. Sounds to me like any psychiatrist would diagnose you as a textbook case of Schulze Syndrome."

Michael chuckled.

"I guess I can't argue with that," he said. "Let me ask you a question. You work with these people who have Schulze Syndrome. You ever consider that maybe they aren't delusional? That they're tuned into some deeper understanding of reality?"

"Interesting thought," I said. "So where'd you hide the bong?"

Michael took a gulp of whiskey, then set the glass back down.

"You've seen how The Slain fear me," Michael said. "If I'm delusional, then it's a very convenient delusion for your purposes."

"So far. But if you're mentally unstable and throwing yourself in the middle of this, your presence could turn dangerous in a hurry."

Michael leaned forward.

"You want to talk practicalities?" he said. "I'll give you two pieces of practical advice. The first is that I'm not the enemy. I'm here to help. The second is that you've already caught onto something, and you're fighting it. Don't."

I picked up my glass and drained it.

"The One Who Takes," I said. "Their representations of him. The one we saw out in the woods. And the one we saw today."

"That's right," said Michael. "So what about them?"

"They were both sculpted with a chainsaw."

A little while later, I was drunk in a bar. That hadn't been my plan. My plan was just a beer or two.

You know that cliche about things rattling around in your head? That's how I felt. Except they weren't rattling so much as clanging, and they had jagged edges. I needed to smooth them, to quiet them down, just a little.

So when I got back to my apartment, I parked my car then walked to a nearby watering hole for a couple beers. And since I was having a couple beers, I figured I might as well have a couple shots to go with them.

I blame Elvis Presley for the rest of it. On my way back from taking a leak, I glanced at the jukebox and saw that the selections included Elvis' version of "How Great Thou Art." I listened to it as I finished my latest beer. Then I ordered another beer and a shot. Since the song sounded so good, I decided to play it again. Once it was over, I wanted to hear it still one more time. And again.

The last time I was heading from the jukebox back to my barstool, a guy wearing a bandanna and a camo jacket at one of the tables looked at me and said "What's your problem? Would you quit playing that goddamn song?"

He and the guy across from him were giving me displeased looks.

"Aw come on!" I said. "This is a great song! Then sings my soooooul! My Savior Lord to theeee ..."

I had some kind of idea that by doing singing along loudly to the jukebox, I'd clue everybody else in to what a great song that was and they'd all start singing too. Instead, someone grabbed me by the back of the collar and the belt and shoved me toward the door.

"Allright, that's it," the bouncer said. "Just get the fuck out of here."

Then I was through the door and out on the sidewalk. I stood up and made an assessment. Some skin off my palms, but I seemed alright otherwise.

It wasn't the first time I'd been thrown out of a bar for getting drunk. That always made as much sense to me as getting thrown out of a barber shop for getting a haircut. Since that argument seemed unlikely to get me readmitted, I walked home.

I unlocked my front door and started up the stairs, singing "Then sings my soul, my Savior Lord to theeee..."

I thought maybe I should shut up. But then I figured it wouldn't be a problem. I had the building to myself for the time being.

My first-floor neighbor would be working the night shift at a factory by now. I turned a corner in the stairs, where the second-floor apartment was located. Vacant for the time being. Good thing, too. The previous occupant, a strung-out-looking guy in his 20s, had taken to knocking on my door in the late-night hours, pleading for a few dollars. I guess it wasn't for rent payment because the landlord tossed his ass out.

I went up the last set of steps to my apartment and staggered inside. I knew exactly what I was in the mood for, and found it in the kitchen.

The muse for countless poets and artists. Or so my friend — kind of a pretentious dork but basically a good guy — who'd given me the bottle of absinthe to pay a poker bet had told me.

TOM JERKFACE: I have been unable to establish the identity of the friend to whom he refers here. Interestingly enough, I myself also once gave him a bottle of absinthe under similar circumstances.

I poured out a little bit into a glass. You can't drink too much of that stuff at once. I lit a cigar. Then I opened a window, because the cigar smoke can get kind of oppressive inside.

I felt relaxed. All that other shit could wait for now. It had been a long goddamn day and I was tired.

The motion detector light in the alley alongside my building went on. I looked out the window. Two guys near the head of the alley.

One of them said, loudly "Damn! I wish we didn't drink all that tequila!"

Just a couple harmless drunks. Who felt the need to announce their status as harmless drunks right after they set off a motion detector light.

Nope. Not buying it.

I put out the cigar and ran back to the storage room behind my kitchen. Found it. My heavy metal flashlight. I also grabbed a snowshovel and an extension cord.

I went through my apartment door, turned and locked it. My heart was going, that feeling of drunken laziness long gone.

I ran down the stairs, pausing beneath an overhead lighting fixture. I smashed it with the snowshovel. Closed my left eye and told myself to keep it closed.

I went around the bend in the stairs and smashed another ceiling lighting fixture. It was just about total dark in the stairway now.

Turned on the flashlight. Left eye, still closed. I ran down another flight of stairs leading to the basement door. Fished in my pockets and brought out the keys my landlord had given me. Dropped the snowshovel.

Not much down in the basement besides a furnace. I didn't turn on the light. Just the flashlight. Left eye closed. I ran across the basement to the backdoor and opened it. Made myself do it very slowly and quietly. If my suspicions were correct, there was probably somebody camped out on my fire escape in case I tried to run for it when his buddies kicked down my door.

Still carrying the flashlight, I ran around the other side of the building, where there was no motion detector light. I heard glass breaking.

I should have run. Even then, in the back of my mind, I knew that. Go to the police. Get help. Just get out of there.

At that moment, though, a louder and thoroughly illogical voice in my head was saying something along the lines of "You now what? Fuck 'em!"

I reached the sidewalk and ran to the front door of my building. Sure enough, the glass in the front window was broken and the door hung open.

I turned off my flashlight and went into the entranceway. Quietly. Softly. Now I closed my right eye and opened my left. It was adjusted to the darkness and I could make things out pretty well.

I crawled about halfway up the first set of stairs. Slowly, trying not to make any noise, I tied the length of cord to the railing posts on either side so it extended above the steps at about shin level. Then I went back down to the bottom of the stairs.

I heard a loud bang and splintering wood from upstairs. Whatever they were doing to my door, it didn't sound cheap to fix. Yes, they would pay for this.

I yelled loudly "Hey! Who's up there?"

Then I pointed my flashlight, still off, toward the landing on the stairs in front of and above me. It didn't take long. As the thudding footsteps descended and they turned the corner on the landing, I turned on the flashlight and shone it in their faces.

They wore leather masks. Their hands held what looked like short lengths of pipe. I guess baseball bats are hard to hide under your jacket if you're planning to walk around alleys and look harmless.

They paused a moment, shielding their eyes. I turned off the flashlight. Whatever adjustment their eyes had made to the darkness was now null and void.

They hurried down the stairs toward me, one slightly in front of the other. The first one hit the cord, then gave a surprised yell as he tripped over it.

The second one, too close and going too fast to stop, tripped over his buddy and the two of them went down the remaining stairs in a big jumble of arms and legs and impolite words.

I jumped in immediately, bringing the flashlight up and down, up and down. It produced some very satisfying clunks and yelps of pain. Then someone stepped in the door behind me. I turned. He wore a leather mask.

He brought up his pipe. I rushed him, jabbing the flashlight at his midsection. But by then, it was too late. The two behind me on the stairs had already got to their feet and moved in.

They overwhelmed me with their clubs and then with kicking feet. As I headed for the floor, a thought occurred to me.

"Yeah, they would have somebody across the street keeping an eye on the front door, wouldn't they?"

I wasn't sure how long I was out. I had an impression of floating in some vast, cathedral-like space. Then I opened my eyes.

I lay in the middle of the street. I stood up and looked around. It was still night and I was alone.

An orange, flickering glow came from somewhere. I turned my head to the west and saw fire. In the middle of the street, from the looks of it.

I walked toward it. Off to both sides of me, the garbage had really piled up along the sidewalks. There was movement in it, too. Rats. Blunt-snouted, scaly-tailed critters the size of cocker spaniels writhed around in the stinking piles.

When I got closer to the fire and the light cast more illumination, I noticed something else in the garbage piles. Human bodies. Men, women and a few children. Some in better shape than others. I realized these were the people who had been killed in the Halloween Parade Massacre, and in the attack on the baseball stadium.

I was now close enough to see the light's source, which was a huge bonfire burning right in the middle of the street. Behind it towered the immense figure, nearly as tall as the buildings on either side, of a man with a horned steer's head.

All around, men in leather masks danced and cavorted. Jumping in the air and twisting their bodies. Some of them stood to the side, banging baseball bats and chains on cars or pavement in a repetitive, staccato rhythm.

I looked at the buildings, figuring that the noise and the light would have people at their windows. The windows were darkened, but the fire gave off enough light to reveal a man in a leather mask standing behind each one of them.

I looked toward the fire again. The silhouette of another man, one with long hair and a robe, stood in front of it and pointed at me. The animated corpse of Friedrich K. Schulze.

The giant figure with the steer's head began to move toward me with long, slow strides. I turned to run.

Down the middle of the street, I went. Arms pumping. Chest burning, I tried to suck enough air to keep going. It became harder to breathe because of the searing heat. I realized the buildings on either side of me were bursting into flames as I passed them. Soon, the fire would overtake me and burn the whole city to the ground.

Standing in the street ahead of me was another man. When I got close and saw the raw, bloody wound between his fat thighs, I knew it was George Hoffman — his skull caved in and his empty eye sockets glistening.

"You can laugh at me if you want," Hoffman said. "But I know what I seen."

And then I was back in Cabot's basement, the night I went there to get Paul Bacon. Something was coming for me in the darkness. Something bigger than any man. Making that keening wail.

"AAAAaaaaaAAAAAAaaaaaaAAA!"

I reached the stairs and began running up them. The thing was closing in on me. I was running ... so ... goddamn ... slow ... like I was underwater.

Little by little, the blackness lightened, becoming a muddy grey. And I gradually realized that I was in pain. An intense, grinding ache in every part of my body.

I opened my eyes. Everything was bright and shiny. White curtains surrounded me. I detected a kind of low-level bustling going on around me.

Sister Pilar sat in a folding chair, watching me.

"The emergency room," she said as soon as my eyes settled on her. "One of Michael's volunteer patrols investigated the broken door and found you lying in a puddle of your own puke. I'm curious. When I told you to find Cabot, what part of that did you interpret as 'get drunk and get yourself beat up?' "

I looked down at my body. Four limbs? Check. I guess the fact that I could see meant my eyes were still in their sockets. I made a mental note to check that my junk was still attached as soon as Pilar was gone.

"You know what?" Pilar said. "You really can be a motherfucking pain in the ass sometimes."

I didn't answer. I was trying to get a fix on something. What the goon in the leather mask who walked in behind me had said as soon as the beating started in earnest.

Had I hallucinated that, too? No. He'd said it.

"Rock and roll, baby."

FILE 15

FROM BILLY'S PAPERS

The kid and I bounced around for a while. We wound up in a ratty little Texas town near the Mexican border, attached to an attraction called "Big Rhonda's Live Girl Titty-Tacular!" As you might surmise, desperation had long since settled in.

We pitched our tent in the parking lot of the former Shriners' lodge in which Big Rhonda and her retinue had set up shop. Said retinue included a pair of identical twin mud wrestlers and a woman capable of shooting ping pong balls from her vagina with surprising accuracy.

Rhonda decided that a resident freak show might contribute to the general air of bohemian decadence to which she aspired. My only goal was to earn enough money to get us on the road again. After several weeks, even that humble aspiration began to resemble an opulent daydream.

I was less than pleased when Big Rhonda approached me with an ultimatum. She'd concluded that her show and mine were too thematically dissimilar and informed that I was required to "sexy it up" should I wish to continue our association. After pondering the substantial quandary of how one sexies up a display of desiccated and deformed animals, I settled on the manatee. I recalled a bit of oceangoing lore I had once read concerning sailors at sea for lengthy periods of time, brains addled by sexual deprivation and grog, mistaking manatees for mermaids.

I placed a new placard on the manatee display, renaming it a "mermaid" and describing it as "the oceanic temptress who drove sailors of old mad with desire." I considered it a stretch, and was surprised when an emaciated, pathetically drunk man who had stumbled across the parking lot from Big Rhonda's show offered me $200 for half an hour alone with the mermaid.

It's a troubling fact of life, what a man will assent to in the throes of financial desperation. In a further ironic twist, my assent would aggravate rather than alleviate that desperation. Because it was precisely while I was standing outside the tent, trying to mentally block out the appalling groans emanating from within, that the police staged a raid on Big Rhonda's for legal violations too numerous to recount here.

The kid and I were charged with "facilitating sexual contact with a dead manatee."

"That's an actual charge?" I asked the district judge.

"It happens more often than you'd think," he replied.

So it transpired that I wound up in a jail cell, contemplating the grim prospect of a fine we couldn't possibly pay, when things became even worse. The public defender gave me some shocking news.

Police going through our tent during the raid had located a large bundle of cocaine. This being a border town, they didn't take that kind of thing lightly and the kid and I both faced hard time. The public defender looked disbelieving at my protestations that the cocaine wasn't ours and I had no idea where it had come from.

Later, the guards escorted me to a back room where a slight, bespectacled man with a pencil moustache awaited me. He identified himself as "R9" and informed me it was within his power to extract us from the situation. I voiced my suspicions that he had gotten us into it in the first place, and told him to go fuck himself.

R9 mentioned the kid and the kind of things that befall good-looking, long-haired young men in prisons. I listened to what he had to say.

He told me he wanted the kid and me to work for him. Or more specifically, for an outfit that he described only as "The Agendum."

And thus the kid and I wound up, of all places, back in Batley.

FILE 16

Pilar put me up in the Hope House for a week.

I told myself, and her, that I was there to keep an eye out for her. We both knew that was bullshit. I was useless.

You could say I was lucky. I needed some stitches in my upper lip. I had a broken nose, but no other fractures. I guessed my assailants figured, rightly, that they had limited time to pound on me before somebody spotted the broken door. They made their point and then got out quick.

For the record, my junk was still attached. Just barely. One of them, probably in retaliation for the stunt on the stairs, gave me a good shot in the nuts. Let's just say "black" and "grapefruit-sized," and leave it at that.

Aside from that, the damage assessment consisted of bruises starting with my face and extending pretty much uninterrupted to the soles of my feet.

Pilar gave me a cane for the first couple of days to help me get to the bathroom and back when necessary. She brought me food and drink. She moved a TV into my room and stayed with me while we watched movies. She had good taste in movies, for a nun.

She wouldn't let me have any booze or cigars, but that was OK. I didn't really want them right then. Besides, the doctors gave me some painkillers that were enjoyable in their own right.

She told me The Slain appeared to be lying low. You could say the whole city was lying low. Pretty much every public event, from high school sporting events to garden club meetings, had been canceled. Batley was looking like a ghost town, she said. After work, people would barricade themselves in their homes.

One activity on the increase was Michael's patrols. After the attack on the March for Batley, people were signing up by scores.

At Michael's suggestion, residents and business owners had taken to displaying signs in their windows. They were simple pieces of paper, with the Order of Gabriel wings on them. Michael said they sent a message.

Michael himself stopped by to see me the day after the beating. I was still woozy from the painkillers. He brought me a bottle of whiskey, giving Pilar an apologetic smile and saying: "For when you get better, OK slugger?"

Pilar told me afterward that she'd let Michael know about the threatening note, and he made sure a patrol kept an eye on the Hope House at all times.

After a few days, I cut myself off the painkillers. I wished I had more time to recover, but that's just not how things were.

I forced myself to get out of bed. While the movies played on the TV, I paced back and forth just to use my muscles, first with and then without the cane.

The morning of day seven, I left. Pilar brought me a cup of coffee, a bagel with cream cheese and a slice of cantaloupe for breakfast. I thanked her. Then I gathered up the bottle of whiskey from Michael and the clothes that Pilar brought from my apartment in a big trash bag, and left the bedroom where I'd been staying.

I walked down the stairs, then went looking for Pilar to say goodbye. I opened the door to the main meeting room and ... oh shit.

Pilar was presiding over a meeting of the C.C. support group, which let out with a few low whistles along with exclamations of "Damn!" and "Somebody beat that boy like a rented mule!"

"Sister, I gotta..." I started to say.

"Why don't you sit down and join us?"

"Sister. I appreciate everything. Really. But I just can't deal with this now. I'm sorry."

I shut the door and started down the hallway. Someone called my name. I turned. Thelma Pointer.

"Things getting pretty heavy?" she asked. "There's more to it than you think. I've got a message for you."

I held up my hands.

"Look, lady ..."

"Would you quit with this 'lady' shit? It's me. Dom."

"... I've got a lot on my mind right now. I really can't handle this. I just can't."

I hurried out the front door. My apartment was walking distance, and I headed in that direction to drop off my stuff and take a shower. Then it was time to quit messing around. I needed to see Safeerah.

Ninety minutes later, a bell rang above the door when I entered the small, plain shop tucked into the middle of a nondescript strip mall. I waited. Soon afterward, a slim young woman in a headscarf came out of a curtained doorway behind the counter.

"What you need?" she asked.

"I'm thinking," I did some estimation in my head, "five bags. Probably won't need that many, but just to be on the safe side."

Safeerah arched an eyebrow.

"Five bags? Must be a big case."

I walked into City Hall. An older guy worked the metal detector at this time of day. He just gave me a nod and motioned me past. Good. That night, a meeting of the Public Safety Committee meeting was scheduled. Even the kid with the flattop probably wasn't dumb enough to fall for the pocket knife ruse twice in one day.

Not that I was planning to use the flask in my jacket at the moment. It was a little early in the day, even for me.

I walked into the tax office. A plump, bespectacled woman behind the counter regarded me with a sour expression. I pulled one of the paper bags Safeerah had given me out of my jacket pocket and set it on the counter.

"This is going to be a pain in my patootie, isn't it?" the woman asked.

"Sorry. If you want, I can just leave and take this with me," I said, starting to slide the bag off the counter.

"You put that back!"

She grabbed it and withdrew a small, dun-colored cube. Then she popped it in her mouth, briefly closing her eyes in an expression of borderline religious bliss.

By my admittedly unscientific calculations, Safeerah's peanut butter fudge is approximately 100 times more addicting than heroin. I kept my source secret from the countless front-office employees who'd begged me to tell them. Knowledge is power.

The information I was about to request was public, and supposedly available to anyone who came in the office and asked for it. But since the local records system was apparently designed by a brain-damaged Neanderthal during a mescaline binge, it was good to have some office workers helping you out. And I wasn't above greasing the wheels, so to speak.

As it turned out, however, it wouldn't have been necessary. All I had to do was mention George Hoffman, and that set the women in the tax office buzzing. He'd been in the week before last and paid off every cent of back taxes on his property. Next thing you know, he turned up dead. Another of life's bitter ironies, although nobody in the office seemed particularly grief-stricken that he was gone.

Next, I climbed the stairs to the city administration office. Actually, it was a suite consisting of a wide open area with most of the major city offices branching off it, including Buck's. His secretary, Linda Goldberg, was holding court at a desk in the middle.

She did a pretty good job at stifling the gasp when she looked up and saw my face. Even after a week, I still looked pretty banged up.

I asked her if Buck was in. She said he was coming in later that day, in anticipation of that night's Public Safety Committee meeting. They'd asked her to put in some overtime sending out a reassuring form letter in response to an avalanche of panicky inquiries from city residents about recent events.

She didn't look pleased. She looked even less pleased when I told her what I wanted, though she lightened up when I put not one, but two bags of Safeerah's fudge on her desk.

The city's spending records came in two forms. One was headache-inducing microfiche, loaded on a grimy viewer in a small, bare room way in the back of the suite. The other was cardboard boxes containing reams of paper, most of which had a fine coat of dust that made me sneeze when I went through them.

Linda brought out what I needed and even offered to get me a cup of coffee, which I accepted. Safeerah's fudge was working its mysterious mojo. Then I settled in, going over columns of numbers and dense paragraphs full of the strange moon-man language that people feel obliged to use in official documents to show just how gol'-danged important it all is.

I was in there for a couple of hours when Linda showed up. She said Ernie Bixler was on the phone and wanted to talk to me.

"What does he want?" I asked.

Linda rolled her eyes.

"Who knows? He's out of town. He called up and wanted to know what's going on. I mentioned that you're here. He said he wanted to talk to you. Would you like me to transfer it in here?"

She pointed to a battered-looking old phone in the corner. I said that would work for me. Linda left the room and I waited. The phone rang.

"Ernie?" I said as I picked it up.

"They used me."

"Fine, thanks for asking. How are you?"

"I don't have time for this. I think … I think they used me."

I asked him to hold on a second. I closed the door and went back on the line.

"Ernie, where are you?"

"I'm at a hunting lodge in Haddon County. My father used to bring me here every year. I was always so happy here."

His voice had a quavering tone, as though he was fighting to get control over himself. For a few seconds, he just breathed into the phone, not saying anything. Then the words came out in a rush.

"When I started doing my radio show, people listened to me for the first time in my life. That's all I wanted. For people to listen to me. Then I ran for office and I won and people treated me like I counted for something. But I think they used me."

"Who used you? Ernie, I think this conversation would be a lot more productive if you said something that makes sense."

He told me he was planning to stay out of town until he figured out what to do. Then he told me he'd said all he was going to say and hung up. I went back to work.

At lunch, I grabbed a cheeseburger and another cup of coffee at a sandwich shop around the corner. On the way back, I picked up a pen and a pad of paper at a corner grocery to jot down some notes.

I also swung by the police station. I'd memorized Sanderson's schedule and knew he'd be out. I checked in with Officer X, and told him (or her) I needed him to check something out for me. He did. I told him I owed him one. Then I went back to the little room in City Hall and continued my research.

By the time I was done, the various city administrators and support staff were putting their jackets and hats on, and preparing to head out. Linda looked like she was hard at work, though.

I asked her about it, and she said she would be at the Public Safety Committee meeting that night. Since there seemed little point in going home for a couple of hours then coming back, she was going to finish up some work.

"Please tell me you're getting overtime for this," I said.

"I am," she said.

She still didn't look happy. I told her that Ernie Bixler wouldn't be there that night, and that cheered her up a little.

I got to my car and checked my watch. Ty, I knew, would be giving one of his Farm Team classes at Moondog Organic Produce. I had enough time to drive down, talk to him and make it back for the committee meeting.

I drove south, leaving the city and then the small ring of surrounding suburbs. The evening sun, just taking on that mellow autumn quality, shone orange on the rolling hills. The leaves on the trees covering them weren't turning color yet, but would be before long. I passed into farm country, with fields full of cornstalks interrupting the woods, dotted with barns, houses, and silos.

After a while, I pulled off the main road onto a smaller one. Then one that was smaller still, driving carefully because it was only wide enough to accommodate one vehicle and the trees lining it didn't provide much visibility.

Then the trees were gone and the road led into a wide, open valley. Immediately to my left was a white, wooden farmhouse. I was surprised to see about 40 or so cars, vans, and pickups parked alongside the road or on the lawn. I recognized Ty's pickup among them.

I pulled in, got out of the car and walked around the house.

In front of me stretched a big field. Off to the right, fences marked smaller squares, where a variety of plants grew, some attached to stakes.

In the field in front of me, a bunch of people bustled around, setting up for some kind of event. From the looks of things, it would be a big one.

Several guys with hammers were putting the finishing touches on a bandstand. A couple of women painted decorative leaves on a sign in front of a wooden booth that read "Organic Food and All-Natural Fruit Juice." And on top of a rise, a burly, younger guy carted a wheelbarrow full of softball-sized stones so an older one with long white hair and a beard could arrange them in a large circle.

I approached the women painting the sign. Both were in their 20s. One wore a peasant blouse and long skirt. The other in a tie-dyed T-shirt and cut-off shorts.

The one with the tie-dye looked up, gave the start at the sight of my beat-up face that I was starting to get used to, then forced herself to smile.

"Are you here to help set up?"

"Set up?"

"For the Faerie Festival?"

"I'm here to see Ty Bacon. Any idea where he is?"

She pointed toward a rust-colored barn.

"On the other side of the barn," she said. "The pavilion."

I walked around the barn, and saw another structure consisting of a wooden roof held up by posts. The kind used for picnics in parks.

When I saw what was going on, I stopped and just gaped. Ty was talking to about a dozen young men sitting in a semi-circle on the ground. They were a pretty hard-looking bunch. I didn't see Ezekiel.

What surprised me was Ty himself. He wore a get-up that made him look like a bit player in some medieval costume drama. A vest of some coarse cloth with no shirt underneath. Knee-high leather boots and leggings.

His face was painted white, like a mime. When I got closer, I saw that it was a skull design, with dark circles around the eyes and lines at his mouth representing bared teeth.

Even more surprising than what he was wearing was what he was doing. Even when he taught the martial arts classes in his garage, it was rare for Ty to say more than a few sentences at a time. And those tended to come out in a tone so soft it bordered on a mumble.

But he was talking to this crew in a loud, singsong voice, gesturing with his arms like some amped-up Pentecostal preacher.

"It all comes down to FEAR!" he said, shouting the last word while pounding his right fist into his left palm.

"Fear," he went on "is about control. If you fear an opponent, he's got you trapped. You're done before the fight's even started. It's not about acquiring courage. It's not about adding anything. It's about subtraction. You discard the things you don't need. And you don't need fear."

He gestured toward the fields.

"What we're setting up for here is an observation of Samhain. For ancient people, it was a festival of the dead. But it wasn't frightening to them! Oh no! See, these days, we separate ourselves from death. We hide from it. We shut it away in back rooms and let professionals deal with it and pretend it's not there. But for ancient people, death was all around them. They accepted it as part of life!"

At this, he raised his arms as if encompassing all the fields around him. Then he went on.

"Samhain was once the most important feast of the year for the Celts. It marked the harvest. But it was also a time when they could commune with the dead. They welcomed the dead and honored them, just as you'd welcome an old relative. They acknowledged the dead and knew they'd one day be among them, so death held no fear for them!"

At that point, he looked over and spotted me. The young guys at his feet followed his gaze. The looks they directed at me weren't friendly.

Ty smiled for a second, then looked shocked.

"Holy shit!" he said. "I heard they jumped you. Are you alright?"

"Yeah," I said. "Sister Pilar took good care of me. Not like I had any good looks to ruin."

Ty turned back toward the young guys and said "I guess we can wrap it up for today. Everybody got a ride home?"

They nodded, some looking sulky about the end of the sermon, and wandered off.

"You never give us a talk like that," I said.

"Yeah. These guys — they're young. They've been through some bad times. I try to give them some guidance. Maybe I get a little carried away sometimes."

I made an exaggerated show of checking out his costume.

"New look for you?"

He gave a sheepish grin.

"Samhain's not 'til the end of the month, but I try to get in character. I'm one of the dead, back to pay a visit."

"Pretty heavy for a faerie festival. I pictured bobbing for apples and hayrides."

"When the public's here, things are more low-key. But at night, some of the people who hang around here hold our own celebration. We're a little more ... old-fashioned."

"I thought Luanne was the one who's into costumes and folklore."

"The fairie lore? To tell you the truth, I'm the one who got her interested in it. I don't talk about it a lot. You know, you say the word 'fairie' and guys laugh. They don't understand what it's about."

Ty told me how when he and Luanne first left Schulze's complex, he felt dazed and disoriented. He'd never really felt like he fit in. And after their experience locked away in the clinic, he felt even more alienated form the world around him.

He started reading up on European folklore. And what really stuck with him was the stories of changeling children.

Those were children who'd been stolen away by the fairies to their land. A lot of times, so the stories had it, they'd leave their own children in place of the stolen ones. Those fairie children would grow up to be strange and fierce and frightening.

"I thought about what it would be like for those kids," Ty said. "They find themselves in a world where everything's strange to them. But people think they're strange. I guess, I don't know, those stories made me feel less alone or something."

He looked down at his feet, like he felt awkward. Then he looked back at me.

"Anyway, I'm glad you finally made it down here for one of our sessions. You're welcome to train with us any time. Any particular reason why you came here today?"

"Yeah, now that you mention it. I was looking for Ezekiel."

"Ezekiel? Why?"

"I just needed to talk to him. Any idea where he is?"

"He hasn't been coming around lately. That's how it is with these guys. They come and go. It's pretty informal. I understand he's been staying at his grandparents' house."

He gave me an address. I thanked him and turned to leave.

"Feel like hanging around?" Ty asked. "I'll be here late helping set up for the festival. We could always use an extra hand."

"I've got to get back for a Public Safety Committee meeting," I said. "Have to take a raincheck."

I turned toward the barn. A man stood there, watching me and Ty. Draped over his shoulders was a long green cape. On his face was an elaborate mask made to look like it was composed of leaves. He turned and disappeared around the side of the barn.

"Who's that?" I asked.

Ty smiled.

"He likes to get in character, too. That's the Green Man. He runs the show around here."

"Yeah, but who is he?"

Ty's smile widened and took on a mischievous quality.

"The Green Man," he said. "Until Samhain's over, that's who he is."

The sun was setting as I walked to my car. The crew in the field had abandoned their various tasks and joined the guys working on the big, stone circle. They planned on a bonfire, from the looks of it. A big one. I started my car and drove off.

I got to City Hall a little early. The evening was unseasonably warm and I considered leaving my jacket in my car. But then how would I sneak my flask in? I met Luanne on the sidewalk out front. Paul was with her.

"My God!" she said, when she saw me. "I heard about what happened to you. Are you OK?"

"I'll live."

I looked at Paul and smiled, as much as the stitches in my mouth would permit..

"You're bringing him to sit through a municipal committee meeting?" I asked. "You know, that meets the legal definition of child abuse in some states."

As we walked up the front steps, she explained that she'd picked him up from school where he'd had a karate club meeting, and had to go straight to City Hall. Earlier that day she'd called Buck, who offered to let Paul use his office to do some homework.

I looked around, and was surprised at the number of other people showing up. About a dozen were heading up the front steps and into the main entrance. The public safety committee meetings were always open to anyone who wanted to attend, but they weren't ordinarily what you'd call the hottest ticket in town.

The kid with the flat-top manned the metal detector. I waved Luanne and Paul ahead of me, then watched them dump out their change and anything else that would set off the detector and walk through.

My turn next. I took off my jacket. My pocketknife set off the metal detector, then ... Eh, you know the drill.

I walked up the steps to the meeting room and was surprised again to see at least 50 people already present — milling around and talking to each other. Becky Gaffigan was there, keyed up like a ferret on meth, talking to anyone who'd tolerate her.

"Do you really think Cabot's behind it?" she said in a hushed voice. "He has powers, you know. If it's really him, guns won't do any good. He's released whatever he was keeping in that house!"

We still had about 15 minutes before the meeting's scheduled start. I wandered over to Buck's office. Paul sat at Buck's desk, textbook laid out in front of him, looking around with wide eyes like he was in the Oval Office or something.

"You've got the run of the place," Buck was telling him with a kindly smile. "The bottle of brandy's in the bottom drawer. Help yourself."

"Just kidding," he added quickly as he caught the look on Luanne's face. "But seriously, could you do me a favor and pick up any calls that come in on my phone? Just write the information down on that pad. People call me day and and night to complain about one thing or another. The burdens of office. You'll find out. I've got a feeling you'll be in charge some day."

He winked at Luanne. We talked a little bit, with Buck giving me the by-now-obligatory questions about how I was doing after taking a look at my face, and the two of them filling me in on what had been going on in town during the week I was laid up.

It wasn't much more than what Pilar had told me. The Slain hadn't done anything. Michael's patrols were keeping an eye on the streets and everybody else in the city was waiting and scared.

Then Buck and Luanne and I wandered over to the meeting room. Michael stood outside. He was talking to Jack Lange, who I noticed wore a T-shirt under his sportcoat. Lange got a startled look on his face when he saw Luanne, probably recalling the ass-kicking he'd recently suffered at her hands, and ducked inside the meeting room. Buck followed him.

Michael must have picked up on the puzzled looks on our faces, because he immediately started to explain.

"Lange wanted to tag along," he said. "He's kicked in a lot of money to the citizen patrols, so I said he could. He even got us these spiffy T-shirts."

He opened his jacket to show us his black T-shirt with the Order of Gabriel wings on it. Above the wings, it said "Order of Gabriel." Underneath it said "Citizens Patrol. Batley, Pennsylvania. Protectors of the City."

"Protectors of the City?" I said. "Sounds like you should have your own line of action figures."

"Lange's idea," Michael said.

"What's up with all the people?"

"That was Lange's idea too. He had some fliers printed up and distributed around the city. Guess he liked the idea of having a crowd out here for our big debut."

He moved his head in closer and lowered his voice.

"For the record, I know he's an asshole. But he might be useful."

"I guess there's a first time for everything," I said.

Then the three of us headed inside. Lou Evans, Susan Rothman, Burt Chandler, and Linda Goldberg were already seated at the dais. They looked uncomfortable, not used to facing a standing-room-only crowd.

Lange sat up front with a group of five guys, all of whom were wearing the Order of Gabriel T-shirts under windbreakers. The group included Drew Schicklgruber and Tim Rourke. The other five glanced around self-consciously. But Lange leaned back in his chair with his legs splayed out in front of him, arms folded, looking very pleased with himself. Michael walked over and sat down with them.

Buck stood up in the front of the room, and asked the crowd to take their seats. He started off by explaining that Ernie Bixler couldn't show up because of a family emergency, so he'd chair the meeting. He also said Sanderson had bowed out to help with the increased police patrols he'd been sending out lately.

Chandler kicked things off with a report on the garbage. He said the last of the backlog had been cleaned up and carted off to the landfill. For now, the city was still renting out the trucks, but he had some people in his department shopping around for permanent replacements.

Sue Rothman said the strain on the police department was also putting a strain on emergency medical services. A lot of the calls they responded to were in rough neighborhoods. If there was a shooting or a stabbing, police would go in first and secure the area before the emergency medical technicians got in.

Lately though, the overstretched police were taking longer to get there, which was playing hell with her department's response times. Evans spoke up then, saying firefighters were having pretty much the same problem. Buck said he'd talk to the other council members, and maybe come up with some interim solutions.

Then Buck asked Michael if he had anything to contribute.

Michael said he did. Everybody in the room visibly perked up as he stood.

"We know the police have a lot on their hands," Michael said. "So we put together this citizen group to help them keep an eye on things."

Lange stood.

"We're going to be out there fighting those bastards!" Lange said. "Remember, we're putting ourselves in harm's way to protect you and your families. Keep that in mind if any of you feel like giving us an attitude."

"Jack!" Michael said. "I'm talking here. You mind?"

Lange clearly did, but he sat down anyway.

"Jack is pretty enthusiastic about this, as you can see," Michael said. "He's right. Our goal is to protect you. But we're going to need your help to do it. We're all part of this effort, together. Now let me explain a little bit about what we have in mind."

He told Rothman and Evans he'd like to sit down with them soon, to see how his citizen patrol volunteers could help them.

Then he walked over to a poster-sized map of the city set up on an easel, and said he would explain some of the plans he had set up for the citizen patrols.

"I've been working with some of the folks over in the planning office," he said. "We want to make sure that the major routes in and out of the city are under observation at all times. We've also been studying some shortcuts The Slain might use to get in and out, like the night they attacked the patrons of Liam O'Shaunnessy's."

He pointed out where different routes had been marked out in colored magic marker.

"I'm pleased to say that we now have more than 200 volunteers on our roster. For organization purposes, I've divided them into four teams: Team Raphael, Team Uriel, Team Raguel and Team Remiel."

Lange said "Ah! The names of Archangels."

"That's right," Michael said. "I thought they would be easier to remember that way."

"Yeah," I said. "Team Raguel really rolls off the tongue."

The people on the dais shot me irritated looks.

"Alright," Buck said, looking my way. "I guess we might as well hear from you next. I know you've been under the weather lately. Will you be able to do this?"

"Never better."

"Glad to hear it. Your boss told me you've been investigating the recent incidents in the city, with an eye toward finding Gary Cabot."

"Yeah," I said, and glanced toward Michael. "I have reason to believe he's tied in with The Slain."

"I think that's a safe assumption," Buck said. "Any progress?"

"While I was laid up, I made a few phone calls. I had a chance to talk to Tim over there." I nodded in Rourke's direction. "It appears that when Cabot was living here in town, contrary to appearances, he wasn't living alone."

Buck looked over at Tim for confirmation. Tim stared at the floor for a moment, as if embarrassed. Then he spoke.

"I delivered groceries to his house. I didn't want to, you understand, but a small businessman like myself can't afford to turn away customers."

"It's OK, Tim," Buck said. "So what about these deliveries?"

"Well, I never really thought much about him. Just delivered the groceries, and he'd mail me a check every month. But he was getting more food than one person could eat. Enough food for at least four people."

"Toward the end, I was keeping an eye on his house," I cut in. "He had short-term visitors, for an evening or overnight. But aside from Paul Bacon, I didn't see anyone else coming and going. There were no stockpiles of food there, so it was going somewhere."

"Interesting," Buck said. "What else?"

"I'm looking into some other leads. But that pretty much sums it up."

"That's all you have?" Buck asked. "Some grocery orders?"

He shook his head slightly, then glanced at his watch

"I received a letter the day before last from the governor, pledging his support," Buck said. "The state government isn't in great financial shape now, but he's looking into getting us some assistance from the State Police. I'm sorry, I seem to have left the letter on my desk. Linda, would you mind?"

Linda said she wouldn't, and walked out of the room.

"I have something to ask."

That was Luanne, standing up at her seat and addressing the room.

"In all this talk about Citizen Patrols and protecting the city, I haven't heard anything about the homeless population. The Council of Churches is doing what it can, but we don't have the resources to keep track of them, or house them all. We need to make some kind of arrangements to protect them."

"I think I can handle this one," Lange said. "Look, doll, we've got our hands full just looking out for all the law-abiding, tax-paying citizens of this city. We can't be wasting resources babysitting a bunch of deadbeats who don't contribute anything to the community. That's just the way it is. Anything else?"

"Yeah," Luanne said. "You're the load your mother should have swallowed."

The room let out a collective gasp. Lange was on his feet.

"Listen to me, you little whore!" he yelled. "Maybe you haven't noticed, but things are changing in this town! We're providing security, and that means we're calling the shots! If you don't learn to show a little respect, you're going to find yourself in big trouble!"

Luanne was pissed. She clenched her jaw and her face was already turning red. Before she could say anything, though, Michael stood and got right in front of Lange. Lange's not short, but Michael still towered over him.

"You. Apologize. Now," Michael said, his voice soft and menacing.

Lange stared up at him. His King of the Room vibe was gone, but he wasn't backing down yet.

"Apologize?" Lange said. "Maybe you don't realize who you're talking to, but …"

Michael grabbed the lapels of Lange's sportcoat and yanked them hard, nearly taking Lange off his feet and pulling his face close to his own. The roomful of people gasped again.

"I know exactly who you are," Michael said, his voice still low and measured. "You're a worthless piece of shit who's about to get his ass stomped unless he apologizes. Right. Fucking. Now."

Michael let go. Lange, face red as a dog's hard-on, looked at Luanne and gulped.

"I'm sorry," he said. Then he left the room as quick as he could without breaking into a run.

I've gotta say, I've seen people look more displeased than Luanne did at that moment.

Michael turned to the five guys in their Order of Gabriel shirts, who were looking very stunned.

"I guess now's as good a time as any to bring this up," Michael told them. "I want to make one thing very clear about the Citizen's Patrol. Our job is to protect the people of this city. Period. Whatever kind of personal shit you've got going on, leave it behind when you're on Citizen's Patrol. I hear of any of you — any of you — using this organization for your own agenda, you're going to have a problem with me. And trust me, you don't want to have a problem with me. Is that clear?"

I've never seen such eager nodding before in my life.

Michael turned to Luanne and opened his mouth. Whatever he was about to say got cut off when Linda came running back into the room. She was out of breath, and looked ready to cry.

"My God! Help! The boy!"

I'm not sure who ran out first, in the frenzy of people hurrying from the room and toward Buck's office. All I remember during the rush into the administrative office suite was the sound of Luanne's panting voice saying again and again "Oh no! Please! Oh no! Please!"

And then we were standing outside Buck's office. Me, Lou Evans, Michael, Luanne and Buck. So were the guys in Michael's Citizen's Patrol. A handful of people from the meeting room were behind us, too, Becky Gaffigan among them. No time to worry about that now.

The lights were off. Paul stood in front of the desk, silhouetted by a small fire burning on top of it, made from a pile of papers.

Paul let out a long, low growl. Then he spoke. His voice sounded vacant, whispery, and strangely high-pitched.

"I am The One Who Takes," he said. "I have come back. I will fuck you all as you are dying, and savor the delicious warmth of your flowing blood on my cock."

"Paul?" Luanne said, choked. She took a step toward him. Paul raised his arms and a jet of flame shot out in front of him. We all jumped back. I realized he was holding a lighter in front of an aerosol can.

"I am The One Who Takes!" Paul yelled, his voice a ragged howl. Then he sprang for Luanne. He caught her off-guard and knocked her to the floor.

As Luanne screamed, he clawed at her face, foaming at the mouth and making animal snarls.

I stepped in, but Michael was there first. He lifted Paul off Luanne and threw him down on the floor. He pinned the boy with a knee on his chest, keeping his face out of range as Paul continued to snarl and squirm and claw.

Michael reached under his leather jacket and came out with the black knife I'd seen earlier. Luanne, who'd now gotten to her knees, screamed.

"No! Don't hurt him!"

"I'm not going to hurt him!" Michael yelled. "Stay back!"

Michael bent down, held Paul by the neck and shouted in his face.

"I command you, leave this boy alone! In the name of all that is holy, I cast you out!"

He pressed the flat side of the knife against Paul's forehead. As the boy continued to buck and howl, Michael looked up at me.

"In God we trust, all others pay cash," he said.

Paul stopped moving, and went limp and quiet. Michael let go of his neck and climbed off him.

Paul looked around, sluggish and disoriented as though he just woke up from a deep sleep.

"What ... what's going on?" he asked.

Luanne started crying and hugged him, hard.

Lou Evans stepped forward and took Paul by the shoulder. He held up three fingers in front of his face.

"How many fingers am I holding up, son?"

"Three, why?"

Lou suggested I find Susan Rothman. I hurried back toward the meeting room. The entire crowd was now gathered in the hallway outside, ignoring Rothman and Chandler's attempts to tell them the meeting was over and shoo them out.

This was largely due to Becky Gaffigan, who was giving the astonished crowd a breathless account of what she'd seen in Buck's office.

"I tell you, that boy was possessed!" she said, reedy voice echoing off the surrounding marble. "It was The One Who Takes! The god The Slain worship! Michael drove him right out!"

I caught Rothman's eye and inclined my head toward the hallway leading to Buck's office. She got the hint and headed that way.

The others caught it and converged on me, demanding to know what happened.

"Nothing," I told them. "The boy was just feeling sick, that's all. He's going to be OK. No big deal."

Their voices rose in protest and they began crowding in on the hallway, intending to head back there en masse to take a look for themselves.

"No!" I said. "There's a sick kid in there! They're taking a look at him and they need space! Back off, please!"

Suddenly they all went silent. I didn't realize I was that persuasive.

Turned out I wasn't. I realized Michael was standing behind me. Just the sight of him sent the small crowd into awestruck stillness.

"He's right," Michael said. "Everything's under control. If you all crowd back there, you're going to create a safety hazard. There's nothing more to see tonight. I'm going to ask you all to please go home."

"What happened?" a young woman asked.

"Was the boy really possessed?" an older man asked.

Michael exhaled deeply, then reached a hand up to massage the back of his neck. He looked drained.

And that, an unspoken confirmation, seemed to stun them more than anything Michael could have said. Nobody spoke. Becky Gaffigan began weeping softly.

"Listen," Michael said. They listened.

"What specifically happened back there doesn't matter," he said. "What matters is what I'm about to tell you. I was hoping I could spare you this. But there isn't time. We don't have that luxury. The truth is that there's a battle coming. A battle for the soul of this town. And we can win it. I say 'we' because you've all got a role to play in this.

"But you're going to have to be brave. And you're going to have to be strong. And there will be times when I tell you to do something and you're just going to have to trust me and do it. Do you understand?"

He looked directly at Becky, who was trying to get her crying under control. She nodded.

"Can you be brave?" he asked. "Can you do that for me?"

A note of tenderness had crept into his voice. She managed a little smile and nodded again.

"Good," Michael said. "For now, go home. You'll hear from us soon about what you can do to help. Look out for each other. If you do that, we can win this."

Quietly, looking scared but uplifted, they headed toward the exit. Michael and I walked back to the office where the others waited.

A little while later, Michael, Luanne, and I stood in the room where earlier I'd been going through the records. The door was shut, and the old overhead fluorescent lighting fixtures gave off an illumination at once glaring and dimly inadequate.

In another room off the office suite, Susan Rothman and Lou Evans were giving Paul a look-over. Lou had already demonstrated his professional expertise in Buck's office by handily beating the flame out with his jacket, then dousing the smoldering scraps of paper with a pot of cold black sludge that somebody had helpfully failed to empty from the office suite's unplugged coffee maker earlier that day.

I caught Buck, a bit of a neat freak, wincing slightly at the sight of his desktop when it was all over.

Paul had gradually emerged from his sluggish trance, becoming awake but confused. One second, he said, he'd been doing his homework at Buck's desk. The next, he'd been lying on the floor watching a bunch of panicky people scuttle around a dark, smoky room and demand to know if he was alright.

Susan Rothman asked Luanne if Paul had any history of seizures. Luanne said no, but she paused first. I could tell Susan noticed it.

I suggested that we get Paul to an emergency room, pronto. Rothman and Evans both agreed.

Luanne, unable to entirely suppress the panicky desperation in her voice, said she didn't think it was necessary.

Evans and Rothman looked about to argue. But I noticed Michael and Buck exchange a glance and a nod.

"I believe it's up to the family, and the boy," Buck said. "He doesn't seem to be in any immediate danger."

Paul, confused as ever, deferred to his sister and consented to the cursory examination in the other room.

Buck, Burt Chandler, and the Citizens Patrol guys asked if anything more was needed from them. Michael said no, reminded those on patrol that night to meet at the staging area at the Community Rec Center in a couple of hours. They all looked relieved to go. None would look directly at Michael, but kept sneaking glances that conveyed varying combinations of awe and fear.

Then Michael motioned Luanne and me into the back room. Luanne immediately turned on Michael.

"What was that? What did you do?" A barely controlled weepy hysteria that I'd never heard from her before was leaking out with her words.

"Guess you'd call it an exorcism," Michael said. "I've had training. A lot of people think it's about doing some kind of ritual. But really, it's more about asserting your will over the entity than anything else. In a very real way, it's like getting control over a vicious dog."

"An exorcism?" I said. "Isn't that a little hokey even by Batley standards?"

"I don't know what else to call it," Michael said. "I can't explain it. I can't tell you whether I'm really casting out an unclean spirit or not. All I know is that in circumstances like this, it sometimes works."

"Should we call Dr. Pigeon?" Luanne asked Michael.

"Dr. Pigeon left town a few days ago," Michael said. "Things are about to get really hot around here. He's a brilliant man. Brave, too. But being in the middle of the shit is not his specialty. We can call him if need be, but we want to avoid that. He's too valuable to lose."

"But what about Paul?" Luanne asked. "Did you cure him?"

"Far from it," Michael said. "Whatever Cabot did to that boy was obviously very damaging. This looks like something far more serious than Dr. Pigeon would be able to handle in outpatient treatment. I know you don't want to hear this, Luanne, but the boy may have to go away for a while. For his own safety and for your family's."

Luanne looked as if she was about to cry. I glanced back and forth between her and Michael.

"So she knows..." I started.

"About Doctor Pigeon and my organization?" Michael said. "Yes. I told you before, I suspect both of you are going to have very important roles to play before long. She knows everything you do."

"So she knows jack shit."

Michael rolled his eyes.

"We've been through this," he said. "I've already revealed a lot more than I should have at this point."

"Great," I said. "Since you're on a roll, how about you tell me what's up with that knife?"

He pulled the Godknife out of his belt and laid it on the table.

It was made out of one piece, and primitive looking. Like something you'd see a wax caveman wielding in a natural history museum display.

A sharp elongated triangle formed the blade, topping a narrower and thicker hilt. No ornamentation, unless you count the cloth tape wrapped around the hilt, obviously recent and likely to provide a better grip.

It looked like someone had cut it out of shiny black rock a long time ago, and it bore lots of chips and scratches. Still, it looked suitably strong and sharp.

"What's it made out of?" Luanne asked.

"Obsidian," Michael said. That would explain how he got it past the metal detector.

"It's called The Godknife," he went on. "Don't ask me who originally named it. Nobody knows. It's ancient. Most don't know of its existence. Some collectors of these kinds of things have forked over fortunes, literal fortunes, for forgeries of it.

"One of the forgeries has an entire goddamn temple devoted to it. It's located on the top floor of a skyscraper with very limited access. Old rich men with cancer or impotence pay large sums of money to stand in its presence in the hopes of being cured."

"So what's its backstory?" I asked.

"If I gave you the full story, even leaving out the parts that are pure bullshit, we'd be here for hours. I will tell you this. Until recently, it was in the hands of The Slain, and some good people died to change that. See, they fear this knife. Some will tell you it's all they fear."

"Why are they afraid of it?" Luanne asked.

"Because legend has it that this knife once killed The One Who Takes."

"What do you mean the knife killed him?" I asked. "That's their god, isn't it?"

"The particulars are a little fuzzy," Michael said. "All this supposedly took place before anyone got around to inventing a system of writing. But according to legend, The One Who Takes was once a flesh-and-blood creature. And somebody killed him ... it ... whatever. With this knife."

Michael glanced at his watch, then picked up the knife and tucked it back in the sheath under his jacket.

"I have to be somewhere," Michael said. "I'll be in touch." He left.

Luanne and I checked on Paul, who was still confused, but otherwise apparently fine. The two of them left. I told them I had one more thing to check on.

I went back to Buck's office. Linda was still there, cleaning up. Her hands shook.

"So what happened to the lighter and the can?" I asked her.

She gestured toward a shelf on the wall.

"Mr. Rockbaugh put them there," she said. "I ... I just don't want to touch them. He said he'd take them out in the morning."

I walked over and looked at them. It was an aluminum can of insect repellant. The lighter was one of those old-fashioned metal types, where you spin the wheel and a big flame stays burning as long as you keep the cover open. Perfect for the job.

"Do you smoke, Linda?"

"Haven't for years. They banned smoking in the building. It got to be too much trouble."

"Does Buck?"

"Not that I know of. Why?"

"I'm just wondering where Paul found this lighter. Any idea what a can of insect repellant would be doing in the building?"

She thought for a couple of seconds.

"Now that you mention it, I don't," she said. "Maybe he brought it in with him."

"Yeah, maybe."

As soon as I was out of Linda's sight, I pulled out my flask and took a drink of Scotch. Paul hadn't brought the can into the building. The lighter, either. I'd been there when he and Luanne emptied their pockets and went through the metal detector.

So how did somebody sneak them into the building? I didn't know. But it wouldn't take a genius to get them past security. The pleasant, mellow burn making its way down my gullet was evidence of that.

The kid who works the metal detector was gone when I walked out the front doors. I started down the front steps. Then a female voice called my name.

I turned. It was Veronica, the redhead from Pinky's crew. She looked pale and frightened – a stark contrast from the expression of pouty-lipped self-assurance that usually occupied her face. In fact, she looked like she might start crying any second.

"Veronica? What's wrong?"

"Pinky asked me to find you," she said. "He's in the hospital. I asked around, and heard you might be here."

Not long after, I walked into a semi-private room at Batley Community Hospital. The bed near the door was unoccupied. Pinky reclined in the one by the window.

An elaborate stainless-steel device elevated one of his legs, encased in a cast and metal braces. His face was banged up too, with two black eyes. He held a phone to his ear.

"Yeah, I know you were scared," Pinky said, irritation in his voice. "That's generally the effect when someone shows you a knife and says he's going to cut you if you don't talk. It's kind of the whole point of threatening somebody with a blade."

Pinky was silent for a minute, the annoyance on his face becoming more pronounced.

"Shit. Are you ... crying? Call me back when you pull yourself together."

He hung up the phone, then looked at me.

"Bob," he said. "Nice kid, but I'm starting to think he doesn't have the stones for this line of work."

"He tell them where to find you?" I asked.

"Yeah. I tried to tell him to quit beating himself up over this. If he was going to talk anyway, and he was, he might as well do it sooner rather than later. But he seems to think he should have let them hurt him first as, I don't know, penance or something. I told him if he was dumb enough to do that after all I taught him, I would have gone around and kicked his ass myself."

He leaned back against his pillows.

"These stupid fucking kids."

"The Slain?" I asked.

"Three of those freaks in masks. They came around to the motel where I've been staying."

"Any idea why they came after you?"

"Who knows? Psychos."

"Anything I can do for you?"

"Yeah. Find them. How's that going?"

"Got some leads. Be easier if you cut the shit and told me everything."

"Like what?"

"Your involvement."

He stared straight ahead, his face not registering anything.

"They didn't pick you randomly," I went on. "When I talked to you after the poker game, you tried to point me in the right direction. I figured you'd tell me the rest when the time was right. From the looks of it, I'd say that time has come."

"I have no idea what you're talking about."

"When I told you about the one I took out at the Warm Hearths festival, how'd you know he wasn't carrying ID? I didn't tell the police that."

"You must have mentioned it. Or maybe I just assumed ..."

I stood.

"If you're going to waste my time, I'm outta here."

"Sit down," he said.

I sat. Pinky lay back against the pillows with his eyes closed. He stayed like that for a long time. His eyes remained closed when he began speaking.

"I knew they'd have no identification on them because those were the procedures when I did the job for them."

"What job?"

"Fifteen years ago. When I helped them organize the Halloween Parade Massacre."

FILE 17

Here's the story Pinky told me while I sat by his hospital bed in his semi-private room at Batley Community Hospital.

Twenty years ago, Pinky was finishing up his postgraduate program from a very prestigious university at the age of 19 when he came up with a business model. He began advertising his services as an "industrial cryptographer."

His pitch to business clients went something like this: Every form of technology used to transmit sensitive information gets breached sooner or later. If you're relying on the latest advanced technology to convey your corporate secrets, all you're doing is gambling that somebody hasn't yet come up with a way of intercepting it.

But long before even the most basic technology came along, going back to the earliest days of recorded history, people had secret ways to transmit information. With Pinky's assistance, his corporate clients could tap into that ancient knowledge.

Pinky's brand of encoding corporate secrets became a trendy management concept, and very profitable for him.

And, technically speaking, everything he told his clients was true. He was, in fact, drawing on age-old concepts for transmitting secret information. The duplicity came in two forms.

The first was his implication that he had some particular expertise to bring to the table. In truth, his "industrial cryptography" technique consisted mainly of simple substitution ciphers, not much more sophisticated than the type commonly used by kids clubs who meet in backyard treehouses.

He got around this by dressing up his presentations with technical-sounding terms that he pulled out of his ass, like "neurophasic comprehension mechanisms" and "semantic obfuscation paradigm," and nobody was any the wiser.

The second form of duplicity was a fundamental flaw in his business plan, which was that Pinky had access to the cipher keys that his clients used, making him capable of exploiting their inside information.

Pointing this out to his clients probably wouldn't be good for business, so he kept quiet about it. Besides, he never took advantage of the situation. He was making good money, so he had no reason to.

Until he got romantically involved with a fashion model who had a wild streak and an appetite for cocaine that strained his by-then-considerable bank account. She persuaded him that real men don't play by somebody else's rules. The federal prosecutors who busted him didn't see it that way.

He was sentenced to five years in a minimum security federal prison. His lawyer told him he'd be out in two. But something strange happened soon after his arrival. A guard told him he had a visitor. Instead of taking him to the regular visitors' room, the guard took him to a small, cinderblock room furnished with a table and two chairs.

In one of the chairs sat a small man with thick glasses and a pencil moustache. The man said he went by "R9," and that's all Pinky needed to know.

R9 said he represented a private firm that specialized in "applied behavioralism." R9 and his associates had been impressed with his work, legal and otherwise. They were prepared to get him out of his sentence if he would work for them. Pinky thought the whole thing sounded weird and declined.

At 3 a.m. two weeks later, a guard awoke him and transferred him to a holding cell. He later boarded a van which took him to a small, remote landing strip.

From there, a jet full of convicts flew him to a transfer center in Oklahoma City, followed by an equally harrowing ride that ended at a maximum security prison in Texas. He was placed in a cell with a large, tattooed man who explained in detail the plans he had for his pasty ass. A guard then collected him and took him to a room virtually identical to the small one in the minimum security prison, right down to R9 sitting across the table.

R9 once again made him the job offer. This time, he accepted.

Two days later, he took a limo from Baltimore Washington International Airport to a furnished apartment in Batley, Pennsylvania. On the kitchen table when he arrived was a set of keys, along with a typed note instructing him that the new but unflashy car parked outside was his. Also sitting on the table was an envelope containing a large amount of cash.

Two days after that, as he'd been instructed during a phone conversation with an unfamiliar voice, he rang the doorbell to a local house at 4 p.m. on the dot and heard a deep, gravelly voice yell "Get your ass in here!"

He opened the door and walked inside.

"What's with the shirt?"

That came from a dark-skinned black man sitting at a table. He had wide shoulders and a broad chest, and wore a white dress shirt open at the neck. A ring of gray hair circled his bald head, and a pair of round, metal-framed glasses sat low on the bridge of his nose.

"Are you TM438?" Pinky asked.

"No. The rest of you can play around with your idiotic code words if you so desire. I'm Billy. What's with the shirt?"

Every syllable out of the man's mouth sounded like a growl.

"The ... the shirt?"

"Yes. Your pink shirt."

He looked down at the pink polo shirt he'd purchased from a local department store the previous day.

"It's just ... just my shirt."

"Well get over here, Pinky. I'm supposed to train your worthless ass."

Pinky walked over to the table. He heard gunshots and was startled before he realized it was the sound of a television coming from a stairwell behind them.

Billy jumped down from his chair. For just a second, Pinky was disoriented because he thought Billy had jumped into a hole in the floor. Billy, it seemed, was a dwarf.

Billy stalked over to the stairs and barked "Hey kid! Turn down that goddamn TV! I'm working down here!"

Billy then walked back to Pinky, who was trying not to stare.

"Something wrong?" Billy asked.

"No! Not at all."

"Good. The kitchen's over there. Get me a beer from the fridge, then we'll start your training."

"Can I get a beer for myself?"

"No."

When Pinky returned from the kitchen with a bottle of beer, Billy was seated at the table again. Spread out in front of him was a deck of cards, several quarters, a cardboard box of salt, a small pile of pills and a glass of water.

Pinky took a seat across the table from him. Billy then picked up one of the quarters and held it up between his right thumb and forefinger. He reached forward with his left hand, closed his fist around the quarter and brought his left hand up in front of Pinky's face.

"Where's the quarter?" he asked.

Pinky pointed to his closed left fist. Billy opened it to reveal that his left hand was empty. He then opened his right hand to show the quarter on his palm.

He demonstrated for Pinky what he'd done, slowly this time. When he reached with his left hand, seemingly grabbing the quarter with it, he'd dropped the quarter into his right palm.

"It's obvious now, isn't it?" Billy said. "Why did you think the quarter was in my left hand?"

"I don't know."

"Of course you don't. It's because my left hand was moving so your eyes followed it. When your caveman ancestors were running through the forest in their little pink loincloths, they had the same brains you do now. Except I assume they were considerably more intelligent than you are, or they wouldn't have survived a week.

"Regardless, something moving in that forest, whether it was prey they could hunt or predator hunting them, was more likely to have an impact on their short-term survival than something that wasn't moving. Over the generations, their brains became hard-wired to pay more attention to moving objects.

"I'm going to teach you to use that principle for offense and defense. And I expect that will be an arduous process, because I've already ascertained that you're dumber than dogshit. But if you don't remember anything else, remember this. The eye always follows the moving object."

In the hours ahead, Billy repeatedly demonstrated that principle, both with the quarters and the cards. Then he showed Pinky how to use those techniques to drop the pills, over-the-counter painkillers it turned out, into the glass without the owner of the glass noticing. Then he moved on to secreting pinches of salt – meant to replicate whatever granular powder was necessary for the job at hand – and dropping them into the glass.

At one point, Billy looked at his watch.

"The Russian and The Suit should arrive soon. They want to welcome you to the fold."

"Who are The Russian and The Suit?"

"Assholes."

After another hour or so dragged by, the doorbell rang and Billy told Pinky to get the door. Standing on the front steps were a dapper man with an elaborate black pompadour and a dark, three-piece suit. Next to him was a sad-eyed, lanky man with a hangdog face and close-cropped brown hair, dressed in jeans, a sweatshirt and an army surplus jacket.

"You must be GP827," the man with the pompadour said, offering his hand. "Welcome to The Agendum. I'm T5. This is S87."

GP827 was the name by which the voice on the phone had told Pinky he would be identified. He now recognized the voice as belonging to the man shaking his hand. The man's words were friendly enough, but delivered with a sarcastic edge that made Pinky uncomfortable. The other man nodded and said "Hello" in a soft, accented voice.

Once inside, the man with the pompadour – The Suit evidently – wandered into the kitchen. The Russian, whose manner was much friendlier than his companion's, smiled at Pinky and asked Billy "We hear he is quite smart. He is working out good?"

"You heard wrong," Billy said. "You sent me an imbecile to train. You people never fail to amaze me. Hey! Did I say you could have one of my beers?"

This last was directed at The Suit, emerging from the kitchen with a bottle in his hand.

"No," The Suit said, taking a chair across the table from Billy. "I don't believe you did. By the way, I've got a message from The Professor."

Pinky had already gathered that the others in The Agendum called R9 The Professor.

"He's starting a new program," The Suit went on. "The kid's going to be an important part of it. The Professor's sending him away for special training."

"Tell him to suck my dick," Billy said. "The kid works for me."

"No, see, you've got that wrong," The Suit replied. "The kid works for The Agendum. And you work for The Agendum. And if The Professor says that's how it's going to be, that's how it's going to be. Or else you know what happens."

The Suit then looked at Pinky and winked.

"See, Stretch here sometimes has a little trouble understanding the chain of command. But don't worry. We'll get him straightened out. By the way, got some reading material for you."

He handed Pinky two sheets of paper.

TOM JERKFACE: The report at this point will include transcriptions of several sheets of paper with the following notation inscribed across the top in felt-tip marker: "From Pinky." All were photocopies. The originals of the first two sheets, as follows, were typed. The rest were written in what appears to be ballpoint pen. They will be labeled accordingly.

WELCOME TO THE AGENDUM

Congratulations! Because of your unique capabilities, you have been chosen to join a dynamic team of individuals engaged in a goal-focused endeavor destined not only to make a profit, but to facilitate some groundbreaking research in the field of applied behavioralism.

CORE EXPECTATIONS

* You will be contacted by representatives of The Agendum, who will inform you of operating procedures and provide you with instructions. You are to obey those procedures and instructions without question.

* You will be compensated in cash, via means to be explicated by The Agendum's representatives, and deposit it in a specified account. You will not attempt to deposit the aforementioned money with any other financial institutions.

* You will be provided with the specifics of a false biography, by which you will identify yourself to local residents inasmuch as necessary. You will minimize your contact with aforementioned local residents, inasmuch as is possible without arousing suspicion.

* In your dealings with other participants in The Agendum, you will maintain a positive attitude, as numerous studies have cited the aforementioned attribute as an essential component of proactive, effective endeavors. Said positive attitude will include, but not be limited to, a demeanor of good-natured jocularity in your interactions with other Agendum personnel.

* You will communicate nothing to any individual who is not involved with The Agendum about its procedures, activities or existence. Written communications, including this one, are to be promptly memorized, then physically destroyed.

* You will not attempt to leave the immediate geographic area, unless you are provided with explicit instructions to do so.

* Failure to comply with any of the aforementioned core expectations will bring severe consequences, up to and including grievous physical harm and death.

* Most important of all ... have fun!

TOM JERKFACE: *The following is a transcription of the second sheet of paper labeled "From Pinky."*

AHOY THERE MATEY! IT'S A GET-ACQUAINTED DINNER!

Welcome to The Agendum! As we get started on Project Anchovy, now seems like a good time to relax, get to know each other and enjoy some barbecue. Join us tomorrow for our Get-Acquainted Dinner at Buccaneer Barbecue, located at 1408 Route 26, Batley. Festivities start with a cocktail hour at 5 p.m., featuring tunes by DJ Pugnashiz. Dinner starts at 6 p.m. Vital instructions on Project Anchovy will be dispensed. Participation is compulsory, and failure to attend without a valid excuse such as life-threatening illness will bring consequences up to and including grievous physical harm and death. Dress is casual; come as you are. Or should we say – ARRRRR!

When Pinky arrived at Buccaneer Barbecue the next afternoon, the hostess showed him to a lounge decorated with ropes and fishing nets, and a bar shaped like a pirate ship. The bartender and wait staff wore pirate costumes, and looked vaguely embarrassed about it.

In the corner, a table bore the sign "DJ Pugnashiz," and a skinny, pale teenager in a pirate costume with several piercings in his lower lip played dance music. Nobody danced.

About three dozen people stood around the room, all but three of whom were men. They were mostly white, between the ages of about 30 and 50. Pinky knew none of them except Billy, who sat in the corner glowering and drinking one beer after another. All wore paper badges that said "Hello My Name Is" followed by a combination of letters and numbers written in felt tip marker. Except for Billy, who had written "NONE OF YOUR FUCKING BUSINESS."

A few made tentative attempts at conversation, but for the most part everybody spent the hour standing, drinking in silence and looking warily at each other. Finally, The Suit and The Russian entered and ushered everybody into a dining room.

The Suit and The Russian took their seats on either side of The Professor, at a table occupying the front of the room. Also at the table was a long-haired, bearded man wearing a velvet smoking jacket. Pinky was surprised to recognize Friedrich K. Schulze, whom he'd read about in the newspapers.

At the front of the room stood a dry erase board reading "Grossman and Grossman Podiatry Associates Employee Appreciation Luncheon"

DJ Pugnashiz, who served as their waiter, took everybody's order. Pinky got the Cajun-fried cheesesteak poppers.

Toward the end of the meal, as DJ Pugnashiz bustled around refilling water glasses, The Professor stood and held up his hands for silence – which wasn't really necessary since nobody was speaking anyway.

"Well everybody, I'd like to say a few words," The Professor said. "I hope you're all enjoying your meals, courtesy of our pirate friend here. Tell us, should we pay you in dollars or doubloons?"

The Suit gave a big, forced laugh. DJ Pugnashiz, who was refilling Pinky's water glass, muttered "Gee, I never heard that one before."

"I want to tell you all that I'm very excited about this endeavor," The Professor went on. "The level of talent gathered in this room is very impressive, and I predict that Project Anchovy will be a great success.

"By operational necessity, none of you will be apprised of every aspect of Project Anchovy, but I can provide a general overview. Our clients have commissioned what's essentially a real-world study in population-level applied behavioralism.

"I realize that not all of you are familiar with the terminology of applied behavioralism, so allow me to provide you with an illustration of what we'll be doing. Perhaps you've noticed this board."

The Professor gestured toward the dry erase board.

"From this, I think we can assume that the good people of Grossman and Grossman Podiatry Associates used this banquet room earlier today, where they presumably also received excellent service from staff members attired as pirates.

"I will ask you to picture that scene. Rank-and-file employees sit alongside managers. People who work and interact with each other each day. As is always the case with such groups of people, both official and unofficial hierarchies of command will prevail and they will conduct themselves accordingly.

"Now, I will ask you to picture something a bit fanciful. Imagine that in the midst of their meal, the room comes under attack by a real band of pirates. I realize that this seems strange, but that's the point. At once, these people who were previously going about their day-to-day lives find themselves under attack, embroiled in a struggle for their survival, all in an alien context that makes no sense to them. They're frightened and utterly disoriented.

"Within this context, how would they conduct themselves? Would they observe those hierarchies of command, those countless nuances governing their daily interactions of which they aren't even aware? Or would that all go out the window, so to speak? Would their immediate priority be defending themselves or protecting others? Would they band together for purposes of defense, or would they abandon any semblance of social order in their blind panic?

"Now picture something similar happening to the entire population of a metropolitan area. As I'm sure you can imagine, possessing clinical evidence as to how people would react in that situation could be of enormous tactical benefit to certain parties. And that's precisely the study that our clients want us to carry out."

Pinky raised his hand.

"Excuse me," he said. "Who are our clients?"

The Professor ignored Pinky, but The Suit glared at him.

"They're the ones who pay us," The Suit said. "That's who our clients are."

The room was totally silent for a few seconds. Then The Professor went on.

"In addition to Project Anchovy," he said. "We will conduct the behavioral experiments that form the core of our enterprise. The focus during our time here will be induced identity disassociation. This will necessitate employing techniques that T5 here …"

He nodded toward The Suit.

"…has succinctly if inelegantly termed 'woo woo shit.' "

The Suit gave a pretty game approximation of a warm-hearted chuckle.

"Toward that end," The Professor went on, "we've acquired some expert consultation. We have not bothered to assign Mr. Schulze here a code name, as I assume his fame precedes him. Would you say a few words Mr. Schulze?"

The Professor sat and Schulze stood.

"Infamy, I believe you mean," Schulze said. He looked nervous and drawn, but he clearly liked being the focus of attention.

"I will ask you all a question," Schulze said. "A show of hands, please. How many of you are familiar with Gilgamesh and Enki?"

Nobody raised a hand.

"Now, how many of you have heard of The Lone Ranger and Tonto?"

Every hand went up.

"Gilgamesh was the hero of an ancient Mesopotamian epic poem," Schulze said. "The king of the city of Uruk. Enki, a wild beast man of the hills, was his companion. His sidekick, if you will. The Epic of Gilgamesh is among the earliest surviving works of literature. Yet the pairing of the civilized hero with the sidekick representing a closeness to nature survives in the stories of The Lone Ranger and Tonto.

"Why have these archetypes survived the millennia? Because mythical archetypes are an intrinsic part of who we are. They address something inherent in our very being, and thus they hold power over us.

"Making use of these mythical archetypes, tapping into them, can be a very powerful tool indeed when it comes to influencing human behavior. And they will be an integral part of our behavioral studies here."

DJ Pugnashiz, who was carrying a tray of dirty plates past the head table, said "Enkidu."

"I'm sorry?" Schulze said.

"Enkidu was Gilgamesh's companion," DJ Pugnashiz said. "Enki, also known as Ea, was the Sumero-Babylonian god of the waters upon the earth."

Schulze cleared his throat.

"Well I guess I stand corrected," he said. "You're a very well-informed young man."

"Yeah, whatever," DJ Pugnashiz said as he exited through the swinging doors."

"There goes your tip, you snotty little fuckwad," The Suit said.

TOM JERKFACE: The following is a transcription of the third sheet of paper labeled "from Pinky," written in ballpoint pen.

REGARDING PROJECT ANCHOVY

This is the first of what will be periodic updates on Project Anchovy. I feel compelled to once again remind you that preserving or copying this bulletin will bring severe consequences.

Our secret transmission system is now in place, courtesy of our cryptography consultant. Some of you have complained that it's cumbersome to transcribe these documents. In response, I must emphasize that security is a consideration we cannot afford to take lightly.

I'm pleased to report that we are ahead of schedule in establishing our operational headquarters for Project Anchovy here.

You may have wondered why we've chosen this location. It is because our clients provided us with very specific population characteristics for the metropolitan area they wished to see tested. In all cases, Batley fit the bill with only negligible variations. Those specific demographic parameters as follows:

White: 57.8 percent
Black: 25.1 percent
Hispanic: 14.2 percent
Asian: 1.4 percent
Miscellaneous ethnic (swarthy): .5 percent
Miscellaneous ethnic (non-swarthy): .25 percent

In addition to preparing for Project Anchovy, we have taken in a number of test subjects for our studies in induced identity disassociation, which are proceeding admirably.

Once again, allow me to congratulate each and every one of you on being part of a winning team. And remember, TEAM stands for "Together, Everyone Achieves More."

FILE 18

FROM BILLY'S PAPERS

Dear Billy, It's me, Sally Bacon. I hope this letter gets to you. My children and I are in trouble. I truly believe that if anybody can help us, you can. We are at the Friedrich K. Schulze Foundation's Spiritual Healing and Exploration Clinic. They keep calling us "guests." I've come to understand that we are really prisoners.

I know that you're aware of the location of this clinic, because I've seen you here. I don't think that I was supposed to. They let me out in the yard, where I'm allowed to walk around or sit on one of the benches. I'm always under observation by at least one of the staffers here. If I spend too much time close to the fence, they make excuses to pull me away. Nobody has yet overtly threatened me or my children with harm, but I have no doubt they would resort to that, so I don't push it.

Recently, I glimpsed you through some of the vines that cover the fence. You were in the company of two men whom I gather are the flunkies of the man who seems to be in charge. That man tells me his name is "Terrence," though I'm certain it's not his real name. He has a pencil moustache. I don't like him.

I thought of calling out to you. Then it occurred to me that maybe you were being detained against your will as well and I might be making trouble for you. You looked angry. But then again, you always do. (I love you dearly. You know that, don't you?)

After I saw you, I positioned myself behind the vines, hoping to hear what was being said without being seen. I overheard a conversation between two men who work here.

One of them said: "The Professor says the other carny gets a car, too. It's out back and it's gassed up. Give him the keys when you go by to talk to him. He lives with the dwarf at the place on Maple Street."

The other asked if "the dwarf" would be present and was answered in the negative. To which he replied: "Good. I don't like that dwarf. He's a crabby son of a bitch."

I knew then beyond a doubt that he was referring to you.

They allow me certain indulgences here, in exchange for my compliance. Among them is the ability to select books from the Batley Public Library that they pick up for me. They also allow me access to snub-nosed scissors and glue from an arts-and-crafts room they have here.

I used to volunteer at the Batley Public Library, and I know the librarian there. Once, as an experiment, I left an envelope with her name on it in the pages of a book. Inside was a note.

I didn't want to give her too many details, because I don't want to put her in danger. But I asked her to put a mark on a specific line of a specific page of a book I was ordering if she received my note.

If she did, I instructed her, I would conceal this letter in the binding of the book when I returned it. I asked her to deliver it to you somehow without reading it herself. I pray she's indulged me in that regard.

Where to start? Since I saw you last time, Billy, my life has fallen apart. Ken left me. He was in the hospital, recuperating from an accident. One day when I went to visit him, he was gone. He left a letter for me, telling me that he'd been carrying on an affair behind my back and decided to leave me for good.

Billy, I've made some bad decisions in my life. I thought that I'd put it all behind me. I thought that I'd reached a stable place where none of my past mistakes could hurt me anymore, and I could finally be happy.

When I read that note, it was as though all of those years I'd spent pulling my life together counted for nothing, and I was back in the same lonely, desperate place I thought I'd never see again. Around that time, budget cuts for the city health department forced my supervisor to lay me off. I took a job cutting hair. It paid the bills, but I hated it.

If it wasn't for my children, I don't know what I would have done during that time.

You've never met my children, Billy, but they really are the most lovely, perfect creatures who've ever lived. Luanne is 18 now and Ty is 16. They're very precious to me.

For their sake, I made myself go on. I tried to keep busy, so I'd have as little time for brooding and self-pity as possible. I began performing again, and even sent some demo tapes out to radio stations. Nothing came of it, but at least I tried.

As I mentioned, I volunteered at the library. And it was in that capacity that I became acquainted with, of all people, Friedrich Schulze.

This was when he'd just come to Batley, and announced his plans to build the clinic. At the time, nobody quite knew what to make of it.

One of my responsibilities at the library was "events coordinator." Whenever a prominent author passed through town, I'd try to persuade him or her to give a lecture or conduct a book discussion group.

When my supervisor suggested I contact Mr. Schulze, I hesitated. I knew of his reputation from the newspapers.

I'd never encountered him at the carnival. I made an effort to avoid him, in fact. I know you didn't like him. But then you don't like anyone, do you darling?

I expected him to be deeply unpleasant at best, dangerous at worst. What I found, to my surprise, was that he was a perfectly charming gentleman. He was very well-read, unfailingly courteous and possessed of a wry and self-deprecating wit.

He asked me to join him for coffee and I consented. Over coffee, this man with a reputation as a voracious sexual beast made a half-hearted and endearingly awkward pass at me. When I made it clear that I wasn't interested in him that way, he passed it off with good grace. I quite liked him. We talked for hours.

He recognized that he wasn't at all what I expected, and said he was used to it. He acknowledged that he had nobody but himself to blame for his reputation.

When he was younger, he said, he'd done some questionable things. But he never regarded himself as debauched or evil.

He simply didn't want to content himself with the dull, circumscribed existence he felt others had laid out for him, and wanted to see what else life had to offer. That desire led him to some places and actions that society considered taboo.

He began playing his fearful reputation to the hilt as a means of armoring himself against the condemnation he faced. And found that the role of wicked iconoclast afforded him some leverage and a certain degree of power in society, to say nothing of a substantial income.

As time went by, he felt trapped in his own role. That was why he began traveling with the carnival, in order to see the world around him and reconnect with it.

He said he didn't regret anything he'd done, because he'd learned from it all. He saw the impulses that led to his earlier excesses as potentially good things that he simply lacked the experience and wisdom to refine when he was younger, and now he could do something positive with them.

Billy, I was amazed because I could relate so much to what he said! At times, it was as though he was looking right into my soul and telling me about myself!

He said he had returned to Batley with the idea of starting a new chapter in his life. He wished to drop his cartoonish villain trappings and devote his life to the genuine study of mythology and folklore. But not dry, academic studies so much as an open-eyed appraisal of what mythological archetypes mean to us as individuals and as a society.

His goal, he said, would be to help people who have problems in their lives draw on certain universal archetypes to heal themselves, and perhaps better their lives and their communities.

I became very excited as he spoke. I hadn't intended to, but I began telling him about my own life and the problems I'd faced.

Friedrich informed me that soon he would establish a place in Batley, a healing center, where people like me could get past our problems and help others by the methods we had just discussed. I told him I couldn't possibly afford something like that, but he said he would arrange for free care in my case. His goal wasn't to make money, he said, but to help people like me.

If you're reading this, Billy, I have no doubt that right now you're rolling your eyes and muttering under your breath about my stupidity. Yes, I was terribly naïve. All I can say is that I was at a very vulnerable point in my life and desperate for help, no matter where it came from.

Friedrich welcomed me to the clinic when it first opened. He introduced me to Terrence as his right-hand man, and said I could trust him.

Something strange happened that first day. Friedrich pulled me to the side at one point and looked around as though he was afraid we'd be noticed. He asked me if I'd like a personal tour of the grounds. I said I would. He grabbed me by the arm and practically pulled me at a run out one of the doors.

As we stood on the lawn, he said in a low, whispered voice "There's something I have to tell you. You need to …"

Just then, another man who appeared to be one of Terrence's personal assistants exited the door we'd come through. A very insolent man who was always dressed in an expensive-looking suit.

"And there's the man himself," the assistant said, placing a hand on Friedrich's shoulder. Friedrich looked very startled.

"Like I was saying," Friedrich said, "you need to trust the people here. I think you'll do very well."

Then the man in the suit escorted him back inside and that was the last I ever saw of Friedrich.

I dealt mostly with Terrence, who at first seemed very kind and understanding. I showed up at the clinic several times a week to take part in small-group discussions about various mythical stories and characters, and what lessons we might apply from them in our day-to-day lives.

I found it enjoyable and interesting, but nothing ground-breaking.

Terrence said the majority of people at the clinic were there on a residential basis and suggested that's how I would derive the most benefit. I told him that simply wouldn't work for me, between my children and my job.

Then something very frightening happened.

As you know, Billy, I've done things in my past that I'm not proud of. In particular, I've made some very bad decisions where men are concerned. Yet I can't say I regret any of it, because I have my two beautiful children as a result.

Ty's father, in particular, was a very shady character. He took off soon after Ty was born. I haven't seen or heard from him since, and have no desire to.

One day when the children were out I was home alone, practicing my guitar. I heard a crashing noise. When I ran to see what it was, I found a man kicking in my door. I screamed and tried to run for the phone but he caught me and put a hand over my mouth.

The man was dirty, with long hair and a crazed look in his eyes. He said Ty's father had disappeared with a shipment of drugs and accused me of hiding it. I told him that I didn't know what he was talking about and hadn't seen Ty's father in years, but he refused to listen. He called me a "lying bitch," and said I'd better have the drugs when he came back or he'd hurt me and the children.

I went to the police. They took down a description of the man and said they'd keep an eye out for him. But I had to tell them I had no idea who the man was or what had become of Ty's father. I left the police station with little hope they could do anything.

Soon after, my car was vandalized. I left work and found my windshield smashed. I became very frightened when Luanne told me a man who fit the description of the one who'd kicked down our door appeared to be following her on the street one day.

The next time I saw Terrence, he said I looked upset and asked me what was wrong. He listened very sympathetically, then told me he might be able to help.

He said I could stay with them for a short time. Just until this man, whoever he was, moved on. They had excellent security, he said, and nobody would have to know we were there. They would even pay the rent on our place for however long we had to stay.

I said that seemed a bit much. But Terrence replied that Friedrich, who was away on a spiritual expedition, considered me a personal friend and had personally instructed him to assist me if need be.

I took him up on it. What choice did I have? Luanne had just graduated and Ty was about to start his summer break. I myself had no reservations about leaving my hair-cutting job.

Although Terrence said it wasn't necessary, I insisted on working in the kitchen. The food was excellent, and the building was beautiful. Ty, Luanne and I all had our own rooms, in a different section from the general population. At first, it all seemed like a wonderful arrangement.

Terrence said they offered programs that might be of interest to Ty and Luanne as well. One of his aides, a quiet-spoken man with a Russian accent, gave martial arts classes and Terrence asked if Ty might be interested. Ty has always loved martial arts, so of course I said yes.

He asked me if Luanne had decided on a career yet. I said she was looking around but to my knowledge hadn't decided on anything. Terrence suggested a course that he described as "interview skills." When I pressed him for details, he said it would deal with "effective interpersonal communication" and might be useful in a business setting. I asked Luanne if she was interested and she said she would give it a try.

As for myself, in between stints working in the kitchen I continued to take part in group discussions about mythology and read study material they provided me. Terrence perceived that I took a particular interest in mythology from a feminist perspective, and suggested I take part in a regular discussion group dealing with that topic.

I had one-on-one sessions with Terence as well. He spoke of applying the lessons toward a spiritual breakthrough of some kind. On numerous occasions, he used some variation of the term "opening the soul gate."

Such talk would have been enormously appealing and fascinating to me when I was a younger woman. But I've experienced a lot since then, and don't give that kind of thing much credence anymore.

One aspect of life in the clinic I found odd from the very beginning was Terrence's insistence that all residents undergo regular medical examinations. I thought this rather intrusive. But since the clinic was being so generous to us in all other respects, I chose not to voice my feelings on the matter.

During one of our individual sessions, Terrence asked me if I'd found any one character in my readings who resonated with me in particular. I told him the fairie queen, Mab.

Depending on which interpretation you subscribe to, Mab may have originated as an actual flesh-and-blood Celtic queen, or a pagan goddess later identified as a fairie after descendants of her original worshippers converted to Christianity.

Shakespeare mentioned her in "Romeo and Juliet" as a tiny creature who influences dreams. But my image of her came from a myth that she led the Wild Ride on Samhain Eve, at the head of a fierce retinue of fairie hunters on horses. I pictured myself as Mab – savage, beautiful and strong. Not wicked so much as untamed. That image stayed with me and I told Terrence. In subsequent sessions he encouraged me to keep my mental focus on that character and that image.

Every night, once I had assisted with dinner preparation, the children and I would sit down at a table in the kitchen and talk. They began speaking of some things that concerned me. Ty spoke with boyish enthusiasm of his martial arts training with the Russian gentleman. Unlike some of his previous martial arts training, he characterized it as "the real deal," and recounted how he was learning to break thumbs, legs and necks in hand-to-hand combat.

Luanne, meanwhile, told how she was learning subtle tricks to gain psychological dominance over interrogation subjects. Worrying me even more than the subject of her lessons was the fact that she received them from the man I mentioned earlier who wore expensive suits and had a very abrasive manner.

My concerns didn't turn to outright fear until one afternoon when I was sitting in a common room, working on a crossword puzzle. I began to have difficulty concentrating. The puzzles clues at once seemed impossibly complex and deeply profound. I became very much aware of tactile sensations such as the pencil in my hand and the feeling of the chair against my body. The sounds around me took on a pinging, echoey quality, like sounds you would hear underwater.

I remembered those sensations. When I looked up and saw shifting patterns in the sunlight coming through the windows, I knew for sure what it was. The onset of an acid trip.

Years ago, well before Ty and Luanne came along, I experimented with LSD. People had told me it would give me amazing spiritual insights. I found the experience more akin to sitting through a movie that has flashy special effects but no real substance.

At the moment, though, I wasn't thinking of it in such objective terms. I didn't know where my children were, but I was terrified they would see me in that condition. I was also afraid because I didn't know who would have slipped me the dose or why.

I Iran to Terrence's office. I told him what was happening and begged him to put me someplace where I could ride it out without my children seeing me.

Terrence took me to one of the rooms they called a "meditation chamber." It was just a small, dimly lit room with soft couches and cushions and patterned curtains on the walls.

I have fractured memories of what happened next. I remember Terrence locking the door with a key, then trying to tell me that I was experiencing the "opening of the soul gate." I became almost hysterical as I insisted that wasn't the case, and that I'd been given a dose of LSD.

In condescending, avuncular tones, as if speaking to a frightened and rather stupid child, Terrence contradicted me.

"The opening of the soul gate can be frightening, Sally, but it's a good thing. Mab is trying to reach you. She's trying to help you achieve your true potential. You want that, don't you?"

I did my best to shut out his voice. I drew on my yoga training, concentrating on my breathing and forcing myself to relax one muscle at a time.

Terrence said he would leave me by myself for a while. He left and the lights went out, leaving me in pitch darkness. I heard a soft, female voice then.

"Sally. It's me, Mab. I'm within you. You and I are one. Can you feel me?"

I covered my hands with my ears and the voice was muffled. I had enough presence of mind to know that if it was really an auditory hallucination, my hands over my ears would have no effect on the volume. There had to be hidden speakers in the room.

I focused on my breathing. In. Out. In. Out. Whatever was happening, I would deal with it when the drug had worn off and I was once again capable of rational thought.

I don't know how much time I spent in the darkness, with that insistent voice coming out of the hidden speakers somewhere. It felt like days.

Finally, Terrence unlocked the door and let me out. Some attendants took me to my room. They gave me a glass of orange juice which must have been laced with a sedative, because I fell asleep right away.

As soon as I awoke, I didn't waste any time. I went straight to Terrence's office.

"Where are my children?" I said. "We're leaving right now."

He tried to calm me.

"The opening of the soul gate is a very profound experience and it may be upsetting at first," he said.

I looked him in the eye and forced myself to speak in calm, measured tones.

"It was not the opening of the soul gate," I told him. "It was a dose of LSD that somebody gave me without my consent. Bring me my children. We are leaving."

"I simply cannot allow that right now," Terrence said. "You're at a very vulnerable stage. There are liability issues."

My calm broke. I stood and began screaming.

"How's this for a liability issue? I'm liable to tear your dick off and feed it to you if you don't bring me my children right now!"

He must have pushed a button I didn't see, because the Russian man came in. He put me in some kind of wrestling hold that completely immobilized me. I struggled and shrieked and screamed, trying to claw at him, to bite him, to stomp on his feet or kick him in the groin. Anything.

Terrence arose from his desk with a hypodermic needle in his hand. I screamed louder still as he jabbed it into my buttocks.

An irresistible torpor soon overtook me and the Russian man assisted me down the hallway to my room, with one of my arms slung over his shoulders as though I was a drunk friend he was helping to get home.

He laid me down on my bed. Before I lost consciousness, he put his mouth close to my ear and whispered.

"I do not like to do this," he said. "If I had the choice, I would not. Please do not cross him. He is very dangerous man."

They kept me locked in my room for a few days. I could tell they were slipping sedatives into my food at first. I said nothing. The sedatives stopped, and I assumed it was a test to see how I would react. I forced myself to be calm.

Eventually, Terrence came to speak to me. As much as I wanted to dive straight for his throat, I instead told him everything I thought he wanted to hear. I told him I was sorry for how I'd reacted. I must have been panicked because I was frightened by the sheer wondrousness of it all. Mab was speaking to me, and telling me profound truths. I'd opened the soul gate. My whole life had changed.

I resumed my work in the kitchen. One day I happened to glance out the window and saw Terrence talking to several men outside on the grounds of the clinic. He appeared to be issuing instructions. Despite his haircut, I recognized one of them as the man who'd kicked in my door and threatened me about the shipment of drugs.

That evening, Ty, Luanne and I met up for dinner once more. I'd never noticed before, but several of the kitchen workers who handled cleanup never let us out of their sight. Luanne asked if I was feeling better after the bout of illness that had prevented me from having dinner with them for several days.

I told Luanne that I was feeling fine, and she told me I was lying. I asked the two of them if their respective instructors ever talked about the purpose of their lessons.

"Yeah," Luane told me. "They say that once me and Ty are trained, we'll be able to do jobs for them."

Billy, staying under control at that moment was the most difficult thing I'd done up to that point. I lowered my voice, but I could still feel the tremor in it that wanted to become a scream.

"Listen to me very closely," I told them. "You are not going to do jobs for them. These are bad people and we need to get away from them."

Since then, we've managed to communicate to each other in bits and pieces, always keeping in mind that we're probably being observed. I've told my children to play along as I've done. Every time I take a bite of food or a swallow of water, I pray it's not drugged.

I refuse to give up and will continue looking for a way out. But Billy, if you get this, please help us.

FILE 19

Pinky asked if I could get him cup of water. I went to the bathroom, filled up his cup and gave it to him. He swallowed a pill, a painkiller most likely, and washed it down.

"So did you come up with a code for them?" I asked.

"Technically, it wasn't a code. It was a cipher. But yeah. Everybody on the team had a lawn ornament of some kind. Mine was a plastic frog. When I'd look out my window and see it was facing a different direction from the way I'd left it, I knew they had a message for me.

"I had a locker at a commercial storage place. When I'd open it, there'd be a piece of paper with a number on it between one and nine, and a key for another locker at another commercial storage place. In the second locker, I'd find the message."

"What was the number?"

"The key to a substitution cipher. See, you'd want a magazine that would be available around here, but not wildly popular."

"Like Saltwater Fisherman Monthly?"

"Yeah. Like that. There's a monthly column in there called 'Gone Fishin'.' Whatever the number was, you'd count that many words into the column, and the first letter of the word would substitute for 'A' as the first letter of the alphabet. If it was 'F,' then 'G' would be the substitute for 'B,' 'H' would be the substitute for 'C' and so on."

"Sounds complicated."

"It's not. The old Lone Ranger radio show used to have something similar. Hell, maybe Schulze's speech at the Get Acquainted Dinner gave me the idea. A real cryptographer could have cracked it in about 30 seconds, but I guess that didn't occur to them. It was just a pain in the ass to transcribe. But I had to give them something. I had a feeling that telling them I didn't really know what I was doing wouldn't be a good idea."

"So what did you have to do with the Halloween Parade Massacre?"

"Yeah, I was getting to that."

Pinky spent the better part of a year living in Batley. Every day, he'd look out his window to see if the plastic frog had changed positions. When it did, sometimes the messages were just updates on how things were going. Sometimes they were orders to perform various errands or report for a face-to-face meeting.

He considered making a break for it. Just jumping in his car and driving off. He could never quite get up the courage. But he did hang onto some of the communications from The Professor, despite the frequent and explicit warnings not to. He hid them behind a rafter in his attic, just in case they might give him needed leverage against The Agendum someday.

He continued his training sessions with Billy. Occasionally, he'd see a long-haired young man wandering around the house whom Billy addressed as "kid," usually in irritated tones.

After several months, Billy said he was still hopelessly incompetent where sleight-of-hand was concerned, but his skills were adequate to meet the very low standards that The Agendum required.

After that, Pinky's duties included regularly showing up at Schulze's local

Spiritual Healing and Exploration Clinic.

Nobody from outside was permitted in the clinic, but Schulze made no apparent attempt to conceal his involvement. To the contrary, he was in the news a lot as a considerable and very vocal group of local people objected to his presence in their community.

That struck Pinky as odd, given the secrecy that characterized everything else about The Agendum. One time he asked The Russian about it, and was told that Schulze's presence guaranteed a steady influx of human test subjects for the clinic. When he tried to get more details on what exactly they were doing, however, The Russian clammed up.

Aside from showing up for the occasional press conference or seminar, however, Schulze didn't seem to spend a lot of time in Batley. Pinky never saw him at the clinic.

The clinic consisted of two buildings. One was a slightly smaller house that they called the "administration building." Pinky occasionally saw people coming and going from there, but he was told that under no circumstances was he supposed to talk to them, and vice versa.

The clinic proper, where Pinky worked, looked like a ritzy but rustic hotel from the outside. On the inside, it looked like a mental hospital. Albeit a high-class one with hardwood floors, tasteful window treatments and the smell of disinfectant kept to a faint background whiff. The type of place where rich people might send their trust-fund drug addicts to dry out.

Day and night, people wandered the hallways, some looking pretty dazed. He saw rooms stocked with what looked like medical equipment. Some doors would be locked. And if you put your ear close to them, you could sometimes hear muffled screams.

Pinky's job on those occasions was to pass himself off as a member of the custodial staff, and occasionally slip a small quantity of powder into someone's cup of coffee or glass of water.

There was a kitchen on-site where residents had their meals prepared. If they wanted to slip something into someone's drink, Pinky wondered why they couldn't just do it there. He once asked The Russian, who never said a lot but seemed like the most approachable member of The Agendum. The Russian said The Professor made it clear that some of the residents must not guess that they were being drugged.

To allay any suspicions, The Agendum slipped the drugs into drinks from communal sources such as water coolers and coffee pots.

Those occasions were rare, though. After he gave them the message transmission system, they didn't seem to have a lot of use for Pinky. He spent most of his time running menial errands.

He'd make arrangements for contractors and services at Schulze's clinic. Stuff like lawn and laundry services. Sometimes, one of the other team members would drive him out to a location such as a farm or a garage in another city so Pinky could drive a car back to Batley. On those occasions, they warned him to be very careful about obeying all traffic laws and not to get pulled over.

More than once, they sent him down to Baltimore-Washington International Airport to pick up men arriving on flights from various locations around the United States.

For the most part, he and those men didn't exchange any more words than were strictly necessary. One notable exception was a guy with a scraggly beard and tattoos on his knuckles who said he'd just served a long spell in prison, and asked if Pinky would give him just an hour to buy a piece of ass. He even offered to pay Pinky and let him have sloppy seconds. But Pinky declined and the man sulked the rest of the ride home.

He'd get regular updates from The Professor, meticulously deciphered at his kitchen table, about how things were proceeding. Flawlessly, according to every message. The Professor frequently hinted that Project Anchovy was nearing readiness, without specifying what it was.

Late one night, a hammering at his door woke Pinky up. Standing outside were The Suit and another man Pinky remembered from the Get Acquainted Dinner — a skinny bald guy with glasses. He barely recognized The Suit, who wore workboots, a flannel shirt and jeans. He told Pinky that his "hocus pocus shit" was needed, then instructed him to throw on a pair of jeans.

To Pinky's confusion, The Suit presented him with a Confederate flag T-shirt, a denim jacket, a pair of tinted aviator frame glasses, a dark wig and a baseball cap, and told him to put them on. He was even more confused when the bald guy brushed some spirit gum on his upper lip and stuck a fake moustache on.

Pinky followed The Suit and the bald guy in his car south across the Maryland state line, eventually stopping in the pickup-filled parking lot of a run-down bar in the middle of nowhere. Finally, The Suit told him what the job was.

Pinky protested, saying he'd be recognized. The Suit assured him he wouldn't be. Pinky asked why Billy couldn't do it, since he was far more skilled. The Suit laughed.

"A black dwarf in a redneck bar like this?" The Suit said. "I think he'd get noticed. One more thing. Hand me your wallet."

"My wallet?"

"You play rough for us, you don't carry ID – real or fake. That's a rule."

Pinky handed over his wallet. The Suit gave him $20 and instructed him to buy a beer.

"None of those fruity drinks you usually get," The Suit said. "Don't want to stand out."

Pinky walked into the smoky interior. The place was busy but not packed. He took a seat at the bar. He ordered a bottle of beer, drinking carefully so he wouldn't dislodge the fake moustache. He checked himself out in the mirror and had to admit that The Suit was right. He barely recognized himself.

Good thing, too. Several seats to his left sat the man with the scraggly beard and the knuckle tattoos he'd picked up at the airport. The man was obviously drunk and talking to a skanky-looking female bartender, his voice loud so as to be heard over the country music playing in the background.

"C'mon baby, you think I'm small time?" he was saying. "You wouldn't believe what I'm doing now. We're tapped into some ancient evil shit. We're going to bring a city to its knees! You like that, sweet thing?"

He reached for her. She slapped his hand away and retreated to the far end of the bar. Pinky reached into his jacket pocket and palmed the small vial of powder it contained.

Before long, the man got up and staggered for the men's room. Under pretense of checking out the jukebox, Pinky walked by the man's seat and stealthily dumped the powder into his beer. From the back of the bar, he watched the man retake his seat and drink from the glass. Pinky left the bar and touched the brim of his cap once outside, as instructed.

The Suit walked into the bar without glancing in his direction. Since he was curious and hadn't been told not to, Pinky went back in to see what would happen.

The man was already unconscious with his head on the bar, not responding as The Suit put an arm around his shoulder and shook him.

"He a friend of yours?" the bartender asked.

"My brother-in-law," The Suit said. "My sister sent me out to look for him. Sorry about the trouble."

He put a couple bills on the bar, which seemed to satisfy the bartender. Spotting Pinky, The Suit said "Hey buddy, mind giving me a hand?"

The two threw the man's limp arms over their shoulders, then hoisted him up and out the door. They dumped him in the back of The Suit's car.

When he was driving the bald guy back to Batley, after The Suit had driven off in another direction, Pinky asked: "So what do you think will happen to him?"

"Don't know," the bald guy said. "But I wouldn't be selling him any life insurance right about now."

They drove the rest of the way back in silence.

A new task got added to Pinky's list of chores. He was to scan the classified sections of the local newspaper every day and notify The Agendum whenever an apartment along Main Street became available for rent.

One day, he was told to go out and rent one. Beforehand, The Russian provided him with a false identity and several fake documents testifying to his identity as a 55-year-old industrial boiler repairman. He met again with the bald, skinny guy from the night of the Maryland bar, who applied some latex makeup that Pinky had to admit really made him look the part. He informed the kindly old landlady who took his security deposit and first month's rent that he traveled a lot for his job, and probably wouldn't be around much.

And then it was late October, 15 years ago. After months of communications from The Professor promising that Operation Anchovy was getting increasingly close, The Suit and The Russian stopped by Pinky's place to brief him on his part in it the following night. Then they left.

Pinky was numb. He considered going to the police. But The Suit had made a point of mentioning more than once that they "had people" in the local police department. Was it just a bluff? Could he take that chance?

Maybe he could make a break for it. They'd assured him that they'd be keeping an eye on him, but that might be a bluff too. Then he thought of his last glimpse of that scraggly-bearded man's body on the back seat of The Suit's car. Not dead yet, but the difference was purely academic at that point.

It was going to happen anyway, he told himself throughout the day. His getting killed in a futile attempt to prevent it wouldn't accomplish anything, he told himself through the sleepless night. Some people might get hurt, but maybe not. He told himself that last one the next afternoon as he let himself into the apartment he'd rented and positioned himself on a balcony facing Main Street. Besides, he was just an observer. It wasn't like he'd be doing anything.

The Halloween Parade is a big deal in Batley. Hours before it started, people were already lined up along the streets, sitting in folding or plastic patio chairs they'd set up the night before. Entire families sat on blankets with picnic coolers at the ready. Vendors made their way up and down the streets, selling popsicles and balloons for the kids.

The kids. So many kids.

To distract himself, Pinky reviewed again the checklist of things he was supposed to look for when it happened. Keep an eye on authority figures, such as police officers or other uniformed emergency workers. Do members of the crowd continue to obey them, or ignore them altogether?

To what extent do people look out for others? Do they attempt to protect strangers, family members and companions, or do they abandon them in their own single-minded pursuit of survival?

Pinky was advised to keep a particular eye out for what The Professor's instructions called "micro-communities" – small groups of people temporarily banding together for protection.

And most important of all, what was Pinky's assessment of the crowd's overall rationality? Did they take steps that were logically consistent with addressing the threat facing them, or did they abandon all reason in their blind panic?

Pinky would be expected to write a report eventually, but not that night. He was under explicit instructions to wait a period of several days to let his impressions sink in.

At this moment, a number of other observers like Pinky would be stationed in other apartments along the parade route, ready to make observations of their own.

Just as dusk started to settle in, the first parade marchers came along and continued in a seemingly unending stream. High school bands and grade-school baton-twirlers. Members of civic groups waving from the backs of trucks. Beauty contest winners waving from open cars. Local political clubs throwing handfuls of candy to the eager kids on the curb.

So many goddamn kids.

The first explosion went off.

It was to Pinky's left, at a distance. If he hadn't known to expect it, he would likely have assumed it was just part of the parade sounds. Then another one. To his right, this time, and closer. The parade halted. Members of an antique car club sat in their vehicles, glancing around, puzzled.

On the sidewalk, meanwhile, ripples of panicked confusion swept down Main Street. Everybody suddenly on their feet. Jostling each other with gradually increasing urgency as more explosions went off.

Then the rifle shots started ringing out and all hell broke loose. The people began surging down side streets. Along the larger streets, they would find flaming barriers. And along random smaller ones would be men in frightening leather masks, shooting at them with handguns or assaulting them with blunt weapons.

The human waves below Pinky increased in their frequency and violence. The antique cars, the papier-mache-decorated floats, all abandoned now as parade participants joined the mass trying to get out. People clawing at each other. Mothers holding desperately onto screaming kids.

The kids.

Pinky was in his car, driving. His throat was raw.

He'd ended up in his car somehow. How? Oh yes. He'd left the apartment. It was furnished when he rented it. Cheap fiberboard stuff. Ugly picture of fruit above the couch. He would have removed it if he really lived there.

His throat was so raw.

He'd gone out into the hallway because he couldn't watch anymore, and then stumbled down the stairs. His knees weren't holding up too good and he almost fell several times. He'd wandered down an alley. People were running up and down it, screaming. He heard sirens.

As he made his way toward where his car was parked beyond the parade route, he was dimly aware this might be one of the alleys where a gunman would be stationed. It didn't really seem to matter.

He'd made it to his car, parked down an abandoned side street, put the keys in the ignition and driven off. He was driving still. His throat was raw.

Then he remembered. It was raw because he'd been screaming. He'd been screaming "Save her! Christ Jesus for the love of God please save her! Somebody!"

Because a girl, maybe about 14, had gone down while he was watching. And she was screaming on the sidewalk as she was trampled, over and over again.

For a moment, she'd reached an arm up to a boy, maybe 17. The boy had glanced at her and then turned away to continue trying to shove his way out of the crowd. The girl got trampled some more and she'd stopped moving.

And Pinky had run out into the street, amid the screaming and clawing and jostling, knowing already that he was too late. Because the girl was dead by the time he got to her. He'd dragged her limp body into the alley and left it there because he didn't want it to get trampled anymore.

Maybe that 17-year-old boy would grow to be an old man. Maybe his kids would visit, and they'd bring his grandkids. And his kids would say go in the living room and watch the football game with grandpa because grandpa's such a sweet old man and he loves you.

The grandkids wouldn't know and grandpa wouldn't even remember that there'd been a second – just a second – when he could have saved a girl screaming on the sidewalk from being trampled to death. And he'd turned away instead.

That boy wasn't guilty. None of them were. Thousands of people killed her, therefore nobody did.

Pinky pulled over and threw up violently by the side of the road.

Now his throat was even more raw. He wanted something cold to drink. For some reason, he found himself thinking about the beers in Billy's fridge.

Hours later, he was sitting at Billy's kitchen table, drinking another beer. He couldn't quite remember how many beers he'd had, or how long he'd been there. He and Billy hadn't said much. They'd mostly just sat, not looking at each other, drinking beers.

Then Billy said "I need you to do something."

FILE 20

FROM BILLY'S PAPERS

The Professor's office was redolent with that musty, back-of-the sinuses stink that some old buildings get. I dislike that smell intensely.

I sat in a leather chair, directly across a highly polished wooden desk from The Professor. My legs stuck straight out. But with my full-sized torso perched in that chair, I could look straight into the reptilian eyes behind his thick glasses.

Polished wood and plush upholstery surrounded us. All of the objects on his desk, I noticed, lined up at precise right angles. Said objects included a pad of paper, a paper clip dispenser and a stainless steel fountain pen set that looked suitably important, efficient and unused. I calculated how close I might get to his windpipe with one of the fountain pens and arrived at the answer: an insufficient degree before the Russian attack dog standing behind me did something I'd find decidedly unpleasant.

And thus I had to content myself with giving him stinkeye as he steepled pale fingers and favored me with the variety of tight-lipped smile favored by pedophile uncles.

He had requested my presence at the clinic to teach a group of workers some basic sleight-of-hand. Earlier, about 20 people perched in folding chairs in the basement and watched while I gave them the same basic instructions I'd given Pinky. After regular instructions, Pinky was becoming marginally less abysmal. This group was, to an individual, nothing short of painful to watch. I finished knowing I'd done little to enhance the effectiveness of The Agendum and not feeling unduly troubled about that fact.

Afterward, The Professor summoned me to his office.

"So," The Professor said. "T5 tells me you expressed some reservations about our proposal regarding your colleague."

"If by 'colleague' you mean the kid and if by 'expressed reservations' you mean informing him that you can suck my dick, the answer is 'yes' on both counts."

His eyes flicked over my shoulder, conveying a message. As I remained conscious and uninjured, I surmised that message was "Let it go."

"You speak your mind without reservation," The Professor said. "That's an attribute that can be of ample benefit to an organization, assuming it's utilized in a proactive manner. I would advise you to keep that in mind. And yes. By 'colleague' I did, in fact, mean the young gentleman to whom you refer as 'the kid.' We've reviewed our assets and concluded that he might serve a role of substantive importance within The Agendum."

"What role might that be?"

"I needn't go into specifics now. Suffice it to say that he will leave for three months, during which time he will be under the tutelage of Mr. Schulze."

"And what the fuck, precisely, can Schulze teach him? The finer points of being a freak and a pervert?"

"Regardless of what you may think of Mr. Schulze, he has demonstrated that he possesses certain – at the risk of sounding melodramatic, I suppose you might characterize them as supernatural powers.

"We've determined that it would be useful to have somebody else who was also capable of utilizing Mr. Schulze's particular skill set. He indicated to us that only certain people are capable of practicing his arts, and he identified your colleague as one of those people. We will house your colleague at this facility for a month, where he will receive rudimentary training in certain skill sets we require of all our employees."

"And what 'skill sets' are those?"

"Things such as interrogation skills, basic self-defense …"

"The kid can take care of himself. I taught him."

"I have no doubt. That's why he'll only be here for a month. Then he will train under Mr. Schulze. While you may have reservations, you should understand certain realities. An efficient operation must maintain a proper structure. Each member plays an equally valuable role, but certain lines of authority must be properly delineated."

I laughed and looked at him hard.

"You're saying I don't have a choice. Why don't you stop wasting our time? I've already inferred that the reason you're delaying me here is so your people can get to him and give him your pitch without me around."

The Professor looked surprised. Then he gave me an extra-smarmy rendition of his pedophile uncle smile.

"You are a live wire, aren't you?" he said. "Well, I suppose that concludes our business for now. S87 will show you out."

While I walked along the vine-covered gate that surrounded the clinic, I wondered again what exactly was going on in there. During my occasional forays to the clinic, I did not mix much with the "residents," as The Professor called them. From my observations, they did not seem to be there against their will. But in light of my mandate to teach other members of The Agendum sleight-of-hand for purposes of surreptitiously slipping narcotics to residents, I was willing to go out on a limb and assume the clinic's functions were less than benign.

For the time being, I could do nothing about that. Early on, under guise of bragging about The Agendum's scope, The Suit had taken care to mention in the presence of each of us that they had eyes and ears in the local police force. It may have been a bluff. Were it not for my concerns about the kid's safety, I likely would have called it.

As it was, I'd been biding my time and looking for a chance to get myself and the kid a safe distance away before alerting authorities to what was going on in the clinic. As none of the "residents" appeared to be in mortal danger, I'd decided to wait and lull them into a false sense of security while simultaneously keeping an eye out for opportunities. While unwarranted hesitancy is never an effective course of action, this struck me as a situation in which unconsidered actions made in haste would be ill-advised.

Now, it seemed, my hand would be forced. The kid and I would have to make a break for it before they got hold of him.

While I drove home, violating speed limits to an imprudent degree, I wondered what I'd find. The kid had been acting sullen, like a teenager forced to stay in his room. I'd informed him on multiple occasions that the whole idea was to keep him out of sight – and thus out of mind — of these people. At length, I'd grown weary of repeating myself.

Fuck him. The kid wasn't stupid. He could figure out that I was right, whether he was happy about it or not.

When I returned to the house, a blue car was parked outside. It was unoccupied and looked like a new model. Inside, I found the kid sitting at the kitchen table, smoking a cigarette.

"When did you start smoking?" I asked him.

He shrugged.

"So where are they?" I asked.

"They've been and gone," he replied.

"Whose car is parked outside?"

"Mine," he said. "They left me the keys. Said it's for my use."

"Good," I said. "We'll be able to use it. It's time to stop dicking around. We need to get out of here."

I outlined my strategy. It wasn't foolproof by any means, but we were short on time. We would split our money. Then we would drive out of town, taking the cars in two separate directions. I'd double back, try to shake off any tail, and we'd rendezvous at a rest stop on the turnpike. We could ditch one of the cars. At the reststop, we would be surrounded by people. That would likely serve as a disincentive for them to try anything. And then ...

He held up a hand to cut me off.

"No," he said. "I'm not going."

"Kid, what the hell are you talking about?"

"I'm 22 years old and my name is Gary. Stop calling me kid."

"Goddamn it, what is wrong with you? We don't have time for this now!"

"Yes we do, because I'm not going. This is my decision, not yours, and I'm tired of you telling me what to do. They said I could be an important man in The Agendum, and I want to see what they have to offer me."

I stared at him, incredulous, as he stubbed out his cigarette in the saucer he'd been using as an ashtray.

"Are you entirely fucked in the head?" I yelled at him. "Do you really believe these pricks are going to do right by you?"

He stood, sending his chair clattering to the floor, and shouted back at me.

"You're saying you did right by me? Broken down carnivals! Scuzzy sex shows! That's all you have to offer me! I'm done!"

I could feel the next words emerging from my throat in a low growl.

"You ungrateful little shit. You begged me to take you in! And I did! I taught you everything you know!"

"And I've worked off that debt a hundred times over!" he shot back. "Busting my ass! Putting up with you and your goddamn attitude! Getting bossed around and yelled at day and night! Now I've got a chance to get out! To be treated with respect! And you're telling me not to take it? Fuck you, little man!"

He stomped into the living room and picked up a suitcase. Then he left the house and slammed the door behind him. Outside, I heard him starting the engine and driving away.

"Well, shit," I said to the empty kitchen.

The next day, a scared-looking older lady who said she was the local librarian showed up at my door with a hand-delivered letter. After that, I was very busy.

FILE 21

FROM PINKY

It has been said that some dream of success, while others wake up and work hard at it. Now all of you may officially consider yourselves members of the latter group. Allow me to extend my sincerest compliments to you on a job well done.

Project Anchovy is far from complete. The lion's share of the work, which will consist of compiling data, analyzing it and collating it for our clients, remains to be completed. Many of you reading this are close to completing your involvement with the project.

Although your involvement with The Agendum, I hasten to add, is not necessarily finished. We may find it necessary to make use of your skills at some future date, at which time we will contact you. And, it should go without saying, you can consider our prohibition on discussing any of this with anybody not involved with The Agendum to be in full effect. That prohibition includes but is not limited to family members. I'm certain that by now, you are all well aware of the consequences that will attend a failure to abide by this prohibition.

Still, the fact that work remains to be done takes nothing away from the extraordinary accomplishment that your efforts have already made possible. As I've previously noted, Project Anchovy will not only be of tactical use to our clients, but serve as groundbreaking research in the field of applied behavioralism.

For obvious tactical reasons, we cannot publicize the nature of our research at this present time. This is unfortunate. But I have no doubt that future generations will consider our work on a par with such advances in human knowledge as penicillin and theoretical phrenology.

To show our gratitude for your hard work, we will include a cash bonus in your next payment, as well as a coupon good for a free haircut at a local stylist. You've earned them.

By the way, most of you have yet to submit your reports. Don't forget, now!

Two nights after the Halloween Parade, Pinky sat in a parked car along a wooded road. He wore a dark, hooded sweatshirt over a dark T-shirt, with a knit hat pulled down low over his ears. As disguises go, he figured it wouldn't meet the skinny, bald guy's standards. But it would have to do for now.

It wasn't the same car The Agendum had provided him. That was sitting in the parking lot of a local department store where Pinky sometimes went to buy stuff.

After it got dark, Pinky had driven there just like he had many times in the past. He went through a set of swinging double doors in the back, where the men's room was located off the store's stockroom. In the men's room, Pinky had taken off the light-colored windbreaker and slacks he was wearing over his dark sweatshirt and jeans, and dumped them in the trashcan. Then he'd put on the knit hat, left the bathroom and ducked out a rear exit.

In a back parking lot used by employees was the other car Billy told him would be there. Pinky didn't know how Billy arranged it, and didn't want to know. The door was unlocked, and the keys were hidden in a crumpled paper towel under the passenger's seat.

The gas tank was full. That was good. After he picked up the new car, he'd spent an hour driving around aimlessly. He wanted to stay on the move. The city was still in an uproar after the Halloween Parade, and someone sitting around in a parked car for no particular reason might make people nervous. Finally, as he neared the designated time, he drove to the wooded road as Billy instructed.

Before long, he spotted a woman running toward the car in his rearview mirror. She wore jeans and a T-shirt. She threw open the rear door and got in the backseat. She had long, brown hair. She looked terrified.

Pinky pulled out into the road, turned on the headlights and drove. Not too fast.

"Down," he said, and she lay down in the backseat.

He heard her shivering. For a moment, he thought about taking off his sweatshirt and giving it to her, but stopping seemed like a bad idea. He turned up the heat and continued driving.

He went to a location he'd suggested and Billy had approved. It was the parking lot of a public park outside the city. No other cars were there at night. And it was located on a ridge that overlooked the approach road. If anybody was following him, Pinky would be able to see. Nobody was.

He gave her his sweatshirt then and asked if she was alright. She said she was. At one point, she asked if it would be OK if she went behind some nearby bushes to pee. He said no problem. He told her she could take a nap if she wanted. She said she wasn't sleepy. They didn't say much more.

Finally, a couple of hours past midnight, he looked at his watch. Billy had been very specific about the timing. Pinky started the engine again. Before long, he arrived at the street behind Billy's house.

"We're here," he said.

She started to hand him back his sweatshirt, but he told her to keep it

"Thank you," she said.

Then she opened the door and ran toward a rear gate in the wall surrounding the house. Somebody swung it open. It was dark and Pinky couldn't see who it was. The nearest streetlight was out. He guessed that wasn't a coincidence.

Pinky made straight for the nearest entrance to the Pennsylvania Turnpike. He wished he could floor it, but knew that getting pulled over would be about the worst mistake he could make.

On the Turnpike, he drove west. He had plenty of cash. He planned to head for Pittsburgh, regroup, and then move on from there. At the moment, he figured long-range plans were a luxury he didn't have.

His gas was getting low, so he pulled over at a rest stop. We went inside, gave the man behind the counter some cash, then went back out to refuel. A car pulled in at the pump behind him. Pinky finished fueling and replaced the nozzle on the pump.

Something hit him in the kidneys and his knees buckled. Then he was being hauled into the backseat of the car behind him.

The Russian was in the backseat. He pressed a knife against the side of Pinky's neck.

"Stay down and be quiet," The Russian said. His voice and manner were mild as ever, but Pinky knew better than to be reassured by that.

"Car keys," The Russian said. "Now."

Pinky fished them out of his pocket and handed them to the Russian, who in turn handed them to somebody in the front passenger seat. The passenger door opened and closed, then Pinky's car drove off.

Their car started. For a long time – hard to judge how long, seemed like an eternity – Pinky rode hunkered down in back with The Russian watching him closely. Pinky tried to talk once.

"Look, I…"

"Quiet," The Russian said.

At length, Pinky heard branches brushing along the car. Then it stopped.

"Out," The Russian said.

Pinky sat up. The bald, skinny master of disguises was at the wheel. He looked scared.

As Pinky exited the car, The Russian said to the bald skinny guy: "You finish your report?"

"Not … not yet."

"Finish it. Very important. Now wait here."

They were in a clearing in the woods, along with another car. It was the one Pinky had left in the department store parking lot.

The headlights on that department store car went on, and The Suit stepped out. He was smiling and holding a handgun.

The lights shone on Billy, who was duct taped to a tree. Sitting on the ground in front of Billy was a shotgun.

Both The Russian and The Suit pointed their guns at Pinky.

"Pick up the shotgun," The Suit said. "And stay facing away from us. You try to turn around, you're dead."

Pinky walked over and picked up the shotgun.

"You ever use one of those before?" The Suit asked.

"No."

"It's easy. You point the business end at the little dickwad taped to the tree and pull the trigger. No fucking around. Just do it."

Pinky looked at Billy. He felt paralyzed.

Billy looked him in the eye.

"I'm dead anyway," Billy said. His voice sounded small and choked. Not like his normal voice at all. "You might get out of this alive."

Pinky pulled the trigger.

"Good. Now drop the gun," The Suit said.

Pinky dropped it, then turned to face them.

"Pleasure working with you," The Suit said. "We'll be in touch if we ever need your services again."

"What do I do about …."

"That's your problem, killer," The Suit said, and climbed into the passenger seat of the car where the skinny bald guy waited.

The Russian looked at Billy and shrugged.

"Sorry," he said.

Then he got into the backseat and they drove away.

Pinky ran to Billy.

"Are you alright?" he yelled, knowing even as he said it what a stupid question it was.

Billy groaned. Then he spit up blood. Then he shit and pissed himself. Then he died.

They'd left the keys in the ignition of Pinky's car, along with a utility knife on the front seat. Pinky used it to cut the duct tape.

It was still dark when he walked through the unlocked gate in front of Billy's home and rang the doorbell. Billy was in the trunk of his car. Pinky didn't know the woman who'd been his passenger earlier. Nor did he have any idea what was going on. But she was apparently a friend of Billy's. Pinky was scared and exhausted, and could think of no place else to go.

He waited for a moment. He heard movement behind the door and guessed someone was looking at him through the peephole. The door opened a crack and he saw the woman's face.

"What do you want?" she whispered.

"I'm in trouble. Can I please come in?"

He sat on the living room couch and told her what had happened. She left the room, and returned a little while later with instructions.

He parked behind the back gate, leaving the trunk open, and walked around the corner. He waited 10 minutes, constantly glancing around, feeling more vulnerable than he ever had in his life. Then he returned to the car. The trunk was shut. He checked anyway to make sure Billy's body was gone. Then he drove off.

Pinky stuck around Batley. At first, he was afraid they might come after him again if he tried to leave. He assumed they were keeping an eye on him. He never saw any of them again, aside from one guy he'd glimpse around town from time-to-time — an older guy with a thick, gray beard and a badly scarred face. Also, a guy with a mullet and a good-looking woman with long brown hair, who'd both been teenagers when he saw them around the clinic. Come to think of it, that woman looked kind of like a younger version of the lady he gave a ride to that night.

He needed to make a living, and he found a way to turn the sleight-of-hand skills Billy taught him into an income. After a while, he assumed The Agendum had forgotten about him. He hung around Batley anyway, just because he didn't have anyplace in particular to go.

Then a few weeks ago, he'd opened his door to find a package on his porch. In it, along with a plastic frog lawn ornament, was a simple typed note reading: YOUR SERVICES ARE NEEDED ONCE MORE.

He got his first signal to pick up a message two weeks later. He picked it up, hoping for another meeting and intending to alert the police. What he found was a manila envelope containing photos of Mako, Veronica and Bob, the "kids" in his crew. The photos had all been taken in public places, apparently without the knowledge of their subjects. Their respective street addresses were written on the back of each photo. Also in the envelope was a message that when uncoded proved to consist of two sentences: "If you try to leave town or tell anyone, we will hurt them. Await further instructions."

Pinky never saw any of them, but several times he picked up coded messages that made references to a plan that had been in the works for at least two years, called Project Shadowboxer. None of the messages specified what it was.

About three weeks before the Warm Hearths Festival attack, he got his first specific order. He was supposed to pick somebody up at BWI Airport, and start calling around about dirt bike dealers in the Washington, D.C., area. He didn't do either of those things, and ignored all further calls for him to pick up messages. He stopped answering his phone.

A week before the festival attack, Pinky went into the men's room in the bar where he held his poker games. When he returned to his seat and lifted his drink, he saw a message penciled on the napkin under it.

"Payphone in back hall. 15 minutes. Or they get hurt."

When the phone rang and Pinky picked it up 15 minutes later, he recognized The Professor's voice.

"You know," The Professor said with a slight chuckle, "we've had men come close to fistfights over who gets to carry out surveillance on Veronica. But we're keeping an eye on all three of them. And on you. We can use your expertise."

"Listen," Pinky said. "I'll keep my mouth shut. I'll even stick around town if it makes you feel better to know where I am. But that's it. I want no part of whatever you're doing. You leave me alone and I'll leave you alone."

"You'll leave us alone? That sounded like a threat." The Professor didn't sound frightened or even angry. He sounded amused. "We expended a lot of time and man-hours training you. From the looks of things, you made a pretty good living with what you learned from us. If you'll pardon me, I must say you're being something of an ingrate."

Pinky swallowed. His mouth felt dry. He said: "Whatever it is you're doing, I know you've got a lot invested in it. And I can blow it for you. I know how you operate. I know your tricks. You just stay away from my kids and leave me out of it and I'll keep my mouth shut. By the way, I made arrangements. Something happens to me, people in a position to cause you serious grief are going to find out what you're up to."

Then he hung up. He was bluffing. But he hoped The Professor and his crew would figure it wasn't worth calling that bluff.

He stuck around town. He wanted to keep an eye on the members of his crew to make sure they were OK. He didn't want to tell them what was going on, figuring that might endanger them. And he had a feeling telling them to get out of town wouldn't do any good.

Pinky packed a couple of suitcases and moved into a motel room on the end of town, realizing as he did so that it was pretty weak as far as defensive strategies go.

He was right. He entered his room earlier that day to find a pair of men with leather masks waiting for him. They broke his leg with a baseball bat.

"How can I take them down?" I asked Pinky.

"You can't," he said. "They've got too many resources. Too many connections. Too much money."

"It's hopeless?"

"Maybe not. There's a word we use in my line of work. It's called 'slough.' It means the scam is blown. Maybe somebody in your crew has fucked up. Maybe the mark is onto you. Maybe a cop has wandered in to get a beer. Whatever the reason, the potential risk is now greater than the potential benefit. Someone says 'slough,' you beat it for the nearest exit and don't look back."

"So you're saying ..."

"You can't take them out. But if you make it cost more for them to stay here than to go, they'll go. Simple economics."

I started for the door when he called me back. He handed me a large envelope filled with sheets of paper.

"Transcriptions of messages from The Agendum," Pinky said. "Some are old ones from 15 years ago. Some are new ones. I had them hidden in a safe place. I told Mako where to find them, and he brought them here. You might find them useful."

"They watching us now?"

"It's possible."

"What will they do to you if they find out you gave me these?"

"They'll throw me a 'Get Lei-ed in Hawaii' party. Margaritas. Hot babes in grass skirts. They're swell that way. Just do me a favor. Don't let them hurt my kids."

I'd heard Pinky fake a hundred different types of emotion when pulling off one con or another. But I'd never before heard the raw fear underlying those last six words.

FROM PINKY

Welcome to The Agendum! Or should I say welcome back?

This is a bulletin specifically for those of you who were previously involved in the great success that was Project Anchovy. I regret that I cannot welcome each of you back personally with a hearty handshake, as befits a reunion with a respected colleague. Unfortunately, the logistics of our current projects preclude this.

I hope you've all fared well in the years since we last worked together. Personally, I've lost a bit more hair. And quite often these days, I feel as though my pants are a bit too tight. But I am otherwise fit and happy.

I trust you all recall the basic procedures by which we operate. Your silence is crucial. One change worth noting is that we now actively discourage communication between those involved in The Agendum when it does not pertain directly to the job at hand.

Regrettably, our previously lax policy in this regard resulted in some unforeseen difficulties.

Perhaps I should provide a few particulars about our current endeavor, which we have dubbed "Project Shadowboxer."

It is an inevitable and regrettable side effect of the milieu in which we operate that the public at large cannot know of our accomplishments. For "Project Anchovy" is widely considered to be a groundbreaking study in the field of population-scale manipulation technology, and its findings have come to play a major role in the operational strategies of our clients.

Project Shadowboxer will be a follow-up to Project Anchovy. We will take some of the findings of Project Anchovy and test them in a somewhat different set of circumstances.

Whereas Project Anchovy's focus was on a small-scale population's response to an acute mortal threat potential paradigm, Shadowboxer will focus more on a large-scale population's response to a long-term mortal threat potential paradigm.

The overall intent of The Agendum will likely play little part in your individual duties. As before, we will contact you if and when we need you to do something, and we will expect you to perform that task to the best of your abilities.

Yes, challenges certainly lie before us.

But remember that being part of a winning team is a reward in itself.

FROM PINKY

Before I go any further, I would like to clarify something in my last missive. I had stated the following: "And quite often these days, I feel as though my pants are a bit too tight." That was intended as a jocular reference to my weight gain since Project Anchovy. It was not a reference to anything else. Grow up, T5.

With that out of the way, the purpose of this missive is to notify you of a wonderful opportunity that has come our way.

If you will indulge me, I would like to provide you with a bit of backstory that involves my past career, providing fee-based professional consultation.

It was in this capacity that I was asked to participate in some some behavioral studies pertaining to a pharmaceutical drug. As neither botany nor chemistry are my fields of expertise, I will not detail its components. It was derived from a mildly hallucinogenic compound used in the religious ceremonies of several primitive, hill-dwelling cultures.

The drug derived from it was not hallucinogenic, but in clinical trials was found to have promising results for treating both obesity and depression. Accordingly, its manufacturer marketed it to pregnant women, both to help them lose weight and cope with postpartum depression. A subsequent audit of the clinical studies found that they were fundamentally flawed, and concealed a statistically significant number of deaths by childbirth among the test subjects, but this would not come to light until years later.

The drug was pulled from the market soon after its release. This was not due to health concerns, but rather to a controversial advertising campaign featuring the tagline: "I hit her because she got fat."

A number of years after its release, an international group of its users joined in a class-action lawsuit. I was hired by the manufacturer to study an odd and singular purported side effect that had only recently come to light.

Children of mothers who had taken the drug were exhibiting an effect that some medical professionals likened to an epileptic episode. With different stimuli serving as a trigger, the children would lapse into a trance-like state. They would be conscious but unresponsive, and remain in that state for spans of time ranging from several minutes to an hour or more. They would eventually emerge unharmed but with no memory of what had transpired.

It so happened that I was asked to conduct tests on a boy who was so afflicted. The boy in question was 12 years old, and being raised by a single mother. His IQ was quantified in the low-average range and a comprehensive examination revealed no other physical, mental or psychological anomalies. He was, in short, a healthy and thoroughly unremarkable preadolescent boy.

Still, my tests yielded some results that were nothing short of remarkable when I placed him in a hypnotic trance. (I have been trained in hypnotism and have made use of it on occasion, but have generally found the phenomenon to be of little practical applicability.)

This boy, first of all, demonstrated astounding mental feats while under the influence of hypnotism. He instantly recalled 30-digit numbers when so instructed, and also proved capable of memorizing the order of an entire shuffled deck of cards after viewing it for a mere instant.

I tried one more experiment, with results of similarly weighty implication. I had procured a dead rat from a laboratory, and placed it on my desk in plain sight, next to a vial of powdered sugar.

The boy's mother brought him into my office and then left to wait outside. He was visibly upset at the sight of the dead rat. I apologized to him for leaving it there, stating that the rat had been sick and I had put it out of its misery with the powdered cyanide in the vial. I warned him not to go near the vial, as the poison it contained was quite deadly.

I then put the boy in a trance. This was quickly facilitated as I had conditioned him to go into and out of hypnotic states in response to a seemingly innocuous word combination, which is clinically known as employing a "trigger phrase." I instructed him to conduct himself as normal when his mother reentered the room. Subsequently, I called her in and poured her a cup of coffee. Then I apologized and asked her if she would be so kind as to get a form from my receptionist.

As my receptionist delayed the boy's mother outside, I instructed him to pour a quantity of the powdered sugar, which he believed to be cyanide, into his mother's coffee. He did this with neither protest nor hesitation, then afterward watched her drink the coffee with no apparent emotion.

I did not include this incident in my official report, for obvious reasons. The lawsuit was eventually settled out of court. The boy and his mother, unfortunately, died not long afterward in an automobile accident.

I retained a portion of the drug for many years afterward. Once I went into my current line of work I sensed the commercial potential of producing another version of that 12-year-old boy I described. The main barrier was the fact that I had no access to a pregnant woman to whom I might administer the drug.

As it happened, just such an opportunity came about almost by accident during the course of Project Anchovy. Unfortunately, through a set of circumstances that I need not go into here, we lost track of both the mother and the child.

But just recently, we learned of the child's location and have initiated action to utilize this knowledge for profitable purposes.

We may or may not call upon you individually to assist in this element of our enterprise, but we wanted you to be apprised. It just goes to show that from an individual seed of hard work grows the tree of success, and it has many branches.

FILE 22

I spent some time sitting in a coffee shop off the hospital's main lobby, nursing a lukewarm cup of watery java while I read through the papers Pinky gave me.

I'd parked near the emergency department when I arrived on the assumption that's where Pinky would be, so my route out took me past it. I happened to look through the emergency department's glass doors as I walked by and did a double take.

I went in. My buddy Tom, the newspaper reporter, was sitting in one of the chairs, holding a compress to his eye. He looked banged up, but not too bad.

"Holy shit!" I said. "What happened to you? You OK, buddy?"

"They've already looked at me," he said. "Just a few abrasions and contusions. Nothing serious."

"What happened?"

"The Slain," he said. "They accosted me on the street. It would appear they took exception to my column calling them cowards. But if they think this will intimidate me, they are sorely mistaken. I am a journalist. I must write the truth, and consequences be damned!"

TOM JERKFACE: This is an accurate account of our conversation at the hospital. I was indeed assaulted by 10 members of The Slain earlier that day.

It happened as follows. I had finished up work at 6 p.m. and was walking to a nearby tavern for a bit of liquid refreshment, as is my wont.

Whilst I proceeded along the side street behind my office, 10 men sprang out of an alley and into my path. One of them, the apparent leader, stepped forward.

"You're going to write shit like that about us, you're going to pay," he said.

I looked him straight in the eye.

"Your mouth is writing checks your body can't cash, hoss," I said.

He hesitated for a beat or two, clearly intimidated by my icy coolness. He and his minions advanced. I took a breath, marshaling my chi energy. Then I sprang. My fist whistled through the air like a steel whip ...

PUBLISHER'S NOTE: At this point in the narrative, Mr. Jerkface describes how he sustained several minor injuries in the ensuing fight, but eventually drove off all 10 of his assailants with his superior martial arts skills. According to Mr. Jerkface's account, several attractive young women who just happened to be passing by stopped to observe the fight with evident admiration, and afterward insisted on giving him their phone numbers. I have opted not to include Mr. Jerkface's account because it is at notable variance with a police report filed on the incident.

The police report relies heavily on an eyewitness account provided by one Leonard Watson, whom Codorus Press' researchers have determined is the homeless gentleman referred to in the first file. According to Mr. Watson, Mr. Jerkface was, in fact, assaulted on a sidestreet behind his newspaper. But there were two attackers, not 10. And they soon desisted out of apparent pity and disgust because of Mr. Jerkface's copious begging and weeping. Mr. Watson quoted one of the assailants as stating the following: "Ah, fuck this. It's like kicking a Chihuahua."

I clapped Tom on the shoulder.

"Well take care of yourself, buddy," I told him. "Anything happens to you, I don't know what I'd read on the shitter."

I started to walk away when I thought of something.

"You know that little recorder you use for interviews? You got that with you by any chance? Any way I could borrow it?"

He said he did and I could, then fished a little black box about the size of a cigarette pack out of his jacket and handed it to me. He asked me what I needed it for, and I told him I just had a hunch I could use it.

I went through the exit leading onto the back parking lot. Warm night. Like summer, almost. Someone called my name. It was Ken, sitting on a bench outside the hospital door.

He said he'd finished his physical therapy more than an hour ago and Luanne was supposed to pick him up. He'd tried calling, but hadn't been able to reach her. Could I drive him home?

I pulled my car around. I tried to help him to the car, but he insisted on limping over with the help of his cane and awkwardly working himself into the front passenger seat. We were quiet at first. Then Ken spoke.

"I don't like this," he said. "This isn't like her."

"Yeah, I've got a bad feeling about it too," I said. "You mind if we take a pass by the place before we pull up?"

"Not at all."

I drove slowly down their street, but not slow enough that we'd draw attention. The house was lit up. Luanne's car was in the driveway out front, but not Ty's pickup. I figured Ty was still down at the farm.

"How about if we take a drive around the block?" I asked.

Again, slow but not too slow, taking it all in. I made a right at the end of the block, drove down a couple more blocks and pulled into a side street.

"You see them?" I asked.

"The cars? Yes I did."

"Anybody ever park like that before?"

"Not that I can remember. This isn't good."

The otherwise abandoned block the Bacons occupied had an alley running down the middle. Parked in both entrances to that alley were apparently abandoned cars, effectively barricading it. Each one was parked a couple of yards from the intersection, so they wouldn't be obvious to somebody who just happened to be driving by.

Only two open passages to the Bacons' block remained. One was the driveway in front of their house. The other was an alley that started just past their backyard garage, and led to the street behind the house. Somebody, from the looks of things, wanted to funnel any foot or motor traffic along a very specific path.

"What now?" Ken asked.

"Not sure I want to call the police yet. The way they're backed up these days, I'm guessing they wouldn't exactly dispatch a SWAT team if I call about some bad parking. I want to take a look first. Can you drive?"

"Might give me some trouble but I'll manage."

I helped him into the driver's seat, and he didn't object this time. He gave me his baseball cap, which I pulled down low over my face. He also gave me his dark green windbreaker. It was shabby and too big for me, with sleeves that hung down past my hands. Perfect. It concealed the heavy metal flashlight I held tight against my forearm.

I scraped some grime from the gutter and rubbed it on my face. I took a pull from my flask, swished it around in my mouth and spit it out. Might as well smell the part.

I spotted a bottle under a bush, which had once held some cheap wine, and carried it with me to complete the effect. I walked toward the back alley leading to the Bacon house, taking care to stagger as I did.

By the time I got to the alley's entrance, Ken had already pulled the car over at the end of the block. If I didn't come back out, he was going to get help. I tried to find comfort in that. It wasn't working.

I took a step into the alley. A light shone up ahead, near the intersection with the crosswise alley. But back here, it was pretty dark. Another step. Then another. I heard movement and spun around. In the alley's dim light, I could make out that the man was tall and had a ponytail. The "fire policeman" from the Walk for Batley. He didn't seem to recognize me.

"Hey buddy," I said, slurring my words. "Think you can help me out? Just need a couple bucks for something to eat."

"Get the fuck out of here," he hissed, giving me a violent shove. "Now!"

I stumbled, staggered a few steps in the opposite direction, then turned to face him again.

"Come on man," I whined. "Just one dollar! That's all …"

He advanced, flicking his wrist. I heard a click and saw a flash of metal. Filed-down lockblade, by the sound of it. Maybe just trying to scare me, but I wasn't taking that chance.

I threw the empty wine bottle at his feet, smashing it. He looked down. I got him in the side of the head with my flashlight. It made a sound like metal striking a rock that's wrapped in cloth. He went down.

I crouched, flashlight held at the ready. If he had any friends in the immediate vicinity, now would be the time they'd rush me. Nothing.

I turned on my flashlight and looked around. Nothing suspicious, as far as I could see. That was suspicious in itself. I slowly made my way toward the lighted intersection with the other alley, sweeping the flashlight beam back and forth as I went.

When I got I got close to the intersection, my beam picked up something the streetlight hadn't. A wire.

I panned the flashlight over to the side and took in what the wire was attached to. Then I let out a long, low whistle.

Soon I was back at the mouth of the alley with Ken, who'd driven the car there when I waved him over. I'd dragged the asshole with the ponytail back by the car. His hands were ziplocked behind him and for good measure I'd tied his bootlaces together. It wasn't exactly Houdini-proof, but it would do for the time being.

My plan was to drive all of us to the police station immediately, but Ken absolutely refused. Before we did anything else, he wanted to cut that tripwire.

"I'm more qualified to deal with this than anybody they could get on short notice," he said. "And those are my children in that house!"

I gave up arguing and helped him get down the alley with his aluminum cane.

I handed him my flashlight so he could check out the setup himself. He shined it along the glistening tripwire that would have been invisible otherwise. One end was tied to an electrical meter, about knee-height, on a building flanking the alley. The other was attached to a bundle of three paper-wrapped cylinders taped to another electrical meter.

"What's with the sacks?" I whispered, pointing to the semicircle of burlap bags surrounding the bundle.

"Tamping," Ken whispered back. "It's to direct the force of the blast at whoever triggers it. Funny. For all the trouble they took to set this up, they sure didn't go out of their way to conceal it. Oh well."

He dug in his pocket and took out a multipurpose tool that looked like a Swiss Army knife on steroids. He unfolded a hefty-looking pair of clippers.

"I can't get down to the ground myself," he said. "You'll have to give me a hand."

I clasped my arms around his chest and lowered him to a sitting position facing the wire.

"Now get back behind the car," he said.

"No. I'm not leaving you here alone."

"Good thinking. If I make a mistake, you'll be able to pick me up and carry me away before it goes off. We'll probably have time to stop for beers and pizza. Get back there, goddamn it!"

I went, and watched him from behind my car. A cold trickle of sweat ran down my back. After a minute or two, an eternity, he signaled me by swinging my flashlight back and forth and gestured for me to approach.

When I got there, the trip wire was cut. I grabbed him under his arms and hauled him to his feet. He leaned on his cane.

Just then, we saw headlights and heard a motor. Ty's pickup pulled into the driveway. Behind him was Michael on his bike.

Ty got out of the truck and started toward the front door. He'd changed back into regular clothes and had cleaned off the skull makeup. I was going to call him when I heard the front door banging open. A guy with a leather mask ran across the front lawn and into our alley with Ty chasing after him. Instinctively, I stepped between Ken and the running man.

When the guy got to the spot in the alley where the trip-wire had been, he gave a jump, continued running a ways then dropped to the ground, tucking into a fetal position. Ty ran after him, bent down, grabbed a handful of his shirt and hauled him to his feet.

At that moment, it registered on Ty that me and Ken were there. He looked back.

"Dad?" he said. "You OK?

The guy Ty was holding slashed at his face. He'd taken advantage of Ty's momentary distraction to pull a knife. Ty had just enough time to draw back and raise his shoulder, which was where the knife hit.

He lost hold of the guy, who ran off. Ty made to run after him when Ken shouted.

"No son! Don't be a fool! He's got a knife!"

Ty started toward us. I was about to ask about his shoulder when he said "Oh shit! Luanne and Paul!" and ran for the house.

For a second, the indecision was killing me. I wanted to run after Ty to check on Luanne and Paul. But I couldn't leave Ken outside by himself if the guy with the knife was still running around. I helped Ken along, as fast as we could move, to the front door and then inside.

Paul and Luanne were duct-taped to a couple of chairs. Duct tape covered Paul's mouth, too. A strip of tape hung loose next to Luanne's mouth, where Ty had pulled it free.

"Michael!" Luanne shouted. "The kitchen!"

I ran back to the kitchen and found it totally trashed. The table was tipped over and chairs were smashed. A cabinet had been knocked off the wall and shattered plates covered the floor.

Ty was looking through the back door that led out to the yard.

"Michael must have chased them out this way," Ty said. "I should go look for him. He might need help."

"Michael can take care of himself," I said. "You'd be better off sticking around, in case they come back."

We went back in the living room, where Ken had already taken the tape off Paul's mouth. Now he used the multipurpose tool I'd seen in the alley to cut away the duct tape holding Paul to his chair.

"Where's the phone?" I asked. "I'm calling the police."

"No!" Luanne practically screamed.

"Luanne, come on," I said. "We need to..."

"No police! I'll explain later! Please!"

I was stunned. Had Luanne Bacon said the word "please?" Ty and Ken also seemed taken aback. But she was clearly upset and neither seemed inclined to argue. I persisted.

"Luanne, I know you're upset," I said. "But whatever your reasons, you need to understand that everybody in this house is in danger right now. Ty chased a guy down the alley, who's probably getting a bunch of his buddies together as we speak. So how about ..."

"Don't think they'll be back," Michael said, striding in through the front door. "They like to strike and run. Not like them to stick around someplace where they've been run off. Here, let me give you a hand."

He bent down to where Luanne was bound to her chair, pulled out the God-knife and began carefully cutting at the tape.

I tried to argue my case again. But Luanne was becoming even more unhinged in her insistence that we not call the police, and none of the others were backing me up. So I dropped it, hoping to at least hurry things along so we could get everybody out of the house and relocated someplace safe.

Ken finished up with Paul. I noticed a big, wet stain in Paul's lap. He saw me notice and turned red.

"I had to go real bad and I couldn't hold it," he said. "I tried ..."

"Shit, buddy, that's nothing to be embarrassed about," I said. "How long did they keep you here?"

"A couple of hours," Luanne said. "We came home from the meeting and they were waiting for us."

Knowing Luanne, I would have expected her voice to be filled with rage. But it wasn't. She just sounded frightened and sad.

"Did they say anything?" I asked.

"No!" Luanne looked sharply at Paul.

"Uh, no. They didn't say anything," Paul said, blushing even deeper. "Hey, can I go. ..."

"Oh course," Ken said. "And he's right. There's nothing to be embarrassed about."

Paul practically ran out of the room anyway.

"I'll go make sure he's alright," Ken said, and followed after him.

Blood trickled down Michael's face. A long gash – not deep, by the look of it — ran the horizontal length of his forehead. He pulled a bandanna out his jacket pocket and tied it around his head, stanching the blood.

"You OK?" I asked him.

"Yeah. There was one here in the living room when I got in. I chased him out into the kitchen and two of his buddies jumped me. One of them got me with a knife. I managed to fight them off long enough to get out the Godknife. That sent them running. I chased them for a few blocks, but blood was running into my eyes and I lost sight of them."

"Good thing you happened to be along," I said.

"Yeah. I'd been meaning to talk to Ty about teaching a self-defense class for the citizen patrols. I drove down to that Moondog Farm to discuss it. He was just finishing up for the night, so I suggested we come back here and bring Luanne in on the discussion."

Luanne, by now free from her chair, looked at Ty's cut shoulder, which his sleeveless T-shirt left exposed.

"You're bleeding," she said. Again, that sadness in her voice.

Ty looked down at his shoulder as though he had forgotten about the cut.

"Probably be a good idea to take you to the hospital and get it looked at," I said.

"No!"

That came from Luanne. To my surprise, she started crying.

"It doesn't look too bad," she said, wiping at her eyes. "We can take care of it here."

"That's right," Michael said. "Got any disinfectant?"

Luanne left, then returned with a bottle and some gauze.

"I couldn't find any bandages," Luanne said. "Can you just hold it in place?"

"We can improvise," Michael said.

He stripped off his leather jacket. Then he took off his own T-shirt and cut it into strips with the Godknife.

Luanne gave a small gasp when Michael took his shirt off. His muscles were big as a bodybuilder's, but without a bodybuilder's rigidity. They flowed and coiled like enormous pythons under his skin with every movement. Tattooed the length of his back were two giant wings. These weren't the abstract wings on the Order of Gabriel logo. Each line of each feather was tricked out in intricate detail.

Michael poured disinfectant on the gauze and held it against Ty's cut. He handed the strips of his T-shirt to Luanne.

"Here," he said. "You do it."

She continued crying, and shrank back a little. Michael touched her chin, raised her face and looked into her eyes.

"Come on," he said, his voice more gentle than I'd ever heard it. "He's your little brother. He's hurt and he needs your help. You can do this."

"Yes," she said, her voice very quiet. "Thank you."

She tied the strips around Ty's shoulder, holding the gauze in place. Michael threw his leather jacket back on over his now-bare torso.

"I left one of them trussed up out there," I said. "We should check on him."

"Good idea," Michael said. "Luanne can come with us. Ty, why don't you stay with Ken and Paul, just in case?"

Ty nodded.

Outside, the guy with the ponytail was missing. I said his buddies must have carried him off. Michael agreed. Luanne barely seemed interested.

I started back toward the house, but Michael waved me and Luanne toward the garage instead, saying he needed to talk to us. We walked in a side door. And Michael, who knew the layout pretty well by then, switched on the overhead light.

He looked at Luanne and spoke in a very soft voice.

"They told you, didn't they? That's why you didn't want Ty going to the hospital. You were afraid the hospital would notify police that someone came in with a knife wound, and they'd investigate."

She nodded.

"I suspected for a long time," Michael said. "I didn't want to believe it, and I wanted more evidence before I accused him. There's no point in denying it anymore. I know you want to protect him. But other people might get hurt or killed."

She nodded again. Then she broke down and sobbed loudly. Michael put his arms around her and she cried against his chest. After a few minutes, she composed herself and Michael asked her what happened.

After the meeting, she and Paul stopped off at home. She was going to make them dinner, then drive to the hospital and pick up Ken.

Four men in leather masks waited for them in the living room. Before she had a chance to do anything, they had a knife to Paul's throat and threatened to cut him if she made any noise or tried to make a break for it.

Once they had Luanne and Paul taped to the chairs and gagged, one of them looked at Luanne and said.

"Your brother failed us. This is the price you pay."

"Shut up!" one of the others said. "Maybe she doesn't know."

"Bullshit, she knows," the first one said. Then he looked back at Luanne and held his knife in front of her face.

"For all we know, it was her idea," he said. "Ty was a good servant of The One Who Takes. A good leader. If he didn't start skimming from Amos Keller, there wouldn't be any problems. Was that your idea, bitch? Huh? Get a little money for yourself?"

They started talking among themselves then, analyzing the situation. It seemed this Amos Keller had been supplying them with stolen cars for their operation. But the last payments came up short. Now Keller was threatening to make trouble for them, which they couldn't afford at that stage of the operation. A lot of their talk was about whether it would be easier to pay off Keller or fight him.

And they blamed Ty for the whole thing.

Luanne told the story in a flat, emotionless voice, as if she was beyond crying at that point. Michael nodded.

"Makes sense," he said. "Ty knew he was playing a dangerous game. He probably wanted to set aside something extra for you and the guys in case he didn't come out of this alive."

"I don't understand," I said. "You're saying Ty's one of their leaders?"

Michael continued looking at Luanne.

"You have to understand something about your brother," he told her. "He's not a bad man. These people — they have ways of getting into your head. I know so much about it because I used to be one of them."

Luanne gasped, and stared at him open-mouthed. Michael blew out a deep breath, then shuddered.

"It's not easy for me to talk about," he said. "They got to me when I was young. I'd been in trouble most of my life. No family. In and out of juvenile homes. They gave me structure. Something to belong to. You'd be amazed, the way they can twist things around in your mind."

He massaged his temples, as if the memories caused him physical pain.

"I did things for them. Bad, bad things. The Order of Gabriel rescued me. Now I've devoted my life to stopping them. If all my efforts, every danger I face, spares one child from going through what I did, it'll be worth it."

"But ... Ty?" Luanne said.

"They give you a sense of purpose," Michael said. "Make you believe the most warped, evil things are right. And they teach you how to keep it all hidden from everyone around you, even the people closest to you, until they need you. In Schulze's clinic, they worked on both of you, right? Were you together when this happened?"

"No," Luanne said. "They'd take us off in different parts of the clinic."

"Whatever they did to Ty, it sunk in deep," Michael said. "Think about it. He knows martial arts. He knows explosives. He was like a time bomb himself, just waiting for these people to activate him. And Cabot obviously did something to Paul when he was keeping him at his house. Neither of them is beyond help, but we need to act fast. Especially for Paul."

Luanne stared at the ground for a long moment.

"What do we do now?" she asked.

"My organization has a way of dealing with these situations," Michael said. "We'll have to keep Ty under observation. Make sure he doesn't harm anyone else."

"Please don't hurt him!" Luanne said.

Michael's voice softened.

"That would be an absolute last resort, and only if he's putting somebody else in grave danger. We've got inpatient treatment for people like Ty. Deconditioning. It's not easy, but it works. Hey, I turned out alright if I say so myself."

That got a small, sad smile from her.

"But Ty's clearly got influence over Paul," Michael went on, "So we need to get Paul away from him as soon as possible. Who are Paul's legal guardians?"

"That's me and Ty," Luanne said. "The courts have Daddy listed as incapacitated because of his mental problems."

"We can handle that," Michael said. "I've got forms at my house. We can work out the legal particulars later. The most important thing is to get Paul away from Ty and someplace safe. Can you bring him to my place now?"

"Can we have a couple hours?" Luanne asked. "I need to talk to him. Get his things together."

"I don't know how safe that is," Michael said.

"You said they probably won't come back tonight," I told him. "I'll be here to keep an eye on things. We'll keep Ty away from Paul. And I'll give you a call if there's any trouble."

"Please?" Luanne said. "The idea that we'll be breaking up the family ..." her voice broke."

Michael put both hands on Luanne's shoulders and looked into her eyes.

"It's OK," he said. "Just don't be long. And remember, the worst is over. It's going to be alright."

He lowered his face to hers and their mouths locked for a short but intense interval. They pulled away from each other, both looking flustered and surprised.

"I'll take care of everything," Michael said. He left.

I fished in my pocket, found a cigar and lit it. Then I addressed Luanne.

"He's full of shit, you know."

"What?"

"You brother is innocent," I told her. "He has nothing to do with any of this."

"What are you talking about?"

"Amos Keller. That's a name I pulled out of my ass. A story I made up. And Michael's the only one I told it to. Everything he just told us — everything he's ever told us — was a goddamn lie."

Ten minutes later, Luanne was yelling at me. Telling me I was the one who's full of shit.

I was trying to explain to her what Pinky said, the papers he'd shown me, what I'd uncovered that afternoon during my research at City Hall. It wasn't easy because she kept breaking into near-hysterical tirades.

"A con artist told you some crazy story and you believe every word of it?" she said. "And so what if you told Michael some made-up story? What if The Slain were talking about another Amos Keller?"

I took another drag on my now-dwindled cigar.

"So you're telling me there really is an Amish gangster named Amos Keller, same as the one I made up?" I said. "Now that would be an ironic coincidence, wouldn't it?"

"Michael cares about us!" she said. "He's the only one who ever really did! Why should I trust you instead? You just come around stinking of booze, asking questions and making wisecracks! Who are you, anyway?"

I didn't respond. I let her seethe while I removed my flask from my jacket, took a swig and then offered her one. She just glared, and I put it away.

"Let me ask you something," I said. "Michael walks into the house where three armed men are waiting. He gets into a life-or-death fight with all three of them in the kitchen. We're talking big fight! Furniture smashed, cabinets knocked off the wall. They run outside and he chases them for three blocks and then he runs back to make sure you're alright. We can assume he's running full-speed the whole time. It's a warm night. He's wearing his leather jacket. Wouldn't you expect his T-shirt to be soaked with sweat?"

She didn't say anything.

"It wasn't, was it?" I asked. "When you handled those strips he cut to make the bandage, they were bone dry, weren't they?"

She didn't say anything for a moment. Then she started to speak but I held up a hand to silence her.

"Wait a second," I said. "Did you hear something?"

I went over the door and opened it. Now the sound of shouting and crashing from the direction of the house was plainly audible.

Luanne and I both ran at full speed through the back door into the kitchen. Ty held Paul in a full nelson. Paul thrashed around, and Ty visibly struggled to keep him under control without hurting him.

Ty's T-shirt had a ragged hole in the chest and he was bleeding.

"I am The One Who Takes!" Paul shouted, his voice high-pitched and crazy. "You will all die! I'll laugh as the maggots devour your eyes!"

"He bit me!" Ty said, his eyes wide. "We were watching TV on the couch, waiting for you two to come in. All of a sudden, he freaked out and went for Dad! I pulled him off and he bit me!"

"I am The One Who Takes! I will fuck your rotting carcasses!" Paul screamed, and then he started growling like a wild dog.

"What were you watching on TV?" I asked Ty.

"What?" He looked at me like I was crazier than Paul.

"The TV! What were you watching?"

"I dunno. The public channel. Some kind of documentary about angels."

Then it hit me. I put my face up to Paul's and yelled loud enough for everyone in the room to hear me over his growling.

"In God we trust, all others pay cash!"

Paul's growling ceased immediately and his body went limp. Ty caught an arm around his waist before he dropped to the floor and set him in a chair.

Paul shook his head like he was trying to wake himself up from a nap, then looked up at us.

"What's ... what's going on?" he asked.

Later, Ty, Luanne, Ken and I sat around the kitchen table. Two of the kitchen chairs were broken, so we'd brought a couple in from the living room.

Paul had been sent to his room so we could talk. He hadn't been happy about it, but Luanne made it clear that now wasn't the time for an argument.

"I know about post-hypnotic suggestion," she said. "When we were in Schulze's clinic, one of the top guys there – a real asshole who was always wearing a fancy suit – gave me some instructions in how to use it. But he said its uses were limited."

"I think Paul might be a special case," I told her. "It can be triggered with a word or a phrase. When he was in City Hall, I figure someone called him on the phone while we were in the meeting and said it. It would have to be something he wouldn't be likely to hear under normal circumstances. I take it you've picked up on Michael's thing about angels?"

"Well yeah," Luanne said. "It hasn't exactly been subtle."

"So it might have been one of those obscure angel names," I said. "Remiel or Gotohell or whatever. Paul must have heard it on the TV and it triggered the hypnotic state again. I figure someone programmed him at the Pigeon Clinic."

I got up and grabbed myself a beer from the fridge. I was thinking about kindly old Dr. Pigeon. With his short stature, thick glasses, slight paunch and bald dome. He must have shaved the pencil moustache somewhere along the line.

"Is he safe now?" Ty asked.

"It eventually wears off on its own," Luanne said. "That's what the asshole in the suit told me, anyway. We might not want to take him to any Bible readings for a few days."

"But you're asking if he's safe?" I said. "The answer is no. Not yet. These people want him bad. And so I can get a better idea of what we're up against, I'd appreciate it if one of you would tell me what exactly went on in that clinic."

Nobody spoke for a long time. Then Ken did.

"I guess that's my job," he said.

He looked at Ty and then at Luanne.

"Why don't you two go out and keep your brother company?" he said.

Luanne pulled the exact same petulant face Paul had when he left the room earlier, which I thought was kind of funny.

"Hand me one of those beers from the fridge, would you?" Ken said, after they'd left.

And then Ken told me his story while we sat at the kitchen table.

FILE 23

FROM BILLY'S PAPERS

Three months after the kid's less-than-gracious departure, I sat at an upstairs window, looking through a hole I'd cut in the cheap, plastic blinds. Our last conversation that concluded with the slamming door made it patently obvious that the kid underestimated me. Yet it would be the very epitome of foolish arrogance on my part to entirely discount the possibility that I'd underestimated him as well.

In preparation for this moment, I'd spent weeks conducting myself with a rigorously predictable routine, having readjusted the training schedule for various pupils foisted upon me by of The Agendum in order to allow for it.

At precisely 5 p.m. every day, I would leave the house and drive to a local news agency. I would purchase four newspapers from around the country, as well as the Times of London.

For the next few hours, I would sit at a bar and read the newspapers. In that interval, I would order a sandwich and fries for dinner and nurse no more than four beers. I did not want to become drunk, but bar staffers tend to look askance at patrons taking up valuable real estate without making it worth their financial while. Hence the beer.

I would return home at precisely 10 p.m., and would not bother scanning the street while I walked up the driveway. Unless I had misjudged the kid to an extent that would render all of my preparations moot, there would be nothing to see.

If the kid was observing me, he would have taken careful note of my regular schedule and planned accordingly. Which meant the time had come to introduce a subtle deviation or two.

In recent days, I had gone to neither the news agency nor the bar. I had parked my car on a sidestreet, donned a hooded sweatshirt and made my way through a series of surreptitious routes to the back door of the house.

I would then spend the ensuing hours sitting at the blinds and watching. At 9:30 p.m., I would return to my car in the same stealthy manner, throw the hooded sweatshirt back in the trunk, and arrive back at the house at 10.

I was rather surprised that I had to wait four whole days before spotting the kid's spiffy blue car as it made a pass along the street at 5:30 one afternoon. I could clearly discern him in the driver's seat. He would be circling, on the watch for casual bystanders, and I estimated that I had sufficient time.

I ran down to the kitchen and positioned myself beneath the kitchen table with the long, overhanging tablecloth. It was a sturdy piece of furniture that I'd retained all of these years because it could easily bear the weight of a glass case containing a deformed, preserved animal or three.

I'd never bothered mentioning to the kid that it was a relic of the seance show with which I'd once assisted Gypsy Sam. On the underside were handholds. The underside once also included several straps that had been long lost to the years. I'd recently replaced them.

I'm not as young as I was in the days of those bogus seances, but I still had little difficulty hoisting myself against the underside of the table, securing my hands and feet in the holds, and affixing the straps across my waist and shoulders to hold me in place.

In the old days, I would have spent my time beneath the table listening to Gypsy Sam droning on in his sonorous, medium's voice about the messages he was receiving from the great beyond, sending me cues through subtleties of phrasing. I would then employ my knuckles to provide the appropriate rappings against the underside of the table. For now, however, my goal was only to remain unseen.

I heard the door being unlocked and opened. Footsteps proceeded through every inch of the house. In the kitchen, he went through all of the cabinets. I would assume he looked under the table. If so, he did not perceive my presence.

At length, he exited the house. I stayed in place. He reentered and ascended the stairs. For an hour, the intermittent buzzing of power tools sounded from above. Then he descended the stairs and left once more. I heard his car outside, starting up and driving away.

To be on the safe side, I remained under the table for another 30 minutes, then let myself down. I ran to the window and confirmed that his car was gone. If I was correct in my assessment, he would have much to do in a short period of time. I ascended the stairs, and looked at what he'd done to my bedroom. It was much as I expected.

I put on my sweatshirt, which I'd hidden in the back of a closet, and retraced the route to my car. Then I drove to the news agency, purchased the three newspapers I estimated I would have the time to read, and went to my customary bar.

When I returned at 10 p.m. and walked up the drive, I reminded myself to look startled when it happened. As an afterthought, I took my car key off my ring and hid it under a bush out front. I didn't think he would bother to move my car, but it was better to prepare for every contingency.

He wasn't downstairs. I would have been sorely disappointed if he was, as it would have indicated a distinct lack of strategic foresight on his part.

Everything was in its normal place. Or most things. He probably assumed that I wouldn't notice the new doorknob installed on the basement door with the keyhole in it. Now he was capable of locking somebody out of that basement. Or locking something in. The knob didn't turn. I put my ear to the door and detected a noise. It was indistinct, but there was no mistaking it. Something very large was moving around down there.

I saw no point in delaying the inevitable, and ascended the stairs. When I was in the doorway to my bedroom, a voice spoke behind me.

"In the room. Now."

I turned and saw him. He'd emerged from the bathroom directly across from my room, with a fierce expression on his countenance. He held a long, slim blade in the vicinity of my throat. A sword of some kind.

"Kid? What the ... ?"

"Gary. My name isn't 'kid.' In the bedroom, Billy."

I backed up, palms facing him in an "I-don't-want-any-trouble" gesture.

When I backed into the room, he swung the door shut. Metal clicked. That would be the kid affixing a padlock onto the hasps I'd found installed on the door earlier that day when I investigated after his departure. I ran forward and banged on the door.

"What the fuck are you doing?"

I gave the door a few kicks, though I knew it would do no good. This was an older house, with none of that hollow-core luan that passes for building material nowadays. It was solid oak. The kid would have figured on that.

I heard him descending the stairs, and commenced banging even louder.

"Answer me, you little shit!" I hollered. "You let me out of this room right now or so help me I will kick your fucking ass!"

Over the years, I had yelled at him, berated him and insulted him, but I had never before physically threatened him. Despite everything transpiring at that moment, I still felt a pang of regret for having done so.

I then took stock of my surroundings. He'd installed a sturdy sheet of plywood over the window. I tested it, and found it would not budge. He'd provided amenities for me as well, including a bucket that I presumed would serve as a toilet, sanitary wipes, a few sandwiches and some bottled water.

I took a paperback book off my night table and settled myself down on my bed to read, having nothing else to do for the time being.

I might as well relax, as in the near future I would have very much to do indeed.

FILE 24

Ken said it reminded him of one of those optical illusions. Where you can either see the silhouettes of two faces looking at each other, or a vase in the shape of the space between them. And at first you can only see the faces, and can't see the vase for the life of you.

Then suddenly the faces are gone and you can only see the vase. And you don't know how you could have ever seen the picture differently.

That's how it was for Ken during those days at the veterans hospital with his eyes bandaged. Things he never understood before were now so clear to him. And other things, concrete things on which he'd once based his entire life, just weren't there anymore.

It was just one of those crazy, out-of-the-blue things. They'd been in the woods upstate for some National Guard training exercises. No big deal. Ken had looked forward to it. It was like camping out with buddies.

The State Police showed up. They got word that someone trained in explosive ordnance disposal was there, and they needed help urgently.

A local paranoid nutjob got served his divorce papers that day. Declaring that the whole thing was engineered by the Zionist Occupation Government, he'd taken his ex-wife and two kids hostage in the basement of his house, which was rigged with explosives. And during a brief phone conversation with police, he said he'd shoot them within two hours unless the Jews relinquished their control of the International Monetary Fund.

When Ken got to work under the watchful eye of several flak-jacketed sharpshooters, none of them knew that the guy had already gone into a soundproof chamber in his basement, stuck a gun in his mouth and sprayed the ceiling with his brains. All Ken knew was the guy's work, which showed plenty of skill and a certain weirdo artistic flair. The front door was a deadly Rube Goldberg contraption of electronic and mechanical feints and ruses, which Ken sweated over for the better part of an hour, knowing full well that every minute could mean the death of a woman and two kids.

He had no clear recollection of what happened when he was defusing the bomb in the front hallway. One minute he was tinkering with a circuit, the next he was in darkness and pain, with consoling yet professionally detached voices telling him he was in a hospital.

In the days ahead, those voices told him that his chance of recovering full sight in both eyes was excellent.

Rebuilding his face would take longer. The structure was largely intact and he could expect to regain full function of all his facial muscles. As for aesthetics, well, plastic surgery was advancing by leaps and bounds every day. So down the road, who knows?

It didn't matter to Sally. He knew this because she told him so, putting her lips close to his ear during her visits and telling him that she loved him and would stay by him no matter what happened.

That was more painful than anything else he'd undergone. Because he knew she meant it. And he knew he had to leave her.

He was no good for her. He didn't deserve her. He thought about that often, in the darkness and the logy haze of painkillers. Such a lame cliché for most people. "I don't deserve you, honey!" So painful when it was true, and you knew it.

Life had been good following his divorce from his first wife. After he retired from the Snippers, in between stints with the National Guard, he tried his hand at a couple of different business ventures. Finally, he hit paydirt with "Bub's," the sports bar he'd co-managed with his old buddy and teammate Bubbles McBride.

"Why'd he change his name to 'Bub?' I guess he heard a few too many 'blowing Bubbles' jokes in his day."

That line was usually good for a hearty laugh and an insistence on buying the next round from the local politicians and businessmen who would patronize the place just for a chance to tell their golf buddies that they were out having a beer with Ken Bacon the other night.

Ken would be the first to admit his job title of "assistant manager" was a stretch, since his responsibilities mostly involved hanging around the bar and being everybody's pal. But what the hell, he brought the customers in, same as the miniskirts Bub required the waitresses to wear.

And those waitresses? Damn! "The dessert tray," as he and Bub used to call the exclusively female waitstaff. Tasty little treats just sitting out there on display, waiting to be sampled.

Given those circumstances, he still didn't fully understand why he fell so hard for Sally, the city health inspector.

He met her one weekday afternoon, after the lunch rush. He put some Fats Domino on the phonograph and lit a cigar hand-rolled by a Cuban national they kept on staff solely for that purpose.

Then he poured himself a Drosselmyer's and tucked into his Caesar Salad, which was basically a big pile of chicken, cheese and creamy dressing with some lettuce at the bottom. But technically it was still a salad, making it healthy by default. No doubt about it, he thought. America's a great country.

Then she walked into the room with her dark dress and her clipboard, saying she needed to talk about the unacceptably high acid content in the lettuce bins. She was older than he usually liked them. Had a kind of leathery look about her. "Rugged," you could almost call it. But damn if she didn't make it look sexy.

"What? Like hydrochloric acid?" he asked. "You're saying we've got a mad scientist on staff?"

"I've never dealt with you before, Mr. Bacon. I was told you're assistant manager and this is your office?"

"It's the cigar lounge. But since I spend most of my time here, I guess you could call it my office."

"Is that Fats Domino you're playing?"

"Why yes, it is."

"I'm impressed."

"I'm impressed that you're impressed."

"Did you know that John Lennon and Paul McCartney said there would be no Beatles if there was no Fats Domino?"

"And that would be a bad thing because ... ?"

She smiled, leaned forward and patted his hand.

"It's uric acid. The big tub full of water in the walk-in cooler? The one used to store the lettuce that's in your salad right now? Somebody's been pissing in it. Since Mr. McBride seems to run things around here, I suggest you tell him that failure to provide adequate bathroom breaks for kitchen staff is a serious labor violation. I also suggest you give 'Rubber Soul' a serious listen before you pretend to know jack shit about music. Thank you for your time, Mr. Bacon."

He steamed about her attitude all day. He also bought "Rubber Soul." And he had to admit she was right. It sounded pretty good.

He found himself looking forward to her visits. She consented to come back after her shift one evening for a drink. They'd laughed and laughed. It was worth it, even if Bub gave him a hard time later for spending the entire evening tucked in a corner booth with Sally instead of schmoozing with Batley's alpha males at the bar.

They were married within a year. He sometimes questioned his wisdom in taking that step. He had his pick of far younger women who were in far better financial shape.

Not that they ever struggled, but Ken realized early on that he'd never own the sports car he'd been saving up for.

She had kids, for God's sake! Teenagers. She'd had them from two different marriages. One of those marriage ceremonies was performed by a minister in her neighborhood church in Batley. The other was performed by a self-described incarnation of Siddhartha Guatama living on an artist's commune in Colorado. Turns out the Buddha had a notary public's license. Neither marriage worked out.

Ty and Luanne had traveled around the county with her when she was trying to make it as a singer, setting up her amp and guitar any place that would hire her. She often performed for free, just for a venue and a chance that somebody in the music business would hear her. It never happened. She waited a lot of tables.

Finally, she decided that she wasn't getting any younger, the music career just wasn't going to happen and the kids needed a more stable life. She moved back to Batley and got her county inspector job.

Ken and Sally got married in the local court clerk's office. Their honeymoon was a long weekend at a nearby bed-and-breakfast. Nothing elaborate. That was just fine by them.

She worked her city job, and did some volunteering at the local library because she loved it. Every summer, she'd do seasonal work at the carnival that came through town. For a spell during her youth, she'd traveled with the carnival, and said she liked to relive those days. She always worked for a grouchy dwarf named Billy.

Ken found Ty and Luanne off-putting at first. But he soon realized that they were just scared. They were new to this life. Living in one place. Everybody coming and going at set hours. People giving them funny looks because of their hair and their clothes. Eventually he'd come to love those kids, with their strangeness and their toughness.

He loved Sally, too. She was kind and funny. She made love with an openness and a physicality so intense that it frightened him at first, before he came to enjoy it more than anything else in the world. He'd never before been big on domestic-type stuff, but he learned to treasure those family outings to the ballpark or the movies or the miniature golf course on weekends, with the kids in the back seat and Sally leaning on his shoulder on the drive there and back.

He fucked around on her constantly.

Sally never found out about it, to his knowledge. He knew she wouldn't stand for it if she did.

But what the hell, he was taking good care of her and the kids. They were damn lucky he'd come into their lives.

Besides, would you say a guy is cheating on his wife if he jerks off once in awhile? That's practically all the occasional raised miniskirt in the cigar lounge amounted to. A quick act of release with no long-term consequences. He was a man with a big appetite, that's all. No harm, no foul.

When he was lying down in the hospital, bandaged, listening to her voice, he realized that his whole life he'd been nothing but a charming asshole. Now he was a hideous asshole. He had nothing to offer her. The best thing he could do for her was leave.

He left a letter for her at the nurse's station. He told her she had full access to all their assets. But he was going. He'd met someone else and that's all she needed to know.

He walked out of the hospital with a duffel bag full of clothing and some basic toiletries. His face was a real detriment for hitch-hiking at first. Then he learned to use it to his advantage. He bought a cane from a drugstore and hobbled dramatically whenever a car came by. Few people lacked the heart to pull over for this poor man who was obviously so badly hurt.

In truth, face aside, he was in better shape than he'd been since he quit baseball. He'd become soft in the intervening years. Living on the road, getting manual labor when he could find it, missing meals when he couldn't, made him lean and hard. He grieved for Sally and Ty and Luanne every waking moment, but knew it had to be this way.

He'd never intended to return to Batley. Loneliness drove him back.

Bub's had a new corporate owner who kept Bub on as manager. That turned out to be a good thing, because the rest of the staff was new and didn't remember Ken from his former life. They certainly didn't recognize him as the handsome young man with an arm thrown over Bub's shoulders in the photos over the bar.

At Ken's request, Bub gave him mostly jobs that kept him away from the customers. Bar back. Working the grill. Occasionally, he'd step in as bouncer in the bar. Ken was still physically imposing. And these days, his face alone was usually enough to scare the martini-induced belligerence out of anyone.

One Sunday night a month, which he'd request off for that very reason, he'd go to another bar called Rusty's Bar and Grill for open mike night. And he'd hear Sally perform.

Rusty's is a long, dark place with an upper level in back that gives you a view of the stage. He figured he could see her coming a mile off if she wandered up his way, and be out the exit before she got there. She never did.

From a distance, he was sure, she wouldn't recognize him. He barely recognized himself whenever he caught a glimpse in any reflective surface. His hair had gone long, and he had a thick beard. Now he habitually wore a baseball cap pulled down low over his face.

Once a month he'd sit there with his beer, watching as she picked up her guitar and sat on the stool behind the microphone.

She had a beautiful voice. High and strong. Sadly, she always insisted on singing her own compositions. Even Ken had to admit they were pretty terrible.

TOM JERKFACE: *Following are the lyrics to a song called "The Faerie Queen's Lament," which was included on a demo tape titled "Tears of the Unicorn" that Sally Bacon recorded and sent out to various regional radio stations. To my knowledge, none of them opted to play it.*

Twas chilly and misty on a midwinter's morn
Whilst I dwelt forsaken, alone and forlorn
When then to my meadow there came a fair lad
To me he did giveth the best love I'd ere had.

Chorus: Oh hey nonny nonny, my true love is gone.

Then came the bleak day in the Meadow of the Queen
When a brazen young harlot by my fair lad was seen
Off he did chase her, like foolish young hare.
And if I'd have caught him, a fat lip would he wear.

(Repeat chorus)

But I'm no longer lonely, for with me there dwell
A fair prince and a princess, and I love them so well.
Of my lad I know nothing. I think that mayhaps
He's alone and impoverished, with a case of the clap.

(Repeat chorus)

Then came the open mike night when she didn't show up. He was disappointed. She didn't show up at the next one, or the next one, and he got a weird feeling of panic. He called the city bureau where she worked, identifying himself as an old college friend who wanted to say hi. They told him she'd been laid off.

At the library, they said she'd left on extended leave, and they didn't have much more information. Ken did something he'd never allowed himself to do before. He drove by the house he'd once shared with them. It looked empty, but not abandoned.

He was surprised how deeply it affected him – not knowing where she was. Not being able to occasionally catch a glimpse of her. He obsessed about it at work and brooded about it in his little shithole of an apartment after work.

One day he was taking his lunch break in the cigar lounge. His lunch breaks no longer incorporated cigars or Fats Domino or a bent-over waitress or a pretty lady with a clipboard who could have been the best thing in his life if he hadn't fucked that up to hell and back. Just him and a grilled chicken sandwich.

Billy walked in, and climbed into the chair facing Ken.

"Are you insane?" Billy asked him.

"What the ... excuse me?"

"Sally and her children are in trouble. They need help. I may require assistance in providing said help, and I've considered recruiting you in that capacity. But I have reservations. Hanging around town. Stalking her. Not telling her you're here. That's fucked up."

"You know who I am?"

"I read people for a living. It's going to take more than that new mug of yours to throw me off. Now, let's return to the subject at hand. If I'm going to bring you in on this, I'll need to know I can rely on you. I repeat. Are you insane?"

"No," Ken said. "I've just been going through a bad time lately is all."

"Well I hate to tell you friend," Billy said. "But I think it's about to get worse."

FILE 25

Ken stood outside a house in the woods not far from Batley. He thought again of the driver's license in his wallet and the birth certificate photocopy in his jacket pocket, both giving his name as Ken Benson.

Ken hadn't seen the point of that. Why a fake name that's practically the same as his real one?

Amid a lot of invective directed at the stupidity of white people in general and of Ken in particular, Billy told him that was the entire point.

This whole thing was taking place in his hometown. What if someone on the sidewalk says "Hey Ken" when he told them his name was Jack? And if someone called him Bacon instead of Benson, his new bosses might just assume they'd heard wrong.

So that's what it said on the driver's license and birth certificate. Courtesy of a black kid with glasses thick as ice cubes and a living room full of comic books, physics texts and computer operating manuals which Ken had leafed through in the 60 minutes or so it took him to get his new identity.

The kid seemed competent. The license and certificate looked good to Ken. But would it hold up with these guys?

He started to hand both of them to the man with the Russian accent.

"You know what? Who cares?" That came from the Russian's companion, a man with a shiny pompadour and an expensive suit. "If you're going to work for us, it's because you get things done. That's a lot more important to me than how pretty you look on your driver's license."

He turned toward a third man standing slightly behind him. He was maybe in his early 30s, with barroom brawler muscles.

"Sonny Liston here's gonna take a poke at you. Let's see how you do."

"What are ..."

The guy charged at Ken. Bad move on his part. Picking off assholes charging the mound had been his specialty. Just a step to the side. A palm —- not a fist, a palm – at the base of his nose. Let the guy's momentum do the rest. And that sumbitch is going to be lying on the ground, bleeding from each nostril.

Which is exactly how "Sonny Liston" ended up.

"Good," the man in the suit said. "Welcome aboard."

The man held out his hand to shake. Ken didn't take it. The man dropped his hand.

"Fine," he said. "You got looks and charm. You're a goddamn movie star. You also have explosives experience?""

Ken nodded.

"Might be useful. And you know what happens if you try to get cute? Let's put it this way. Your predecessor decided he was going to get laid in Maryland, even though he was told not to leave the area. Well he didn't get laid but he sure got fucked!"

At that, he started laughing loudly. He punched The Russian on the shoulder.

"Not bad, huh? He didn't get laid but he sure got fucked!"

The Russian sighed deeply.

Most of Ken's work centered on security. At Schulze's clinic, he spent a lot of time sitting in a room with a one-way mirror, watching as the professor talked to some poor sap or other. He'd set up recording equipment to capture the whole exchange. If things got violent, he was supposed to run in and intervene. They never did on his watch, though.

The first time he did this, the subject was a timid young woman who seemed to be in a slight stupor.

"Could you describe your experience?" The Professor asked.

"It's hard to explain," she said. "I'd just finished a study session in the library..."

"You've been instructed to study Nyx, correct?"

"Yes."

"And you've done your meditations? The communing ritual?"

"Well, I did what Mr. Schulze said to do in that video. But I didn't seem to get anything out of it. Then yesterday when I finished my study session, I stopped by the lounge for a cup of coffee and went outside to drink it. And I felt — I can't really describe it — like everything was connected somehow. Me and the sky and everything moving in the earth."

"How long did this last?"

"I don't know. One of the orderlies put me in the meditation chamber and for hours, I was just ... like I was completely out of myself. Then I ... I thought I heard a voice. Telling me that Nyx and I were one."

"It will happen at random intervals," The Professor told her. "That's how it is when you open the soul gate. You're on the verge of a higher consciousness now. Some of the things you experience will be frightening to you. But you must persevere if you're to complete your spiritual journey. Do you understand this?"

Ken was amazed The Professor could get all that out with a straight face. He heard variations of that spiel over and over. The Professor telling people who'd obviously been slipped a drug that they were experiencing the "Mind Gate," through which they'd play host to their "mythical identity."

But some of the stuff he saw was genuinely scary. There was a group of residents in the clinic that other called "the ghosts." Those were people who'd been kept on a regimen of barbituates and amphetamines through IV tubes, and put into a coma-like null state for days. During that time, some additional procedures were done to them that nobody described to Ken.

In time, most of them would suddenly begin talking in a different voice, claiming to be a recently murdered man or woman. They were kept separate from the rest of the residents.

One time he watched as Ty received a training session in hand-to-hand combat from The Russian. He was amazed to see the man maintain his gentle manner even as he described in detail the mechanics of snapping an opponent's neck.

Once he watched The Suit give Luanne a lesson in how to conduct an interrogation. He instructed her about subtle facial tics that could signal whether a subject was telling the truth or not.

He never saw Sally. Billy, who was spending more time at the clinic now, said he'd run into her occasionally. They'd pretend not to know each other.

When Ken saw Luanne and Ty, he'd wanted to run in the other room, grab them and make a run for it. But he knew it wouldn't do any good. He'd never find the other two in the time it would take for the rest of the hired muscle to reach him.

He knew for a fact that cameras were pointed at every major exit. They started giving him an overnight shift at the clinic, sitting in the room and watching those cameras.

He knew something else was afoot, too. The Professor kept making references to something called "Project Anchovy." A bunch of elites in The Agendum seemed to be selected for it. As far as Ken could tell, they tended to be the most vicious and unhinged of his new co-workers.

It pained him, seeing the interviews with people like that young woman told to study Nyx. But he was afraid of the threat from The Suit that they had somebody with the local police. His biggest fear was that they'd catch on to him and Billy, and there'd be nobody left who knew about what was happening to Sally, Ty and Luanne.

He promised himself that once he and Billy got the three of them out, he would go straight to the police. Whether it did any good. Whether it got him killed.

Billy thought they should keep face-to-face meetings to a minimum, so they kept in touch mainly through a letter drop system they'd worked out with Bub's help. As long as they did their jobs and didn't leave the city without permission, The Agendum let them come and go as they wanted. In fact, Ken had to admit, they were downright accommodating when it came to time off.

In Bub's, a single-occupancy unisex bathroom back behind the pool tables didn't get used much. Both Ken and Billy had keys for the paper towel dispenser. They'd leave letters on top of the paper towels. Each had designated days to go into Bub's, so they'd never be seen in there at the same time.

The presence of the toilet was an added advantage. After reading each others' letters, they could flush them. Though Ken admitted that he'd held onto a few of the letters, even though he knew it was a bad idea, hiding them in the sole of his shoe. They were notes from Sally, which Billy smuggled to him. He showed them to me afterward.

TOM JERKFACE: The following is transcribed from three separate photocopies of hand-written notes, labeled "Sally note from Ken."

The first note.
I ASKED BILLY TO BRING YOU THIS NOTE. WHEN I SAW YOU TODAY, I KNEW THAT WAS YOU. YES, YOU CAN COME AND SEE ME TONIGHT. WE HAVE A LOT TO DISCUSS.

The second note.
I KNOW YOU TOLD ME ONLY TO SEND YOU NOTES IN AN EMERGENCY. BUT I FEEL I NEED TO TELL YOU THIS BEFORE YOU COME TO SEE ME AGAIN. FOR SO LONG, I THOUGHT OF WHAT I'D TELL YOU IF I EVER SAW YOU AGAIN. I REHEARSED LONG SPEECHES IN MY HEAD. NOW I BARELY KNOW WHAT TO SAY. THANK YOU FOR HELPING US. I KNOW THE KIND OF MAN YOUR ARE, AND I KNOW YOU'LL DO THAT REGARDLESS OF WHAT I SAY. I HAVE NO REGRETS ABOUT WHAT WE'VE BEEN DOING. YOUR VISITS HAVE BEEN A GREAT COMFORT TO ME.

STILL, I DON'T WANT TO FEEL AS THOUGH I'M MANIPULATING YOU FOR YOUR ASSISTANCE. I'M SORRY, BUT THE ANSWER TO THE QUESTION YOU ASKED ME LAST NIGHT IS NO. WHEN THIS IS OVER, WE WILL NOT GET BACK TOGETHER. MY DECISION HAS NOTHING TO DO WITH YOUR ACCIDENT. I TOLD YOU BEFORE THAT DOESN'T MATTER TO ME AND I MEANT IT. I UNDERSTAND WHEN YOU TELL ME WHY YOU FELT LIKE YOU NEEDED TO LEAVE US LIKE YOU DID. IT STILL DOESN'T MAKE SENSE TO ME. YOU CAUSED ME AND MY CHILDREN A LOT OF PAIN, AND I WISH YOU WOULD AT LEAST HAVE TRIED TALKING TO ME BEFORE TAKING IT UPON YOURSELF TO BRING THAT PAIN INTO OUR LIVES. BUT THAT'S NOT THE REASON EITHER. THE REASON IS THAT I'VE LEARNED THINGS ABOUT MYSELF. WHO I AM AND WHAT I WANT FOR MY LIFE AND MY FUTURE. YOU'RE JUST NOT A PART OF THAT ANYMORE. MY WORDS MAY SOUND HARSH. I DON'T WANT THEM TO, BUT I HAVE TO TELL YOU THE TRUTH. IT'S ALSO TRUE THAT I STILL LOVE YOU AND ALWAYS WILL.

The third note:
I'M PREGNANT. OH GOD. WHAT DO WE DO NOW?

FROM PINKY
    Greetings everybody. I'm afraid I have a delicate subject to broach.
    We've encountered a rather awkward situation that we are now in the process of investigating. Please understand, I am not making accusations against any of you. For all we know, one of our residents may have been responsible.
    Still, the following must be said. Contact of an intimate nature with clinic residents, except that necessitated by medical procedures, is prohibited.
    The case that prompted this warning, fortunately, appears unlikely to compromise our work here. Quite the contrary, we believe it may have provided us with a hitherto unforeseen business opportunity.
    Happy accidents aside, such circumstances have the potential to facilitate unwelcome complications at a very crucial juncture of our project. To sum up: When around clinic residents, let's keep our hands to ourselves. Nuff said?
    In other matters, Project Anchovy is proceeding according to schedule. In the near future, you will all be furnished with a detailed schedule of our evacuation, which we will initiate at the project's conclusion.
    I must emphasize that adherence to the evacuation schedule is no less important than any other element of the operation. You must leave town at the prescribed time and in the prescribed manner. Failure to do so has the potential to jeopardize all of the hard work we've done here. Even after Project Anchovy has taken place, we will treat unscheduled departure attempts with appropriate severity.
    Just remember: The key to successful teamwork is less "me" and more "we!"

    Ken knew Project Anchovy was going to be something big. He just hoped that whatever it was, nobody would get hurt.
    As deadline approached, he got more details about the evacuation. He found out something about the people in the "administration building," for example.

They were patsies.

They consisted of an acupuncturist, an aura reader and an energy healer. When The Agendum set up, those people got a letter from Friedrich K. Schulze inviting them to be part of his clinic. They'd be provided with ample, rent-free space to conduct their practices. All Schulze asked was that they not go into his clinic, because the nature of his work required his patients to be kept in strict isolation.

Little did the acupuncturist, the aura reader and the energy healer know that the clinic's paperwork listed them as clinic administrators, as investigators would discover after the Halloween Parade Massacre.

None of them served time, though. They managed to convince prosecutors that Schulze set them up. And Schulze would turn up dead in New Mexico.

Two days before the scheduled start of "Project Anchovy", a group of them moved to the house in the woods where they'd first interviewed Ken. In addition to Ken, The Suit, The Russian and The Professor, they had about five guys.

It was a broken-down-looking place. Three stories. Probably nice once, but nobody had taken good care of it in a long time. The front yard was full of rusted-out cars and other junk.

They kept Sally, Ty and Luanne locked in separate rooms on the third floor. They brought them meals and periodically escorted them to the bathroom.

The Russian complained that it was a difficult place to secure. The Professor told him not to worry. Nobody would be looking for them there. Besides, they'd only be there for a few days, then they'd move on.

The Suit complained that it would be a lot easier if they'd left Ty and Luanne behind at the clinic. He was willing to call their training program a failure anyway. Without drug-induced behavior modification, they were too willful. With it, they'd likely be too zonked.

The Professor said the woman wouldn't go anywhere without them. Less trouble for now to oblige her. Because no matter what else happened, they needed her.

No radios or televisions were permitted in the old house. Once an hour, Ken or one of the other men was required to take a handgun and patrol the property's perimeter.

The night of the Halloween Parade Massacre, The Professor got a phone call. He was on for about half an hour. He said little. When it was over, he hung up, looked at The Russian and The Suit, and said "Gentlemen, Project Anchovy was a success."

He cracked open several bottles of champagne and insisted that everyone drink a glass. He even ordered that glasses be brought to the woman and the teenagers locked in their rooms upstairs.

The Professor got a little tipsy. In a voice choked with emotion, he told them they were as fine a group of men as he'd ever worked with, and he was proud to know them.

Two days later, Ken drove into town on an errand. He was to go to an abandoned house and pick up some boxes of supplies.

As soon as he made it into the city, he pulled into the parking lot of a strip mall. He called the house in the woods. He told them he had a flat tire. He'd take care of it. No problem.

Then he made another phone call. Billy picked him up, driving a car with special extensors that allowed his short legs to reach the pedals.

On the drive, Billy told Ken about the Halloween Parade Massacre. It was the first Ken had heard of it.

Sitting at the kitchen table, telling me this story, Ken said he'd asked himself a question many times over the years. What would he have done if he'd known what Project Anchovy was? If he'd had any idea about the bloodshed and the deaths they planned, would he have gone to the police anyway – knowing there was a good chance he'd blow any chance of Sally and her children getting out safely?

No matter how many times he asked himself that question, he still had no answer.

That day, listening to Billy describe what happened as they drove in the car, Ken's reaction was even greater fear on behalf of Sally and her children. He knew these people were monsters. He just hadn't realized how monstrous.

Billy drove Ken to a small house on the edge of town. One of the men involved in The Agendum had been living there, although he didn't appear to be there now. Behind the house was a free-standing garage, big enough to hold six cars. The Agendum took advantage of it to store some of the stolen cars they'd been using.

Now that Project Anchovy was over, nobody seemed too worried about them. The keys were even in the ignition.

Ken drove one of those cars to a parking lot and left the keys under the passenger seat in a crumpled paper towel. Billy drove him back to his car. He gave Ken a hammer and a sharp chisel, which Ken used to make a hole in one of the tires. With Billy's help, he was able quickly replace it with the spare. Ken hid the hammer and chisel in the waistband of his pants. He picked up the supplies as instructed and drove back.

At around 9 that night, it was Ken's turn to walk the perimeter around the old house where they were sequestered. At selected spots, he was to blink his flashlight twice to signal those in the house that everything was OK.

When he was parallel to the side of the house, he ran toward it. He shielded the flashlight with his hand as he examined the metal basement door set flush with the ground. They'd put a shiny new chain and padlock on the handles, holding it shut. But they hadn't bothered to replace the hinges on the door, which were none-too-sturdy to begin with and now heavily rusted. He broke the hinges with the hammer and chisel Billy gave him earlier.

As he walked around the back, he paused to blink the flashlight twice in the direction of the house. Then, again shielding it with his hands, he swept it toward the trees, keeping it low.

There, at the head of a small trail, was Billy. Ken pointed in the direction of the basement door. Billy took off that way.

Other side of the house. Pause. Two blinks of the flashlight.

Around to the front of the house. Facing it head-on, across an expanse of junked cars, scrubby bushes, rusted lawnmowers and a crumbling swingset.

He didn't blink the flashlight. Instead he crept forward, taking refuge behind a bush. He waited, counting off the minutes in his head. Three minutes. Five. Eight. Ten.

By now they'd be paying attention, wondering if there was an easy explanation for the signal failing to appear, or whether they should be concerned.

He raised his gun, pointed it at an angle perpendicular to the house, and fired two shots. Immediately, lights started turning off in the house windows. He couldn't hear anything, but he knew there would be a lot of activity. They would be moving Sally, Ty, Luanne and The Professor to the basement, where they'd be safe from stray bullets. A guard would remain in front of the closed basement door in the kitchen at the top of the steps, but it would be just the four of them in the basement. That was the drill. They'd been over it many times.

Ken waited another few minutes. They'd be outside, trying to get a fix on him. He fired a couple more rounds. Giving them no doubt of his position.

He looked around. Where would they try to flank him, he wondered? The rusted pickup over his left shoulder? The clump of gnarled trees a few yards to his right? They had a lot to choose from. Ken never did have any knack for all that creeping-around bushcraft shit. And it was all academic anyway.

He fired another shot. Then he shone his flashlight on his watch without bothering to shield it this time. A few more minutes. Ty, a tough kid even before he started getting personalized instruction from The Russian, would already have punched The Professor into unconsciousness. Wouldn't Ken have liked to see that!

Billy, from the outside, would have helped them quietly move the basement door aside. And now, with all attention focused on the unknown threat in the front yard, Billy would be leading them on a furtive run through the backyard toward the trail.

The trail would take them out to the road. There, they'd split up, with the expectation of not seeing each other for a while. Sally hadn't liked that idea at all, but finally had to admit the sense of it. If they got away clean, fine. They'd be able to get back together eventually. But if one car got intercepted, maybe the other could get away.

Ken looked over his shoulder, away from the house. Beyond the property was a field, then some woods. A part of him momentarily yearned to make a break for it.

No. Having them search around the property was the last thing he wanted now. He wanted them zeroing in on a specific point. Right where he was sitting.

Sally hadn't been informed of what was coming next. Maybe she'd balk, maybe she wouldn't. Either way, it had to be done.

A flashlight beam shone on him.

"Movie star? What the fuck are you doing?"

It was The Suit's voice. Ken would wager that at least four guns were pointed at him right then.

Again, the brief yearning. All he needed to do was raise his gun. Not even fire it. Just raise it.

He dropped the gun.

As they moved in on him, for no reason in particular he found himself thinking about a day when he was still dating Sally, not long before they got married.

He'd taken her and the kids to a miniature golf course. Neither Luanne nor Ty had ever held a putter before in their lives. Ken gave them a long lecture on how to handle one, and how to line up their shots.

On the first hole, if you got a hole-in-one, it was good for a free ice cream cone from the concession stand. Ty knocked one right in. Then Luanne stepped up, and damn if she didn't hit a hole-in-one too!

And Ken? He'd completely whiffed it. His ball didn't come anywhere near that hole. Sally, Ty and Luanne all teased him mercilessly about it when they got their ice cream afterward. Then they'd gone to see a movie.

That had been a very good day.

They beat him in the front yard of that ramshackle house in the woods, then dragged him inside. They hauled him down the steps of the basement, where they'd apparently already figured out what happened.

They cuffed him to a chair, and forced him to swallow drugs that turned the world into a hellishly vivid nightmare. Then they went to work on him with a cigarette lighter and a pair of pliers.

They asked him the same question over and over. "Where are they?"

At one point, The Suit grabbed a handful of hair at his temple and pulled his face in close.

"Look at me asshole! No! Don't you look away! Was the dwarf involved?"

Ken didn't say anything, but The Suit saw the answer in his face. He let go and said "That little fucker."

It went on for hours. Eventually, Ken talked. He didn't tell them the full story of his marriage to Sally and his fake identity. He had just enough command of his mind to hold onto that. He told them only that he'd been involved with Sally and he wanted to help her. He'd been told that Luanne and the kids were going south and planned to head for the Mexican border. He said that was all he knew.

And it really was all he knew. That's what Billy had informed him, and instructed Ken to spill eventually.

"These people know how to fuck with your head so thoroughly, you will no longer be able to make a distinction between what's true and what isn't," Billy had written in a letter that Ken immediately tore up and flushed. "All you need to know is that Sally, Ty and Luanne are heading to Mexico. Tell them that. Don't tell them too soon or they won't believe you."

They left Ken cuffed to the chair for a long time, alone in the basement. His mind was still swirling from the drugs. He remembered that the darkness outside had given way to daylight when they returned and discussed among themselves what to do with him.

The Suit got angry at one point.

"That's not the problem!" The Suit said. "It's the disposal that takes time! You can't just dig a hole in the yard anymore. And we really need to get moving. I say we dump him downtown. What's he gonna do to us now?"

Later still, The Suit kicked him out a car door into a back alley in downtown Batley.

"See ya, Movie Star," The Suit said. "Stay handsome."

Then he drove off.

Ken couldn't say for sure how long he was living on the streets. It was like trying to wake up from a nightmare. He had a vague sense that there was something important he needed to do. But he couldn't quite pull his thoughts together.

Sinister voices spoke to him from out of sewer grates and alley openings. Shifting shapes stalked him from behind bushes and parked cars. At times he was very cold and hungry. Somehow he found places to go where he could get warm and get something to eat. Places that smelled of unshowered men and disinfectant.

He was in one of those places once with a lot of other men, doing nothing, just sitting and not being out in the cold. A man walked into the room and pointed at him.

"That him?"

A girl was behind that man. Luanne. She ran to Ken and threw her arms around him. She cried onto his shoulder for a little bit. The she took him to the apartment where she was living with Ty.

For the better part of a year, Ken worked to get his head together. He paced a lot and watched a lot of television. Eventually, he was able to understand what Luanne and Ty told him about that night they escaped from the house.

Billy drove them to the apartment building where they were staying now, giving them instructions along the way. He handed them keys to the place then sped away, leaving them on the curb.

For three months, Ty and Luanne went stir crazy in the apartment. Ty would venture out on rare occasions with a hooded parka pulled over his head, to buy provisions from a corner grocery or clothes from a thrift shop that was within walking distance. All paid for from an envelope of cash they found taped to the underside of the living room couch.

Billy told them to give it at least three months, living like that. If they suspected for an instant that they were under observation, they'd need to jump on the next bus out of town immediately, and resign themselves to the idea that they might never see their mother again.

Once a week, Luanne would borrow the parka. She would walk to Bub's, order a soda at the bar, then go into the bathroom behind the pool tables.

She would open the paper towel dispenser and find a note that said "STAY." If it said "GO," if it wasn't there at all, she would have run home, gotten Ty, and the two of them would have left town.

On one of her excursions to the restaurant, keeping an eye out all around her as usual, she saw a homeless man who looked like Ken disappearing into an alley down the block. He was gone by the time she reached the alley.

She began combing all the homeless shelters in town looking for him. Fuck caution.

A few months after she found Ken, she went into the bathroom at Bub's and opened the paper towel dispenser. The note said "YOUR MOTHER IS DEAD. I'M SO SORRY."

Luanne sat on the toilet in that bathroom for a long time with her head in her hands. Then she walked home.

"Who wrote the notes?" I asked Ken, as we sat at his kitchen table.

"I don't know," Ken said. "Billy kept a lot from me. Intentionally. He said the less I knew, the less they could get out of me. I assumed it was Billy leaving those notes. For years, I never knew what happened to him. When you found Paul living in Cabot's house, I was so happy. But I was sad, too, when I learned that they found Billy's remains. I'd hoped Billy made it away and was doing alright for himself. He was a brave man."

Ken said they'd originally planned to leave town, but he was still recovering from his ordeal in the old house's basement. Ty and Luanne both got jobs, because they were running out of money. Ken tried to work too, but he couldn't seem to marshal his thoughts enough to make it through an eight-hour shift.

Months turned into years. Nobody showed up looking for them.

Ken went on disability. They pooled their funds and bought the house. And they kept their mouths shut, in the hopes The Agendum had moved on and would leave them alone.

I took a pull off my beer. Then I sat back and took a long look at Ken. If you could kind of put your mind and your eyes out of focus at the same time, you could just about catch a glimpse of the cocky ladies' man sitting around, holding court in his very own cigar lounge. Before the facial scars. Before the fractured hip and the cane. Before the woman and the kids and the lighter and the pliers and the whole experience that tore up his mind and left him to rebuild it the best he could.

"OK," I said. "I understand you wanted to protect the kids. And yourself. And I'm willing to believe you didn't know what they were planning with the Halloween Parade Massacre. And I'll accept that you figured it was all over, and you were hoping they wouldn't come back.

"But they did come back, didn't they? Or did you think it was just a coincidence that another bunch of assholes calling themselves The Slain came into town and starting fucking shit up. You knew a bunch of people got killed the last time around. What I want to know is, how come you didn't tell anybody what you knew?"

"We did."

That was Luanne walking through the kitchen door.

"Were you out there listening?" Ken said angrily.

"I know it all already," Luanne said. "And you know what? I already guessed that you and Mom had a sex life. I'll get over it."

"Who'd you tell?" I asked.

"Michael, for starters," she said. "He seemed to know so much about what was going on already. I trusted him."

"Did he tell you that you were 'chosen?' " I asked.

She said nothing.

"He told me that too," I told her. "Makes you feel real special, doesn't it? I'll bet he said the same thing to everyone he wanted to manipulate."

"He told us The Slain were linked up with The Professor and his operation from day one," Luanne said. "He said The Slain based their tactics on his behavioral studies."

"That's bullshit," I said. "The Slain never existed, except as part of some crazy shadow puppet show these people were putting on."

"You think I haven't figured that out?" Luanne said. "I wanted to believe him, OK? I was scared. It was good to have someone who knew what was going on and what to do about it."

She paused for a moment, looking at her folded hands on the table.

"Besides," she went on, "I got to a point where I was scared to go to the police."

"Because Michael kept dropping hints, putting it into your head that Ty was involved."

She nodded.

"You said Michael for starters," I said. "Did you talk to someone else?"

"It was Michael's suggestion."

"Mayor Rockbaugh."

She looked up in surprise.

"How did you know?"

"You could say it's a hunch."

I got up from the table. I took out my wallet and handed her a card.

"That 24-hour number? That's Sister Pilar. Call her now. Take Paul over there. Take Ken while you're at it. Then meet me back here."

"Where are you going?" she asked.

"Call it a visit from a concerned constituent."

FILE 26

She insisted on giving me a plate of homemade oatmeal cookies. But that's not what broke my heart. You know what that was? The cookies were warm! She took time to warm those cookies so they'd taste better.

Bess Rockbaugh handed me those cookies on a flowered plate as small and delicate as a communion wafer, with shaking hands.

She wore a flowered nightgown and her hair hung down in long, white braids. Bess Rockbaugh was still a beautiful woman, with her strong jawline and her hazel eyes.

She apologized once again for that unseemly fuss she made when I first knocked on the door. You know. The hour and whatnot. Silly really.

She walked out, closing the living room door behind her. Buck reached for a shelf crammed with stuffed animals, ceramic children and commemorative glasses. He got a pair of those glasses and set them down in front of us. I took a look at mine. It was from the dedication ceremony of the downtown historic butter churn replica.

"I don't suppose you have ..."

He gestured in the direction of the pocket where I keep my flask.

"You have the expensive stuff stashed in here somewhere, Buck. I suggest you get it."

"Now look here! I've been very civil, considering that you bang on my door at this hour and upset my wife, but I hardly think ..."

I reached down to the coffee table, grabbed a magazine and displayed the cover for him to see.

"You do your saltwater fishing in the creek out back?"

He said nothing.

"I spent some time going through municipal records today," I said. "A year-and-a-half ago, you introduced an ordinance approving a contract with the Pigeon Clinic to provide 'behavioral services' for the city. You know how much the city's paid them since then? Zero. Goose egg. Not a single cent from the municipal budget has gone to that clinic. Pretty good deal if you ask me. Not many medical professionals out there working for free these days."

"So you know,"" Buck said.

"You know what I could never figure out?" I said. "How Cabot was able to beat it out of town so fast. He was unconscious and trussed up when I left his house. I called you. You called the police. But somehow before the police got there, he managed to wake up and get himself freed and pack up his stuff and get out of town without leaving a hint of where he was going.

"How'd he manage that? It's because the police weren't the first people you called, were they? So how about you get the goddamn Scotch and tell me what really happened."

Buck walked over to a large, brown teddy bear on an end table, turned it over, and extracted a bottle from its furry hindquarters with a deft efficiency that would have made any customs agent proud. He poured us both glasses. Then he began to talk.

Bess was the smartest, sweetest and deep-down the toughest girl a fella could wish for. But she had what folks used to call a "nervous disposition." A few times, she needed to go away for treatment. She took prescribed medication. It helped her.

This all started at a time when people didn't talk openly about such things. The rumors started around then.

It was mostly just foolish gossip. Every time some two-bit lunkhead got steamed over a parking ticket and decided to run against Buck for mayor, he'd bring up that rumor again. Bess was a sick-in-the-head drug addict and her husband covered up for her.

Sure, it made Buck angry. But he'd beat the tar out of them in the election and then they could drag themselves and their jackass stories elsewhere, thank you very kindly.

Charlie Kettner. Now he was different.

Kettner ran a local chain of furniture stores. Between that and his rumored financial stake in several back-alley handjob parlors, he did pretty well for himself.

Buck never paid him a lot of attention. Then Kettner asked for Buck's help in making some changes in the city's zoning laws that would benefit Kettner, but nobody else. Buck refused. Kettner pulled out his checkbook and offered to make a contribution to Buck's re-election fund. Buck threw him out of his office.

Kettner challenged Buck for mayor, with that son-of-a-bitch former president of the Batley Businessmen's Association Tim Cassidy as his running mate. Suddenly, those rumors about Bess were everywhere. Buck found out why. Turns out Kettner had hired himself one of those bigshot campaign consulting firms. Calls were going out asking people around the city if they'd participate in a telephone poll.

One of the questions was: Would you object if you found out an incumbent office holder used taxpayer money to cover up a family member's drug use?

Buck got so mad, he even considered bringing up Kettner's daughter – a well-known juvenile delinquent – in the campaign. But that would be wrong.

The little fella with the glasses and the pencil moustache who visited Buck in his office one day said he represented a group of investors who were looking at Batley for some future business opportunities that looked a lot more promising if he remained mayor. They wanted to fund his campaign.

The man explained that their future investments would be a very good thing for the city. For a number of reasons, they didn't want competitors getting wind of their plans. In order to cover their involvement, they might not abide by every little quirk of campaign reporting requirements. He hoped Buck could live with that. Buck could.

They funneled money to Buck by various sources. He deposited the money in a fund they'd set up called the BCKATC (Beat Charlie Kettner and Tim Cassidy) Fund. Buck's campaign made a dramatic recovery and he beat Kettner soundly.

A year later, another man showed up in Buck's office, claiming to represent the same consortium of investors. This man wasn't so polite. He had one of those haircuts that greasers used to sport back in the day, and he wore a flashy suit.

He wanted Buck to make a phone call to Kettner, telling him he'd back that zoning change after all.

Buck demanded to know what was going on. The man said there'd been an incident out at the carnival traveling through town that involved Kettner's daughter. They needed her to change her story. Kettner told them he could make it happen if they could do something for him. It was complicated, the man said. Buck really didn't need to know all the particulars.

He showed Buck some paperwork related to the recent mayoral campaign. The letters BCKATC really stood for "Beatrice C. Kline Addiction Treatment Center."

Misappropriation of campaign funds is illegal, the man explained to Buck. Hell, people in town would likely forgive him, looking out for his wife like that. Probably be hard on Bess, though. The way people would look at her in the supermarket and whatnot.

Buck made the call.

Kettner never did get to make use of the zoning change. He packed up his family and left town without explanation not long after the whole affair. Buck suspected The Agendum saw Kettner as a liability because he knew too much, but they had no particular use for him. By that time, Kettner's departure was scant comfort.

A year later, the man in the suit showed up in Buck's office again. He said he and his colleagues were ready to get started on a business enterprise they had going. They might need Buck to run some interference for them when it came to dealing with local agencies. No need to worry, really. What they mainly needed was for people to stay out of their way, and let them do what they needed to do.

Bess had one of her episodes the day before the Halloween Parade that year, and hadn't been up to attending. Buck was standing on the reviewing stand with the other council members when all hell broke loose around them.

Buck ran through that crowd in a blind panic, his only thought that he had to get home and make sure Bess was alright. She wasn't there. An envelope was on his kitchen table. In it was a note. It read: "Do what you need to do. If you tell anybody about us, we will hurt her."

They brought her back three days later. She wasn't right for the better part of a year. In a way, she never recovered. To this day, she would still get hysterical if left alone in a dark room.

"Did she even know what was going on?" I asked.

"I told her it was a kidnapping for ransom situation," he said.

"And she believed that?"

"She tries not to think about it. She gets out of sorts if something reminds her, so she mostly just blanks it out."

He drained his glass and refilled it.

"She's a lot of trouble sometimes, no question," he said. "But I don't know what I'd do if something happened to her."

We sat silently for a minute or two, drinking the Scotch.

I asked if Bixler was in on it. Buck said when The Agendum contacted him about two years ago, they told him to endorse Bixler. It pained him, but he did it.

No, Bixler wasn't in on it, although he got the impression that Bixler eventually sensed he'd been used as a pawn.

Bixler wasn't the sharpest tool in the shed, no question about that, but in his own way he meant well.

Buck himself didn't understand what they wanted with Bixler, until he saw the destabilizing effect Bixler's "Feet to the Fire Campaign" had on the city.

That made The Agendum's job easier.

And Chief Sanderson?

No, Buck said. He believed Sanderson also had a feeling that something was going on behind the scenes. But he wasn't in on it.

We drank in silence for a little bit longer.

"Paul Bacon is only 14," I said. "Did you think about that before you helped them organize that stunt tonight? Positioning him by the phone so somebody could call in with the phrase that would trigger his episode?"

"I didn't know what they were planning," Buck said. "Michael just told me to have him at my desk, and tell him to answer the phone. It didn't make any more sense to me than anything else they told me to do."

"Bullshit!" I said, suddenly angry. "You're sitting here acting like you're just some poor, innocent dupe! But you knew their stunts got people killed in the past! You knew they wanted Paul for something, whether or not you knew specifically what it was! And you went along with it anyway!"

Buck waved a hand, trying to get me to lower my voice. But I wasn't done.

"You know what? You said you don't know what you'd do without Bess. The people who had family – Kids! – trampled to death during the Halloween Parade Massacre would probably have said the same goddamn thing about the people they lost!"

"Please! Keep your voice down! Bess'll hear you and she's upset enough. I didn't know what they were planning," he said. "And 14 years ago, they told me they were done with this city. I thought maybe Bess could be safe and they'd just leave us alone."

"You thought wrong," I told him. "That's why you asked me to investigate, isn't it? You hoped I'd find out about them but not about your involvement?"

"I don't know what I was thinking," Buck said. "I just knew I couldn't stand by while they did something like that again. I thought … I hoped … I don't know. They used me."

He sat quietly for a moment. He looked very tired and old right then.

I was about to start in on him again. Then something occurred to me.

"They used me, too," I said.

"What do you mean?"

"Paul Bacon," I said. "Those anonymous letters to Sister Pilar, with the picture of Paul. They wanted me to get him out of Cabot's house, so they could get to him."

"That would mean …"

"I don't know what Cabot's involvement is in all this," I said. "But he's not with them. He never was. He was trying to protect Paul."

"I don't understand."

"You don't need to. Here's the deal. I know who their point man is this time around. You do too. It's Michael. If you can run interference with Sanderson, I think I can deliver him giftwrapped for you, same as I did with Cabot. I just need to know that when I call you this time, your next call is going to be to the police."

Buck looked toward the door where Bess had exited.

"You worried about her?" I asked. "Last time around, people got killed. Who knows what the fuck they've got planned this time? What would Bess think of you if she knew you had a chance to stop it and you didn't?"

"Alright!" Buck said. "Enough. Yes. I'll take care of Sanderson. You just take care of Michael. Anything else you need from me?"

"Yes."

I pulled out my flask, and filled it from his bottle. It was going to be a long night.

FILE 27

FROM BILLY'S PAPERS

I slept later than I intended to the next morning, because the plywood over the window kept the room darkened. I breakfasted on one of the sandwiches the kid left me, and reflected that it was good I'd be well-rested in advance of what I needed to do.

I urinated in the bucket that served as my toilet. Then I sat on the bed with my paperback again and listened to the kid moving around downstairs.

At one point, I heard his feet mount the stairs and pause outside my door. I pounded on it again, cursing and threatening and demanding that he let me out. I knew it was expected of me, just as I knew that the kid would not comply. His feet descended the stairs once more.

I put my ear to the door and detected a wavering yowl, most decidedly not originating from the kid. Soon after, the opening and closing of the front door was audible.

I looked at my watch and waited another ten minutes.

Then I pulled back the fitted sheet from the bottom of my mattress to reveal the large hole I'd cut there. I pulled out the variable speed reciprocating saw I'd purchased from a local hardware store the previous day. I had removed stuffing to make room for it, and it made a big, hard lump in the mattress. No matter. It wasn't like I'd ever used the bottom third of my mattress. I plugged in the saw, hoisted it, depressed the trigger and cut out the lower panel of the oak door.

I picked up my paperback, crawled through the hole, dusted the sawdust from my pants and proceeded down the stairs. In the living room, I climbed onto the couch and resumed reading. An hour later, a key turned in the lock and the door swung open. The kid stood there with a pair of plastic grocery bags in one hand and a cane in the other.

"You'll have to replace the bedroom door," I said, setting down my book. "And empty the piss bucket."

He dropped the grocery bags and kicked the door shut behind him. Then he gripped the head of the cane and withdrew the slim sword blade I'd seen the night before.

"You might as well put that away," I told him. "I know you have Clem stashed in the basement. He was staying with Schulze and you brought him home with you. I was expecting it."

Too astonished to put the sword away, he gaped at me with wide-eyed incredulity as the blade hung limp at his side.

"What? How did you …"

I motioned toward the chair across from me.

"Sit down, kid. We need to talk."

He finally recovered his voice.

"My name isn't kid," he said.

"Fair enough," I said. "Gary. Take a seat and I'll tell you about it."

He resheathed the sword cane and let it drop to the floor. He then sat in the chair and I recounted what had happened after he walked out three months ago.

From what The Professor told me, I knew I had a month to find Schulze and confront him before Gary arrived at his place. I began visiting liquor stores and purchasing bottles of cognac. After each purchase, I would loudly speculate that I must be the only one in Batley who drinks the stuff. At three stores, that statement met with disinterested nods. At the fourth one, the man behind the counter told me that wasn't true. In fact, they delivered a case of it to a place on Wheatley Street once a month.

I knocked on Wheatley Street doors, saying I sought a friend who'd moved into the neighborhood recently, and was unsure of the address. They directed me to a house set well back from the sidewalk, with a gated driveway, as the only one housing a recent arrival.

When a thick-necked man I recognized from the sleight-of-hand class at the clinic inquired about the nature of my business from the other side of the fence, I reminded him that I was with The Agendum and told him that Schulze was an old acquaintance of mine. The man lowered his voice to inform me that The Professor was very explicit in his orders that nobody see Schulze. He could convey a message if I liked. I declined and walked away.

The next evening, while I observed from a bush across the street, a pair of young men pulled up in a pickup, loaded several large cardboard cartons of groceries onto a hand truck, and wheeled them through the gates. Back in my car, I followed the pickup back to a downtown grocery store.

The next week, I followed that truck and learned its route. The week after, I followed it again. During a delivery that delayed the two men in a house, I dug groceries out of a carton and threw them in the bushes, then hid in the bottom under the remaining groceries.

The truck hit a few more stops before the two men unloaded my carton, one of them bitching about the weight.

Schulze's voice said: "Did you remember the frozen pizzas? Thank you. Here's a little something for you. And you."

The door closed. Schulze's footsteps approached my carton and he began unloading the groceries. He froze when he uncovered me, mouth hanging open, brain manifestly unable to process what his eyes conveyed. I exploded out of the box, grasped his robe where it opened at his neck in both of my fists and pulled him over.

He was already bent over at the waist, his weight forward, so we both toppled over in a cascade of groceries. Cans rolled across the floor while I hauled him to the ground and jumped onto his chest. My left hand grasped his scrawny neck, my thumb pressing down on his windpipe. In my right, I brandished my razor before his eyes.

"What do you want with the kid?" I hollered.

He choked, gasped and sputtered. I released the pressure on his windpipe an iota.

"Start talking! What do you want with the kid?"

"I don't!" he managed to get out. "I don't want him! It's all their idea! I have nothing to do with it!"

"Are you lying to me, motherfucker? If you are, I'll carve you up like a side of beef!"

"It's them! It's all them! They said they want me to train him as my assistant. But that's a lie. He's my replacement."

"What do you mean 'Your replacement?' "

"They think I haven't figured it out," he said. "I'm a liability now. They can't just cut me loose because I know too much. They want me to train my replacement first."

He gave a short, bitter laugh. The fact that he laughed as he lay on the floor with my razor hovering a hairsbreadth from his face made me believe him. Only a man already reconciled to his own death would do such a thing.

I allowed him to get up and sit in a kitchen chair, first ensuring that I was between him and the door. I instructed him to keep his hands where I could see them and emphasized just how badly I would injure him should he attempt to run for it.

I was not unduly worried, as he looked incapable of anything more strenuous that shitting himself. He was even more emaciated than when I had seen him last, and appeared to have aged decades. His manner was antsy and tremulous, like that of a drug user overdue for a fix. I gave him permission to light a cigarette, which he did with trembling fingers.

"To begin," I said, "am I correct in assuming that our mutual involvement in this unholy clusterfuck is not coincidental?"

"Yes, you're right," he said.

"You gave them my name."

He nodded.

"I ought to cut you up for that alone."

"I wouldn't blame you for it," he said. "For what it's worth, I didn't set out to harm you. I was desperate. I was trying to buy time."

From the doorway leading into the rest of the house came a high-pitched, indistinct and wavering shout.

"What?" Schulze said in response.

The shout came again.

"I can't … I'm sorry … I can't understand what you're saying," Schulze called back. "I'll be there in just a little while, OK?"

"God," he said, creasing his forehead in exasperation. "It's like taking care of a toddler. A toddler who eats like a damn elephant."

I recognized the voice.

"What the hell are you doing with Clem?" I asked him.

"I'm not sure myself."

It all started that day at the carnival in Batley, when police arrested him in his trailer with a teenaged girl named Alice Kettner.

"I had no idea she was that young," he said. "I would have said she was 19. 18 at the youngest."

"That's quite a relief," I told him. "For a minute there, I was under the mistaken impression that you're a twisted lowlife who was trying to slip it to a teenage girl young enough to be his daughter."

He merely sighed. The man clearly had no fight left in him.

"I'm not proud of it," he said. "All I can say in my defense is that I didn't think I was committing a crime, and I didn't mean to hurt anyone."

The marijuana dealer sharing Schulze's cell after his arrest at the carnival had given a whoop of incredulity when the latter recounted his misadventures. Kettner's daughter? He wasn't sure which was more astounding, the depth of Schulze's stupidity or the depth of shit into which he'd inadvertently stumbled.

With the gleeful perversity of those who truly relish conveying bad news, the dealer filled him in. Her father was a local bigshot, with a good deal of money and no reservations about investing it in personal vendettas. The pot dealer advised to Schulze to grow eyes on the back of his head while he was in Batley.

Schulze found himself unable to get hold of Skunk. The next day, he learned that his recent employer was in Batley Hospital, the victim of a severe beating. He also discovered that the local district judge considered him a flight risk because of his transient status, and refused to set bail.

That struck Schulze as strange, and he sensed something ominous afoot. That suspicion intensified when a guard carrying a baton walked by his cell and spoke in a quiet voice.

"So you like playing with little girls? Got a message to deliver from that one's father. See you later, scumfuck."

He banged his baton against the bars, then continued walking.

Not half an hour later, another guard informed Schulze that his lawyer was present. Schulze had never seen the small man with the thick glasses and pencil moustache awaiting him in the meeting room.

The man said he'd long been an admirer of Schulze's work, and had been looking for ways to incorporate certain principles into his own business enterprise. He was prepared to offer Schulze a consultant's job, with a very generous compensation package. As an added bonus, a kind of welcome-aboard gift as it were, they could make his current legal troubles disappear. All he had to do was say yes.

They set Schulze up in the house. They told him they were embarked on a major study in applied behavioralism that would probably take a few years to come to fruition. In the meantime, they wanted to establish an ongoing study program in what The Professor called "externally induced behavioral modification."

When Schulze used the term "brainwashing," The Professor regarded him as one might a loudly flatulent mourner at a state funeral.

"That is a very crude and archaic term," The Professor said. "It implies a negation of the cognitive process. What we do is the exact opposite. We enhance the cognitive process in a proactive and productive manner."

Soon, Schulze had bigger problems than getting his semantic nuances straight.

The Professor, it seemed, was very well versed in Schulze's books and fascinated with his descriptions of ritualistic magic used to monitor events from a great distance, bring misfortune and death down upon one's enemies, control people's thoughts and actions, and evoke powerful cosmic forces.

The professor wanted Schulze to show The Agendum how to do those things. The problem facing Schulze was his inability to do any of those things himself.

"So you were always full of shit," I said. "What about all those stories about traveling the world and learning occult secrets?"

"It was all P.R.," he said. "I made one trip to India. I paid a few street magicians to show me their tricks. Then I spent the rest of the time holed up in my hotel room with a case of the shits."

He put out his cigarette and lit another one.

"These days," he said, "I spend a lot of time going over in my mind how it all happened. How I landed in this situation."

His family was loaded, but Schulze had been a socially awkward, strange-looking kid. He had few friends, and no aptitude whatsoever in dealing with the opposite sex.

By his second year of college, he was still a weirdo, a loner, and a virgin. His entire life changed one night when he responded to a rare party invitation.

He found himself at a fraternity mixer, filled with boisterous young men and women clearly having a better time than himself. He imbibed two beers, which represented a copious amount of alcohol for him in those days. He'd inhaled from a joint that somebody passed him. Then he'd staggered to the party's periphery to slump against a wall and attempt to regain his bearings.

A girl approached, appearing as out-of-place as he did. Her clothes, lipstick and long, straight hair were all the deepest black. Schulze found her incredibly sexy, and mourned her inaccessibility.

Later, she told Schulze that she'd attended only because women were granted free admission and free beer. Schulze wracked his brains to think of a smooth opening line.

"Hello," he said. "My name is Friedrich Schulze."

"Interesting," she replied, sounding distinctly uninterested. "No relation to Otto Schulze, I take it."

"You mean the author of 'A Friend for the Knowing Ones?' Yes. He was my ancestor."

Schulze had always found that part of his family history embarrassing. If not for the marijuana and beer, he would no sooner have mentioned it to a girl than he would have referenced his furtive masturbation sessions in his dormitory room.

Now, however, the girl in black lipstick regarded him with undiluted fascination.

"Reeeeaaaally!" she said. "You have to tell me about it!"

She took him to her tapestry-lined apartment, redolent of incense, where she lit candles and another joint, and begged him to regale her with stories of his magician forebear.

With the joint and years of comic-book-reading serving as inspiration, he wove tales about the dark knowledge that only his family possessed. Their wearing of ceremonial robes and performance of arcane rituals at pagan worship sites in the countryside, during which they would call forth ancient gods. Their mastery of astral projection, allowing them to send their spirit bodies into dimensions beyond human understanding and there view things that would drive an ordinary man mad with terror.

Nothing of what he said pertained in any way to Otto Schulze's book, which was more about using chicken fat to cure warts. But apparently her knowledge of "A Friend for the Knowing Ones" was minimal, because she ate it all up with a spoon.

The darker he made the stories, the more visibly excited she became. When he began speaking about the ritualistic sex magic, she practically tore his clothes off and he lost his virginity in the resultant bruising carnal frenzy.

Thus began the career of Friedrich K. Schulze, Master of the Occult.

When he was arrested and expelled from the university where he taught for a time, he worried that the poontang express had run out of track. But his notoriety only swelled the ranks of women regarding him as a kinky thrill. He seemingly could do no wrong. On a whim and out of a sudden desire to see more of the country, he decided to join the carnival.

"I had plenty of money from my trust fund, and I was pulling in even more with my books," he said. "And there I was, traveling around the country, getting laid like a rock star in every town. I couldn't believe how good I had it."

As the days went by, however, he found himself thinking about his life and what it amounted to. He wasn't getting any younger. He was having a good time, but what had he to show for his time on the planet other than some books filled with bullshit, salacious news articles, and a coast-to-coast trail of discarded condoms?

He'd once relished the notoriety of being the Most Evil Man in America. In time, he began to feel stirrings of sadness when he'd be out walking in public, and see a mother recognize him and then pull her child by the arm in the opposite direction. Or when he would attempt a genuine conversation with one more thrill-seeking young woman, only to find her hungry for another fabrication about ritualistic goat killings in the Schulze family manor.

He always emphasized the weird and the grotesque in his books and act because that's what sold. The rubes don't pay to see herbivores. But underneath it all, he nursed a genuine interest in mythology and folklore. He formed an idea of using his family money to start a series of study centers for mythology.

"They would be about helping people overcome problems by studying sacred stories from different cultures, and seeing what lessons they could apply to their own lives," he said, describing it at the kitchen table.

Then he gave a sad little smirk as he lit yet another cigarette. It all made perfect sense to him at the time, he said. He envisioned spending his golden years as a revered figure. Friedrich K. Schulze: Scholar, Humanitarian and Visionary. It had a better ring than Friedrich K. Schulze: Aging Sicko and Pussy Hound.

In the carnival's off-season, he drafted study guides about different mythological figures, drawing from his university courses. In retrospect, he thought those guides might have saved his life.

When The Agendum snapped him up and asked for genuine displays of magic, he stalled them and searched with increasing desperation for a way out. Soon, though, it became patently obvious to all concerned that Schulze couldn't deliver what they'd brought him in for.

Having seen his act, The Professor believed that Schulze really did have paranormal powers. Schulze encouraged that. He told the professor it was a matter of genetics. Some people were born with those powers and some were not. It wasn't something that he could teach just anyone.

That left the question of why The Agendum should keep Schulze around, since he had nothing to offer and knew too much to let go.

Though they didn't spell it out for him, he'd seen enough to realize obsolescence did not get one a gold watch and a pension from this crew.

Schulze had spent the whole previous night pacing and rehearsing before the morning he went into The Professor's office and made his pitch.

Much of his paranormal expertise, Schulze explained, came from the power to influence people's thoughts and perceptions. How did he do that? By tapping into the primal power of myth. Certain archetypes triggered different responses in people's brains. If The Professor really was interested in "externally induced behavioral modification," as he called it, perhaps he'd like to hear

Schulze's plans for a treatment center. A clinic, as it were.

A week later, The Suit told him the plan was a go. He slapped Schulze on the back and said: "Congratulations. Maybe it was worth the effort setting up your fat friend to take the fall for you after all."

"My what?" Schulze said.

Schulze found Clem living in a county-run shelter. The social worker who oversaw it told Schulze in confidentiality that nobody who worked with Clem believed he was mentally or even physically capable of doing what that city councilman's daughter claimed. They managed to get him out of the county prison and enrolled in a program to rehabilitate "mentally challenged" inmates.

The government grant that funded the program was set to expire and nobody was sure what to do with Clem. If nobody signed on as his legal guardian, he might have to go back to the prison.

Schulze stared at Clem, who was laboriously drawing something on a piece of construction paper with a crayon, and asked the social worker to bring him the forms.

Once Schulze gave The Professor his study guides, they didn't consult with him much on the setup of the clinic. They did come to him from time-to-time with requests, though.

If they were trying to frighten a population with a theoretical enemy, what attributes would that enemy have? What would that enemy's name be? What would that enemy look like? Also, they decided they needed a good sleight-of-hand artist. Schulze knew people from the carnival. Whom would he recommend?

Eventually, they opened the clinic. Schulze's existing fan base provided test subjects, but The Agendum wanted more. Much more.

Schulze told them he had a new book coming out, which would be the culmination of his career as both an artist and a mage. The Agendum waited for the publishing date, with plans to use it as the start of a campaign to bring in new test subjects.

"By then, I had enough clout with my publisher that I could pretty much wipe my ass on a sheaf of paper and they'd print it," he told me.

That, in effect, is what he did. Schulze intentionally made "When the Ancient Ones Feed" so weird, disgusting and off-putting that it would drive away followers instead of drawing them.

He knew his plan had been successful when The Professor told him they were canceling a planned clinic expansion. And he knew it was over for him when they suggested he find a trainee. He told them it wasn't that simple. It might take years to train a replacement. They told him he had two months, and to pick one.

"Why did you pick the kid?" I asked him.

He glanced toward the room from which Clem's voice had emerged.

"I knew he was friends with Clem," Schulze said. "Since I had to bring in somebody anyway, I thought it might as well be somebody who could take care of Clem. In light of what Clem went through because of me, I thought I owed him that much."

"Do you honestly believe any of this makes up for what you did?" I asked him.

Some fight remained in him after all. He straightened his back and raised his voice.

"Do you think you're any better than I am?" he said. "Look at you! You've spent your life preying on people!"

"Ah bullshit! I scammed people for pocket change at carnivals! People came to you for help and you served them up to these fuckers on a silver platter! Are you trying to tell me that's the same thing?"

His shoulders slumped. He lit yet another cigarette. And as he did so, I reflected upon the night I made the kid leave Clem behind and wondered if Schulze had a point.

"No," he said. "I don't think that makes up for what I did. But I have some other plans. And I think I could use your help."

We talked for hours, during which we devised a system of communication. Until recently, they'd given him relatively free rein. That changed with the publication of his book. Now the guard stood outside and he wasn't permitted to leave. They'd told him it was for his protection because they'd received threats directed at him, none of which explained why he wasn't allowed to take or receive phone calls.

He suspected they were reading his mail at first. But since he typically got such a large volume of it, they appeared to have become lax in that respect.

So whenever he received a manila envelope with a certain return address that didn't exist in the real world, he would know it was from me. Inside would be a decoy letter, and a real single-sheet letter hidden between the outside of the envelope and a piece of another manila envelope pasted to the inside. If I did it right, it would be undetectable by touch and stand up to a cursory glance inside the envelope.

Schulze, in turn, would send out letters to me hidden in copies of "When the Ancient Ones Feed," sent to P.O. boxes that I'd list in my hidden letters.

"You'll end up with lots of copies of 'When the Ancient Ones Feed' as souvenirs," he said.

"What would I want with that piece of shit?"

He smiled, displaying nicotine-stained teeth.

"Say what you will," he answered. "As far as I'm concerned, it's the best thing I ever wrote."

By then, the sky outside had darkened. I hid in the bottom of a plastic trash can as he put a trash bag full of crumpled newspapers on top of me. He wheeled the trash can up to the gate, and the guard took it to the curb. I waited for what seemed a prudent interval, then extricated myself and drove away.

"He gave me updates on what you were doing," I told Gary. "It sounds like you spent a lot of time sitting around and watching TV."

"I was keeping Clem company," Gary said. "When Friedrich was doped up, there wasn't much else to do. He showed me some tricks, and showed me how he runs the business. He mostly lets his lawyers handle that. About all he does is send out cryptic letters to followers. Can I ask why you went through this whole pretense?"

I jumped down from the couch and picked up the sword cane, turning it over in my hands.

"Where the hell did you get a sword cane, anyway?"

"Pawn shop. Are you going to answer my question?"

I removed the sword blade and flexed it in my hands.

"You see, kid … Gary … I never saw any meanness in you. Maybe that's not a bad thing, in and of itself. But the world's not a nice place. When you're looking out for others, sometimes you have to be a little mean on their behalf."

"I didn't think you'd let us take in Clem," he said.

"I know. You were right. I wouldn't have."

"When I first joined that carnival, nobody else would talk to me," Gary said. "He was my only friend. Ever since I abandoned him, it's eaten at me like acid every day."

"I knew you wouldn't leave him behind again," I said. "And since I knew you wouldn't listen to reason, I wanted to see if you could do what's necessary to protect him and yourself. I talked about meanness. These people? The Agendum? They're mean in a way that men like you and I can't even comprehend. Now they're in our lives."

"This was a test?" he asked, his voice going quieter.

"What was your plan?" I asked him.

"Make a run for it."

"They would follow."

"I'd throw them off."

"How?"

It seemed he had a horse trailer hitched to a pickup in a garage outside of town. Both were recent acquisitions. Before leaving, he would take off in his car to Shooter's Row, where the local junkies hang out. He'd explain he was offering good money for one of them to do a job that was not of the hand or blow variety.

He would drive said job candidate to this house, hand over the keys to the trailer that had served us since our carnival days and was still parked out front, and explain that it must be driven to a destination in Baltimore. He would tell him it was only legal to drive on certain roads, otherwise it would get impounded. He would map out for him a winding, eminently visible route out of town.

Gary, meanwhile, would retrieve the pickup, load Clem into the horse trailer, don a disguise and leave town.

"And you would expect this junkie driving our trailer to abide by those instructions?" I asked.

"Absolutely. For him, the trailer is pure gold. The moment he gets down to Baltimore, he's going to exchange it for high-grade smack. I wouldn't even bother to give him a real address."

"Backup plan?"

"I pay another one of the junkies. I tell him I'm heading north. But I need him to call police about a reckless driver that almost hit a kid, with a car that fit my description. I'd leave the car hidden in the garage when I drove out of town in the pickup with the horse trailer."

"What if the junkie put it together that people were trying to find you and tried to work an angle of his own?"

"He could tell them we were headed north if he wanted. We'd be headed west."

"What about me?"

It seemed he had a hammer and a screwdriver hidden in the room. Sooner or later, I'd go through everything in that room, find them, and remove the pin hinges on the door.

"How would I reach the top one?" I asked.
"By pulling the desk over. I measured it."
"What if I didn't figure it out?"
"You would have."
"What if I didn't?"
"You would have."

I nodded. Then I held up the sword with which he'd threatened me.
"Allow me to demonstrate something."

I placed the tip of the sword against the floor. Then I stepped on the side of the blade. It bent like it was made of tinfoil.

"This was your chosen weapon?"
"I didn't want to hurt you," he said.

I threw the bent sword down on the ground.

"Haven't I taught you anything? Godammit! You can't think like that! Never pull a weapon you aren't prepared to use! If the other man has a hidden weapon and he thinks you're willing to use yours, do you think he'll hesitate to use his? I'm not going to be here to tell you these things, kid, and you better get a lot smarter in a hurry if you're going to take care of yourself and your friend down there!"

He looked down toward the basement. And then he just kept his head down. Ah hell. I walked over the coffee table and picked up some manila folders.

"These are yours," I said, and handed them over.

He leafed through the papers they contained. I told him it was information on stashes of our money. One was a conventional bank account. Two were envelopes full of cash in safe deposit boxes. One was disguised as the assets of a company that consisted of nothing more than a post office box in Delaware. And one was an offshore account.

I looked down at the bent sword on the floor, then I cleared my throat.

"Look," I said. "I know I'm not the easiest son of a bitch on the planet to get along with. That's just how I am. But for what it's worth, I looked out for you the best I knew how."

Gary leafed through the papers for another few seconds. Then he set them down on the coffee table.

"You were right all along," he said. "These people are rotten."
"Yes, I assumed you would come to that conclusion once you got a first-hand look at their operation."
"What should I do, Billy? I'm scared."
"There's nothing inherently wrong with fear. Oftentimes, it's a rational response. It can keep you alive. As for what you do — it's going to be your call from now on. But if I were you, I wouldn't make a break for it. Not yet. These people seem to be done here for now. They're already pulling up stakes. And I'm about to do something that's going to spook them and give them an added incentive to depart.

"This religious cult leader gig? It's a good scam. You'll have a home. If you play it right, you'll pull in enough money to support the two of you. If things go sour, you can still make a break for it. Just be sure you keep your guard up. You're on these people's radar now, and I won't be around to keep an eye out for you."

"Where are you going, Billy?"

"Remember Sally? The friend of mine who used to help out with the show?"

"Yes. I liked her."

"She's mixed up in this and she asked for my help. I have things to do. And there's an excellent chance that I won't be coming back. I'm going to need your help."

I explained to him what I needed him to do. He paid careful attention and nodded. When I was done, I started for the front door.

"Billy?" he said.

I stopped and turned.

"Thanks," he said. "You know, for everything."

I couldn't think of what else to say. I just said "Don't mention it."

Then I departed to meet Ken.

FILE 28

FROM PINKY

Have received complaints about time it takes to transcribe messages. Asked to shorten them. Will give babies their bottle. Found good candidate to oversee next phase of study. Background with underground religious militia groups. Oversaw numerous domestic terrorism operations, never caught. Was serving term in federal prison for steroids trafficking. Made offer. He accepted. Expertise in explosives and martial arts. Will update as necessary.

I stumbled a little as Luanne and I walked through Michael's doorway, holding onto the frame to steady myself.

"Easy there, cowboy," Michael said, and looked at Luanne. "He didn't drive did he?"

She shook her head. I shut the door behind me. I noticed a dainty little table sitting by the door. Probably to set mail on and maybe a vase of daffodils or something. Michael definitely hadn't furnished this place. I wondered if it got annoying for him, living here. Or was he used to living in other people's settings? Other people's lives?

Michael motioned us to sit down on the couch, then sat in a chair facing us.

"You started to worry me," he said. "You were gone awhile."

He cut a quick look at Luanne.

"But that's OK," he said. "I know this is difficult. Keep in mind, though, this is the best thing for Paul and for Ty. And for you."

He picked up a clipboard and a ballpoint pen from an end table and handed them to Luanne.

"The forms are there," he said. "I've been on the phone with Dr. Pigeon. We'll still have some legal details to take care of, but this will get the ball rolling and we'll be able to get Paul someplace safe immediately. Is he in the car?"

Luanne shook her head again. A crease appeared between Michael's eyebrows.

"So where is he?" Michael asked.

"Someplace safe," I said. "Away from you."

Luanne finally spoke, her words a soft, drawn-out hiss.

"You bastard."

The crease between Michael's eyebrows deepened.

"I don't under…"

"We're onto you, Michael," I said. "You and your buddy Dr. Pigeon. You were behind it all."

Michael stood, walked over to the front window and slapped his hand against it. Then he turned quickly and directed his next words to Luanne.

"I don't know what this drunken fool has been telling you, but your family's in real danger. And right now, I'm the only one who can …"

"Shut up!" Luanne screamed at him. "I'm done listening to you!"

Michael's whole bearing changed then. He looked relaxed all of a sudden. Casual. A guy having a couple of people over for a visit. He walked back to his chair and sat down.

"I guess that's it, then," he said. "So tell me. How long have you known?"

"Well, I didn't really know until tonight," I said. "How long did I suspect? Since the beginning. Or really, since the attack at O'Shaunessey's. You told me it was your first time in the bar. But the attack happens and in the middle of it — in a span of seconds — you manage to figure out the layout of the place to a point where you know to head out that side fire exit and back in through the kitchen door? Bullshit. You'd cased that bar out beforehand. The whole thing was choreographed so that bar full of local bigshots would see you chasing The Slain out the front.

"Same as when you just happened to show up during the ballgame to take out Dudek. Guess I beat you to it that time. But it didn't really make a difference, did it? You still got to pose for a bunch of shit-scared people. Don't fear, citizens! I've got it under control!

"Same as when you chased off The Slain at the creek during the March for Batley. Although there, I guess they were supposed to pick off a few people with rifles before you chased them off. Sister Pilar ruined that part for you, didn't she? But what the hell. Same deal. You still got to come across as the man here to protect us."

Michael got up from the chair again and went to the window.

"I guess George Hoffman was kind of an ingrate, huh?" I said. "Your bosses must have paid him pretty well, considering all they wanted him to do was stand up at a city council meeting and tell a scary story, then keep his mouth shut. Enough to pay off the back taxes on his property and buy a new truck, anyway. What was he doing? Threatening to blow the whistle if he didn't get more? Of course, even after you killed him, you found a use for him. Gotta hand it to you. You people are efficient."

Michael continued to stare out the window.

"I'm wondering," I said. "When your boys jumped me at my place, how come they left me alive?"

Still facing the window, he spoke.

"If it was up to me? They wouldn't have. My boss thought if we got the Freak Foundation on our side, it would bolster our credibility. And he thought you might be useful."

"Kind of like when he conned me into getting Paul away from Cabot?"

"Yeah. Kinda like that. I tried to tell him that you and that nun were nothing but a pain in the dick, but he wouldn't listen. He always figures he knows better. I guess that's why he's the boss and I'm not. Since you kept interfering, he let me take you out of the way long enough to really get us established in the city."

"So all that bullshit," I went on. "The Slain. The Godknife. The Order of Gabriel. Was that part of a script they gave you or did you make it all up?"

"A little of both," he said, still not turning from the window. "Dr. Pigeon? That's not his real name. They never told me what his real name was. Calls himself R9. Everyone else calls him The Professor. He gave me the basic storyline. The Slain. The One Who Takes. He said Schulze came up with all of those details a long time ago.

"But he encouraged me to improvise. He asked what I was interested in. I told him warrior angels. Always have been, ever since I was a kid. He told me to build off that. The Order of Gabriel and The Godknife were my ideas. He liked them. He said they had 'mythological resonance.' Said all of it was what he called 'archetypal psychological triggers.'

"He's always saying stuff like that. Never have been able to figure out if he really knows what he's talking about, or if he's just nuts. Doesn't really matter to me. I'm in it for the money, and he delivers."

"What was the point of all this?"

"No idea," Michael said. "Some kind of behavioral study they were doing for clients. Never found out who those clients were, but I guess they were paying a lot. I had to do reports. Tell him how people reacted to me. How they acted in general. I was supposed to get the whole community going along. The boss was real pleased with the way it was going."

"Glad to hear it," I said. "Sounds like you might pick up a nice Christmas bonus. I guess the reason you brought Lange on board was because you knew he'd act like a psycho prick as soon as he got some power, and make you look reasonable by comparison?"

"Tell the truth, I didn't plan that at all. It was what you might call a bonus," Michael said. "They told me to bring in what they called 'social leaders.' You know what's interesting? The more I ..."

"Don't mean to cut you off," I said. "But you can look out that window and keep us talking all night if you want. They're not coming."

He turned to look at me.

"Your buddies in the dark sedan across the street," I said. "Your backup. I guess when you slapped the window, it activated your alarm system. Since it's not going to notify the police, I assume it's supposed to call them in. But they're not coming. The guard who works the front gate has got it locked down."

I looked at my watch.

"By now, they'll have tried to get in and failed. The man at the gate will have called the police, let them know the men in the car are making a disturbance. Ritzy place like Heritage Estates, full of Batley's 'mover and shakers,' as you call them? The police'll come. No question. And whatever your buddies tell them, they've still got a stolen plate on their car. Had it checked today with a contact I've got on the police force. Since nobody's going to crash the party, we might as well talk."

Michael walked back to the chair and sat down. By then, I'd already pulled the little recorder Tom gave me out of my jacket.

"By the way, I got a recording of everything you said back there," I told him. His eyes went wide.

"So here's the deal," I went on. "You're getting off pretty light here. We've only got one demand. Leave town. We don't care what you do after that, as long as you get out of Batley and leave Luanne and her family alone. Because good luck trying to run your operation now that we're onto you."

In a quick motion, Michael reached under his chair and pulled out a handgun. He pointed it at us.

"Throw me the recorder," he said. "Then your car keys. We're going for a ride."

Luanne gasped. We looked at each other. Then I looked back at Michael.

"No," I said.

"You think I'm fucking around?" Michael asked. His voice was still calm.

"I think you're living in the wrong neighborhood," I told him. "You live downtown and fire a gun, maybe you'd get lucky and everybody'd pretend they didn't hear a thing. Not here. Not among the rich folks. They hear a gunshot in their neighborhood, they'll all be on the phone telling the police exactly which house it came from. And remember, the police are already on their way."

He was quiet. Just staring at us and holding the gun.

"Doing some calculating?" I asked him. "You could tell them we broke in and you were defending yourself. Maybe you could make that work for me. Maybe. But Luanne? That's going to be a harder sell. Especially since Sanderson suspects you to begin with. Don't forget, you'll need to explain how we made it past your fancy schmancy alarm system."

"Shut up," he said.

"And federal prison?" I said. "That steroids rap was a felony, wasn't it?"

His eyes went wide again.

"Don't know what kind of strings Dr. Pigeon pulled to get you out of that," I said. "But you're still a convicted felon. Just holding that gun is illegal. Firing it? Leaving two bodies on the floor? Now that's going to be a mess. In more ways than one."

"I said shut up!" His voice wasn't calm anymore. Not by a long stretch.

"You could ditch the gun, right?" I said. "Maybe claim somebody else did it. Except you're in a gated community with security cameras on all the exits. They'll know nobody left. And a gun's not a joint. You can't flush it when the police show up. You could throw it in the neighbor's bushes. Drop it down a storm sewer. Wherever you stash it, they'll find it sooner or later. It's a nice place to live, except now you're trapped in here."

"Just shut the fuck up!" he was yelling now.

"What's the penalty for bringing the law down on The Agendum? Grievous bodily harm or death? The second you pull that trigger, you're fucked and you know it."

I stood and put the recorder back in my jacket pocket.

"Well, sounds like you've got a lot to figure out," I said. "And by my estimates, you've got only minutes to do it. Good luck."

I turned my back to him and started toward the door. At that point, I figured I'd hear one of two sounds. One of the sounds? It would likely be the last one I'd ever hear. I heard the other one. The click of him unloading the gun's magazine. Followed by a couple of thuds as he hurled the gun and the magazine into the kitchen behind him. He didn't want anybody else using that gun and wasn't likely to give us a chance.

Immediately, I picked up the dainty little table by the front door. When I turned, he was already coming for me. I threw the table at him, aiming for his shins.

Bullseye. He tripped over it and crashed to the floor. As he got to his hands and knees, I kicked him in the face. Hard. His head shot back and blood spurted from his nose.

Luanne was on her feet, watching with a stunned look on her face.

"Run!" I yelled.

Michael shot forward like a cannonball, hitting me in the chest and knocking me to the floor. Then he was on top of me with a hand on my throat. I tried to take a swing at him, but his arms were too long and his face was out of reach.

I grabbed his arm and tried to move it. Nothing doing. He was stronger even than I'd anticipated. He squeezed and the room started to go gray.

I let go of his arm and grabbed onto the little finger of the hand gripping my throat. I bent it back furiously and felt it snap. He gave a howl and let go. His weight lifted from my chest.

I sat up, tried to claw for his eyes. He'd already repositioned himself and a knee slammed into my face, sending me sprawling. He was on top of me again with a hand raised. In it was the Godknife.

Before he could bring it down, Luanne had a hold of his arm.

Goddamn it! What the fuck was she still doing in here?

She got him in a wrist lock. Her technique was excellent. Ty would be proud. She twisted. He gave a yelp and dropped the knife.

He backarmed her. He was still on his knees and didn't have a lot of leverage, or else he probably would have hurt her bad. Even so, he sent her flying backwards, knocking over a lamp and then hitting the wall. She ended up sitting on the floor, looking dazed, blood streaming from her nose.

He turned away from me and made a move toward her. I threw myself forward and grabbed him around the ankles. He fell to the floor again, cursing in a very non-angelic manner.

"Run, goddamn it!" I yelled at Luanne.

She got to her feet. Michael started to get up, but I jumped onto his back, bringing my elbow down on the back of his neck. Hard enough to knock him out, I thought. Maybe even hard enough to kill him.

Michael just grunted, hit the floor for a second, then lifted himself back up. Luanne was on her way toward the door.

One last shot. No matter how strong an opponent was, he'd still pass out if you sunk a chokehold right. Ty had told me that many times.

I wrapped an arm around his neck. Got a hand on the back of his head and squeezed.

He was standing up and there was nothing I could do to prevent it. He was crazy strong. Roid strong. And then I was flying through the air and hitting the floor hard.

His boot came down and stomped on my stomach. An explosion of blinding pain engulfed my whole body. I couldn't breathe. I curled up and gasped like a dying fish as he ran toward the front door.

No air. I was suffocating. Drowning on dry land. Didn't know what was worse, the lack of oxygen or the pain where he'd stomped me.

With one last effort, I managed to throw myself forward and hook an arm around his ankles. He fell again as Luanne made it out the door.

He turned on me, then. His fist slammed into my face. I had no strength to fight him off this time. He punched me again. Bright lights went off in my head and I dropped limp to the floor.

I waited helplessly for the next punch but it never came. He was on his feet, running toward the door again. The knife in his hand.

He opened it. Standing in the doorway was Ty.

Before Michael could react, Ty slammed a palm into his face, driving him backward into the living room.

Michael never got a chance to recover. Ty was on him – a flurry of elbows, knees and shins operating with the merciless efficiency of a threshing machine. Goddamn, he was magnificent.

Michael went to the ground. Ty gave him a couple more shots to the side of his head with his knee. To make sure he stayed down.

Ty ran over to me, helped me kneel and then bent me forward with my head between my knees so I could catch my breath. Then he assisted me to my feet.

"Are you OK?"

I managed a nod. I was breathing again, my breath coming in ragged gasps.

John, the guard from the front gate, was there then. His massive frame filled the door as he entered the house. Luanne walked in behind him.

Ty nodded at John, who walked over to where Michael lay on the floor, pulled his hands behind his back and snapped a pair of plastic cuffs on him.

"Damn!" John said as he got a look at Michael.

I was thinking more or less the same thing.

Michael was limp. Unconscious and breathing, although the breathing sounded funny. Beneath the mask of blood, snot and spit that covered his face, Ty had done some structural damage.

John, Ty and Luanne looked at me as I sat on the couch, gradually getting my breath back. I pulled my flask out of my pocket, took a drink and immediately felt better.

I looked at John.

"You call the police?" I asked him

"Nah. I did what you said."

The last time I'd come to Heritage Estates, when Michael tried to make me believe Ty was with The Slain, I'd asked John to keep an eye on the sedan. Around the time I'd tapped the window on Michael's house, before he'd jumped me outside, the men in that car had driven up to the gate. All residents get a card for guests to use at the front gate, and they had one of those.

I'd asked John to get the license plate number if the car pulled up, as I expected it to.

Night security worked in two-man shifts. One kept an eye on the gate and one patrolled Heritage Estates for any sign of trouble.

As luck would have it, the other guy on tonight was a friend of John's, willing to back him up. The minute John saw the dark sedan approaching, he locked the gate. The other guy was keeping an eye on it now, by camera. I'd warned John not to put himself or his buddy physically close to the gate, in case the guys in the car tried to make them open it at gunpoint.

As we'd find out later from the security cameras, the guys in the sedan honked their horn for a while, circled Heritage Estates a couple of times, then took off before the police showed up.

"Should I call the police now?" John asked.

"No," I said. "I'll call the mayor. He'll take care of it. You remember your story?"

"I was on patrol," John said. "I saw a disturbance. I came to investigate. I saw this man," a nod at Michael "attempt to assault this woman." A nod at Luanne. "Then this gentleman," a nod at Ty "intervened before I got there."

"Good," I said. "Ty?"

"I drove you two over and I was waiting in the car. I got out to see what was taking you so long. Just when I got to the door, Luanne ran out with Michael after her. I got between them, he took a swing at me and I defended myself."

"Good," I said. "I think his gun will go a long way toward helping us sell this. Buck will probably still have to do some heavy lifting."

"What about the recording?" Luanne asked.

"It's illegal in Pennsylvania to record people without their consent," I told her. "I was betting Michael didn't know that. Figured it would get a reaction out of him."

I took a deep breath. It hurt to inhale but I didn't think I had any broken ribs. I sure as shit got a reaction out of him. Me and Luanne debated whether or not to bring Ty in with us from the beginning, but decided he'd be more valuable as the ace up our sleeve.

I got to my feet and walked to the door. I peeled off the piece of duct tape I'd stuck on the frame when I pretended to stumble on my way in, to keep the door from latching. I didn't know if it would lock automatically, but I didn't want to take a chance.

"So how about your story?" I looked at Luanne.

"We went in to talk to him. He didn't like what we had to say. He attacked us. That's what happened. Why do we need to go over this?"

"Because it seems like you have some trouble keeping to a script!" I said. "Why did it take you so long to get out of the house? The plan was if Michael tried anything, you were supposed to head straight – Straight! – for the door! What the fuck were you thinking?"

"You're talking to me about plans?" Luanne said. "Remember saying he wouldn't have a gun because nobody's really after him and it would be too much of a risk? I also remember you saying that if I had to run for the door, you'd take care of him while I got Ty! Looked to me like you weren't taking care of shit! Looked to me like you were getting your ass kicked!"

"Hey!" Ty said.

She went quiet and looked at him.

"Back off," Ty told her. "Considering that he was still recovering from a beating when he went into that fight, I think he did pretty good for himself."

We were all quiet for a little bit as I took another pull from my flask.

"Ah, you're just trying to make me feel better," I said.

Ty grinned.

"You're right," he said. "I am just trying to make you feel better. You were getting your ass kicked, buddy."

He, Luanne and John all laughed. These fuckin people. Geez.

"What now?" Ty asked.

"First things first," Luanne said.

She walked over to Michael and spat on him.

"That's for my family, motherfucker," she said.

Before I called Buck, I made a quick search of the house. The basement door had three heavy locks on it. Something important down there, no doubt. I would have liked to check it out myself. But I didn't have the expertise, the equipment or the time to get past those locks without the police knowing what I'd done.

The locked desk drawer on the second floor was another matter. One locked drawer in the entire house? That looked interesting. And indeed it was, once I'd taken my picking tools out of my wallet and opened the almost insultingly easy lock.

I found several magazines. One, big surprise, was "Saltwater Fisherman Monthly." The rest were porn of a variety suggesting that getting beaten, cuffed and spat on wasn't as unpleasant an experience for Michael as I might have hoped.

I found sheets of paper with five different addresses in cities surrounding Batley, each with anywhere from three to seven names listed under them. One of them was Ezekiel. I pulled out the pen and the pad of paper I'd used for making notes in City Hall earlier that day and wrote them down. I also wrote down an address in Philadelphia that had no accompanying names or any other explanation.

I put everything back the way I'd found it. Except for one piece of paper that I kept. It listed an address in Florida, under the heading "G.C."

FILE 29

I never understood why the climate draws so many people down to Florida. For me, it's the least appealing part of the place.

In the days since our fight with Michael, the temperature dropped in Pennsylvania. We were getting those real nice, crisp fall days. I found the sun, heat, and dampness in Florida kind of oppressive.

Don't get me wrong. The state has plenty to recommend it. I'd already hit a couple of roadside barbecue joints that were better than anything I could get up north. And on the passenger's seat of my rental car were three sacks of their sweet-as-candy grapefruits. One for me, one for Pilar and one for the Bacons.

Besides, I thought as I fiddled with the rental car's radio in search of a decent station, it was good to get a break from all the commotion in Batley.

Turned out I missed the big prize in Michael's basement, which was where he kept the automatic rifles and explosives. Law enforcement types were keeping pretty tight-lipped. They'd put out word to the effect that Michael was heading up some kind of end-times religious cult. According to the official account, all the attacks by The Slain – who were really Michael and his followers – were meant to punish Batley for turning away from God or something. And they were acting alone, police said.

It was all bullshit. I tried to share what I knew with both Sanderson and the team of federal investigators who came to town after Michael's arrest. They made it clear that they didn't have time for my crazy-ass conspiracy theories.

I had to admit, I didn't have a lot to back up my claims. Pinky made himself scarce as soon as he got out of the hospital. Buck was playing innocent and refusing to see me. His word carried a lot more heft than mine. Ken said he'd be willing to talk about what he'd experienced. I didn't tell Ken this, but I suspected a guy who'd spent the last decade on disability for mental health problems probably wouldn't get any more of an ear than I did.

Ty and Luanne? Nobodies as far as the people who mattered were concerned, and they had exactly as much proof as I did.

I hoped the investigators would eventually get the full story from the rank-and-file members of "The Slain," who turned out to be the names on the lists I found in Michael's desk.

They were a mix of regional and out-of-state guys. Most of them had criminal backgrounds. Nothing extraordinary. Assaults. Armed robberies. That sort of thing. These guys were grunts, not criminal elites.

They'd told their neighbors in the various towns where they set up in rental houses that they were crews of contractors, brought in for a temporary job. Technically, I guess you could say that was true.

A few of them, Ezekiel included, made a break for it before police raided their houses and were still on the loose. The rest got picked up. Police found their weapons and their leather masks in the houses.

All I could get on the radio was top 40 pop or Jesus stuff, so I gave up and drove in silence. Evening was coming on. I had to admit, this part of the country got some damn pretty sunsets.

I'd turned off the highway about 20 minutes ago. I was driving down a road in dire need of repair, passing occasional trailers and houses that didn't look to be in much better shape.

I spotted a little rancher on my left and confirmed the number on the mailbox when I drove by. Yep. When I got to the next driveway, I turned around and headed back toward it. That's when I thought of something that really should have occurred to me a lot earlier. What exactly was I going to say to him?

Hey buddy! Haven't seen you since I broke into your home and knocked you out. So, how ya been?

I pulled off to the side of the road a few yards short of the house. Maybe it would be good if I could case it out a little beforehand.

I walked up the dirt driveway, which had a pickup with a Florida plate parked in it. Off to one side was a trailer, still with its Pennsylvania plate.

As I got closer to the house, I could hear yelling. Cabot's voice.

"What do you think I am, your personal chef? I've been working all day while you've been sitting here watching TV! You know what? Don't eat it! Just go hungry if you want! I don't care!"

A couple of seconds later, a screen door on the side of the house banged open. Cabot emerged and sat down on a concrete step in front of it.

His long hair was gone, replaced by a crew cut. He'd grown a beard. He was wearing a red polo shirt, jeans and sneakers.

He lit a cigarette.

"Hey," I said.

He started, and turned toward me. I expected to see fear or anger. Confusion at the very least. Instead he looked like I was someone showing up for a tiresome but necessary appointment that he'd penciled in on his calendar, but slipped his mind until that moment.

"Oh, it's you," he said. "I've been following the news about what's going on in Batley. I assumed you'd show up sooner or later."

"Look," I said. "About you and that kid. Paul. I thought … I mean, I've figured out …"

He nodded and interrupted me.

"Yes," he said. "I've learned some things since then, too. You might as well come in. We should talk."

He took a big drag off his cigarette, then flicked it onto the dirt driveway. He walked back in the screen door, holding it open for me.

The kitchen was little, but neat. On a table was a plate holding a chicken breast and steamed vegetables, with a can of beer next to it.

To our left was a darkened room. A sound came from it. A kind of high-pitched, keening wail.

"AAAAaaaaAAAaaaaaa!"

It came again. I listened closely, and realized it was a word.

"GAAAaaaAAAaaarrry!"

Cabot went to the entrance of the room.

The high-pitched voice came again. The words were draw-out. Indistinct. But if I concentrated, I could understand them.

"Gaaaary? I'm sorry."

"It's OK, pal," Cabot said. "I'm sorry I got mad. I know you don't like the food. But the doctor said if you don't lose more weight, you're never going to get better. You understand that, don't you?"

"Uh-huh. Who's there?"

"We've got company," Cabot said.

He motioned me over and I looked in the room. It was dark, except for a flickering TV showing a cartoon. A couch faced the TV screen, with a tray table in front of it that held a plate like Cabot's and a glass of milk.

In the darkness, I could barely make out the man sitting on the couch. Just a shadow, really. Bigger than any man I'd ever seen before. Next to him on the floor sat a portable respirator with a tube leading from it to his face.

"Hi," the enormous man said. "My name is Clem."

"Hey Clem," I said. "Nice to meet you."

Cabot walked back into the kitchen and I followed him.

"Beer?" he asked.

"Sure," I said.

He handed me a can from the fridge. He pulled a wry face and said "I thought you might want to open it yourself."

"It's OK," I said. "And I'll try to be a better house guest this time around."

We sat down at the table. The keening voice came from the darkened room again.

"Gary?"

"Yeah?"

"It's really good."

"Thanks, pal. Glad you like it."

Cabot gave me a sad smile.

"He never did learn how to lie convincingly," Cabot said. "That's strange, because he sure had some great teachers."

"The same Clem from your carnival days, I take it?"

Cabot nodded.

"We go way back. He was my best friend when I was younger. I look out for him. Mind if I ask what you're up to?"

"I'm compiling a report," I said. "About everything that's happened. The man who asked me to prepare it, well, I think now he'd just as soon I didn't. And I don't know if anybody else is going to read it."

I shrugged.

"I just feel like somebody needs to write down everything that happened," I said. "Call it a personal project."

Cabot took a pull off his beer.

"It's been awhile since I left Batley," he said. "How is the old place?"

I told him the whole story, about what went on since he left. I told him about the attacks by The Slain. And Michael. And Pinky. And our visit to Michael's home, from which my ribs and face were still hurting.

Cabot ate his dinner as I talked, nodding from time to time. Once he took a break to get Clem another glass of milk and a single cookie.

When I finished, he said: "So Paul is safe."

I nodded.

"Good," he said. "I liked that boy. I guess he didn't like me much. I can't say I blame him. I felt bad, keeping him cooped up like that. I was making arrangements to send him someplace better."

"Where?"

"I had a lot of contacts from all over through the International Society for Mythical Studies and Personal Development. I found a place for him to stay. Someplace he would have been treated well. I think he would have liked it."

"Where?"

"I would have kept him hidden for maybe a year until the heat was off, then arrange for him to go back to the family he was living with in Colorado. I guess it all worked out in the end."

"Where?"

"Someplace safe."

I smiled.

"Playing it close to the vest. Billy taught you well, huh?"

Cabot looked toward Clem's room.

"I don't know," he said. "He tried to keep any one person from having too many pieces of the puzzle. That way if The Agendum got hold of anybody and made them talk – and he said nobody could hold out forever – the others would be safe.

"Sometimes I wonder if he took it too far. If I'd known about you and you'd known about me, we could have helped each other. But then I remember that Billy was just operating on the fly, trying to piece the whole thing together as he went along. Besides, that was how his mind worked. In his world, survival was about having that one piece of knowledge the other guy doesn't. Of course, he did take care of me and Clem."

"One thing I'm wondering about," I said. "If I had drunk the Scotch that night I went to your place, what would have happened to me?"

"I was going to drive Paul to where I was taking him," Cabot said. "I couldn't risk putting him on a plane. It took me some time to make arrangements. One of the big logistical problems was Clem. I couldn't leave him by himself.

"I was getting ready to leave soon when you came along. If you drank the Scotch, I would have taken you with us for part of the ride while you were knocked out. I would have left you someplace where it would have taken you a while to find your way back."

I nodded.

"Sound plan," I said. "Another thing. Scotch is my drink of choice. Why did you happen to Scotch on-hand?"

"Because I'm a civilized man."

I decided I liked him.

"So how did you end up with Paul in the first place?"

He told me.

He didn't know the man who dropped Sally off at his place 15 years ago. He never even saw him, and Sally never described what he looked like. Whoever he was, he showed up the next day with Billy's body. Sally met with the man in the living room and afterward told Cabot about it.

Cabot wasn't surprised when Billy came back dead. Billy had told him that he likely wouldn't make it. Still, it was harder than he expected to carry Billy inside, wrap him in a tarp, then take a sledgehammer to the concrete basement floor and bury Billy under it.

Sally sensed his sadness and did her best to console him. She was like that. Very sweet. Very kind. When she hid out with him during her pregnancy, they quickly became good friends. Clem loved her.

Investigators questioned Cabot about the clinic, of course. He was worried, with Billy's body buried under the basement floor. But they never did search the house. Cabot attributed that to the sheer scale of their job at the time. Despite the public's perception of Cabot as Schulze's evil second coming, investigators quickly wrote him off as a fringe player. One more clueless dupe Schulze and his thug friends left behind.

Cabot let them believe that, because of something that happened about a week after the Halloween Parade.

One afternoon, his doorbell rang. Sally made a practice of hiding every time that happened. Cabot was grateful for that when he opened the door and found The Professor and The Russian standing on his front porch.

"May we come in?" The Professor asked, giving him a friendly smile.

When they were sitting in his living room, Cabot asked them if they'd heard from Billy. He figured it would look suspicious if he didn't.

The Professor told him that Billy's responsibilities had taken him somewhere else and he would be there indefinitely. That was all he needed to know, The Professor assured Cabot.

Cabot, on the other hand, could consider his work with The Agendum effectively completed for the time being.

"As I trust you've surmised, Project Anchovy was the main test study we were here to perform," The Professor told him. "Our work with Mr. Schulze, involving the behavioral studies at the clinic, were something of a side project."

"What was the point?" Cabot said. "I've seen the news reports. What you did to those people. Why did you want to make them believe they were a bunch of gods and ghosts and monsters?"

"We didn't," The Professor said. "Our interest lies solely in a field of applied behavioralism known as 'identity displacement.' Our clients have intimated that the ability to impose and eradicate identities at will would be of enormous tactical value to them.

"Mr. Schulze indicated that we might facilitate this more easily by employing certain archetypal templates. Now, we hope to build on the foundation of research we conducted here to fine-tune the techniques, and perhaps impose identities that will be of more operational utility to our clients.

"The research wasn't a waste of time by any means. We discovered, entirely by accident, what appears to be a genuine though inexplicable parapsychological phenomenon in the form of the subjects we've come to refer to as 'ghosts.' We've also gleaned some potentially ground-breaking insight into externally induced behavioral modification principles, with long-term implications that are staggering.

"But our clients, who tend to be pragmatic to a fault, are not interested in long-term research possibilities. Mr. Schulze was an extraordinary man, to be sure."

Cabot took note of The Professor's use of the past tense. He thought about Clem and Sally, and felt his mouth go dry.

"As he demonstrated by surviving extended burial, he did appear to be truly possessed of certain ... powers," The Professor went on. "But it seems that Mr. Schulze was a bit, shall we say, imaginatively optimistic when he described what kind of results his techniques could produce for us.

"Toward the end, we were using his organization as nothing but a means of bringing in test subjects. Unfortunately, Mr. Schulze's behavior ultimately made him something of a liability, and we felt it wise to sever our association with him.

"So for now, we are discontinuing the phase of the operation in which we'd been intending to utilize you. I sincerely regret that we could not have employed you in a more productive capacity, as you seem like a very capable young man. There's every likelihood we'll keep that in mind for future operations. But until then, I would like to present you with what I would consider to be a very generous severance package ..."

He handed Cabot an envelope.

"And a gift."

He gave Cabot a small, giftwrapped rectangle. Cabot unwrapped it. It was a framed photograph featuring a ring of skydivers with linked hands. On it were printed the words: "TEAM. Together Everyone Achieves More."

As Cabot walked them to the door, The Professor spoke again.

"I see that Mr. Schulze foisted his companion off on you. Do whatever you want with him. But keep in mind what might happen to him if you decide to tell anybody about our operation and what you've seen of it."

That was too much.

"He's my friend, you piece of shit!" Cabot yelled. "If you even think about coming after him ..."

He reached out, wrapped The Professor's tie around his fist, and practically yanked the little man off his feet.

The Russian was on him like a hailstorm — elbows, knees and fingers striking and twisting. Then Cabot was face-down, immobile, with the Russian's knee in his back. The Russian had Cabot's shoulder twisted to an angle where a milimeter's move in any direction would tear tendons like wet cardboard.

The Professor bent down and produced a switchblade from his jacket, flicking it open in front of Cabot's face.

"As it happens, this is a perfect illustration," The Professor said.

He walked into Clem's room.

"No!" Cabot yelled. "No, please!"

He heard Clem scream and then begin to cry. The Professor emerged and showed Cabot a drop of blood on the knife.

"That was just a little nick on his face," The Professor said. "No harm done. If you tell anyone, this exact scenario will repeat itself. But the screaming will go on for much longer, I assure you."

Then they left.

With that ordeal over, the next few months were pretty nice. He and Sally and Clem spent a lot of time sitting around watching TV. When Clem went to bed, he and Sally would stay up late, playing cards and talking. He would tell her about life as a carny, and she'd tell him about her travels as a musician. She had no guitar with her, but sometimes she'd sing her songs for him. Songs about unicorns and fairie queens. They weren't very good, but he didn't mind.

Once a week, Cabot would disguise himself. Billy had told him many times about the extent to which people perceive what they expect to, and nothing else. Still, it amazed Cabot when he saw that principle in action. A flannel shirt thrown over a country music group T-shirt. A pair of jeans and workboots. A baseball cap pulled low over his face. Suddenly, the notorious black magician whom the whole town feared and hated looked like a guy who'd show up to resurface your driveway. And he could walk the streets, all but invisible.

He'd go into Bub's and order a beer at the bar. At some point, he'd go into the bathroom behind the pool tables. After he dropped off the envelope in the paper towel dispenser, he'd leave. Cabot didn't know who Sally's children were or where they were staying. He wouldn't recognize them if he passed them on the street. That's how Billy wanted it.

A midwife friend of Sally's checked in on her from time to time. Cabot didn't want to tell me who the midwife was, but assured me it was someone who understood the stakes and swore not to talk no matter what.

As Sally's pregnancy progressed, she became weak and pale. She got sick frequently. And she grew quiet.

"Something's not right," she told him. "I can feel it. I think they gave me something in the clinic that's making me sick."

Cabot and the midwife tried to get her to go to a hospital, but she refused. She was afraid. And she didn't think it would do any good.

She contacted her friend Patrice Logan in Colorado and apprised her of the situation. She was pregnant. Ken was out of the picture. He had the kids with him. The baby she was pregnant with wasn't Ken's. The father was a dangerous man and she was hiding from him. Long story.

She was staying with her cousin, Gary. She and Patrice had been friends at that commune. Sisters. Soulmates. (One-time lovers, Cabot suspected, though she never articulated it.) If the worst should happen, could she take the child?

The night of the childbirth, the midwife was there for the whole ordeal. In the end, the baby boy survived. Sally didn't.

The midwife left, trailing tearful apologies, condolences and reassurances that she'd done all she could do. Cabot buried Sally under the floor along with Billy. Clem cried for a long time.

The midwife came by for a few months to help care for the healthy baby, until he was big enough to travel.

Then Cabot took the baby to Colorado. The midwife looked in on Clem to make sure he was OK while Cabot was gone. Still, Clem was upset at being left alone that long. Cabot promised him it wouldn't happen again.

Beyond that, not much to tell. He lived the life of the reclusive evil mastermind everyone thought he was.

Supposedly, he was now in charge of Schulze's mini business empire. He found it was set up as a kind of perpetual motion machine of advisors, editors, copywriters, financial managers and various other white collar contractors who rarely met face-to-face.

Much of Cabot's work consisted of signing forms or penning the occasional essay for some mystical journal or other. For the latter task, he'd look through Schulze's previous writings, pull out a few compelling selections of bullshit, rearrange them into something that looked reasonably coherent, then call it a day.

Every once in a while, on the advice of his business manager in Dallas, he would conduct a corporate retreat. Those were very popular because they were basically weekend campouts with ample booze. Cabot would give a seminar where he'd survive being buried alive, just like Schulze did in his carnival shows.

To his surprise, he found a lot of smart, interesting people in the course of his correspondences with members of the International Society for Mythical Studies and Personal Development. They'd share insights. He even invited a few of them to visit.

"So when I was casing out your place, and I'd see those rough-looking guys paying visits …" I said.

He shrugged.

"There's a certain type I'm attracted to," he said. "It's not like I could go out, hit the bars and meet someone. Not in that town, with my reputation. And I couldn't let anyone settle in, either. I thought about it. But it came down to – What if The Professor comes back? Would I risk dragging someone else into that nightmare?"

One day he got a call from Patrice Logan. No fewer than five times in the lengthy letter Sally had composed to Patrice, she'd begged her to contact Cabot should anything like a certain situation arise. And now it had. Somebody showed up in the town adjacent to the commune where they bought their supplies. A definite out-of-towner, with his flashy suit. He'd been asking around about a boy who met Paul's description.

Cabot made Clem a big pile of peanut butter and jelly sandwiches to sustain him before leaving him alone once more to catch the next flight to Colorado.

When I ran out of his house that night, after the hard-working gentlemen of Security Concepts Inc. failed to stop me, the next thing they'd done had been to run in the house and check on Cabot. They woke him up and got him free.

While they were asking Cabot what he wanted them to do, The Professor showed up. He had several men with him, including an enormous one who looked like some kind of Viking biker.

They told the Security Concepts Inc. crew that they were police, and they should leave. When the security guards balked, The Professor's men pulled guns. Cabot told them to leave. It was OK. He knew these officers. He knew the jig was up, and any bloodshed would be pointless.

The Professor told Cabot to hit the road. He could go wherever he wanted, as long as it was far away and he notified The Agendum when he got there. If he didn't, they'd find him.

As Cabot drove south, he thought about Sally singing one of her awful unicorn songs to Clem. And how he was leaving her son behind with The Agendum. And he hated himself more than he would have thought possible. But you save who you can. That's what Billy told him.

"Aw man," I said. "Suddenly I feel like the world's biggest asshole."

Cabot waved a hand dismissively.

"Paul's still in touch with Patrice," he said. "He found family he never knew he had. It worked out for him."

"How about you?" I asked.

"We're getting by," he said. "Billy put some money aside. Clem's had health problems and his treatment ate up a lot of it. I got a job working at a liquor store."

"I'll check with the Foundation," I said. "We might be able to get you some financial help. And don't worry. It would be discreet."

"I'd appreciate that," Cabot said. "I have something for you."

He left the room and came back with several large envelopes.

"Billy left instructions for me if I ever had to go on the run," he said. "One of them was to stop by a safe deposit box in Maryland. There were some papers in it, including these – an account by Billy of his experiences. I suggest you give them a read."

As I walked to my car, something occurred to me and I turned.

"Just one more thing," I said to Cabot, who was standing in the doorway. "That buried alive stunt. I take it the flag to mark your position is really a tube you can breathe through?"

He tapped his forehead with his finger.

"You're not as dumb as you look," he said.

"Is anybody?" I wondered, putting the rental car in gear and heading toward the airport.

FILE 30

"Who are they?" Luanne asked me.
"I wish I knew."
"Will they come back?"
"Your guess is as good as mine."
"Would you like another beer?"

This time I had an answer, and it was an affirmative one. Luanne and I sat at the kitchen table in the Bacon house. The radio was on, tuned to a country station. Ken was laughing in the living room. Paul must have been giving Ty another beat-down.

I'd dropped off the bag of grapefruits from Florida that evening, and told her about my visit with Cabot. She told me about her interview with Sanderson a couple of days ago.

Sanderson told her what Michael had said. Michael claimed he wanted Paul as a recruit for his end-times religion. She tried to tell Sanderson there was more to it than that. She told him about the hypnotic trances. Sanderson rolled his eyes and asked if she'd been talking to me. That's when she lost her temper with him.

I smiled.

"Wish I'd been there to see that," I said.

"Why did they try to kill Ty?" she asked.

"I can only speculate," I said. "I figure Michael was getting ready to start some new phase of the project. One that was more about him as leader. 'The man behind this is dead. But his followers are still out there. I'm here to protect you, so obey me.' Whatever he had planned, he wanted to make Ty out to be responsible for this and didn't want him around to defend himself. Also, he figured you'd be scared, and more inclined to hand over Paul for his protection."

"Why Ty?"

I shrugged.

"I guess Ty was a good candidate for scapegoat. Martial arts training. Knowledge of explosives. He had a connection to Schulze. And — pardon me for saying this, you know Ty's my buddy — a lot of people around town think he's kind of weird. Added advantage, taking him out was one step closer to getting Paul."

"Why didn't he come after me too?" she asked.

"He needed somebody to sign the paperwork," I said. "Also, I think he had genuine feelings for you."

"I'm touched," she said with a sneer. "You know what kills me? Every time I dropped off Paul at the Pigeon Clinic, they had a nurse deal with me. They played it all off as so natural, it didn't occur to me that I never actually laid eyes on Dr. Pigeon. If I'd ever just seen that little weasel's face, I would have recognized him and …"

"Don't blame yourself," I told her. "I'm sure they went to great lengths to keep that from happening."

The radio started playing some George Jones. Great stuff. We sat without talking for a little bit.

"By the way, who's the Green Man?" I asked her.

"The who?"

"Some guy running around in a mask at Moondog Organic Produce. Ty called him the 'Green Man.'"

"Oh, that's Clyde," she said. "He owns the farm. He dresses like that every year for the Faerie Festival. He gets really into it. You should come out to it. It's a good time."

"Maybe I will."

It was nice sitting in the kitchen with her, drinking beer and listening to country music. I felt good.

The phone rang. I heard Ty getting it in the other room. He came into the kitchen.

His hand was still taped up from the fight. Other than that, he looked fine. Better than me, that's for sure. I looked like roadkill, as Luanne had informed me earlier with her characteristic sensitivity.

"That was the police," Ty said. "They want to talk to us right now."

Ten minutes later, I sat between Ty and Luanne in the front seat of Ty's pickup on the way to the police station. Luanne drove because Ty had trouble operating the shift with his bruised hand. Fall was definitely coming on. The temperature had taken a turn toward the chilly, and it was full dark at 7 p.m.

"I wonder what this is about," Luanne said. "Do you think Michael told them the true story?"

"I doubt it," I said. "It's possible one of his goons did. Maybe Sanderson is ready to hear us out. Is he the one you spoke to on the phone?"

"No," Ty said. "I don't know who it was. He didn't say what it was about. He just said to get to the police station, and to bring you and Luanne along."

I felt like I'd just been dropped in a pool of icewater.

"Wait a minute!" I said. "That's exactly what he said? Get there immediately and bring me along? Did you tell him I was at your house?"

"Huh? No! No I didn't!"

"Then how the fuck did they know ..."

Luanne, face white as a snowdrift, had already put the truck into a tire-squealing U turn in the middle of the street and stomped on the accelerator as she took it back toward the house.

"Go down the back street first!" I said. "Let's get a look at the situation!"

She killed the lights, pulled down the street behind the house and stopped the truck. From there, a van backed into the driveway out front was visible.

Its double rear doors were open and two men carried an unconscious Paul toward it.

"Get out," Luanne told me and Ty. "I'm going to keep them from leaving." She buckled her shoulder belt.

"Paul is going to be in that van!" I said. "Do you really think ..."

"There's no time, goddamn it! Get out!"

Ty and I got out and ran toward the van. The men had already loaded Paul into the back and closed the doors behind them. The van started moving.

The pickup's tires squealed as Luanne took it around the block at high speed. It accelerated with a roar when she hit the street in front of the house and stomped on the gas.

And just as the van exited the driveway, the pickup slammed into the driver's side of it with a loud, metallic thump and breaking glass. The van lifted in the air on two wheels before it came down again hard.

Ty and I reached the van. The back doors banged open and two men with drawn guns jumped down before they realized we were there.

No time for subtlety now. The guy nearest me was a stocky, no-neck type. I clamped a hand on his face and hooked my other arm around his gun hand to keep it pointing away. I drove a knee into his nuts, then swept his legs out from under him. I landed on top of him when he fell, still keeping a firm hold on the gun hand, and pounded my elbow into his face until he stopped moving.

I looked up. Ty stood over the unconscious body of the other guy. Whatever he did, I'm sure it was cleaner and more elegant than my technique.

I stood. Another man came around the corner of the van. The ponytailed fire policeman from the March for Batley. I guess he'd recovered from my clocking him with the flashlight in the alley, because he pointed a gun at us.

I was too far from him. It took only a split second but I saw it happening in slow motion. He raised his barrel. Sighted along it. Ty started to move but he was also too far away. No way. No way in hell.

Suddenly, Luanne was behind the gunman. She grasped his ponytail, wrenching and twisting hard. He stumbled backward, gun firing in a random direction as his arm flailed.

Then Luanne was in front of him, her fists hammering into his midsection and his face. As he fell to the ground and she went with him, she was no longer punching so much as clawing, voice raised in a fierce shriek.

"Leave my family alone! Leave my family alone! Leave my family…"

Ty and I pulled her off. Blood covered the man's face. We were afraid she'd kill him.

Something made her glance toward the house and she screamed again. Not a fierce battle cry this time, but a howl of sheer terror and despair.

"Daddy!"

I looked. Ken crawled toward us down the driveway, blood flowing from his leg.

The sirens had already been there in the background, but now I was aware of them. Somebody must have reported the crash.

I ran toward Ken. A river of blood trailed him. This wasn't good.

We later got the full rundown when we kept up a vigil at the hospital for the next two days. We napped in waiting room chairs. Ate our silent meals in the snack bar. Pilar hung out with us for part of the time, but she had a lot to take care of back in town.

Paul was OK. When they'd kicked down the door, they'd shot him with a tranquilizer dart like an animal. I guess their orders were to leave him unharmed. His unconsciousness may have helped him escape injury in the van crash because his body was totally relaxed.

They apparently weren't so concerned about leaving Ken uninjured. The police who interviewed us in the hospital said Ken tried to fight them off with his cane and one of them shot him in the leg.

The bullet hit his femoral artery. The doctors said he would have had a better chance if he'd been younger and in better health. But he lost too much blood.

I was sitting on a bench with Ty and Luanne near the intensive care unit when a doctor came out and told us.

I stood. Ty covered his face with his hands and his body shook with big, hitching sobs. Luanne put her arms around him and stroked his hair.

She wasn't crying. Not yet. Her face held an expression of steely resolve. She looked like someone staring down a long stretch of road she'd have to walk. And she saw nothing ahead to make the journey easier.

I thought I should say something. But I had nothing to tell them. No bland consolations. No anemic reassurances. We knew what we were up against and that was it.

I walked away. I pulled out my flask and took a long drink as I exited through the double glass doors into the chilly darkness outside.

FILE 31

FROM BILLY'S PAPERS

It is night and I am sitting in my bedroom. I have locked the door, for no reason other than helpless thrall to oppressive dictates of habit. An irregularly sawn hole, after all, represents an appreciable compromise to the door's structural integrity.

I am writing this on an old, portable typewriter that has served me well through years of traveling and sporadic access to electricity.

I feel as though I have taken a brief respite from a game of chess, having left my pieces scattered about on a board that comprises the entire city. An odd match to be sure, in that the various pieces will enact the end game themselves.

I have assisted Ken in freeing Sally and her children. I dropped said children off at a downtown apartment I have selected for that purpose. Sally should be with Pinky for the moment. Eventually, she will end up in this very house.

At this moment, they are interrogating Ken. In several hours, he will give them certain information. They will learn of my involvement and converge on this house. When they do, I will make a break for it in my car and they will chase me. While they are occupied in this pursuit, Pinky will take Sally to this house and The Agendum will be too distracted in chasing me down to take note of this development. The eye always follows the moving object. Gary will take care of her during her pregnancy.

If they catch me, and they have an excellent chance of doing so, they will probably kill me. Let me be clear about my motivations. I am indeed coming to the rescue of a friend who has asked for my help. However, I am doing this for myself as much as for her. They will not own me, as they do so many others. I will die fighting them before I allow that to happen.

Once I am finished composing these notes, I will drop them in a corner mailbox. Their ultimate destination is a safe deposit box in Maryland.

I have intentionally withheld certain information from Gary at this juncture, because the more he knows, the more of a potential threat and thus a potential target he will be to The Agendum. I have instructed him to retrieve this account from the safe deposit box should he ever find it necessary to evacuate.

I cannot know the specific circumstances that precipitated the reading of this account. But I will assume that the shit has already hit the proverbial fan, in which case a full account of what happened may be of some strategic value.

In a separate envelope that I will paperclip to this account, I have enclosed yet another letter for Gary. In it, I have informed him about you, and instructed him to share this account with you if he feels that he can trust you and that you might accomplish something productive with its contents.

Yes, you. The runty little fuck from New Jersey. I'm talking about you.

When I spoke to Schulze, he alluded to a project he'd embarked on immediately after being drafted into The Agendum. He knew The Agendum would do a good deal of harm, so he wanted to use his family's considerable financial resources to establish a foundation tasked with protecting people from their depredations.

Early on, Schulze did an exemplary job of convincing The Professor that he was an enthusiastic supporter of The Agendum, so they did not observe him as closely as they did some of their other conscripts. Schulze let his lawyers and business managers do much of the work. The foundation he established is wider in scope than you probably realize.

When we spoke in his kitchen, Schulze told me he'd concluded that the foundation would require an operational center in Batley.

He knew that running the center would require an individual possessed of a very distinct character and set of talents. He informed me that he trusted my judgment, and asked me to include recommendations in my letters to him if I could think of anybody who fit the bill.

I recommended Sister Pilar Lopez. She has featured prominently in quite a few recent newspaper accounts, fighting for the poor and standing up to the big boys with no apparent fear.

I know that it won't be long before the powers-that-be find her too much of an inconvenience, and expedite her removal from Northern New Jersey. When that happens, I advised Schulze, his foundation would be well-advised to scoop her up.

I calculated that the type of foundation Schulze had in mind would also require someone to perform the dirty work that would inevitably be necessary. And where might we find such a candidate?

I pondered that very question one evening while I read a newspaper and drank a beer at a sidewalk table in front of a downtown bar. I spotted you at another table and didn't take much notice. You appeared to be half in the bag already, and I dismissed you as one more of the aimless drunks who frequent the place.

Not far from my table, a young man set up a folding table on the sidewalk alongside a parked van. On the table was a large, fancy television, and a sign declaring that it was for sale at a surprisingly low price.

Before long, a rickety-looking car pulled to the curb, and an equally rickety-looking old woman disembarked.

She expressed her delighted disbelief at the price of the television, saying it just so happened that she was in dire need of one. The young man said he was happy to be of service. He was able to accept only cash and hoped that wouldn't be a problem. The old woman replied that it wouldn't. She extracted a large wad of bills from her pocketbook, counted some off and handed them to the young man.

And then, a deep voice barked out the words: "Alright! Put the money on the table!"

The television salesman complied. A slightly older man, dressed in a patrolman's uniform and cap, strolled around the corner and closed in on the salesman and his confused customer.

"Didn't you get the message the last time I locked you up, Smitty?" the cop asked. "You're going down for a hard spell this time."

"Oh my!" the old woman said. "I'm not in any trouble, am I? I just wanted to buy a television set."

"You're not in trouble, ma'am," the cop said. "But this is stolen merchandise."

That's when you stood up.

"The uniform's a nice touch," you said. "I mean, it's not the uniform that the real cops around here wear. But it shows commitment on your part. I respect that."

"Sir, if you don't mind, I'm trying to conduct police business here," the cop said.

"Yeah, I've been watching," you replied. "You're at the part where you tell her that the money she just handed over is now evidence in a crime and you'll have to confiscate it but she'll get it back. Were you going to give her a fake phone number, or were you really going to force her to make a trip to the police station to find out she'd been ripped off?"

"Look, mister …."

"I know you guys are trying to make a living," you went on. "But not off people like her. That's just wrong."

You advanced on them as you spoke and by then you stood directly in front of the cop.

"Buddy," the cop said, "if you don't take a hike right now, I'm putting you in cuffs and placing you under arrest."

"Well I'm not going," you said. "You could call for backup, but you don't seem to have a radio. Guess you'll have to draw your gun. Doesn't look real, but you can draw it. The cuffs look real. That a recreational thing? You kinky bastard, you."

He raised his fist, but you straight-armed him in the chest before he could take a swing. He staggered backward, tripped over the curb and fell on his ass.

The other one advanced on you, and you began yelling and waving your hands in the air.

"Help! Somebody is assaulting a police officer! Call 911! Officer down! Help!"

The two men jumped into the van and sped off, one of them yelling "Asshole!" out the window by way of farewell. You turned to face the old woman.

"Might as well take the television," you told her. "I don't think they're coming back for it."

She shook a finger in your face.

"You're a very strange man!" she said in a distinctly bellicose tone. "If you just got me into trouble with the police, I'm going to be very angry!"

She gathered her money from where it lay on the table, replaced it in her purse and drove away. You shrugged and returned to your drink.

I inquired around about you, and conducted some research into your background. In so doing, I ascertained that my initial impressions of you were correct. You're a loser and a drunk. Yet I thought you just might be the right man for the job.

I trust Gary's judgment. If you are reading this, it means he agrees with my assessment of your qualifications. So congratulations. I guess you turned out to be the right man for the job after all.

Take care of the people these bastards have harmed. If The Agendum comes back, try to keep them from harming any more. Fight them if you have to. And if you suspect they might take you out, make sure there's somebody to carry on the fight.

Good luck. You'll need it. Now get back to work. You're not getting paid to stand around with your dick in your hand.

FILE 32

I've decided to go looking for them. Whoever they are. Wherever they are.
 I checked out the lease on the Pigeon Clinic. The trail disappeared in a maze of paper companies. I looked up the old tax records on the building where Schulze's clinic used to be. Same deal.

I'm going to visit the address in Philadelphia that I found in Michael's desk. What the hell. It's an overnight trip by bus. I hate driving and parking in Center City, so I figure I'll leave my car here. I'm not planning anything major. Just going to case the place out.

I wanted to leave right away, but there were a few things to take care of. Ken's funeral, first of all. I was a pallbearer.

Ty, Luanne and Paul were surprised and touched at how many people showed up for it. Ken had a lot of fans and friends from before his accident who didn't even know he was still living in town. The funeral director asked Luanne if she wanted a closed-casket ceremony. She got a little testy with him. However the others remembered him, that was the face of the stepfather she'd long since come to regard as her father. The face she loved.

Ty, like Luanne, took a leave of absence from work. He was staying constantly by Paul's side. Supposedly, he was doing it to guard Paul, in case anybody tried to come after him again.

But sometimes it seemed Ty was clinging to Paul for comfort. He was taking Ken's death hard. He'd become prone to long silences where he'd sit motionless, staring off into the distance, until Paul brought him out of it by suggesting they go somewhere or do something. Almost like Ty had reverted to childhood and Paul had become the adult.

I also had some work to do with the Foundation's other clients before I left. Winter would come before long, and I had to get the Japanese war god Bishamon signed up for home heating assistance. And Perkunas, the Lithuanian thunder god, needed help filling out the forms for a state program that got him a discount on his cholesterol medication.

Altogether, it was three weeks before I could finally hit the road. Pilar picked up a ticket for me and I paid her back. She said members of religious orders get discounts, so it only cost me $70.

TOM JERKFACE: *There's a slight discrepancy in the account here, as bus tickets between Philadelphia and Batley cost only $50.*

When I stopped by Pilar's office, she asked if I was sure about this.
"It's no big deal," I told her. "I'm just taking a look around. I'll only be gone a day. Two at the most."
"I'm still worried," she said. "I wish you wouldn't do this."
"I have to."
"I know."

I told her I'd pick her up a Liberty Bell snowglobe. We shook hands. Then she gave me a kiss on the cheek. Then I left.

My next stop was the Bacon house. Luanne was alone. She said Paul suggested that he and Ty do some volunteer work at a soup kitchen downtown. He'd confided to her that he thought the activity might be good for Ty. She was proud of Paul. He was being so mature about this. She was a little worried about Ty, but she knew he'd get over it. He always had a brooding streak, and he was just dealing with it in his own way.

She was bustling around, cleaning up. She said she'd been so busy with the funeral and everything that she hadn't really taken the time to keep up the place.

I asked how she was doing. She said she was holding up alright. It was still sinking in. I didn't tell her this, but I guessed she was coping in her own way, too. The house already looked plenty picked-up to me. I figured it seemed empty to her and she was trying to fill it up with activity.

She asked how I was doing. I told her fine. And I was, according to the doctor who took a look at me when he redid the stitches in my lip and reset my nose. No major fractures or damaged internal organs, from what he could see. I was still sore and bruised, but I'd survive.

I told her I was catching a bus that night. She said she knew. Pilar mentioned it to her on the phone that morning. She told me to wait a minute, and walked out to the kitchen. She carried a paper sack back into the living room.

"For the trip," she said. "Food's expensive in the city. I made you a tuna salad sandwich and carrot sticks. There's a fruit cup in there for dessert, with a spoon. There's also a can of Ginger Ale if you want something … to … drink. Yeah. Well, the can's in there anyway. Do what you want with it."

"Thanks," I said.

"Take care of yourself."

"I always do."

"No you don't," she said. "That's why I'm worried."

I looked at her for a long moment.

"Keep an eye on things while I'm gone?" I asked her. "You mind doing that?"

"What? No. I …I guess not."

"Thanks," I said again.

I had one more stop to make.

I found Thelma Pointer. Or Dom Russo. Whoever she was. He was.

He was in a bar on Shimmel Street. Guess he just felt more at home there these days, surrounded by people more-or-less in his same predicament, gender-wise. A small black woman sitting at the bar, reading the Batley Daily Needler. The only other patrons were a gray-haired man with blurry tattoos on his wrinkled forearms, an enormous blonde with a bouffant hairdo at the end of the bar, and a couple thickly muscled Latinos in tight dresses shooting pool.

I took a stool next to Dom and ordered a beer. He folded the paper and put it on the bar.

"Looks like you took a beating," he said. "Didn't I teach you anything?"

"Yeah. You taught me how to fall. You taught me how to do a proper kata-gatame. You ever do a lesson on not pissing off some juicer who's the size of a truck? Cause that might have been of some use to me."

"You always did have more balls than brains," Dom said, taking a swallow from his beer.

"So what's up?" I asked.

"Not much," he said. "You know, Ed moved on."

One day recently, Dom told me, Ed woke up in the room at the Hope House where he'd been staying temporarily. Except he said he wasn't Ed anymore. He was the man who occupied that body before he'd checked into Schulze's clinic. He packed up his stuff and left.

Dom went into his room afterward and picked up on a smell.

"What kind of smell?" I asked.

"A smell made up of lots of different smells," Dom said. "It smelled like fried food and spilled beer and cigarette smoke. Diesel fumes, too. And puke. There was definitely puke in there somewhere."

"Sounds nasty."

"No, it was kind of a good smell," Dom said. "There was something sweet in there, too. It took me a little while to recognize it. You know what it was? It was funnel cake."

We both took swallows of beer.

"Let me ask you something," I said. "Say you get old and die in Thelma Pointer's body. What happens to Thelma Pointer? Or you for that matter?"

"I suppose we both just move on, each in our own way. That's what we all end up doing, sooner or later."

I glanced down at the front page of his newspaper on the bar. It read "City to Hold 'Rally for Batley.'" The story was by Tom. It started: "Rain failed to dampen the spirits of rally organizers who held a press conference at City Hall ..."

"There's something I don't get," I said. "Cabot was faking the whole occult master racket. Schulze was a bullshit artist from day one. The other folks at the clinic were just drugged and brainwashed. But you guys. The ghosts. Where do you come in?"

Dom watched one of the pool players sink a tricky corner shot. Then he spoke.

"The Agendum? They're always looking out for arcane knowledge they can use for their purposes. Just like anyone else, they can be conned. Like Schulze managed. But sometimes they stumble onto something legit. This thing is wider-reaching than you know. That's why some of the dead hang around. We've got jobs to do. For the greater battle."

I shook my head and took a swallow of beer.

"You think I'm full of shit," he said.

"If you'll pardon me, I've been lied to a lot lately."

Dom gave a sort of half smile. He used to do that a lot. Back when he was Dom.

"All experience, all perception, is deceptive," he said. "Everything we know? It comes by way of sensory apparatus that's limited and flawed. We never really know what's going on. We just take our best guess and act on it."

"Mind canning the esoteric bullshit?" I said. "It gives me a headache and I've had a rough couple weeks."

"Remember when we sent a team out to that jiu jitsu tournament in Pittsburgh? That one guy getting everybody with the hip throw?"

"The wiry little Japanese guy?"

"Yeah. And I told you to reverse the throw. But not to think about it because by the time you consciously thought about it, it would be too late. You followed my advice and pulled it off."

"Yeah. And he tapped me out anyway with an arm bar. What's your point?"

He set down his beer and looked me straight in the eyes.

"Do you trust me?"

I let out a long breath. Fuck it.

"Yeah," I said. "I guess I do. What's this message you've been trying to give me?"

"It's not over," he said. "You still have work to do. Be careful. It's dangerous."

"You know, I never would have figured that out for myself. Any other profound messages from on high? Water's wet? Shit stinks? I probably don't want to go home with that blonde at the end of the bar that's got an Adam's apple?"

"Don't shoot the messenger."

"Am I supposed to tip you?"

He swallowed the last of his beer.

"Not necessarily. But if you feel like buying me another beer, I won't stop you."

I bought one for him and one for myself. We drank them. Then it was time for me to leave.

I'm in my apartment now, putting the final touches on this report. I've been working on my account for the last three weeks. Once I'm done, I'm going to assemble it with the stuff that Pinky and Cabot gave me. And then I guess I'll leave it on my kitchen table. I'm not sure what else to with it.

I'm already packed for the trip. Just one duffel bag. I won't need much.

Looking around now, I feel a weird compulsion to straighten up my apartment. For the sake of completion I guess. I haven't even cleaned up from last week when I had some asshole friend of mine over who got drunk and knocked over one of my shelves. I'll bet he doesn't even remember. Having people in your life is kind of a mixed blessing sometimes, isn't it?

Ah, the hell with it. I'll clean up when I get back.

I left myself time to watch the fireworks they're having after the Rally for Batley at the stadium tonight. There's going to be some tight security there, but I'm not worried about The Agendum trying to pull anything. I think they're done with this city. For now. Some of the local civic leader types planned the rally as a combination tribute to those who died, and a big "Hey-let's-pick-up-and-rebuild" gesture. They're going to have speakers and music and a non-denominational prayer service.

It's a good thing, I guess. But I can live with myself if I miss it.

I do want to see the fireworks, though. I even scheduled my departure around them.

There's a bench outside the bus station where I can sit and get a good view of them. The way I've planned it, I'll be able to have a cigar and a few drinks from my flask while I sit and watch.

And right about the time they're over, my bus should arrive. I'll board it and ride out of town.

I like fireworks. They make me feel … I don't know … connected. When somebody puts on a fireworks display, everyone in town turns out for it. Young and old. Black and white. Rich and poor.

Nobody's got a better seat than anybody else. Nobody needs one. And while the show's going on we're not doing anything except standing around together, enjoying those pretty lights in the sky.

Well, gotta go.

EPILOGUE BY THE AUTHOR

He never did come back.
    His car sat unattended in the parking lot of the bus station for days before it was impounded. His landlord eventually placed all of his things in storage and rented out his apartment to someone else. Sister Pilar collected his personal possessions. He didn't have much. Among them were the preceding files. And as I have described in the introduction, they eventually came into my possession.

After I submitted the files for publication and reviewed them, I realized they practically demanded an attempt to put them in context. In the course of doing so, I interviewed some of the people involved in the account.

In short, the book required a coda. I'd go so far as to say a failure to provide one would represent an unforgivable breach of journalistic standards.

My publisher, I regret to say, did not initially see it that way. Motivated by petty considerations of logistics and cost, he tried to dissuade me from including this epilogue in the book you are now reading.

He would soon learn that he crossed the wrong journalist. Despite his craven attempts to avoid me, I located some of his haunts around Batley and finally confronted him in a restaurant.

When I presented him with the hard-hitting information I'd uncovered, he had no choice but to relent. And so, I present my findings and analysis.

PUBLISHER'S NOTE: If Mr. Jerkface's reference to "petty considerations of logistics and cost" alludes to my concerns about his many missed deadlines and cost overruns pertaining to this project, I will not argue the point.

He did not deign to inform me of his decision to include an epilogue until a week before this volume was scheduled to go to a printer who had already exhibited a Zen-like tolerance in the face of Mr. Jerkface's previous delays, but whose patience was wearing markedly thin.

I would emphasize that Mr. Jerkface did not only present the text of the epilogue, but also a list of expenses connected with its compilation. Said expenses included travel costs; bail money necessitated by a public disturbance Mr. Jerkface created at a Florida family restaurant that failed to prepare a club sandwich to his specifications; and a $300 tab from the apparently still extant Big Rhonda's Live Girl Titty-Tacular that Mr. Jerkface included on his expense report under the less-than-enlightening heading of "research."

I explained all of this to Mr. Jerkface over the phone, but he nonetheless made the epilogue's inclusion something of a personal crusade. After he failed in attempts to gain admission to my office, my health club and my country club, he did indeed confront me in a restaurant.

In a state of visible intoxication, he approached my table and greeted me with the following words: "This is just how I expected to find you! A cheap blonde on your arm, gladhanding your fat-cat friends!"

I informed him that the "cheap blonde" on my arm was my daughter, whose high school graduation we were attempting to celebrate, and that the "fat-cat friends" at my table included my wife, my parents, my sister-in-law and her husband, who happens to be the publisher of the Batley Daily Needler.

Mr. Jerkface merely stared at me, his alcohol-befogged brain attempting to make sense of what I'd told him. I then consented to publish the epilogue because it seemed the most expeditious means of hastening his departure. Had I not, I feared he may have taken it upon himself to press his case at my next house party, golf outing or colonoscopy.

The latter procedure, I might add, is considerably more enjoyable than my professional association with Mr. Jerkface has been.

So what is to be said about the account? As much as possible, I've corroborated the objective facts put forward therein.

As I mentioned in the introduction, I'm personally acquainted with many of the people his account mentions by name. Sister Pilar Lopez, Luanne Bacon and Ty Bacon all claimed that the facts presented in it were true. Michael Burk – the full name of the "Michael" mentioned in the account – refused my numerous requests to interview him in prison.

Notably, I confirmed that the city officially contracted with the Pigeon Clinic, yet paid nothing to the clinic for a span of two years. That deal, it turned out, was engineered almost exclusively by Mayor Buck Rockbaugh. When I attempted to ask him about it, Rockbaugh attributed the discrepancy to an unspecified accounting error and refused to discuss the matter further. He also categorically denied the truth of the report, while refusing to discuss it in detail.

Sadly, I did not have much time to pursue the issue. Not long after the events described in the preceding report, Bess Rockbaugh suffered a fatal heart attack. Two weeks later, Buck Rockbaugh entered his office after hours, penned an apologetic note to his constituents, then ended his own life with a shotgun.

Sister Pilar presented copies of the report to the police and to the federal investigators looking into what has come to be known in local parlance as "The Slain Invasion." When that failed to yield results, she presented a copy to the editors of The Daily Needler.

Since I have not been privy to discussions on the matter by either local police or federal investigators, I cannot say why they have chosen to ignore it.

Where my editors are concerned, I know they were reluctant to publish such dramatic claims without more substantive corroboration.

To be fair to my editors, conspiracy theories concerning The Slain Invasion are abundant. For a long time after the events described in the report, it was a rare week when I wasn't contacted by somebody purporting to have the "real story." Some of these people had direct experience with the events, and others were simply armchair observers. Many were local, though I personally heard from conspiracy theorists in Japan, South Africa and New Zealand, to name a few locations.

These people, with varying degrees of logic and evidence, laid the blame on a wide range of political and economic entities, secret societies, religious authorities and ethnic groups. Even today, I will still get the occasional phone call or letter informing me about the hitherto unknown link between The Slain, Freemasons and extraterrestrials.

One theory that I've heard expounded more than once was that Michael Burk was a heroic figure who did, in fact, try to save the city from The Slain and was framed by the shadowy machinations of an equally shadowy cabal of ill-defined villains. Some local people even took to wearing T-shirts bearing an image of Michael's face. Angry, and sometimes violent, responses from other city residents soon discouraged that practice.

Still, on occasion, you will see graffiti around the city pertaining to Michael. At first, such graffiti read: "FREE MICHAEL." Now the graffiti more often than not reads: "MICHAEL DIED FOR OUR SINS."

I wrote in the introduction that it is not my intention to reiterate the basic facts relating to The Slain Invasion, which have been extensively documented elsewhere.

I only mention Michael Burk's death inasmuch as it further illustrates the general conspiratorial mindset that has colored – one might say contaminated – any potential reception of the preceding report, and rendered objective assessment all but impossible.

In his (clearly ghostwritten) account of the affair "Flaming Justice!" by Lockwood & Ferlinghetti Press, former federal prosecutor Jeffrey Derr wrote that the arrested members of "The Slain" other than Michael Burk claimed to have been paid outright as mercenaries, although a handful said they consented to their recruitment in exchange for immediate termination of prison sentences in addition to financial remuneration.

Derr wrote that the latter group appeared to be affiliated with an obscure program that offered certain prisoners reduced sentences in exchange for participation in clinical studies.

According to Derr's account, Michael at first stuck to the storyline that he was simply a religious fanatic carrying out some unfathomable act of retribution on the part of The Almighty.

Michael claimed that his efforts were funded by the American Army of God, an outlawed religious militia group with white supremacist leanings with which he had previously been involved.

The American Army of God has issued a statement disavowing his claims. As Derr points out in his book, their denials seem plausible. The group had previously been known for mosque bombings and assaults on immigrant business owners, but had never engaged in anything as elaborate as The Slain Invasion.

Eventually, Derr writes, Michael intimated that he had a more in-depth story to tell. If this is true, he never got the opportunity to tell it. Michael developed a taste for cocaine while he was in prison. About the time Derr claims he was ready to talk, Michael ingested some cocaine that had been lethally laced with a powerful opioid and died of an overdose.

Derr, predictably, finds a conspiratorial subtext in all of this, as in the events that led to Derr's own personal disgrace and professional ruin. Just as predictably, his written account makes no acknowledgement of the incontrovertible ethical lapses that led to his downfall, including financial improprieties and patronage of a notorious call girl service.

Ultimately, like so much else pertaining to The Slain Invasion, the circumstances underlying Michael's death and Derr's allegations remain unknown.

Before I go any further, I must acknowledge the invaluable assistance I received in compiling the facts presented in this epilogue from the recently expanded Friedrich K. Schulze Foundation. Of particular help was the organization's investigative branch, which now operates under Luanne Bacon's supervision.

It's difficult, certainly, to look at an event such as The Slain Invasion and characterize any aspect of it as "good." But if it did yield one benefit, that came in the form of a funding windfall for the Foundation. The board of directors, charitable groups and many individual donors all responded in the Invasion's aftermath with generous infusions of money. And Sister Pilar, always a canny financial manager, was able to leverage those donations into substantial state and federal grants.

While not exactly flush, Sister Pilar found herself with enough resources to expand on the work once performed by the now-absent operative. Pilar remains the director of the Foundation's Batley operations, and Luanne reports to her. Officially, Luanne's branch is called the Friedrich K. Schulze Foundation Investigative Division. But she and her staff simply refer to themselves as "Freak Foundation operatives."

After making clear in the most adamant fashion imaginable that she expected me to respect his wish for anonymity, Luanne put me in touch with the man identified in the report as "Pinky."

I met him for lunch in a chain restaurant attached to an office park in New Jersey. He informed me that he left Batley soon after the incidents described in the report, and was now working in an office job.

I asked him if he was hiding from law enforcement authorities.

"Hell no." he said. "They set me up in this gig."

After The Slain Invasion, Pinky told me, he experienced a crisis of conscience regarding his years of silence about The Agendum. He was especially troubled about his involvement in Billy's death, and Gary Cabot's taking the blame for it.

Through a series of circumstances I need not recount here, he got in touch with Sister Pilar. She, in turn, put him in touch with the federal prosecutor Jeffrey Derr, who was already embarked on his investigation of The Slain.

Based on what he'd already uncovered, Derr apparently found both Pinky's and Cabot's stories plausible. In exchange for their cooperation with his investigation, he managed to get the charges against both men dropped, and get Pinky enrolled in the Federal Witness Security Program.

I asked him if he was currently participating in any investigation, and he shook his head.

"Once Derr got busted for skimming funds to pay call girls, it all kind of faded away," he said. "I'm still in the program. They still check in on me once a year. But nobody in the government's investigating jack shit, and I've got a feeling it's gonna stay that way. Because if you think what happened to Derr is a coincidence, I've got a bridge in Brooklyn I want to sell you. Somebody really high up wants this whole thing to quietly disappear."

I asked him if he thought the Professor, or anybody else in The Agendum, was affiliated with the government. He said he did not.

"I still don't know what it's all about," he told me. "But that's not the sense I get. My guess? The Professor did some work for the feds at some point. Now he's operating on his own, but it would still be embarrassing for certain people if he gets traced back to them."

He helped himself to a forkful of pasta salad.

"Maybe that means I'd be safe if I just stayed out of this," he went on. "But since I have no intention of doing that, I guess it's purely academic."

In recounting his recent experiences, he informed me that he found his office job unfulfilling, but it paid the bills and the benefits while he pursued what he described vaguely as "side projects."

"When those sonsabitches said they were going to come after the kids in my crew, it scared the shit out of me," he said. "From now on, I work solo."

I asked him to clarify what he meant by that, in light of Luanne's informing me that he was working with the Freak Foundation.

"I'm working with them, not for them," he replied. "That's a big distinction. They're going after the bastards that did all this, and I want to see them got as much as anybody. I'm still solo. But sometimes Luanne and her crew want some advice. Maybe an assist. If it's no skin off my nose, I'll give it.

"I figure they need every advantage they can get anyway. Pilar and Luanne seem borderline competent. But everyone else in that undertaking's an idiot. They even picked up two of my kids. There's a recipe for failure if I ever heard one. How are those kids doing anyway?"

After giving Pinky a full report on the doings of his former associates, to which he listened avidly, I showed him copies of the report's sections that dealt with him. He told me they were accurate. He also told me he had no knowledge or theories concerning the whereabouts of the man who compiled those accounts. Then he insisted on giving me a small amount of cash.

"If you do find him, buy him a beer for me," he said.

While Pinky spoke, a young man in a dress shirt and tie who had been talking loudly at the bar approached our table and gave Pinky a hearty thump on the back.

"Hey Wild Man!" he said. "Surprised you can afford to buy lunch after that bath you took Saturday night!"

He then laughed, said he was kidding, and introduced himself to me as one of Pinky's co-workers. At his approach, Pinky's entire aspect changed. He looked up at the young man with wide eyes and spoke in a squeaky voice.

"Gosh! I never dreamed that poker would be such a ... a complicated game!" he said.

"Ah you'll get the hang of it," the young man replied. "I'm having another game at my place next Saturday. Stop by if you want. Maybe you can win back some of your money."

"I'd certainly like to," Pinky replied in the same squeaky voice. "But please keep quiet about it. I don't think my wife would approve."

"Uh oh!" the young man said, waving his hand in a flogging gesture. "Sounds like somebody's whipped!"

He laughed again and headed for the exit. Pinky watched him leave with a small, predatory smile on his face.

I also went to see Gary Cabot.

Again, Luanne helped facilitate that, although it wasn't as tricky in his case. Cabot, it seemed, had dropped his anonymity. Though he still lived in Florida, he was by then working full-time as a paid Freak Foundation operative. He'd made a number of return visits to Batley, keeping a low profile and staying with Sister Pilar or Luanne when he did. Ty had been down to visit him in Florida a few times for training sessions.

In fact, I recognized Ty's handiwork when I approached Cabot's home on a bright afternoon and found him working out on a heavy bag in his garage. He was dressed in sweatpants and a T-shirt. Rather than his fists, he was using his forearms to land hard, whip-like blows.

"Russian forearm strikes?" I asked.

He turned toward me and smiled.

"You must be Tom," he said. "Ty told me you'd trained with him."

He toweled off his face, drank from a plastic sports drink bottle, then invited me into his house.

He offered me a beer, which I accepted, and we sat in his living room. Whether consciously or not, he appeared to have divided it into two distinct portions.

The part where we sat was meticulously clean, with inexpensive-looking yet tasteful living room furniture and art on the walls.

The other side of the living room contained a bedraggled-looking couch littered with toys that faced a television set. Crayon drawings hung on the wall. None of it looked as though it had been dusted, or touched at all, for a long time.

Cabot read the parts of the report that dealt with him, including the initial break-in and the later visit to the house I was currently visiting. Other than a few minor details, he confirmed that it was all accurate.

When he finished, he said there was someone I should meet and left the room.

I set down my beer on a glass coffee table and walked over to the other side of the room. There, I inspected the crayon drawings. Most of them appeared to be childish representations of airplanes. They all featured two smiling faces looking out of the plane windows.

"He loved airplanes," Cabot said.

I turned around. Cabot stood in the kitchen doorway. Next to him was a broad-shouldered black man with a shaved head, also wearing a T-shirt and sweatpants. The two of them walked into the living room and sat side-by-side on the couch.

"I don't know why," Cabot went on. "He never rode on an airplane in his life. But he was obsessed with them. He always drew the two of us flying. I'd ask him where we were going. He said he didn't know."

"What happened …" I started.

"He died about six months ago," Cabot said. "He's buried near here. It's a nice place."

"I'm sorry."

"Thank you," Cabot said. "He'd been in poor health for a long time. It wasn't a surprise."

I picked up one of the toys from the couch. A plastic monster. Humanoid but bestial, with a comically ugly bug-eyed face.

"Would you mind not touching his stuff?" Cabot asked. "It's just … I don't mean … would you mind?"

"No, of course not," I said.

The black man spoke.

"We gotta clean that stuff up sooner or later."

"I know," Cabot said. "I'm just not ready yet."

The black man put his hand on top of Cabot's and gave it a squeeze.

"It's OK, baby," he said. "Whenever."

Cabot introduced the black man as Craig, who had been a police officer in upstate New York. Craig once got an assignment to go undercover and look for drug buys at a hippie jam band festival taking place in his area.

He'd spend the most of the day cursing his luck over the assignment, and wondering why people would voluntarily subject themselves to that music. Then he gradually began to regard it as the best music he'd ever heard. About the time he discovered that he could see the music, he realized he'd been dosed with something. As it turned out, he wasn't the only one. Somebody managed to slip LSD into all of the drink vendors' wares and just about every one of the 2,000 or so people present got a dose.

Craig was trying to marshal his thoughts enough to get help when a small army of men in ghoulish masks, hoisting blunt weapons, charged from the surrounding woods and attacked the crowd.

Somewhere in the chaos that followed, LSD aside, Craig was certain that he'd spotted a small bespectacled man watching from the sidelines and taking notes on a clipboard. Many others there reported seeing similar note-takers with clipboards afterward.

It made no sense to Craig. He began doing research on his own, and he and Luanne found each other. After he became involved with the Freak Foundation, he and Cabot found each other. Craig was now a paid operative, as well as Cabot's housemate.

I asked Cabot if he was afraid of dropping his anonymity.

"No," he said. "I'm done hiding."

Craig patted him on the shoulder.

"Ty's doing a good job," Craig said. "Gary here's getting pretty bad for a faggot white boy. And I'm packing heat. Anybody wants to come for us can go right the fuck ahead."

When I left, they were both in the garage. Cabot held the heavy bag so Craig could kick it. They were the kind of high karate kicks that Ty advises against using in a real fight. But from the looks of them, I would not have been eager to change places with the bag.

As for the city of Batley itself? If you'll forgive the triteness of the expression, life went on. After Mayor Rockbaugh's death, his former political ally Anne Swanson — whom Rockbaugh had once abandoned to support Ernest Bixler — was elected mayor in a special election. She has served ever since in that capacity alongside councilmen Dan Oliphant and Tim Rourke, owner of Rourke's Grocery Mart.

Bixler opted not to run for re-election. He went back to broadcasting his radio show. However, he changed the format from politics to local sports. He now devotes a portion of each broadcast to ways that people can assist various local charities, with a particular emphasis on assistance for the homeless.

The arrested members of The Slain received a range of sentences, based on the extent of their involvement, their cooperation with prosecutors and the competence of their defense lawyers.

Though Batley certainly has its share of troubles, as does any city, it has not suffered any more attacks of the kind detailed in the preceding account

And the Freak Foundation operative who left that account? Sister Pilar filed a missing person's report. Nothing came of it.

I had the occasion to ask about him during a visit to the Hope House one recent afternoon. Like any reporter, I have sources with whom I regularly check. As Sister Pilar is savvy, knowledgeable and well-connected, she is very valuable to me in this capacity.

The Hope House has undergone some remodeling. When I walked in the front door, I found myself in the portion now given over to the investigative branch.

It held seven desks. All of the furniture and equipment, even the coffee maker in the corner, looked to be second-hand. Every surface, it seemed, was covered with loose papers or bulging file folders.

The only occupants were Mako and Veronica, formerly of Pinky's crew.

Mako, dressed in an oversized T-shirt and baggy flowered shorts, stood by a desk at which Veronica sat. In his hand was a deck of cards.

He smiled when he saw me.

"Hey! Writer man! Get over here. I've got something to show you."

At his insistence I looked at the top card, which was the two of clubs. He set the deck down and instructed me to cut it. He then picked up the cards, riffled them and told me to look at the top card again. The two of clubs.

"See?" he said, a broad grin on his face. "Reversed the cut. Slick, huh?"

Veronica shrugged.

"You're improving," she said.

"You're improving," Mako repeated, his voice a mocking imitation of her southern accent.

Luanne exited from an office door at the back of the room.

"If you're not too busy doing card tricks," she said, "I'm wondering if you had a chance to check on that sensory deprivation cult from Tennessee."

"You know it," Mako said. "I'll write up those reports today. Interviewed three survivors and a couple of escapees. They confirmed that the guru was a little guy, in his 60s maybe, with thick glasses. His head of security had a Russian accent. He wasn't young, but nobody wanted to mess with him."

"Good," Luanne said. "Any luck talking to that cult deprogrammer who investigated them?"

"I tried," Mako said. "The guy's an asshole. I didn't get anything out of him."

"Really?" Veronica said. "I found him quite forthcoming. He provided me with a wealth of valuable information, and you'll have my report shortly."

"Oh sure," Mako muttered. "It's easy when you shake your tits in his face."

Veronica raised an eyebrow.

"I beg your pardon? All of my communication with him was by telephone."

"I meant shake your tits in his face metaphorically."

She blew him a kiss.

"Metaphorically speaking – eat the big one, sweetie."

"Any other leads?" Luanne asked.

"Yeah," Mako said. "I need to follow through on this. Sounds kind of weird. Something about an underground sword-fighting circuit."

"That does sound strange," Luanne said. "Well, we've seen stranger. Please get me those reports as soon as possible. By the way, Ty's doing a training session on grappling this evening. If you brought your sweats and you have time, feel free to attend."

"Grappling with Ty?" Veronica said. "MMMmmm! Sounds delicious."

She then caught the scowl on Luanne's face and quickly added, "Just kidding, honey. I know Ty's a married man."

Luanne was only a year older than Ty's new wife, a chatty, sweet-natured local girl named Doreen. But she'd quickly assumed the role of protective older sister. Ty and Doreen liked to joke about it when Luanne wasn't around.

While I was there, I told Luanne, I'd like to talk to her about her work. She showed me into her office, which was also cluttered with papers.

She brought me a cup of coffee. I thanked her and asked about Ty, whom I hadn't seen much lately. Between his full-time work for the Foundation and getting settled into married life, he didn't have time to conduct the martial arts classes in his garage anymore.

Luanne said he was well. She couldn't believe how domesticated he'd become. He and Doreen were fixing up an old house. Luanne frequently had them over for dinner. Once their kitchen was finished, they'd promised to return the favor.

"Have you heard from Paul?" I asked her.

"Yes," she said. "He's fine. He's safe."

"Can you give me any idea what he's up to? Where he's staying?"

"He's safe."

"I mean, I know you can't tell me specifically where he is. That's not what I'm asking. I'm just wondering if he …"

"He's safe!"

Then she sighed.

"I'm sorry," she said. "I didn't mean to snap."

I assured her it was alright. I should have known better than to push it because I knew what a sore subject it was for her.

One day, Paul left. Neither Luanne nor Ty gave any particulars as to how or where.

Ty, I'd heard, took it hard at first. Paul's departure, so soon after Ken's death, broke his heart. He began drinking heavily, stopped training and gained a lot of weight. Ultimately, it was the opportunity to help Luanne track down the people responsible that pulled him out of it. Soon after, he met Doreen.

I brought the subject around to her work with the Foundation, which Luanne was much more eager to talk about.

"When I started this, I thought the hardest thing would be finding people willing to help," she said. "I have the opposite problem. So many people are coming forward, the biggest challenge is weeding out the genuine witnesses with reliable intelligence from the well-meaning cranks.

"But even by our most conservative estimates, The Agendum has been a lot more active over the years than we would have thought. We now have a volunteer network of more than 500 people in 23 different states, and more than two dozen paid operatives scattered throughout the country. That's not an awful lot, but we're just getting started and growing fast."

"So you've gone national," I said.

"Soon to be international. We've been analyzing reports from South America and Europe suggesting The Agendum might have been active there."

I looked at the piles of paper scattered around her office.

"This looks like a major undertaking," I said. "At the risk of sounding pessimistic, you're still a relatively small and inexperienced group. If the accounts are true, the people you're up against are very efficient and ruthless."

"We're going to win," she said.

"How can you be so sure?"

"The principle of multiple opponents."

That was a term that Ty used in his martial arts classes. A surprisingly large number of students showed up with a firm belief in the documentary realism of martial arts movies depicting a hero single-handedly dispatching scores of opponents at once.

Ty would quickly disabuse them of that notion, informing them that real life doesn't work that way. If you're tough and skilled, you might last against several opponents. More than that and they will overwhelm you with their numbers.

"The Agendum can't keep doing these things to people and not make enemies," Luanne said. "Time and again when I read these reports, I see them using the same methods. They make you feel alone and cut off. And when you're scared and desperate enough, you'll believe their lies just because you need to. They're comforting.

"Our job is to make people aware they aren't alone. They've got The Agendum far outnumbered, but they don't know it yet. We need to organize them. Teach them to see through the lies. The job won't be easy, or safe. But it's necessary. Sooner or later, we'll win."

When I finished my coffee, I went into Sister Pilar's office. She had much to tell me. Still more money was available from the Foundation's board of directors, for a program they were calling the "Community Betterment Project." She'd spent the afternoon working on proposals that the board needed to approve. Some possibilities they discussed included programs for at-risk youth and an expanded homeless shelter. Ernie Bixler had promised to host a fundraising drive on his show to help them get even more start-up money.

As always, before I left, I asked Sister Pilar if she had any word on Luanne's predecessor. And as always, a pained expression crossed her face when told me she did not.

She'd filed the missing persons report, and regularly checked in with various sources and mutual acquaintances.

"I guess that's all I can do," she said. "Aside from praying for him every day. But then, I've done that for as long as I've known him."

So that wraps up this tale, other than one more curious episode that I would relate.

The episode occurred one recent night when I was leaving my apartment building to wet my whistle at a local tavern. I exited the elevator into my building's lobby. The only occupant of the lobby was a shabby-looking individual with long hair and a beard, dressed in an overcoat, whom I took to be a homeless man seeking shelter.

He approached me, his hair hanging in his face, and I looked down to fish in my pants pocket for the dollar I expected him to request. After he stood in front of me for several seconds without speaking, I looked up just in time to see the crazed expression in his eyes.

"Rock and roll, baby," he said.

The air went out of me and my midsection exploded in pain as Ezekiel punched me in the solar plexus. I dropped to my knees, gasping for breath. He swiftly moved behind me, and soon had me in a military choke.

Ordinarily, I would have likely been able to overpower him with my prodigious martial arts skills. But his surprise assault left me quite helpless.

Ezekiel leaned over, mouth close to my ear, and spoke in a gleeful whisper.

"Got a book coming out, huh? Think you're going to tell everything and just walk away? Nuh-uh. We can't have that."

With that, he began squeezing violently. The building's lobby seemed to liquefy around me and everything went black.

I woke up face-down on the lobby's tiled floor. For a moment, I couldn't comprehend where I was or how I came to be there. Then I remembered and sprang to my feet.

Ezekiel lay on the floor several feet from me, alongside a set of stairs leading up to the first floor. He was unconscious, bleeding copiously from his nose and mouth. A smear of blood stained the stairway's metal railing.

Before blacking out, had I thrashed and struck him with the back of my head? Given the angles, that seemed unlikely.

I will not pretend to be an expert at reconstructing crime scenes. Yet it seemed to me that somebody had crept up behind him as he choked me, wrenched him away and then driven him face-first into the railing.

I searched the lobby for my benefactor and discovered a fire exit door hanging open, leading to an alley. I saw nobody outside.

I hurried to my apartment and called the police. Ezekiel was still unconscious when they arrived to collect him.

Afterward, I gave the police the full account. Well, almost. There seemed little point in mentioning what I'd first noticed upon awakening. A smell of Scotch and cigar smoke in the air.

So, my friend, I don't know if it's you I should thank. Let me extend my gratitude just the same, should you happen to read this. I hope I've done justice to your account, and I wish I knew what's become of you.

Whatever you were looking for, I hope you found it. Whatever you set out to do, I hope you accomplished it.

Since I hope to see you again someday, I won't say goodbye. Instead, I'll leave you with the words of an Irish blessing.

"May the road rise to meet you and the wind be always at your back.
May the sun shine warm upon your face and the rains fall soft upon your fields."

And may they always fail to dampen your spirits.

*The Freak Foundation Operative's Report
is the fourth title for Codorus Press.*

*The book is set in Palatino Linotype
for body copy and Gill Sans for titles.*

*Designed by Hermann Zapf, Palatino emulates the
humanist fonts of the Italian Renaissance, which
mirrored the letters made by a broadnib pen. It is
named after Giambattista Palatino, a 16th century
master calligrapher.*

*Designed by Eric Gill, Gill Sans is a humanist
sans-serif font inspired by the Johnston typeface
developed for the London Underground.*

Printed in the United States of America